About the Author

Fiona Walker, whose novels have been *Sunday Times* best-sellers, leads the field as the voice of young, media-aware women. She lives with her two dogs in an idyllic cottage in Oxfordshire. To find out more about her novels, visit Fiona's website at www.fionawalker.com

Praise for Fiona Walker

'Walker's got that feel-good factor' *Mirror*

'Turn down the lights, get yourself a drink and settle back for a belter of a tale, for this is an author who remembers what so many of the current lot forget: you can't go wrong with a really good plot' *Express*

'Pure, gorgeous, expertly constructed escapism' *Minx*

Also by Fiona Walker

French Relations

Kiss Chase

Well Groomed

Snap Happy

Between Males

Lucy Talk

Lots of Love

Tongue in Cheek

Four Play

FIONA WALKER

HODDER

First published in Great Britain in 2006 by Hodder & Stoughton
A division of Hodder Headline

This paperback edition published in 2007

A Hodder paperback

3

A CIP catalogue record for this title is available from the British Library

ISBN 978 0340 92126 5

Typeset by Hewer Text UK Ltd, Edinburgh
Printed and bound by Clays Ltd, Ives plc

Hodder & Stoughton Ltd
A division of Hodder Headline
338 Euston Road
London NW1 3BH

For ue and heila, to whom I owe my livelihood
(and one broken keyboard) with a grateful heart.
And to am, who helped to mend that heart
and make a happy ending come true. ILY.

PROLOGUE

Lady Isabel Belling, known to all in Oddlode as Hell's Bells, looked eagerly around the Manor Farm drawing-room, drinking in its masculinity – sporting prints, leather furniture, sombre minimalism. It had Ely Gates's mark all over it.

He appeared at the door with a tray of coffee things.

'No Felicity today?' She watched him cast around for a spot to land the tray, and stood up to take it from him. 'Here, let me.'

'Thank you. Felicity is taking the boy back to boarding school.'

'I see.'

Ely always referred to his children Godspell and Enoch as 'the girl' and 'the boy'.

'And is Godspell at home?'

'I believe she's with the Wyck boy.'

'Are they *still* courting?'

'Regrettably, yes.'

'How unfortunate for you.' She settled the tray on an over-stuffed banquette.

'It will end before long, no doubt. It's just a rebellion after . . .'

'Quite.'

Hell's Bells poured coffee into two delicate bone china cups with barely a rattle of the pot. Her nerves were steady, despite the subject close at hand. Last year her son, Jasper, had entered into a short, unhappy engagement to Godspell Gates. The parents had been delighted until it abruptly ended with Jasper and Godspell both choosing alternative partners. In Jasper's case, all had worked out rather well, with an attractive if headstrong daughter-in-law who was well on her way to producing a Belling heir. In Godspell's case, the liaison with uncouth local hooligan Saul Wyck was less than ideal.

'The only thing that they have in common is their music,' Ely muttered.

Hell's Bells was uncertain whether music was the correct term for the dreadful din that Godspell's band made, but she said nothing as she passed the coffee across and smiled a rare Belling smile. Ely rewarded her by return, making her heart skip a little.

It was impossible not to be at least slightly skittish around Ely Gates. Once the unrivalled loins of the village, he still retained handsome features and broad shoulders even though his blond hair had turned to steel and his rangy body had started to stoop. Self-made, forthright, impossibly rich and very clever, he filled a room with his charisma.

She crossed her ankles neatly in front of her as though she were a deb and cocked her head winningly. 'To business. The hunt ball.'

'You really think it should go ahead this year?'

'But of course! Just because hunting is temporarily illegal, hosting a ball is not. And the hunt is still at the centre of this community. We must celebrate its survival.'

'Indeed.' Ely was more ambivalent on the subject, but now was not the time to point that out.

'I refuse to let a bunch of lefties ruin any good party.'

Ely, whose capitalist success shrouded a socialist heart, cleared his throat. 'And how may I help?'

'St John and I can't accommodate it at home this year because of the building work. The roof is due to be renovated in March, ruling us out.'

'I really don't think that I have the space—'

'Not *here*, Ely. Far too poky. No ballroom for a start.'

Ely narrowed his eyes as she made his beautifully proportioned Queen Anne farmhouse sound like a shepherd's croft.

'Then where exactly?'

'Eastlode Park.'

Ely's eyebrows shot up at the mention of one of the most expensive country estate hotels in England, a hotel just a mile out of Oddlode, a hotel of which he was a major shareholder.

'Isn't it a little grand?'

'Not at all. I want this ball to be *very* grand.'

'But it's just the hunt.'

Hell's Bells gave him a look that could have struck lesser men dead. 'And Eastlode Park is just an hotel.'

'One of the best in the country, the most élite, fashionable, the most expensive . . .'

'You must be able to get us a good deal,' she pressed him, pulling out all the Belling charm guns with a smile that was part coercion, part despotism and curiously arousing. 'The usual rates are prohibitively expensive. We wouldn't need exclusive use, of course – just the ballroom, formal dinner, waiting staff, perhaps a block of discounted rooms for those who have to travel from London or wherever. I am relying upon you, Ely. The Vale of the Wolds is relying upon you. You are our saviour.'

Put like that, Ely felt his backbone straighten and his shoulders square as he promised to see what he could do. Lady Belling could always bend him to her will, appealing to his innate snobbishness, godliness and just a little bit to his unfaithful loins. Short, squat and bullish she may be, but she had amazing silver eyes, hard-hunting thighs and tremendous class.

Equally smitten, Hell's Bells regarded him through her short but lusciously thick eyelashes. 'There's another point on which I'd like to pick your clever mind, Ely.'

'Oh yes?'

'We desperately need youth for the Wolds hunt. New blood. We need to appeal to a younger generation. Last year's ball was full of dreadful old crusties like you and me.'

'Hmm.' Ely pulled at his cuffs.

'I have asked Spurs and Ellen to help come up with some ideas – after all, they're young – but you are the best business-man in Oddlode. I'm sure your mind is more finely tuned to such things.'

'I would say so.' He returned her patronising smile.

'We need to sell ourselves to the younger generation. Make the VW *sexy*.' Hell's Bells emphasised the modern catchword with a little waggle of her fist. 'They still ride out with us, after all – we get plenty of young eventers and point-to-pointers in the field. We need to get them in their glad rags, adding to the glamour and the coffers. The hunt won't survive long enough for the ban to be lifted unless we get these young'uns to really join in on every level. We want them in their bally warpaint.'

'A unique selling point to attract them to the ball?'

'Exactly! Can I leave it with you?'

'By all means.'

'Jolly good,' she beamed. 'I'll tell Ellen that you're on the case. She'll be thrilled. Not really fair lumbering her with it all when she's heavily pregnant, and dear Jasper is so busy these days.'

Ely gave her another dry smile, doubting that Ellen would feel relieved to have his help. She had, after all, stolen Ely's selected son-in-law from under his nose. They were hardly on speaking terms.

'When is the baby due?'

'Beginning of March. St John is terribly excited – we all are.'

'Surely you can't risk the hunt ball clashing with the birth?'

'We're holding it early this year.' Hell's Bells checked her diary. 'The last Friday in February was the date agreed although, God knows, we'll have to get proper invitations out pronto. Ah! Here we are – the twenty-ninth. I say!'

'It's a leap year.'

'Yes. And that means it's a Look Before You Leap ball. What fun!'

Ely ran a perfectly manicured thumb along his neat white beard and creased his clever blue eyes. 'I have an idea . . .'

I

Magnus Olensen-Willis was not a rock star name. But Magnus had never wanted to be a rock star. He wanted to be a professional musician; a moderately successful singer-songwriter, perhaps. Well respected, certainly – renowned, even. Famous – no way. Or at least that's what he told his family.

His friends the Three Disgraces knew differently. They'd hung around enough at Magnus's band practices and gigs to realise that the dopey blond's dreams lay well beyond the realms of Oddlode's goth-metal ensemble, Roadkill. Fronted by the wailing, white-faced Godspell Gates, the band made a dreadful sound even to the Disgraces' undiscerning ears. Magnus's exquisite guitar playing was lost amid the thrashing din of Saul Wyck's drumming and the string-chewing antics of bassist Ket, just as Magnus's soul-searching lyrics were obscured by larynx-garrotting screams. He had been at sea for months.

Tonight he had finally been washed ashore. Three hours of spats and deafening amp feedback had finally led the man accustomed to under-selling himself to offer an end of season giveaway. 'Either we play it my way or we stop playing.'

At which, Roadkill had stopped playing and disbanded.

'Shit, I should call Saul and apologise,' he told the Disgraces as they adopted their customary positions on the sofas by the New Inn fire, pints of Budvar in hand. 'We're booked to play the Trout in Huntscote on Friday. I don't want to let them down.'

'They're letting *you* down!' wailed Carry, the youngest of the Three Disgraces. 'Tonight was just a joke. You were right to quit.'

Earlier, she and her two elder sisters, Sperry and Fe, had loyally wound their way along the hundred yards of narrow, black-iced lane to watch Roadkill's 'new material' rehearsal. Forsaking their father's warm pub for the freezing, half-finished studios that Magnus and his stepfather were creating out of a burned-out old agricultural warehouse, they had dutifully listened to yet another musical assassination.

'They've just been using you,' Fe insisted, looking up as she rolled a cigarette.

Carry nodded. 'They wanted to get their hands on your equipment and your material and trash it, Mags.'

He shrugged. 'They have their own ideas. But it's not my band. I've got no right to interfere. I'll apologise tomorrow.'

So laid-back that he watched the world over his own feet, Magnus was an infuriating if adorable friend. Loyal, easy-going, sympathetic, funny and incredibly talented. And, occasionally, a total mug.

'They're holding you back.' Sperry didn't look up from texting.

'They don't even *like* you,' Fe reminded him. 'They said so.'

'They said they didn't like my "look".' He ran his hand self-consciously through his blond mop and cast an eye down to his chunky green sweater. 'And perhaps they're right – I look bloody preppy these days. My mother bought me this for Christmas and I have to wear it all of January to keep her sweet.'

'Preppy? C'mon!' Fe snorted. 'You're gorgeous. All the girls fall for you. You're Chris Martin, Brad Pitt and Jude Law all rolled into one. Even our mum says you're like a young Robert Redford – whoever he is.'

'And that's not preppy?'

She tilted her head thoughtfully. 'Well, you could lose the jumper.'

'Thanks.'

'You *were* cooler when we met you.' Again, Sperry didn't look up from texting.

'I've been countrified.'

'You'll be countrified with a different spelling if you get back together with Godspell and Saul. Dye your hair skunk and we'll disown you.'

'Tempting. I might get a bit of action without you three cramping my style.'

'Not with skunk hair, you won't. Anyway, I thought you said you were enjoying being single?'

Having never been without at least one girlfriend until the Three Disgraces came along, Magnus was rather baffled now to find himself with three ravishing chaperones who refused to let another woman near him. They fascinated him, with their confidence and bravado. They also confounded him. The friendship wasn't yet losing its novelty value, but he couldn't figure it out.

Magnus had arrived with his family from urban Essex the previous summer, immediately causing a stir amongst the younger female population of the Lodes Valley. Tall and blue-eyed, he drove a vintage Porsche, talked to anybody, laughed a lot and flirted even more. Rumours quickly spread that he was a musician who'd been in a successful band. The Three Disgraces had wasted no time in befriending him for his own protection.

Savvy, streetwise and cocky, the three girls were the un-official, unholy Trinity of Lodes Valley youth, holding court in their father's Upper Springlode pub. They talked too fast, were the fastest texters around, rode their mopeds too fast along the lanes, fasted a lot to stay thin as rakes but they were resolutely not *fast* – just a little speedy. And Magnus was their new racing mascot. They'd immediately seen something special in him. They adored him. There had been no escape. Had it not been for a lifelong, unwritten pact that they never went after the same man, they would have fought tooth and nail over him. Instead, the Sixsmith sisters fought his corner and kept him willing captive to their charm, protecting him from less worthy female adversaries. Sharp good looks and song lyrics that cut into one's soul lent a quixotic, heroic angle to the dopey, gullible mug who was too honest for his own good. A free-spirited wolf lay beneath that waggy-tailed golden retriever exterior. Magnus had a sex appeal that made him the ultimate fashion accessory. And the Three Disgraces were slaves to fashion as well as friendship.

Magnus had tried to dispel their initial misconceptions as soon as they lured him into their fold. True, he'd always been in bands, but none of them had made it big time. At university, his band had been getting some impressive gigs, but that had all fallen apart when a motorbike accident put Magnus in hospital for six weeks and then forced him to postpone university for a year. Back in Essex, he'd formed a new band, Slackers, with two old school-friends. They had just started to get a real following when the entire family uprooted to the Cotswolds.

'I'm really just a failed engineering student with a limp who lives with his parents and plays guitar. In fact, I'm the kiss of death to bands,' he'd told them.

To their shame, it was the girls who had introduced him to Roadkill, never guessing at his latent talent. They'd just wanted to see him play on stage.

But Roadkill had tried to mould him into a skunk-haired weirdo.

'We think you should go it alone,' Carry told him now.

'And you'll be my Robert Palmer girls, I suppose?' he laughed.

'Who?'

'Forget it – stuff my stepfather likes.' He watched their blank expressions with amusement. With their identikit dark slanting eyes and glossy pouts they would make the perfect Palmeresque backing trio, if only they could be relied upon not to carry on texting throughout a musical number.

'So are you going to do it?' Carry urged.

'Nope. I've always been in bands. I like people around me. I only do it for fun.'

'I play netball for fun,' Fe shrugged. 'Doesn't mean I'd play for a shit team.'

'You *do* play for a shit team,' Carry pointed out.

'Do not!'

Watching them start a squawking match, Magnus knocked back his pint and tried not to think about his half-hearted attempt to quit the band. His edgy, soul-searching songs had been massacred beyond recognition. He knew Roadkill stank as much as its namesake did glued to melting tarmac in midsummer, but he had a rather suicidal addiction to it. He appreciated Godspell, Saul and Ket's carefree attitude and black humour, and the fact they didn't take him seriously. Ever since his accident, he'd struggled for direction. He didn't want to go back to university and his stepfather had thankfully sided with him on that. Graham, who had never gone to university and had made a mint in haulage, saw his stepson doing the same in music production – becoming a sound engineer and taking it from there, through graft and dedication, not a fast-track education. It suited Magnus because it meant he could lazily stay at home and set up his dream studio, gig with Roadkill and knock around with the Three Disgraces.

They had stopped scrapping now and were all looking at him

sceptically. Individually, they were pretty, but not knock-out. Collectively, with their smoky cat eyes, high cheeks and long, gleaming manes, they were electrifying. They had a strange power over him that he thoroughly enjoyed.

Magnus grinned. 'I won't get the skunk hair, okay?'

The cool, smooth faces kept on staring. It freaked him out when they did that.

'And I'll lose the jumper.'

The girls smiled with overpowering effect.

'Give.' Carry held out her hands.

'Yes, give.' Fe put her hands alongside, followed by Sperry.

Sighing, he pulled the sweater over his head and laid it on the outstretched hands.

Without warning, they launched it into the fire and let out shrieks of delight.

'My mother gave me that!' he wailed, watching it woof up in flames.

'Acrylic.'

'Cheap.'

'Probably panic shopping.'

The girls exchanged winks. Somehow, they would turn Magnus into a rock star. The name would have to change, of course, but they wouldn't break that to him just yet. Let him get over the jumper first.

Dilly Gently was a disastrous name to be lumbered with. The love-child of eighties New Romantic turned teenage seductress Ophelia Gently – or Pheely – she supposed she was lucky not to be called 'Softly'.

Now nineteen, she had just about developed the maturity to cope with the funny looks and sniggers she got when introducing herself. Most often she used her full name Daffodil, but it was such a mouthful and she loathed being nicknamed Daffy.

At thirty-five, her mother had not improved much on the name taste front. Baby Basil, born just two weeks earlier on New Year's Eve, was so named because Pheely had been in her larder at the time and had stared fixedly at the Schwartz basil pot throughout her labour. Poor Basil would have been named Schwartz had it not been for the thick mop of blond tresses he had appeared with.

'Why are both my children blond? I have such lovely rich-coloured hair. Dark is so much more dramatic.' She fingered her teak tresses petulantly at the mirror. 'I thought the dark gene was dominant over blond?'

'If it comes out of a bottle, genetics doesn't work that way,' Dilly told her, pulling on her coat. 'I think you'll find blonde and *mouse* are equally dominant. If you want Basil to take after you, I can always pick you up some dye from Boots.' She wrapped a scarf tightly around her neck.

Pheely nobly ignored the sarcasm. 'Are you going out?'

'Just Maddington.' It was what the locals called Market Addington, the closest thing to a metropolis that the Lodes Valley had to offer.

'Oh, goodie! I'll write you down a list.'

'I've got to run for the bus.' Dilly was already at the door, tripping over Hamlet the Great Dane who thought he was going to be taken for a walk.

'I'll text it to you then. Anke's coming round for a coffee and a chat in a minute. In fact, can you take your brother?'

'You *are* kidding?'

'I'll pay you.'

'In that case, I'll take you seriously.'

'Thank you, darling! Darling Dilly Gently.'

'Don't call me that. Just give me the money.'

All the Cottrell offspring had been given Christian names that began with P since time immemorial, and Peregrine 'Piggy'

Cottrell's crop had been no exception. The youngest of his children, however, had rebelled.

When they turned eleven, the twins had agreed that Phillip and Penelope were ghastly 'old' names to be lumbered with. Thus, Phillip had adopted the nickname given him by his elder brothers – 'Flipper' – which, as far as he knew, was something to do with an old kids' TV series that he had never seen. In turn, he had nicknamed his twin sister Penelope 'Nelly', after the elephant. This wasn't because Nell had ever been elephantine, but because she was always running away from home – packing her trunk and trying to leave the family circus.

Now twenty-three, the duo had hung onto those childhood nicknames. With their looks, the twins could have called themselves Sodom and Gomorrah and got away with it. Long-limbed, lean and as graceful as thoroughbred racehorses, they had inherited their mother's jet-black hair and the Cottrell grey-green eyes which were fringed with the longest, blackest lashes in the county. It was universally agreed that the Cottrell twins were the best looking family members, but also the most arrogant. And, for a family renowned for being stand-offish, that made them very arrogant indeed.

Flipper answered to no other name amongst his confidantes. Most of his clients used it, too, although, as a newly qualified equine vet, it caused occasional bafflement. He never explained it, simply introducing himself with a charming self-assurance that made his strange name appear alluring rather than ludicrous.

Nell had dropped the 'y', but she was still resolutely Nell without a pit-stop to Penelope permissible. If any of her family called her by her full name, she walked out of the room. And, while she no longer tried to run away from the circus, she dreamed constantly of escape.

Today was no exception. She was bored, as always. January

was such a dull month – the long, cold posting between Christmas and skiing. All the lovely parties were over, the gifts unwrapped and the mulled wine guzzled. There was nothing to look forward to and nothing to do.

Her parents thought that the cure to her ennui would be to get a job, but Nell was resisting the idea. They had been droning on about it again over breakfast, so she'd escaped to walk Milo, her chihuahua. Given his small stature and proximity to the frost-hardened ground, walking to the end of the drive was about all Milo could take, so he was now tucked up in her big leather bag watching the world go by from under her armpit.

Not that there was a lot of world to watch going by in Fox Oddfield. Action was limited to old Mrs Pickering (known as 'Pickitup') rooting through the hedgerows for hazelnuts and discarded litter, dressed in her usual multiple layers. She looked as though she had randomly stage-dived onto a jumble-sale trestle. Nell recognised one of her father's ancient flat caps and a pair of her mother's ghastly checked golfing slacks.

Giving her a wide berth, Nell trudged through the small hill hamlet and onto the bridle-way that ran alongside the pheasant shoot. Her father had once prided himself on running the best shoot in the Cotswolds, but the woods, coppices and drives had recently been sold, along with a great swathe of family land. The year before that, the London house had been leased out. Times were hard for the Cottrell family. The auctioneering and surveying business started by Nell's great grandfather was struggling to keep afloat.

She missed the Chelsea house. Had it still been available, she would be there now, raiding the January sales and seeing her friends. She'd been furious with her father for letting strangers take it on. It was her bolt-hole.

'We got up to all sorts, didn't we, Milo?' She tickled the nose beneath her armpit. Milo – named after a favourite ex-boyfriend – let out a cold-nosed snort.

Plucking her mobile from her pocket, Nell idly called her brother.

'What do you want?' He was characteristically brusque.

'I'm bored. What are you up to? Got time for coffee?'

'I'm giving a plasma drip to a premature foal. Please don't ring my mobile when I'm on call.'

'C'mon, Flips. When are you free? Daddy's being vile to me again. Says I've got to get a job.'

'You *do* have to get a job – whoa, whoa sweetheart. You're fine. Stand still.'

'He'll get me some ghastly admin job at the estate agency.'

'You know the rules. It's that or find a rich husband,' Flipper reminded her. 'I've gotta go. Why not beg a coffee from Trudy? Or Spurs' pretty wife – you like her. Pour your heart out to one of them, darling one.'

'But only you understand me, Flips.'

'Unfortunately so. Call me later. *Much* later.'

Sighing, Nell stashed her phone away and kicked a frozen divot up in the air.

Flipper had become increasingly distanced lately. Her twin, her beloved best friend of a brother, had a life beyond hers even though they now shared the same big flat in the attic of their parents' house, had the same friends and shared every secret. His job was shutting her out.

At first, Nell had joined her brother in his ambition to become a vet. They had always been fiercely competitive as well as frighteningly close, and they had progressed through the lower rungs of academia neck and neck – twelve A-grade GCSEs, two brace of A-grade A-levels each. Then Flipper had won a place at Bristol as a vet student, and Nelly hadn't. Her interview had gone well, she was equally qualified. The rejection was as hurtful as it was baffling.

Instead of taking up her place at second-choice Liverpool, she had changed her mind about veterinary medicine and announced her intention of taking a foundation course in art, basing herself in the London house with its custodian, great-aunt Grania. There, she had partied mercilessly. The foundation course – which she had scraped through because she was clever and talented despite her chronic laziness – was followed by a journalism course and then an acting course and finally a fashion design course, all funded by her long-suffering parents. Only the leasing of the house had called a halt to Nell's endless search for the perfect niche career. Now she was trapped in the Cotswolds, uncertain what to do.

In London, she had come and gone as she wished, sharing the house with great-aunt Grania who was as deaf as a post and usually three parts cut, enabling her to turn a blind eye to Nell's antics. With a generous trust fund, Nell had lived life to the full.

Now she and great-aunt G were back in the Cottrell bosom, living in separate quarters in her parents' draughty country pile and exchanging looks of mutual pity if they ever passed in a stairwell. The fun years were over. At twenty-three, Nell knew that this was far too soon. She *so* craved fun.

At least coming home had coincided with Flipper's return to the fold to take up a post at Foxrush Equine Clinic. Curiously, being apart hadn't affected their closeness – just as it hadn't when sent to separate single-sex boarding-schools. Throughout his training in Bristol and her dilettante diplomas in London, Flipper and Nell had spoken several times a day and stayed with one another often. Now that they were under the same roof once more, Flipper's dedication to his career left Nell feeling left out. It was the first time she felt that she didn't understand him entirely. She had no such passion. His volatile on-off love-life she could understand – it had always been as stormy and chaotic as her own. His dedication to his vocation was a mystery.

None of the Cottrells was passionate about work. About horses, yes – plus country pursuits, fine food and wine, friends and, most of all, family. Work was a necessary evil. It was one of the reasons the family company was flailing.

Nell was not alone in her lack of direction. It was an inherited trait. Her elder brothers Piers and Phinneas (known as Finn) were barely even part-timers at the auction house as they pursued their preferred pastimes of horse dealing and house restoration respectively. Elder sister, Phoney, was a full-time mother. Her father was practically retired, and doting mother Dibs had never worked in her life.

They all lived together in various wings, cottages and farms at Fox Oddfield Abbey, a decrepit Cotswold stone pile set in a beautiful but ever-dwindling estate. When Piggy had snapped it up in the early nineties 'for a song', he had been full of bold, entrepreneurial ideas. A conference centre, luxury holiday destination, apartments or even a theme park. Of course, nothing had come of it. The family always got in the way. Just like the house they had lived in before – the Manse in Oddlode – it was used and abused like a tatty old pair of gumboots. Now it was falling apart.

She turned to look at it briefly, walking backwards. A huge, ornate slab of eighteenth-century Cotswold stone neo-classicism squatted regally upon the long-gone site of the original twelfth-century Cistercian Abbey. She knew it to be a beautiful house – even Pevsner had raved about its Palladian lines and Corinthian portico. Framed by poplar avenues and lime walks, the Abbey certainly loomed large above little Fox Oddfield, but it did absolutely nothing for Nell and it had never really felt like home.

Piggy liked to live in houses with religious connotations. It assuaged his Catholic guilt.

Nell found the place creepy. It was only having Flipper around that stopped her freaking out up in the attics late at night. In midwinter it was freezing, damp, draughty and deeply inhospitable. She was convinced that her parents had deliberately let most of the house and its farms and cottages go to pot in order to lure the extended family back into the heart of the house. At this time of year, the only warmth in the whole of the Abbey could be drawn from the huge kitchen range and the ever-roaring fire in the main hall.

And this morning, lured into the kitchen at the prospect of thawing out her feet, Nell had been caught between her parents in a skilled pincer movement as they demanded she find gainful employment.

She watched as a fat pheasant squawked its way airborne. Perhaps Flipper was right. Perhaps it was time to find a rich husband. It would certainly beat working for a living.

2

Market Addington wasn't the most exquisite and tourist friendly of Cotswold towns. More workmanlike and agricultural than its near neighbours, Morrell-on-the-Moor and Idcote-over-Foxrush, it still boasted a wonderful array of lopsided, honeyed stone terraces, mullioned windows, grand Georgian shop-fronts and twisting back alleys crammed with cottagey antique shops. But it hadn't the gourmet-and-patterned-welly glamour of Morrell or the picturesque riverside quaintness of Idcote. The weekly farmers' and street markets sold more cheap seed potatoes and bargain fabric than sides of venison and tapestry cushions. The shops were utilitarian and functional rather than over-priced treasure-troves of lifestyle accessories. It even boasted one or two high street chain stores, unheard of in other local thoroughfares.

On a bitterly cold January afternoon, it certainly wasn't at its most attractive or welcoming. Perched high on the escarpment between the Lodes and Foxrush valleys, it was taking the full brunt of a bitter easterly wind that was rattling the tiles and stones on roofs almost disappearing into misty black clouds. Litter scuttled along the pavements, bad-tempered shoppers shouldered their way into the wind without looking where they were going, and unexpected gusts snatched hats from heads and toys from pushchairs.

As Dilly trudged around the January sales pushing the buggy ahead of her, she decided bringing baby Basil shopping had not been a great idea. Little old ladies were dive-bombing her left,

right and centre, collecting windswept Fimbles and Tellytub-
bies that had fallen overboard, then holding them ransom until
they had given Basil a thorough cooing and checking-over.

'Aw, what a lovely little chap – just a few weeks old is he?'

'Two weeks.'

'Looks just like you. So nice to see a young mum these days –
far too many of these modern mothers leave it until they're as
old as forty.'

'He's my brother. Our mother is almost forty.'

At least having Basil in tow meant that Dilly was spared the
usual leering from the Maddington menfolk. They hardly gave
her a passing glance as she pushed Basil along the High Street
pavements. Not that Dilly blamed them. In her shapeless duffle
coat and combats with her blonde hair crammed into a woolly
hat, she hardly cut her usual glamorous figure. And she had no
desire to any more. She was, after all, heartbroken. She had put
on almost a stone in a month, a fact from which she drew more
comfort than just the comfort eating. She liked the warm
blanket it provided around her, insulating her from male
attention as well as the cold.

In truth, the weight had started to pile on some time before
she had been so unceremoniously dumped on New Year's Eve.
It had started to gather forces around her hips and bust as soon
as she started living with boyfriend, Pod, cooking lavish meals
for him, sharing endless bottles of wine, loving the domesticity.
She hadn't noticed at the time. Then, after the terrible day that
he'd left her sitting alone with a three-course meal which he had
never come home to eat, the same day her baby brother was
born, Dilly had found herself singly eating for two. She told
herself that she was binge-eating for both halves of her broken
heart.

She had always been totally ruled by her heart. Even now,
shattered as it was, it dictated her every move – right down to

today's trip to Maddington. Despite the tears, the self-loathing, utter rejection and dejection, and the mourning, grieving, abandoned sense of loss, Dilly's heart kept her moving, refused to let her lie down in her bed and weep for ever as she had tried to. It was a restless beast, far too broken to ever think of loving again, but in need of comfort and protection. And now that the Christmas leftovers and chocolate were eaten up, there wasn't enough comfort eating to keep it satisfied. Dilly's heart needed an armour-plated make-over.

Daffodil Gently wanted to be ugly. All her life she had been admired for her effortless looks – long, curly golden hair; a leggy, busty, flat-bellied figure; big green eyes set in a pretty face. Well, look where it had got her. Heartbroken. Used. Abused. Rejected.

It was time to get ugly. She had ditched her contact lenses in favour of her oldest pair of National Health specs and was dallying with the idea of cutting all her hair off. For someone for whom looking good had always been enviably effortless, looking bad took more work and more thought than she'd anticipated, but she was enjoying the challenge.

Today, she was on a mission to buy herself the cheapest, most hideous clothes she could find – but Basil kept getting in the way. It was typical of Dilly's mother, Pheely, to foist the baby on her daughter at the last minute – turning a quick trip to Market Addington into a marathon involving buggy, nappy-changing kit, unwanted old lady attention and endless mobile phone calls.

On cue her phone rang with *You're So Vain* – a tune Dilly had allocated to incoming calls from her mother's mobile.

'Hi, Mummy.'

'Just checking all well?'

'Same as half an hour ago – I left him outside the Co-op and somebody snatched him.'

'You mustn't joke about things like that. He needs feeding soon. You haven't used up all the expressed milk, have you?'

'I gave it to a wino – after all, it's about forty per cent proof. I can't believe you got so pissed last night when you're breast-feeding.'

Dilly was in a bad mood. She wanted to be mean as well as ugly. All this conspired to make her unusually spiteful. The all-new, heartbroken Dilly was learning to express her anger at last – perhaps too well.

At the other end of the line, Pheely burst into tears. Still swilling with hormones after giving birth in her larder on New Year's Eve a fortnight earlier, reeling from a new child car-crashing its way into her dozy, dilettante life nineteen years after the last one had arrived, and wincing from a hangover after sharing a bottle of brandy with friend Pixie the night before, Pheely was ultra-sensitive to her daughter's black mood and censure.

'How could you *say* things like that? I knew I should never have trusted you with him!'

'That's what I told you, Mum, but would you listen?'

'Bring him home *at once*!'

'I've only just got here.' Glancing across the High Street, Dilly spotted a row of familiar, tatty mopeds parked illegally in a Disabled space. The Three Disgraces were in town. Her heart, which had felt about as low as it could go, managed to sink a few more inches.

'What's happened to you?' Pheely was sobbing theatrically. 'You used to be such a lovely girl, Dilly Gently.'

'Don't call me that!' Dilly rang off in a huff and pushed Basil tetchily towards Dorothy Perkins.

'All right, Dills?'

She started as she realised that Sperry Sixsmith was lounging in the shadows by the Lloyds' cash-point, all slanting eyes, fake fur and glossy mane.

'Hi,' she greeted cautiously.

Dilly had always been wary of the Sixsmith girls. They had never been anything but polite and courteous to her, but she sensed enmity in them, and none more so than from Sperry, the oldest and sassiest.

'This your baby brother?' Sperry was peering into the pram, holding her cigarette at a respectful distance above her head.

'Yeah.' Dilly wondered why she always roughened her accent when she was talking to Sperry, trying to match it to Sperry's husky Cotswolds burr. She supposed it was a pathetic attempt at being accepted. There was a time when she had longed to be a part of their hardened teenage gang, to be just like them. She still held them in awe.

'Cute. Looks like his dad.'

Dilly said nothing, trying to keep her face blank. Not many people knew that Basil had been fathered by local Lothario, Giles Hornton, but the Three Disgraces – who knew everything – were certainly in on the secret.

'So what'y'up to?' Sperry looked up at her, cat eyes assessing the bad skin, duffle coat and National Health specs.

'You know – shopping. Sales. Looking for a bargain. You?'

'Same. Heading for a drink at the Boar in a bit. You want to join us?'

Dilly reeled. An invitation from the Three Disgraces to join the inner circle was sacred.

Sperry checked an incoming text on her mobile and fired out a reply while she waited for Dilly's response.

Feigning insouciance, Dilly held up her own mobile to keep up appearances and tapped out '*Sorry – PMT*' to her mother.

'We're meeting up with Mags. You know Mags, don't you?' Sperry looked up from sending another text.

'Maggie who?'

'Magnus – a bloke. Good-looking fuckwit.'

'Oh, him.' Dilly tried to sound ultra-casual, although she knew full well that, as the best-looking male to arrive in Oddlode since Spurs Belling, Magnus was already a local legend. 'Our mums are close – we've met a couple of times, yeah.'

While Sperry took a call, Dilly scrolled her own phone's menu up and down for something to do. Magnus had always been very friendly to her, but he was far too cool for her to get to know properly. He was well-rumoured to be going out with all three of the Disgraces, which even to bohemian Dilly was excessive. Despite several attempts made by Pheely and Magnus's mother, Anke, to throw them together, he was a part of the scary Sixsmith set and the even scarier Roadkill mob, and that made them a part of two different worlds in one small village.

As soon as Sperry rang off from her call, her right thumb started punching out yet another text.

'Your mum well? After the birth?' She didn't look up.

'Yes – fine.' Dilly carried on scrolling.

Soon they were both beeping away, Sperry sending and receiving texts, Dilly reorganising her phonebook.

It was the modern-day equivalent of Restoration ladies communicating from behind their fans, constructing all sorts of strange, coquettish, lacy ways of wafting air around their faces as they feigned insouciance whilst exchanging gossip in a complicated ritual of one-upmanship.

'You and Pod Shannon split up, I hear?' Sperry took a phone photo of Basil to send to her mother.

Dilly felt the familiar fist punch its way at her heart, smashing it into smaller fractions. Her tear ducts instantly started whooshing round like a Hotpoint hitting the rinse cycle. Somebody had cut her windpipe again. With great effort she blinked back the waterworks and found a few small pockets of air to breathe.

'He dumped me, if that's what you mean.'

'You and Rory going to get back together now?'

'Doubt it.' Dilly read her mother's reply text '*Try post natal – much worse than pre menstrual.*' Was that a peace offering or were they still arguing, she wondered.

'So you've got plenty of free evenings?'

Dilly looked up sharply. Was Sperry seriously trying to befriend her?

'Some.'

Sperry read another incoming text. 'You can sing, can't you? You were in choirs and operas and stuff.'

Dilly winced. She preferred not to be reminded of the years when her mother had forced her to perform star turns, enrolling her in every dancing and singing society in the Lodes Valley. Her *Little Orphan Annie* still haunted her.

'I don't sing much these days.'

'You play an instrument?'

'Piano mostly, but I'm pretty hopeless.' The Grade Six exam had reduced her to tears, and she had smashed her flute over her bedhead when her mother had locked her in her room to force her to practise.

'So you coming for that drink, then? Cheer you up.'

Bewildered by the invitation and the strange line of questioning, Dilly longed to agree, but her tear ducts were filling up again, that fist was using her chest as a punch bag and the air was thinning around her.

'I'm not sure Basil's up to it. He's only two weeks old.' She nodded towards her baby half-brother as an excuse, although she knew that wasn't the full truth of it.

It was Dilly who wasn't up to the Three Disgraces yet. One drink and she'd be weeping all her secrets to the biggest gossips in the Vale. Just thinking about Pod made her unstable, torn between sobbing hysterically on Maddington High Street and throwing a brick through Lloyds' window.

'Shame.' Sperry clicked her tongue against her cheek and sighed. 'Magnus needs cheering up, too. Roadkill have split up.'

'His band?' Dilly was only half-interested.

'Yeah – artistic differences. Godspell and Saul have ganged up against him.'

'Hardly surprising. Godspell is a complete bitch. That band was crap, anyway.'

Sperry whistled in delight. 'And I'd always heard you never had a bad word to say about anyone.'

'Well, you heard wrong.' Dilly lifted her chin defiantly, tipping the waiting tears to the back of her throat and embracing her new mean, ugly stance. 'I'm actually quite a bitch.'

'Oh, I have heard that,' Sperry laughed.

'You have?' she squeaked in a tight voice.

Eyeing her curiously, Sperry reached out a long, bony hand and squeezed Dilly's shoulder. 'Hey, I'm a much bigger bitch. Don't let the bastard get you down. With your looks, you'll get another one straightaway.'

'I don't want another one.'

'We all say that.'

'I mean it.'

'Yeah yeah. You'll fall in love again soon enough.'

'I'd rather fuck my way through a phone directory than fall in love again. He said he was my soulmate, but he was just an arsehole.'

Sperry's phone beeped a text alert, but she ignored it, still looking intently at Dilly, her slanting eyes unexpectedly soft.

'Bitches don't find soulmates. Believe me, I should know.'

Dilly felt tears at minus ten and counting.

As a sudden cold wind howled along Market Addington

High Street, rattling the baby buggy, Basil let out a mewlish whimper of protest.

'Must go.' She let off the wheel brake. 'Bargains to snap up. Enjoy your drink.'

She made it into Dorothy Perkins just in time to whip the first item she passed from its rail, charge into a changing cubicle and, with Basil's buggy poking out of the curtain, she cried as quietly as she could, muffling her sobs and splutters with her gloved hands.

'Low self-esteem,' Sperry told her sisters later over a brace of Hooch and a J20 for under-age Carry. 'She's got all the classic signs.'

'A spoilt brat if you ask me.' Fe sniffed disparagingly.

'Nah, that's what people always say about them, but folk with low self-esteem aren't really spoilt at all. They just display the symptoms.'

Sperry's sisters looked at her in disbelief.

'Look at her – pretty, clever, funny. Granted. But she's never made the most of herself. Yeah, she flirts with men and breaks hearts just like her mum, but has she ever been happy? Ask yourself that. Rory and Pod walked all over her. She needs men to desire her to make her feel good, but it never works. And all that centre of attention stuff is just a sign of how insecure she is. That's why she's got no female friends her own age – why she's never wanted to be our mate.'

'We'd never *have* her as a mate.'

'I would,' Sperry said thoughtfully. 'She's cute when she's angry. And I reckon we could straighten her out.'

'What are you on? Some sort of agony aunt mission?' Fe demanded.

Sperry gave her an enigmatic smile. 'Perhaps I am.'

'Fuck off.'

'What's wrong with trying to spread a little happiness?'

'Christ! Ever since Magnus came along, you've been all do-goody fucking moral crusade. You're just the same with him, banging on about making him take a break from serial mono-gamy to recognise the "real" value of love. What do you know about love?'

'A lot more than you, little sister.'

'Like hell. You love them and leave them,' Fe pointed out.

'Exactly. We all do.'

'What's that supposed to mean?'

Sperry leaned across the table towards her sisters, propping her chin on her steepled-together fingertips. 'Think of true love as the most delicious thing you've ever eaten.'

'Like chocolate?' suggested Carry.

'Like chocolate,' she nodded, 'but not any old Galaxy bar. True love is a really dark, bitter, cocoa-rich chocolate for connoisseurs.'

'Ugh.'

Sperry pressed her palms tighter together, getting into her topic. 'Now I've taste-tested love, but I'm not ready to eat it every day. I'm a Galaxy girl through-and-through and that's just a quick fix. Bitter chocolate lovers are the true passion junkies. To Magnus, being loved is a basic fodder he takes for granted – he just fuels up on it wherever and whenever, like buying a Mars bar at a service station to boost his sugar levels. Except he's being offered connoisseur chocolate all the time, but he grazes on it because he has no idea what he's eating. He treats all love like junk food. He's never been without it until now, and he was on a shit fast-food diet when we met him.'

'Talking of which, I'm starving.' Carry scanned the menu, tiring of her sister's cod psychology.

But Sperry was on a roll. 'Now Dilly – Dilly is all feast or all famine. She's so in love with the idea of loving someone, she forgets to love herself. She feeds love to other people and starves herself. Then, when it all goes wrong, she binges to cheer herself up. She doesn't know how to be loved properly.'

'I thought you said she was looking fat?' Fe sniggered.

'She is. That's because she hasn't got anyone to love.'

'So you're saying she's loving herself now by feeding herself?' Fe sneered.

'Sounds like she just loves food,' muttered Carry, still salivating over the menu.

'It's a metaphor,' Sperry sighed, looking wisely from one sister to another. 'By feeding herself, Dilly is substituting her need for love, but that's not the point. The point is that for the first time in her life, she's bitten off more than she can chew. The point is that Pod was bitter chocolate. He was all grown up and—'

'And the sexiest bastard that ever walked the earth,' sighed Fe, who had harboured a long crush on Pod.

'The point is that Dilly is addicted to love. Without someone to love, she will self-destruct.' Sperry thought back to the image of Dilly wandering along the High Street earlier, unaware that she was being watched, a lost soul in a duffle coat – later racing away to hide her impending tears. Something about her had ripped at Sperry's conscience.

'What has that got to do with chocolate?' asked Carry, confused.

Sperry opened her hands in despair and then slid her head between them. Self-assured, cocky and just a little bit know-it-all, Sperry Sixsmith might be a regular character assassin, but she was also a small-time philosopher and she had got Dilly's measure totally.

The two girls had never been friends, but they had grown up sharing the same small pool of under-age drinking dens and village hall parties, and their paths had crossed on numerous occasions. Sperry knew enough about Dilly's childhood to realise where a lot of her insecurities sprang from, and that her natural good looks came from a very unnatural pairing.

Her mother, Pheely, had been brought up almost wild by gregarious, widowed sculptor Norman Gently. Under-educated and over-exposed to an academic, bohemian party set that treated her as a pet, she had always done as she pleased which had included being happily seduced by ruthless, dynamic Ely Gates. The result was Dilly. Back then, Ely had been a tall, blond village heartthrob by all accounts, although Sperry found that hard to imagine now, given the white-bearded pomposity of Oddlode's self-styled local entrepreneur, church-goer, philanthropist and groin-led moral hypocrite.

Despite providing generously for his only naturally born child, Ely had steadfastly refused to be a part of Dilly's life. Married to the saintly Felicity, Ely had no desire to complicate and muddy his life with a love-child, although Dilly's parentage was an open village secret. Poor Felicity, who could not have children of her own, had never raised a word of complaint at the thousands of pounds spent on Dilly's education and 'improve-ment'. Their beloved, adopted children, Godspell and Enoch, had received similarly generous investments after all.

Not that Dilly's expensive education had made her life easy. As far as Sperry could make out, Dilly's mother had been basically under orders – and great financial pressure – to create a wonder-child in Ely's own image. From ballet classes to extra maths to singing lessons to Pony Club camp, Dilly had been denied nothing in her childhood improvement except friend-ship. Pretty, precocious, hothoused and isolated emotionally, she'd made no lasting friends. She didn't know how to make friends. She just knew how to please her mother. And her education, paid through Ely's business account, was no less destructive to her relationships.

Dilly was sent away to a posh boarding-school – Sperry remembered her disappearing from Brownies. Shortly after that, her grandfather had died, and Pheely had moved from the big house into the little studio cottage in its gardens. A local rumour spread that the hell-raising sculptor was haunting Oddlode Lodge, but the truth was far more prosaic. Pheely was broke – remained so pretty much to this day. Lovable, talented, eccentric Norman had left crippling death duties and personal debts along with a beautiful house and a garden full of sculptures that Pheely refused to sell. Only her daughter benefited from outside funds, and those were carefully accounted. Ely Gates refused to love his child just as he refused to love the mother of his child, but he paid one's way while he dispassionately watched the other struggle to keep afloat. Local legend had it that Pheely had eaten nothing but baked potatoes for that year, working at a local petrol station forecourt to keep afloat while trying to market her own less lucrative artwork. Dilly had run away from school several times in her first term. Devastated by the death of her father, Pheely had sent her back every time, struggling to hold everything together, to appear fearless and in control at a time when Dilly needed her most.

Pheely's relationship with her daughter was complex and volatile. There had been pressure for Dilly to do well in every sphere. Sperry remembered the legendary Gently mother-and-daughter tantrums dating back to fancy dress competitions at village fêtes and flute recitals at harvest festival. Protective and competitive, Pheely had not only wanted Dilly to get all the opportunities denied to her in her own childhood, but had also been desperate for her daughter to prove herself brighter, more talented and more successful than Godspell, on whom Ely doted. As a result, Dilly had turned into a multi-skilled, better-educated and more fucked-up version not only of her adoptive sister, but also of her mother. She alienated her peers by being too bright, too weird, too pretty and too desperate to please. She was cosseted beyond redemption. She and Pheely lived in their ridiculous cowshed alongside a huge, beautiful house that they could no longer afford to run but refused to sell. They did their own thing. Dilly was a 'weird' kid. To her shame, Sperry had blanked her for over a decade as a result. Pheely and Dilly Gently had been seen as a comedy double-act and Sperry had been happy to laugh along at the joke. Only today, seeing Dilly pushing a pram along Maddington High Street, Sperry had done a double-take. Dilly Gently had grown up. She was no longer the weird kid. Life had knocked the soft edges off her prettiness, yet there was still a sad beauty about her which took the breath away.

Last year, Dilly had dropped out of university and dropped adoring, adorable boyfriend Rory for a seductive bastard – the sort her mother specialised in. The only thing Dilly shared completely with her mother was a disastrous love-life. It was the same thing she had in common with Sperry.

'She's addicted to love,' she repeated, grabbing the menu from Carry, too caught up in her own thoughts to notice that Magnus had just limped up to their table in an ancient woolly hat from which a few blond curls licked their way on to the scuffed collar of his old leather trench coat.

'Addicted to love? Don't tell me you've been listening to Robert Palmer?'

'No. Sperry's just been banging on about you, chocolate and Dilly.' Fe leaped up to kiss him, taking the first taste of his cool, stubbly cheek.

'Dilly who?' He stooped to kiss the others, unwinding his long scarf and settling his pint on the table.

'Gently.'

'Diligently. You *are* joking?'

'Ophelia Gently's daughter.'

'Pheely Gently,' Carry corrected. 'Mad as a hare.'

'Of course. The sculptress. She's one of my mum's mates. Crazy bird.'

'As is the daughter.'

'With a name like that, who can blame her? Is she the blonde? Hair like Kidman, lips like Jolie?'

'You've met?' Sperry grinned.

He nodded, wide eyebrows curling together in apologetic appreciation. 'Only in passing. We say "Hi" and I ogle. Nuff said. Why?'

The Three Disgraces lifted their heads from their necks in unison, like meerkats. As those slanting eyes slid past one another, the slim lips barely moved, but the message passed smoothly between Fe and Carry: 'They must be kept apart.'

Sperry, meanwhile, let a small smile play on her slender mouth. 'What you doing this Thursday, Mags?'

'You tell me.'

'Holding auditions for your new band.'

Magnus removed his woolly hat and scratched his head. 'T'yeah. It may have escaped your attention, but I'm already in a band.'

'Not any more. Roadkill's definitely over,' Sperry reported solemnly.

'Says who?'

'Ket texted me today. Saul and Godspell want a fresh start. They're calling themselves Trackmarks. Saul's cousins Jobe and Moses are in and you're out.'

'Why didn't they say anything last night?' Magnus hid his hurt behind a wall of smiles and bafflement, but the girls saw straight through it.

'You were the one who quit, remember?'

'We'll see about that!' He almost upended the table in his haste to get out.

'Told you he'd get even sexier when he's angry,' Sperry smirked at her sisters. 'Just like Dilly. They have so much in common.'

'What are you up to, Esperanza?' Fe asked her sister darkly.

Sperry was right. Dilly and Magnus had a lot in common.

They were both far too biddable and good-looking for their own good. They both had low self-esteem. They both under-valued themselves and held too much belief in others. They hated hurting people. They both adored their mothers, despite ongoing conflict. They had many passing friendships but no confidantes. They were diffident and disillusioned and easily led.

They both owned battered old cars that they cherished. Both motors were too ancient and cranky to cope with a startlingly cold January of frosts and fog. Dilly's heavily dented, twenty-year-old 2CV had died when her mother had driven it into a tree; Magnus's beloved yellow 70s' Porsche had staged a drama queen collapse on a quiet back lane just a few days ago.

And today these two lazy, lost, attractive souls were on the same irregular bus heading from Market Addington to the same village, in a similarly vile temper.

Dilly and Basil were up front, close to the driver, eyes clenched shut – Basil because he was asleep; Dilly because she had just spent forty pounds she didn't have on a truly vile collection of cut-price outfits that made her feel fittingly bad.

Magnus was at the very back of the bus, plugged into his iPod, listening angrily to music made by far more talented musicians than he could ever hope to be.

It was only when they reached the first Oddlode bus stop, by the station – opposite Wyck Farm where Magnus lived – that the two kindred spirits recognised one another. As Magnus

brushed past Basil's buggy, he stooped to retrieve a discarded
Fimble toy and his eyes inadvertently caught Dilly's.

'Hi there!'

Dilly smiled, taking the toy. 'Hi yourself. Thanks. You well?'

'Great.' He pulled out one iPod earphone. 'You?'

'Fine, thanks.' She looked away.

It was their customary patter, except this time he waited until
she looked him in the eye again. One hand stayed on the seat in
front of her, the other on the edge of the open bus door. Dilly
was too busy tracing the seams of the Fimble to notice, but she
was acutely aware that he was still hanging around, too big and
blond for comfort.

'You sold your 2CV?'

'Clinically dead.' Dilly was amazed he had noticed what car
she drove. 'Your Porsche?'

He was chuffed that she'd clocked his beloved old yellow car.
'On life support but basically a vegetable.'

The bus driver started to mutter irritably about 'time-
wasting young twits trying to ask a girl on a date'.

Dilly looked up in nervous amusement. Old ladies were
starting to barrack at the back.

Magnus's friendly blue eyes were smiling down at her, his
broad shoulders relaxed, hands straddling the front seat and
bus door like an eagle's wings clipping two forest pines.

'That's some span.' She looked from his left fingertips to his
right. 'Do you hold up buses regularly?'

'Only when I'm feeling militant.'

The driver stamped on his air brakes noisily, trying to hurry
them up as the old ladies at the back threatened mutiny.

To Dilly's amazement, Magnus turned and apologised to
them all.

'Forgive me. I'm just plucking up the courage to ask something.'

The entire bus fell silent, apart from the high-pitched tones of hearing aids being turned up.

Dilly stared furiously and in terror at her lap as he swooped his mouth close to her ear.

'What's two plus two?' He dropped a kiss on her ear, as light as a breath. And he was gone.

Dilly laughed, genuinely and deliciously, for the first time in weeks.

At least one of the Three Disgraces would have been proud.

As Magnus leaped lamely on to the pavement, he looked up at Dilly through the misted windows and she stared back. A smile broke across two faces. Smiles that cheered up a drab January day. Nothing miraculous, but everything cheering.

3

Dilly crunched hurriedly along the gravel drive to Goose Cottage, dashed around to the back door and let herself in. Tripping her way past the discarded wellingtons in the boot room, she entered the welcoming warm fug of the kitchen. Her glasses steamed up as she closed the door on the cold, damp afternoon behind her, and she watched mistily as Snorkel the collie came flying around the corner, claws skittering across the flagstones in his hurry to greet her.

'Hello! Ellen? It's me!'

A teapot was resting on the top of the Aga and a milk bottle was on the surface. She helped herself to a mug of the golden brew. Not even stewed. Ellen must be close at hand.

Fetching a bar of Galaxy from Ellen's stash in the larder, she wandered excitedly towards the sitting-room with Snorkel at her heels, sipping her tea and steaming up her glasses even more.

'You'll never *guess* who gave me the hottest look on the bus just – oh, hi.'

Occupying the sofa opposite Ellen was an impossibly leggy figure with gleaming black hair and a smooth winter tan. Even through steamed-up glasses, Dilly recognised those wide-set verdigris eyes and that toothy smile.

'Dilly Gently!' came the husky whoop. 'How the devil are you?'

'God. Hi, Nell. You're . . . here,' she spluttered obviously.

'I moved back recently.' Nell re-crossed her long legs,

tipping off the tiny dog that was sitting on her lap so that it landed upside down between two scatter cushions. 'Just temporarily while I decide where to go next. I met Ellen through the Bellings. They've always been great chums with my mob.'

As the mist cleared from her lenses, Dilly took in the long leather boots, tailored shorts and fur-collared little jacket. Matched with the trendy, razor-cut, tufty hair, Nell looked a bit like a principal boy in a pantomime. But Penelope Cottrell had always been so screamingly sexy that the androgynous look just served to set off her huge, smoky eyes and athletic beauty.

'You two know one another?' Ellen was looking from one to the other cheerfully.

'We were at school together for a while.' Dilly felt the years concertina backwards as she remembered the same awestruck wonder hitting her when first meeting Penelope Cottrell – school trendsetter, rebel and all-round idol.

'Not in the same year, of course.' Nell was studying Dilly's drab outfit and dreadful glasses.

'Nell was my dormitory monitor,' Dilly explained. 'The older girls had to check up on the little ones – be their big sisters.'

To Dilly, Nell had been a goddess. Despite being a lax, uninterested and occasionally cruel dormitory monitor, Penelope Cottrell was such a figure of idolatry that having her as 'dorm mon' meant being the envy of most of the other younger girls. Dilly had adored her slavishly. The day that Nell had left had been one of her darkest schooldays.

'God, did I really do that?' Nell had extracted her small dog from the cushions and was cuddling him. 'I'm surprised they let me. I'd been expelled from so many schools by the time I arrived there that Daddy was threatening to get a private tutor in at home, which seemed almost tempting. The nuns at that school were like prison warders.'

'It was pretty draconian,' Dilly agreed, realising that Nell's memories of the school – and her stay there – were far vaguer than her own.

'I think I lasted four terms, which actually was rather a record.' Nell laughed, rolling a finger around her little dog's tiny ear, looking up at Dilly with the same direct silvery-green gaze that she had possessed all those years earlier when getting her to run errands, forcing her to tell lies on her behalf and ultimately swearing her to secrecy. And suddenly Dilly realised that Nell remembered everything just as vividly. How could she possibly forget?

Dilly remembered the exciting controversy that had surrounded Nell Cottrell's expulsion. Rumours had circulated like wildfire – that she had taken drugs, slept with a rock star, got a part in a Hollywood movie. Nell was like that – so glamorous and grown-up and wild that anything was possible, at least as far as her peers were concerned. And Dilly had kept all her secrets for her. To this day, even her oldest school-friends had no idea why Penelope Cottrell had left the school so suddenly under such a dark cloud. They'd had a pact, and Dilly had honoured it.

That they had continued growing up just a few country miles apart didn't mean that their paths had crossed regularly since, particularly as Nell spent most of her time in London as far as Dilly could tell. There had only been a handful of encounters at local horsy events, Young Farmers' balls and chance meetings in pubs – and on those rare occasions Nell usually blanked Dilly completely. She was four years older and that short half-decade was a lifetime apart in village social circles, particularly when you shared a secret that could wreck lives if it ever got out.

And now Dilly had walked into her favourite safe haven and confessional, into Ellen's warm, tatty sitting-room in which she had spent more hours than her own home, only to find her first true idol facing her.

Dilly's life had been peppered with big, doting crushes – on friends and animals, on celebrities and men. She adored to love, to hero-worship and to admire. She believed in soulmates, in forever togetherness and kindred spirits.

Ellen was her most recent idol – a wise, brave, sassy woman who took no nonsense and had bagged the sexiest man in Oddlode. But Nell was her first female love, and first pashes had a special place. Outspoken, undisciplined, flirty, argumentative – Nell was a legend in Dilly's lifetime. She had all the verve and nerve that Dilly felt she lacked with her wetness and kind-hearted weakness. And her beauty was the sort Dilly craved – not her own soft, child-like, Miss Pears' peaches-and-cream prettiness, but a fine, rare, high-cheeked bone structure hewn from Irish peat mixed with full-blooded, aristocratic, old English sandstone.

'So how do you know each other?' Nell was asking Dilly and Ellen, more from politeness than genuine interest.

They answered at the same time.

'I know Dilly's—'

'Ellen's my best—'

'– mother.'

'– friend.'

Nell's wide, straight eyebrows shot up.

'I'm friends with Dilly and Pheely,' Ellen explained kindly. 'So I get the best of both worlds.'

Dilly beamed at her gratefully.

Hopelessly excited and yet unsettled at the same time, she scuttled across to the sag bag in the corner and perched awkwardly on it, reaching out to stroke Finns the cat who was balanced on a sofa arm behind his mistress, flicking his tail disapprovingly.

'What were you saying about someone on a bus?' Ellen shifted her bulk on the sofa, which she was sharing with Snorkel. With her hair scraped back in a ponytail and her make-up-free face glowing healthily from pregnancy and good living, she could have easily passed for Dilly's age – and she knew how to pitch a conversation to suit her younger friend, knowing how much Dilly needed to talk right now. 'It's a good sign if you're noticing boys again.'

It was the word 'boys' that put Dilly off recounting her recent magic moment. It was nothing special, after all; just a heart-lifting little encounter of no consequence.

'Oh, it can wait.' She certainly didn't want to talk about stupid girly emotions in front of Nell. Nor did she want to talk about her heartbreak, a subject she was normally happy to bore Ellen with for hours. 'How are you feeling? Ankles still swollen?'

'No – they're much better.' Ellen rubbed her pregnant belly fondly. 'Being kicked to bits right now, but apart from that I'm feeling great. Even managed a decent night's sleep last night. How's Basil?'

'Gorgeous, heaven and perfection. I took him shopping to Maddington today. He was so good.'

'You have a baby of your own, Dilly?'

'No – no, he's my little brother. Just two weeks old.'

'How cute.' Nell wrinkled her nose insincerely, as though she could smell an unchanged nappy just at the thought.

Dilly licked her lips nervously, yet again aware of those big greeny-grey eyes on her face, uncertain how to play it.

'Basil's the best.'

'Dilly's fabulous with babies,' Ellen sighed happily.

Dilly kissed Finns on the nose. 'I'd love to have children of my own soon. I can't wait.'

'God, really?' Nell laughed in surprise.

'Yes. Absolutely. I want the most enormous family – like yours, I suppose. One day we can all share the Lodge and make it a big, lively home again.' Dilly was aware that she was gabbling breathlessly. Seeing Nell made her feel eight again. She was so shy she could hardly bring herself to even look at her.

'I'm so glad she's going to help us out with this little squirmer.' Ellen shifted again as the baby kicked up into her ribs. 'I think it'll come as one hell of a shock when Heshee pops out.'

'Is that what you're going to call it?'

'No, it's just a nickname. Spurs – like you – kept calling the baby "it" and I corrected him every time by saying "he-stroke-she" – Heshee. It's just stuck.'

'Cool.' Nell cast another curious look at Dilly, who was mauling the big black and white cat on the sofa, and realised that her erstwhile little ally was obviously settling in to join them. Slightly miffed, she re-crossed her long, slim legs and decided to ignore her for now, much as she had all those years ago at school when Dilly had followed her around gawkishly. Then, as now, she had been disturbingly adorable – like a little pet.

Nell was not accustomed to carrying guilt around with her. She didn't subscribe to her parents' devout Catholicism, but going to confession occasionally was certainly a useful way of offloading emotional baggage. That she had never sought forgiveness for what she had done to little Daffodil Gently ten years earlier hadn't particularly bothered her until today. In the decade that had passed, avoiding contact with her had been relatively easy. A little lip service and air-kissing when their paths occasionally crossed went a long way.

And now Dilly was as close as she had come since childhood – claiming best-friend status with somebody Nell had been cultivating for a friendship of her own. It unsettled Nell, who couldn't decide whether to hate her, pity her or feel threatened by her. Most of all, she was thrown by an overwhelming urge to apologise to her.

'As I was saying,' she cupped her lukewarm tea in her hands and leaned towards Ellen, 'my parents are really turning the screw. I've got to get them off my back.'

'Pru Hornton's looking for help in the Gallery,' Ellen suggested. 'That would at least be quite arty.'

Dilly opened her mouth to explain that she had just taken the job in the Gallery, but Nell cut across her.

'I'm not working as a lowly assistant in a glorified gift shop, especially not for that alcoholic. She's psychotic.'

Given such a concise précis of her new job and boss, Dilly snorted with delighted laughter.

'I was thinking of something more media,' Nell went on. 'More high profile.'

'Round here?'

'Why not? Face it, the Cotswolds is the new London. Kates Moss and Winslet are here, along with Madonna and Liz Hurley. Every other barn conversion has a household star living in it or a creative team running a business out of it. Spurs is cashing it in at Con, isn't he? Piers says one of his original cells sold for almost a grand at auction this month.'

'He's doing really well, yes.' Ellen smiled proudly.

Spurs had got together with two old friends six months earlier to do some of the artwork for their latest animated short. It was only intended to be a bit of fun, but the project – originally showcased for free on the internet – had gained almost immediate cult status and soon attracted the interest of a couple of big advertising agencies. Everyone knew Spurs' amazing, hypnotic artwork was the key, but his loyalty to his friends kept him happily working away in a messy, converted attic in Cheltenham each day – and their company, Con, was reaping rewards. Two highly successful advertising campaigns later, the threesome were enjoying a halcyon phase of endless calls and meetings. They had signed for more adverts, a pop video, a series of animations for a cartoon network and they were now negotiating an American deal with their shiny new agent. It had been a crazy six months, going from breadline poverty to the promise of silly riches. In the short term, it paid a generous rent to Ellen's parents who owned Goose Cottage and assured that Heshee would have a good start to life. She was so excited and proud of him, but also hugely protective.

'Now Con would be a fantastic company to work for – I'd love helping them out,' Nell fished with cheerful openness.

'I don't think they have any openings.' Ellen pulled an apologetic face. 'It's just Ron, Dom and now Spurs. They got a lucky break when Spurs came along, but they run a bloody tight ship to stay there. It's early days.'

In fact, Con was crying out for a PA, but Ellen knew Spurs would veto the idea of hiring Nell at source. He adored Nell, but had been the first to tell Ellen not to trust her after he'd introduced them. Ellen had laughed at this at the time, but Spurs had told her to wait and see, explaining that Nell – and her twin brother Flipper – were two of the most charming, entertaining and untrustworthy people he knew.

Nell was swilling the last of her tea dregs around her mug and studying Ellen thoughtfully over the rim. 'Maybe I should do what you've done, eh? Marry a rich man who can look after me.'

'Steady on!' Ellen laughed. 'I married the man I love, for better or worse. Spurs hadn't got a bean when I met him. And I have a bloody good career when I'm not up the duff. I'd happily win the bread. It works both ways.'

In the corner, Dilly sighed dreamily. Ellen and Spurs were

her idea of true romance – willing to sacrifice everything for one another. When they'd met, Spurs seemed destined to marry someone else and Ellen had been poised to travel around the world, but both had fallen so impossibly in love with one another that their futures were fused for ever.

Dilly had thought that's what she'd found with Pod. She had sacrificed Rory for him and he had forsaken his long-term girlfriend for her. Together, they had seemed set to take on the world like Spurs and Ellen, overpowered by blind love. But while Spurs and Ellen were still living their happy ever after, expecting their first baby and looking out for one another in the ultimate loved-up team, Dilly was all alone, heartbroken and horribly disappointed.

She cherished Ellen's and Spurs' relationship. It served to remind her that the real thing was out there – somewhere.

'Maybe.' Nell was unconvinced by Ellen's protest. 'It still helps if they're well connected. Spurs had a very good pedigree, after all.'

Ellen groaned at such cynicism.

'I'm just being practical,' Nell went on. 'The Constantine name may have died out, but the line is the closest thing Oddlode has to royalty. Spurs and his cousin are direct Constantine descendants. My parents were desperate to unite Cottrell and Constantine blood at one time. They were furious when I turned down Rory's proposal.'

'*Rory* proposed to you?' Dilly squeaked.

Electing to ignore her, Nell told Ellen, 'It was years ago – we were just kids. And of course he was much more successful then – eventing at top level, sponsorship deals coming out of his ears, tipped for the Olympics. And, Christ, he was beautiful. But I was too young. He couldn't keep up with me. I broke his heart. I sometimes think that's why his career crashed and burned.'

'He's still the best rider in the county,' Dilly defended.

'The yard is in rack and ruin now,' Nell said 'and his sister has hardly helped, despite all her great plans. Flipper says that every time he's called out there to treat one of Rory's old-timers for blown-up tendons or whatever, he feels like offering to shoot the lot at discount.'

Ellen looked at Dilly and saw the tears swilling around in her eyes.

Nell sighed sadly. 'For the last couple of years, Rory's just been in free-fall. All his friends have noticed, but we don't know how to help him. He drinks too much, shags anything that moves, has already lost his looks and his fortune. I often wonder how different things would have been if I *had* married him. He had such potential.'

'I still don't think a rich husband would help you, Nell.' Ellen stood up with some effort and went to fetch the teapot, stooping to tickle Milo and whisper in Nell's ear, 'Lay off – Dilly can't take it.'

Unaccustomed to such directness, Nell cleared her throat and let the silence condense until they could clearly hear every intricacy of Ellen filling a kettle and lifting the Aga hot lid two rooms away. She fiddled with the tassels on her belt and admired the sharply pointed toes of her designer boots.

Dilly rustled her way into the pilfered Galaxy bar and offered Nell a square.

Nell shook her head with a quick smile.

Halfway through the bar and cheered by her chocolate fix, Dilly eyed Nell over Finns' black and white back and admired the boots too. She admired everything about Nell.

She was stunning: a spellbinding mix of boyish style and feminine wile, all grown up and classier than ever. How one person could radiate such sheer, bloody-minded abandonment and attraction floored Dilly. Nell had never had to make an effort – she had the best of the Cottrell genes and, in a good-looking family, that was one hell of a legacy. But she had something else too. Nell Cottrell had such sexual, animal self-confidence that she commanded adoration without ever needing to bat her long, dark lashes. Nell Cottrell was magnetic.

For all her own supposed vivacity, intelligence and charming dizziness, Dilly felt like a fluffy Shetland pony admiring a Derby winner. She was mesmerised by attraction for the second time in a day, but this time a safer, more heart-warming variety – nostalgic, child-like attraction mixed with apotheosis. She craved acceptance and approval. Such longing was too much for the heartbroken.

With a great swishing of sag bag she flew to the sofa to join Nell, making the cushions jump, Finns claw his way urgently up a curtain and Nell reel back in shock.

'We all adored you at school, you know. Nothing was ever the same after you left.'

'Really?' Nell smiled tightly.

'I thought you'd be a famous actress or model or singer by now.'

'Really?' Nell's ego allowed her to drop her defences slightly.

'Yes – with at least two marriages to hopelessly lovely famous men under your belt.'

'How sweet.' Nell looked around for Ellen, but a phone was ringing and the extension picked up in the kitchen.

'I always wanted to be like you.'

Cornered, Nell looked into the sparkling lime-green eyes and realised that she was hearing the truth. Dilly spoke from the heart – she knew no other way.

Something in the deepest recesses of Nell's memory surfaced. Those bright green eyes shining with clarity and endless optimism, however low life took her and however hard one tried to knock her back. Dilly had been the same as a small, dumpy schoolgirl, crying her way to sleep at night because she missed her neglectful mother and didn't even know the father that she desperately longed to love, then bouncing out of bed the following morning because she hoped the day would make her happier. If Nell had cared enough, she'd have pitied her. As it was, she'd been fighting too many demons of her own at the time to spare the heart.

'You were a good kid.' She patted Dilly's knee, suddenly fighting that ridiculous urge to apologise. 'You've turned out – deliciously.'

'Have I?' Dilly – who had spent two weeks trying to be less than savoury – felt decidedly tasty.

'You surely have.'

Before Nell realised what she was doing, she automatically high-fived the palm that Dilly was holding up.

Dilly burst into laughter. 'You still do that?'

Embarrassed, Nell quickly dropped her hand to her lap and stroked Milo. 'It's something Flipper started when we were kids – he was into the Harlem Globetrotters. I'd forgotten I'd taught it to you.'

Dilly snuggled back into the cushions, tucking her feet beneath her. 'Your family always sounded so fantastic.'

'I beg to differ – Aunt Grania excepted.' Nell's mouth twisted into an enigmatic crescent.

'Of course, your aunt is Giles Hornton's mother, isn't she?'

'The very same.' She looked at Dilly curiously, wondering if she was one of her wicked cousin's many conquests. 'D'you know Giles then?'

'I – er – keep my horse on his land.' Dilly wasn't about to let on that he was Basil's father.

'So you still have a horse?'

'For now.' She shrugged coolly, not wanting to appear like a babyish Pony Clubber. 'I never seem to get time to ride him. I love him to bits, but I'm thinking of selling him.'

'We should ride out together before you do. Go for a blast.'

'I'd love that. I really would.' Maybe she wouldn't sell Otto so hastily to pay for a replacement car. It was a heartless thing to do. He had always been the only constant male influence in her life, even if he was highly unpredictable, exceptionally grumpy and prone to madness.

'It's a date.' Nell checked her mobile as an incoming text tone beeped.

But it turned out to be coming from Dilly's phone.

Auditions for Mags's new band at New Inn on Thurs. Be there at 6 or else. Sperry. Xxx

'A band?' Nell read breezily over her shoulder.

'Oh, it's nothing.' Dilly deleted the message. 'Just something a – mate – wants to rope me into.'

Still, she pressed the phone antennae to her lips, thinking of Magnus on the bus – so utterly blue-eyed and sexily dishevelled and friendly; thinking too of streetwise Sperry and the sudden friendship she could never have hoped to achieve. And here was Nell acting like a lovely older chum. Today was blessed. Being ugly paid off.

With her chocolate sugar rush reaching its peak, Dilly suddenly felt the highest that she had felt since Pod's departure.

'I've always rather liked the idea of being in a band.' Nell was admiring her pointy boots again.

'You should come along to the auditions!' Dilly suggested, forgetting that she'd never intended to go herself. 'What do you play?'

'Oh – percussion mostly.'

'That's brilliant. Women drummers are really cool.'

Nell, who had been thinking more of the tambourine *à la* Linda McCartney, said nothing.

'Can you sing?' asked Dilly.

Knowing herself to be utterly tone deaf, Nell made an enigmatic gesture with her long, slim hands. The band was bound to be a crap, tinny little local affair which she would no doubt want to run a mile from joining. But she had been so bored lately that it might be quite entertaining to see what it was all about, and Dilly's enthusiasm was surprisingly infectious.

'Oh, you must come along to the auditions with me,' she urged now, the green eyes more sparkly than ever.

Nell hesitated, aware that she was in dangerous territory, falling for her old sidekick's adoring charms. Then, as now, Dilly Gently had an uncanny ability to make one feel incredibly good about oneself – so much so that she was hard to shake off, like an embarrassing comfort blanket.

'Is this Mags woman any good?'

'*He's* a Mags guy and he's amazingly talented.' And dreamy, Dilly added silently, wondering if ugly, heartbroken people were allowed a crush and deciding not. Her heart hurt too much.

Nell knew women well enough to read the little lights that beamed out so brightly from Dilly's green eyes – like breaking into a mint Matchstick to find the glistening centre.

'Is he good looking?'

'Incredibly.'

'Hmm.' She lifted Milo to her lips and kissed him, making his eyes bulge.

'How old?'

'I don't know.' Dilly bit her lip excitedly as she realised what her amazing day had been all about. It was fate. It had to be! 'But he's wildly sexy and rich.'

'Really?'

She nodded emphatically. 'He drives a Porsche and runs a recording studio.'

Nell smiled. 'I'll check my diary, but I'm sure I can shuffle something to fit in Thursday. It sounds a hoot. Give me your mobile number and I'll call you.'

In the midst of an exchange of numbers, Ellen stomped back into the room with a rattling teapot and a new-found bad temper.

'My bloody mother-in-law! I could murder her.'

'Don't tell me – she wants you to put Heshee's name down for Eton?' Nell looked up, pressing *Save* for Dilly's number as DILDO GENT.

Hoping that was a slip of the thumb, Dilly saved hers as NELL and planned to assign a special ring-tone to it.

Slopping tea everywhere as she plonked down the pot, Ellen was fuming, her blonde ponytail slipping out from having raked her hand through her hair so much during her recent telephone conversation. 'Hell's Bells just takes the piss, frankly. I agreed to help attract "trendy young blood" to the hunt ball, even though she knows I'm not exactly pro The Cause, and now she's only coupled me with—' She suddenly stopped herself as she remembered Dilly was with them.

'With who?' Nell pressed.

'A friend of hers who has totally hare-brained ideas,' Ellen said lamely as she lowered herself back on to the sofa with an exhausted sigh. 'Honestly, I have half a mind to say I'm going to quit. Spurs hasn't been any help at all – and now this! I'm seven months pregnant. What do I care about a stupid hunt ball? I've never been to one in my life.'

'My parents used to host the hunt bollocks before the Bellings – when we lived in Oddlode Manse and my father was MFH,' Nell remembered. 'I was too young to join in then, but I used to spy from the banisters. There was always lots of fantastic talent there. Daddy was forever dragging naked young couples out of the cupboards.'

'Apparently that's no longer the case,' Ellen sighed.

'I haven't been to one for years – nor has Flipper,' Nell admitted. 'Even my older brothers avoid them and they're hunting-mad. It's all a bit stuffy and the food is dreadful.'

'Exactly.' Ellen shifted awkwardly as Snorkel joined her. 'Which is why my mother-in-law has relocated the whole shooting match to Eastlode Park and asked me to help keep the average age below seventy. So I had already planned a really cool charity auction, a basement "club" in the cellars, better music. But no. My new "colleague" has just rung to announce that he already has the music organised. And you're going to love this.' She rolled her eyes at Dilly. 'It's Godspell's new band.'

'Oh Christ, Ellen!' Dilly tried not to giggle.

'Are you saying a *gospel* group has been hired to play at the hunt ball?' Nell shrieked with delight at the thought.

Dilly shook her head, still trying not to laugh. 'More likely to be a devil-worshipping ensemble. Godspell is the name of the lead singer – she has the worst voice you've ever heard. It could raise the dead.'

'Exactly,' Ellen groaned. 'They're aiming to be more main-stream than Roadkill was, but I ask you! For a hunt ball? Of course Foxy Lady are already booked to do the main ballroom, but this new band are playing all night in the wine cellars along with some local DJ friend of Ely's son who fantasises himself Fat Boy Slim. It's all organised, apparently, without even a by your leave.' She was so livid that she gave away the secret without realising.

'Oh God, it's Ely.' Dilly covered her face. 'I might have guessed.'

'Ely Gates?' Nell looked at them curiously. 'You'll never get him to change his mind. He'll just take over.'

'I know. And it gets better. The ball is being held on Leap

Year day, and Ely has a madcap plan to get as many girls to propose to their boyfriends as possible. Anyone getting engaged that night gets some sort of prize. It's bloody ridiculous!'

Dilly let out a little squeak. 'That's so romantic!' Her mind was already racing ahead to men in dinner jackets and women in glittering dresses dancing together under the Eastlode chandeliers – and to the most beautiful couple of them all, Magnus and Nell, declaring love for one another. A fairytale moment at a Cinderella ball, all enabled by a trainee Fairy Godmother who knew how to read coincidences. Today was very special indeed.

'Bloody cool idea.' Nell was grinning, already composing proposal speeches in her head. No man would be safe.

As she and Dilly turned to look at one another, they both experienced a frisson of excitement.

Ellen, meanwhile, experienced a chilly finger of worry running its way along her spine as she watched the two girls bonding over Ely's ridiculous scheme.

Ellen had seen that animated look on Dilly's face before, just a few short weeks earlier when she had excitedly explained that she and Pod were going to move into the Lodge together, bring the old house back to life and have tens of babies and happiness and laughter into old age.

Ellen was very protective of Dilly. She was adorable, gullible, far too susceptible to love, and a bit of a pain sometimes, but her heart was in the right place and she was basically a good kid. She had few friends her own age, preferring the company of those closer to her mother's generation and, by being friends with both, Ellen was a halfway house as well as a safe house. She'd got used to her hanging around, making herself at home, talking about falling in love and then more recently about her heartbreak. What Pod had done to her had hit her very hard. Only Ellen knew the real extent of the damage.

And Ellen also knew by instinct that Nell, despite being much closer to Dilly in age and background, was not good for her.

The thought made Ellen feel unpleasantly ancient as well as helpless. She knew that Spurs was going to laugh at her later when she told him her fears. He still called Dilly the little wildcat. Men never realised how vulnerable Dilly was. She was too good at flirting and fighting to give away the truth.

Perhaps she was being paranoid, Ellen told herself. Watching Dilly and Nell giggling together on the sofa, talking men and horses, she couldn't help but experience a pang of jealousy as well as unease. She was poised on the cusp of motherhood, daunted by the one-way door that lay just ahead of her, by letting go of her carefree childless years for ever.

Here were two girls eager to play fast and loose and fall in love. They had far more in common with one another than with her. She suddenly longed to phone Pheely.

'I'm going to have to boot you two girls out,' she said tiredly.

'I've got to feed Otto.' Dilly checked the time on her mobile and turned to Nell. 'D'you want to come and meet him?'

'Not if Uncle Giles is there.'

'He'll still be at work, but I know where he hides his dope in the woodshed.'

'In that case I'm definitely coming.' Nell popped Milo in her big shoulder bag and stood up. 'Thanks for the tea, Ellen. Good luck with Hell's Bells' friend and the hunt bullock. Keep me posted.'

'Will do.' Ellen watched them go worriedly, wondering if she shouldn't have tried to discourage the giggly excursion to Giles Hornton's woodshed.

As soon as the door banged behind them, she rang Pheely.

'Your daughter has left the building.'

'Thank God – I'll be five minutes.'

*   *   *

Dilly and Nell counted magpies as they walked along the dusky, poplar-lined drive to River Cottage, a white-painted Victorian hideaway on the banks of the River Odd, tucked well back from the lane behind railed paddocks from which the black and white birds now took off, chattering furiously.

'Seven for a secret never to be told,' Dilly breathed, turning to look at Nell, longing to talk about the childhood pact now that they were away from Ellen.

But Nell set her jaw. 'I only saw six.'

The message was clear. Dilly looked away, chewing her lip nervously, not wanting to ruin the new alliance.

'Then you get gold.'

'A gold ring perhaps? Wow!' Nell spotted a furious face glaring at them over a gate. 'Is this Otto? He's so pink and divine.'

'Strawberry roan and evil,' Dilly corrected.

Otto bobbed his head greedily and tried to eat Milo who was peering out of Nell's shoulder bag.

'I've always adored roans.' Nell reached out to scratch his nose.

'Want to buy him?'

'Popeye would never forgive me.'

'That's your horse?' Dilly asked as she clambered over the gate.

She nodded. 'My brother bred him. He's ugly as sin, but very loyal and totally fearless.' She clutched her coat closer around her, breathing in an approaching frost and suddenly wishing she had just got in her lovely warm car to drive home instead of trooping along to see a horse with a teenager.

'Sorry I'm late, baby.' Dilly fussed around, straightening Otto's rugs and checking his legs before hopping back over the gate and heading into a big ramshackle shed to start scooping feed from metal bins into a big bucket.

Nell was just contemplating leaving when Dilly called over her shoulder:

'Giles's dope is in the log-store over there – look up in the rafters for an old tobacco tin. All the gear's in there.'

Deciding that she might as well stay for a spliff, Nell left Otto who was tossing his head wildly and smashing a front leg into the gate, greedily anticipating his dinner, and found the target. Resting Milo in his bag beside her, she settled on a pile of logs and started to skin up while Dilly hurriedly gave Otto his bucket, shook out some slices of hay and then joined her.

'So we both broke Rory's heart, I gather?' Nell licked the gum of a Rizla and attached it expertly to another.

Dilly ducked her head guiltily. 'He's one of the loveliest men I know, but he's crap with women.'

'He was pretty good with me.'

'That was a long time ago. You said it yourself, he drinks too much now.'

'Still no excuse to dump him from a great height. Only makes him drink more.'

'Is he?' Dilly asked worriedly, tears welling.

Nell shrugged, breaking into a Marlboro Light and scattering the tobacco along her paper cradle. 'He's been better.'

'Oh God.' Her bottom lip wobbled madly.

Nell, who had been preparing to lay into her big time, stopped herself. Making Dilly cry was too easy – always had been. She was long past the days of taking pleasure in others' tears. And Dilly was right. Rory was hopeless with women. He'd been just as hopeless with her. He treated his horses far better.

'What happened?' she asked.

'I really want to settle down.' Dilly stooped to tickle Milo, who was shivering in his bag. 'I know that sounds silly, but I always have. I just loved Rory, but he'd never commit to anything – not even a phone call. He was always lovely and attentive when we were together, but getting together was the hard bit – if I could get him to go out, he only ever wanted to go to his local pub. And he's such a flirt that I knew he was never particularly faithful either, which hurt me a lot. Then I went to university in the north east – Mum kind of pushed me into that one – and I found it easier to cope without thinking about him all the time. Distance making the heart grow fonder is a load of balls. I went out with a few guys just to see what it was like and it was fun.' She paused for breath, letting the lie echo in her ears, knowing that it hadn't been much fun at all. 'Then I met someone else; I mean someone I could really . . .' She burst into the tears that had been waiting to come out for too long to be refused.

Nell lit the spliff, took a couple of drags, blew on the end and waited for the chest-wrenching sobs to turn into snivels before handing it to her. 'So that's why you dropped out of university? Because someone broke your heart there?'

'Not there.' Dilly hiccoughed and wiped her eyes with the cuffs of her fleece, trying to pull herself together. 'Here. But he went back to his girlfriend. He's decimated me.' The sobs started again.

'Poor old you.' Nell took the joint back before Dilly had even had a puff and inhaled deeply. 'Jesus, this is good.'

'My mum grows it,' Dilly said in tearful gulps. 'She's Giles's supplier.'

Nell snorted with giggles. 'Your mother is a drug dealer?'

'Only for friends.'

But Nell was almost on the floor, hooting away. 'Your mother's a dealer!'

'It *is* pretty strong.' Dilly plucked the spliff from her before she set light to Giles's log pile and took a small toke to cheer herself up. Holding the sweet smoke deep in her lungs, she unwound her scarf to tuck over poor, cold little Milo who was still shaking in his bag. Then she cocked her head as she heard a strange sound coming from behind the outbuildings.

'Sshh,' she told Nell. 'Listen. What's that noise?'

Stopping giggling with some effort, Nell straightened up and listened.

There was a strange sucking noise followed by a loud clatter and a cough.

'Fuck – that must be Giles!'

The girls threw the spliff into a water butt and hastily replaced the tobacco tin before straightening their clothes and rounding the corner of the ramshackle lean-to.

But it wasn't Giles. It was Otto. Eyes rolling white, breath coming out in heaves, he seemed to be dying.

'Fuck, fuck, fuck!' Dilly raced forwards as she saw her horse convulsing, his whole body going into spasm. 'What's happening? Oh Christ, it's colic, isn't it?'

'It's just choke.' Nell was fighting giggles again. 'You need a load of water in something like a squeezy bottle to try to flush into him to make him swallow.'

'Are you sure?' Dilly stared at her, frozen with panic and indecision.

Nell bit back her mirth and nodded. 'Really, truly. Go and get the water – I'll massage his gullet and get him moving to try to dislodge it.'

Otto rolled his eyes, the whites flashing in alarm as his neck seemed to turn inside out. But he raised no objection as Nell vaulted the gate and started to rub her thumbs into the soft flesh below his jaws before clipping on a lead rope and turning him in circles, clicking her tongue against the roof of her mouth to urge him on.

Ellen grabbed the Evian bottle from her bag and filled it from an outside tap, groaning as the pathetic trickle from frozen pipes took for ever to come out.

Between them, she and Nell manhandled Otto's chin as high as possible before thrusting the spout of the bottle into the corner of his mouth and emptying it – mostly over themselves.

They watched for a moment or two, but he still convulsed, looking more and more dull-eyed and ill. Watery mucus had started pouring from his nostrils.

'Fill it up again,' Nell ordered, fishing her phone from her coat and dialling Flipper, her laughter gone. He picked up straightaway.

'What now?'

'You busy?'

'How many times? I'm always busy.'

'I have a horse with choke.'

'I'll be five minutes. Which one?'

'Not one of ours – a friend's. She keeps him at Giles' cottage. In Oddlode.'

Flipper's tone became less urgent. 'Is it that bad? You know how to deal with choke.'

'It's bad. Reeling around in a field like a foamy water feature. He needs to be tubed.'

He sighed. 'Get him in a stable. I'm on my way.'

Dilly had started crying again as she rushed back with the water. This time, almost all of it went over the girls as Otto pulled back, lifting on to his hind legs and trying to thrash away in panic. His neck was darkening with sweat and thick foam was pouring from his mouth and nostrils.

Nell tried to calm both her companions. 'Don't panic. I've seen it before and I swear he'll be fine. My brother's on his way. He'll sort him out.'

'Does he know what he's doing?'

'He should. He's a vet. Got a double first from Bristol.'

Twenty minutes later, Dilly watched in wonder as Flipper Cottrell pumped water out of a bucket and into a long tube that he had fed through Otto's nose, ably assisted by Nell, who didn't seem to care that her designer shorts, fur-collared jacket and long suede coat were liberally coated in horse snot.

Dilly wasn't sure whether she was more amazed by the fact that Flipper was a taller, infinitely more masculine but equally beautiful version of Nell and therefore utterly spellbinding, or because he made something so veterinary and messy appear so unbelievably sexy. And whilst Otto didn't appear to be enjoying the show as much as Dilly, he certainly seemed to appreciate the after-effect as the blockage at the entrance to his big belly finally passed and he could at last relax and lean dopily over his stable door.

'Starve him overnight and then turn him out first thing,' Flipper ordered as he pulled off his rubber gloves. 'He should be fine to have his usual hard feed tomorrow, but dampen it down. Better still, divide it into two or three feeds so that he doesn't gobble.'

He towered over her as he barked out these instructions, his stable-side manner brusque and unsympathetic. And yet he was so physically like Nell, Dilly found herself smiling up at him adoringly and fighting the urge to hug him gratefully.

'Thank you.' She could have wept with gratitude. 'You saved his life.'

A pair of familiar Cottrell grey-green eyes regarded her coolly. 'Hardly. But I do have to get back to the clinic to try to save one now. I left a horse on the table to come here.'

'Oh God – you were operating?'

'Just assisting, but it's touch and go and they need all the hands they can get. All the staff are mucking in.'

She hung her head guiltily. 'You shouldn't have come. I could have called my usual vet.'

'Nell asked me to come,' he said simply, reaching out to

hand her his card, his dark-lashed eyes looking straight through her. 'Call me if there are any problems.'

As he settled back in his big, rubber-bumpered silver Audi, Dilly watched a waggy-tailed dog leap from the back seat to lick his face and felt just the same urge. What a hero. Such was his magnetism, he was one of those men that she could have picked out of an identity parade in decades to come even after one short, misty, twilit encounter. And yet she knew for certain that he wouldn't recognise her if she reintroduced herself in ten minutes' time.

Nell reappeared from behind the stable as the tail-lights disappeared.

'Has he gone?' She looked put out.

'He had an emergency.' Dilly tickled Milo, whose bag bed was once again slung over Nell's shoulder. He was wrapped totally in the woolly scarf now, like a doggy burka, just his poppy eyes peering out.

'I was going to offer him some of this.' Nell produced another spliff which she'd just rolled. 'He's amazing, isn't he?'

'He's a brilliant vet,' Dilly nodded. 'You're *so* alike.'

'I'm not a brilliant vet.' She settled her bag on the ground between her feet.

'But you *are* brilliant.'

Nell grinned as she flicked her lighter and watched the flame dance, a little heart of heat in a cold winter afternoon. What a sweet girl.

Who would have thought it? Little, dumpy Daffodil Gently with the name that she had been teased about so mercilessly at school; later, daffy Dilly who was known as a bit of a village boho and bicycle. Silly Dilly the oddball who had so much warmth, talent and no direction, chumming up again with no-good Nell who had precious little talent and was very direct indeed.

'Do you fancy him?' She passed the joint across.

'Who?'

'Flipper, of course.'

Dilly smiled at her feet. 'He's incredibly good-looking. I'm sure I'd be absolutely mad about him if I had any heart left.'

'Flipper mends broken hearts. It's his speciality.'

'I'm not a horse.'

'More's the pity,' Nell giggled. 'Rory might have treated you better.'

'Pod preferred horses, too,' Dilly laughed sadly.

'The one you dumped Rory for?'

'He was a jockey.'

'Figures. Horsy men are all bastards to women.' Nell sighed cheerfully, linking her arm through Dilly's. 'Let's make a pact.'

Dilly held her breath as the unmentionable suddenly got a name-check.

'A good pact this time. Make up for the last one.'

Dilly nodded, taking a huge toke of the spliff, terrified of speaking in case she said the wrong thing.

Nell took it back and blew on the end, a big smile spreading across her face. 'We propose to someone at the hunt ball.'

Dilly snorted with surprised laughter. 'Isn't that more of a dare than a pact?'

'Dare – pact. Whatsitmatter?' Nell took another drag.

'It mattered last time.'

The companionable arm unthreaded itself from Dilly's. 'That was a long time ago,' Nell reminded her, face darkening. 'And I don't ever want to talk about that.'

Dilly winced. She knew she'd say the wrong thing. She watched Otto's face in the gloom of the stable, eyeing her dolefully.

'So what d'you think?' Nell handed her the spliff like a peace-pipe. 'Are you up for it?'

Dilly considered the plan for a moment. It was completely hare-brained. 'We propose to different people?'

'Of course.'

'Do we mean it?' She began to feel the sweet, giddy kick of the dope and started to laugh.

'Deadly serious. We go all the way. And we'll be one another's chief bridesmaids.'

'And make speeches?' Dilly wiped her eyes as the laughter took hold.

'Absolutely. As long as they're funny speeches full of toilet humour.'

They leaned against each other, finding this absurdly funny.

'Whoever bags the richest husband buys the other something exceptionally gorgeous,' Nell cackled.

'A gigolo?'

'Or a divorce?'

They both reeled across to the logs to sit down, knees interknitted and foreheads pressed together, two schoolgirls once again, plotting behind the bike sheds.

'Who are we going to ask?' Dilly giggled.

'Who cares as long as they're rich?'

'But they might say yes.'

'That's the whole point!'

Dilly snorted with laughter.

'Of course, we might be famous rock chicks marrying our movie-star beaux in Vegas by then,' Nell hooted.

'Huh?' Dilly wiped her eyes.

'Mog's band?'

'Oh, *Mags*.' Dilly grinned stupidly, fighting thick-headedness as she desperately tried to appear cool. 'I hardly think we'll be rock chicks in six weeks, do you?'

'C'mon, Dilly – you're supposed to be the dreamy one – so dream a little.' Nell thrust out her arms to welcome Milo who had escaped from the abandoned bag to join them, trailing the scarf like an unravelling Egyptian mummy.

'You don't *really* want to audition, do you?' Dilly asked worriedly, suddenly frightened of the idea of singing in public again.

'Of course! Especially if Mog is as gorgeous as you promise.'

'Mags – and he is. But his band'll still probably suck as much as his last one did.'

'Good, because my singing sucks and I can't even ring a triangle in time to a beat.'

Dilly shrieked with delight.

'Promise you'll do it for me?' Nell rested her chin on her knee and stared across at her, her beautiful face more persuasive than ever.

Just for a moment the *déjà vu* sent Dilly's dizzy head reeling even more.

'The proposal thing or the band auditions?'

'Both. In fact, we're making another pact. I'm not joining his band unless you do and vice versa.'

'Agreed.'

'And Flipper.'

'Flipper?'

'He drums – or he did. Drove our father mad.'

'Hey – we already have a band!'

'Who needs Mog?' Nell held up her palm.

Laughing, Dilly high-fived it. '*Mags!*'

'Mags – Mog – Pod. What's it matter?'

Dilly stopped laughing, her face stricken.

'Sorry.' Nell held up her arms. 'Just testing.'

'Testing what?'

'How heartbroken you are.'

'And?' Dilly asked in a strangled voice.

'Put it this way, I won't ever mention the P word unless you do first.'

Dilly blinked and swallowed the lump in her throat. 'Never?'

'Not ever.'

'Swear.'

'On what?'

'Your life,' Dilly whispered.

Nell's eyes were huge in the half-light.

Ten years earlier, she had made Dilly swear on her life. It was a night neither girl would forget.

'I swear.' Nell reached across and tweaked Dilly's nose as she had so often at school.

There was a long pause in which they studied one another warily, and then both suddenly burst into fresh howls of mirth, grateful for finding one another again, finding a shared secret high on a cold January afternoon, and finding such a surprising new alliance.

4

Somehow, Dilly had lost control of ugly. It wriggled out of her grip on Thursday lunchtime and by late afternoon it was running rampant. She blamed her period, arriving just after midday like a punch in the belly from a prize-fighter. Having a comforting bath only served to give her a hot flush, and her ankles poured blood for hours afterwards from shaving cuts. Bloated, aching, only comfortable in big, flowered pants and an ageing sports bra that flattened her throbbing boobs to her chest, she tried and failed to tone down ugly for the sake of Nell and the auditions.

Spots were sprouting on her forehead and chin like guests gathering at a party. She'd clumsily sat on her NHS specs, twisting the hinges so that they now rested at a jaunty angle on her nose. A harsh, frosty day had turned her curls into a mad, statically charged frizz, and she'd put on so much weight lately that the zip of her only decent pair of jeans burst when she crouched down to pull on her boots.

Cursing under her breath, she waddled unhappily to her mother's wardrobe, trailed by a yawning Hamlet who lumbered on to Pheely's bed and watched her rifling through the rails. The one benefit of being fatter was that she could raid Pheely's capacious clothes although, as she started to flip through the hangers, she doubted there really was a plus to her new plus size if one's shopaholic mother dressed like a hippy. Everything Pheely owned appeared to be velvet, purple, beaded, tie-dyed or all four. It was hardly the look Dilly was seeking to try out for a trendy, urbanite band. She'd promised Nell that she'd make an effort,

Basil was crying again.

Clutching her cramping stomach, Dilly went to see what the matter was – smelling the cause as soon as she went through to the main reception room.

'Poor poopy nappy.' She gathered him out of his crib. 'Let's get you changed, shall we?'

As usual, Pheely had left her daughter holding the baby as she 'popped out for supplies', but Dilly hardly blamed her. With the 2CV off the road, getting anywhere involved either the irregular bus or their temperamental moped. Pheely had taken the latter, which meant that whatever supplies she was fetching would be very limited.

As she gathered the last nappy from the baby-changing kit, Dilly hoped her mother could fit Pampers into the moped basket at the very least. Those and the essential supplies Dilly had begged her to remember.

There was a pounding on the door. Hamlet let out a deep, bass bark from Pheely's bedroom, but didn't shift from his lair, meaning it was unlikely to be a stranger or axe murderer. At last!

Zip still gaping, specs at a mad angle, dirty nappy in hand, Dilly went to answer it. It was bound to be her mother, who always forgot her keys.

'You're a life saver! I need a tampon and nappy cream right now.' She wrenched open the swollen door. 'Although not necessarily in that ord—'

Ruddy-cheeked and dishevelled after fighting his way through the thorn bushes that overran the garden path, Magnus Olensen stood in front of her, smiling amiably from beneath his woolly hat.

'Oh – hi, Dilly. You okay? Do you need me to run to the shop or something?'

'No! Sorry! Hi! Come in out of the cold!' Dilly waved the dirty nappy about, hopelessly flustered.

'Great place.' Magnus whistled as he followed her, taking in the chaotic little lodge which was mostly artist's studio. 'And great baby. Hello, gorgeous!'

He gathered Basil up to his chest, looking very Athena postcard if it weren't for Basil's unpleasant backside.

'I wouldn't – er, I haven't wiped him clean.' Dilly thrust the nappy into the bin and dashed over to collect her little brother from a very clean knitted cream chest.

Magnus pulled off his hat so that his own statically charged blond curls stood on end, too. 'I tried calling, but the number Mum has down in our book is unavailable.'

'It got cut off,' Dilly mumbled as she swept a baby wipe expertly between Basil's waggling legs. 'Mum and I just use our mobiles.'

'Oh, right.' Magnus was still gaping at the huge room – the only real living area in the barn-like cottage – which was crammed to the gills with furniture, books, sketches, moquettes, bags of slip mix, half-finished sculptures under hessian and finished work ready to fire and glaze – all coated with a thick pelt of clay dust. A wood-burning stove glowed a welcoming red at one end of the room, its fierce heat meeting that from the little Rayburn at the opposite end of the room, backed up by a roaring kiln at the centre, so that it was tropically hot compared to the chill outside. He started unwinding his scarf.

'There.' Dilly secured the final sticky tape on Basil's nappy and held him up in front of her, kissing his nose. 'Much more presentable. Do you want to hold him now?' She thrust Basil at Magnus.

He took him awkwardly, woolly tassels dangling over Basil's pink little face so that he looked like he had a grey afro.

'Tea? Coffee?' Dilly bounded towards the small kitchen area

and heaved up a lid on the Rayburn, trying not to dwell on the tampon request. Perhaps he hadn't heard.

Watching her as he bounced Basil around, Magnus wondered if it would be rude to point out that her jeans were undone, and decided it would. He could see the top of a pair of very jaunty flowered knickers, above which Dilly had a little butterfly tattoo. As she placed the kettle on the hot plate, her other hand reached around to tug down her cardigan.

'Nothing for me, thanks – I can't stay. I just came to sound you out.'

'Oh yes?'

Dilly still had her back to him, trying to straighten her glasses.

'Sperry Sixsmith has been going on at me about how well you sing.'

'Oh, I'm hopeless.'

'You know I'm trying to put a new band together?'

'Yes, Sperry said something about it.'

'Did she mention tonight's auditions?'

'Mmm. She texted.' Dilly chewed her lips, trying to pull herself together. This was her perfect opportunity to prepare the ground, mention Nell, assure him that she would be there later with her gorgeous friend and that they were both dying to try out for his band. Instead, she felt stupidly self-conscious and tongue-tied. Whether it was her period arriving or the ugly plan starting to take effect, she'd lost her flirting missiles, that quick flatter-patter, the protective fire that she had always relied upon.

'I'm really hoping to get a good female vocalist on board,' Magnus told her.

'I'd be far too shy to sing in a band.'

He laughed incredulously. 'You're not shy.'

Glasses now even more bent, Dilly turned back to face him,

a tea towel clutched casually to her belly to hide the broken zip. She suddenly felt shyer than she ever had in her life. 'You don't know me.'

Magnus smiled at her, bouncing Basil in his arms. 'Then I'd like to get to know you.'

Dilly gaped at him, at his friendly smile and honest blue eyes lined with the smokiest lashes. He couldn't be for real. Men never said things like that without an agenda – or at least a bit of flirting. He seemed so straightforward, so honest.

She didn't trust him at all.

'Believe me, you don't want to get to know me,' she muttered.

'Why not?'

'I'm deeply boring.'

'So am I.'

'And I don't know how long I'll be staying on in Oddlode.'

'Me neither.' The smile didn't shift as he lifted Basil to his chin and blew kisses at him. 'I'd still like to make music, right up until I make a swift exit.'

'I've only ever sung classical stuff – in a choir. And that was a few years ago. I hated it.'

'So you're not at all interested?' He looked across at her.

Basil was now completely buried in scarf with just two little hands poking out, but he seemed happy enough and was making contented gurgling noises.

Dilly suddenly found herself laughing. 'I'm coming along tonight – with a friend. She's really interested. I might do it if she does.'

'Is she any good?'

'I don't know,' Dilly said vaguely, remembering only too well that Nell had declared herself tone deaf. 'She certainly looks the part. She's gorgeous – a total rock chick.'

'Great.' Magnus's face lit up. 'Just my type.'

Dilly turned back to the kettle, which was now whistling furiously. Now's your chance, she told herself. Tell him how fantastic Nell is.

'I do play a bit of piano – keyboards. Whatever you call it. I might be able to help you out there.'

'Excellent.'

Stop it, Daffodil, she chastised herself tetchily. Stop pushing yourself forwards. You don't even want to be in a band, and you can't risk putting your heart up for grabs again – there's hardly any of it left.

'I hear Godspell has already got a new band,' she said, quickly changing the topic.

He made a sort of hmphing noise behind her.

'Ellen says they're booked for the hunt ball.'

'They're what?'

'I know.' She started to gabble as she fetched a mug and searched through cupboards for the right herbal tea. 'It's ridiculous – but there's going to be some sort of basement party running alongside the main event, with a top DJ and chill-out room and foam for all I know. Trackmarks are supposed to be playing. It's at Eastlode Park so I suppose it might be quite a good night.'

'Hmph.'

'There's even some silly Leap Year proposal thing going on. I think the local press will be all over it. Maybe I could have a word with Ellen. Get your new band on the bill too?'

He laughed hollowly. 'I'm not really a hunt ball sort of a guy. But thanks. You're sweet.'

Dilly felt her shoulders relax. Sweet was fine. She could cope with sweet.

'So who else have you got coming tonight?' she asked as she poured hot water over a peppermint teabag, steaming up her glasses.

'Not sure – the Disgraces have organised it all. Mostly Sperry's work. To be honest, it's more their gig.'

'Are they in your new band then?' She glanced over her shoulder through a mist of glass.

'Your guess is as good as mine. I just do what they tell me.' He raised his free palm upwards in confusion and laughed again, his blue eyes twinkling at her as he rocked Basil in the crook of his arm, still covered in woolly scarf.

Dilly blushed. She felt it hit her face – a big red stain spreading as quickly as the teabag infusing the water in the bag beside her. What was going on? She never blushed.

'You know,' he confided in a half-whisper, stepping towards her as though they were in danger of being overheard. 'I have the strangest feeling that the Disgraces have set me up here.'

Dilly's blush spread to her neck as she tried, and failed, to resist the urge to ask the obvious question.

Turning to face him, she stood on one leg and chewed her lip. 'Are they – um – all your girlfriends or something?'

His direct gaze held hers as laughter creases formed around his eyes.

'Is that what people are saying?'

'Sort of. I don't know.' Dilly blushed deeper.

'Well, they're my friends.' He pondered this.

'And they're girls,' she agreed.

'Indeed they are – which makes them girlfriends. In which case . . .' He closed one blue eye in concentration. 'Yes – they are my girlfriends. But they're not my lovers. Just friends.'

'Oh.' Dilly's blush raged on.

'And I'd like you to be my friend too.' He walked towards her, that direct, honest expression on his face.

'You would?'

He nodded, holding Basil up for her to take. 'I think we'll be good friends.'

Not even a flirty twinkle crossed his true blue eyes – just cheerful enjoyment.

Dilly felt a great surge of gratitude and affection well up inside her as she took Basil back from him and kissed the top of her little brother's downy head. 'I totally agree. Oh.' She looked up as she remembered something. 'It's four, by the way.'

He creased his eyebrows at her curiously.

'Two plus two is four.'

'Ah. Just as I thought. Thanks.'

He was standing very close, so close that when Dilly looked up at him she had to resist a stupid urge to press her hot face into his lovely knitted cream chest. Instead, she pushed her warped glasses higher up her nose and grinned up at him.

'So I'll definitely see you later, then?' he checked. 'With your gorgeous rock-chick friend? Who is a girl, too, and therefore your girlfriend.'

'See you later,' she nodded.

He turned to leave, but his scarf was still wrapped around Basil and he ended up pulling Dilly to the door with him. Laughing, they disentangled the long wolly noose.

'I'd better take your mobile number,' he said at the door. 'Now that we're friends.'

Dilly reeled it off cheerfully and then waved him away, watching him beat his way back through the thorns, her heart hammering happily.

As soon as he had disappeared into the mist, she raced back inside to grab her mobile from her bag, clutching Basil to her chest.

'Ellen, hi, it's me . . . I need to ask you—'

'Come and borrow what you like.' Ellen was accustomed to Dilly raiding her wardrobe whenever she had a big night out. 'None of it fits me right now after all.'

'Wouldn't fit me either now I've put on so much weight,' Dilly said cheerfully. 'That's not what I was going to ask.'

'Oh?'

'It's about the man on the bus.'

'Ah.'

'The thing is – it's someone I know. And he knows I'm heartbroken, which I am, and we haven't flirted at all, but I think he quite likes me, in fact he's just popped around and told me he wants to be my friend and what I was going to ask is if you think—'

'Yes. Definitely.'

'Definitely what?'

'He has the hots for you.'

'You think so?'

'He obviously adores you. Please don't tell me he's married.'

'No.'

'Girlfriend?'

Dilly smiled. 'No. He's single.'

'Good God.'

'Oi! I do *try* to meet single men occasionally.'

'Age range?'

'Twentyish.'

'Good double God.'

'I know – he's a bit young for me.'

'Dilly!'

She bit her lip. 'So you don't think I should set him up with Nell, then? Only I'm really not sure I'm up to this sort of thing yet, and I know he respects that, but men are always in a hurry, aren't they, and he's gorgeous and so is Nell and so I thought—'

'No!' Ellen wailed.

'Not a good idea?'

'Nell is perfectly capable of getting her own boyfriend – in fact I think she already has several on the go.'

'She has?'

'Yes. You keep this one to yourself.'

'Okay.' Dilly's pounding heart was starting to slow at last, the blush finally fading, the endorphin kick receding.

'Dilly, just have fun and take . . . it . . . *slowly.*'

'I will, I will. Oh, Christ, I wish I hadn't thrown my contact lenses away.'

'What *are* you doing?' Pheely asked her daughter when she finally returned.

'Funking up my specs,' Dilly announced cheerfully as she super-glued the last bead on to the rim of her glasses and put them back on. 'What do you think?'

'You look like Dame Edna Everage,' Pheely snapped, gathering a sleeping Basil from where he'd conked out between two cushions on the sofa beside his sister.

Dilly's good mood was shattered in an instant.

'Did you buy nappies?' she asked quietly.

'No. How many are left?'

'None.'

'Oh, well, I'll just have to use tea towels until tomorrow morning.'

'Mum!'

'I did it with you.'

'No wonder I'm screwed up. You're a lousy mother.' Dilly stormed off to get changed, secretly devastated by the Edna Everage comment.

When she re-emerged, she was squeezed into a long denim skirt that had been falling off her hipbones a month earlier, a stretchy green shirt that gaped between the buttons in front and gave her a fat, rolly bra back, and a beaded belt that Pheely recognised as her own.

Still reeling herself from the lousy mother snipe, Pheely

was at her most poisonous. 'Still going for the ugly look, I see?'

Dilly scowled at her as she gathered her long sheepskin coat, trying and failing to do it up. She crammed a fluffy hat over her curls, wound a long shaggy scarf around her neck and climbed into her furry ankle boots. 'Don't wait up.'

'Where are you going?'

'Out.'

The door slammed.

Pheely tipped her head back, scrunched her eyes, and counted to ten to stop herself screaming. She didn't want to wake Basil.

She called Ellen.

'What's got into her?'

'I think she might be falling in love again.'

'Surely not? She still cries herself to sleep over Pod every night.'

'Ever been on the rebound?'

'Not really. I've never been as good at effortlessly pulling men as my daughter.'

'Me neither, but I think that's what we're witnessing.'

'Who is it?'

'I don't know. She said something about meeting him on the bus.'

'Oh, God – low-life. Bound to be a Wyck.'

'Pheely! Shame on you.'

Pheely stifled a sob. 'She'll get hurt again won't she?'

'That's what I'm afraid of.'

'Mum and me used to get on so well – like best friends,' Dilly told Nell as they drove to Upper Springlode. 'But lately we're at each other's throats all the time.'

'Yeah?'

Nell wasn't a great listener, but was happy to let Dilly rattle on.

'I know the obvious thing is to blame it on Basil arriving. Me the jealous grown-up daughter with a new little rival, Mum finding her freedom taken away while I still have mine. But it's not like that.'

'No?' Nell leaned forward to flip through a couple of tracks on the CD changer until she found a favourite.

'No. I mean, we both adore Basil. He's the one thing we have in common. It's just getting on with one another that's the problem.'

'I know the feeling. My parents are a pain.'

'I think it's to do with me going away – first to university, and then when I came back because I fell in love with Pod, we moved into the main house together – with Mum's approval – and she just couldn't cope. I guess she saw that I was grown—'

'Pod?'

'You said it.' Dilly froze. 'You said the P word.'

'Only because you said it first. Anyway, what sort of name's Pod? You can't help but repeat it for confirmation – like Mog.'

'Mags.' Dilly tipped her head back to stop the tears.

'Hey, have a cigarette – light me one.' It was the closest Nell knew to an apology.

Dilly found a packet of Marlboro in the glove compartment and lit two.

'He's really called Padhraig, which is Irish.'

'Ah. Same name as my brother.'

'Which one?'

'Padhraig was between Piers and Phinneas. He died when he was just a baby – long before I was born.'

'I'm sorry.' Stupid tears started to plop out of Dilly's eyes which she swished away.

'I never knew him.'

'Still a brother. I had to wait nearly twenty years for mine, but he's so precious.'

'Being the youngest I'll never know how it works that way around.' Nell lowered her window to flick out a ball of ash. 'Paddy would be nearly forty now.'

Dilly took off her glasses and drew the tears away from her eyes with a finger knuckle, furious with herself for being so wet. 'I had no idea you and Flipper were so much younger than your brothers – like Basil is to me.'

'Mum had loads of problems going to term – miscarriages, ectopic pregnancies, pre-eclampsia. She was told to stop trying to conceive after Finn, but she wouldn't listen.'

Dilly couldn't stop crying. 'I want loads of children.'

'So you say.'

'I so wanted Pod's children.' Tears clawed at her eyes and throat.

'You said the P word again.'

'I know,' she said in a small, sob-stricken voice. 'Trouble is, I keep thinking about the P word.'

'And the P word is back with his ex-girlfriend, yeah?'

'Yes. He had an accident. It was awful – a fire. He almost died. She was there. She saved his life.'

'I guess that gives her first dibs.'

'He'd pretty much dumped me by then anyway.'

'So he was a waste of time.'

'I loved him. We talked about having a huge family and breeding horses and—'

'You're too young for babies, baby. It's time to rock and roll.' Flicking her half-smoked cigarette from the window, Nell cranked up the music, yelling over the din. 'Now stop crying – you'll ruin your voice and your eyes will be puffy.'

Dilly rubbed her nose fiercely with the knuckle of her

forefinger and told herself to dry up. She glanced across at Nell, her beautiful, tempestuous face illuminated by the green lights of the dashboard on her racy little car – that straight nose, the upturned mouth, long neck and impossibly shiny black hair as short as a boy's. She was tough. She was on Dilly's side. She was heaven.

'You're right. Rock and roll.' Dilly watched a fox cross the road in front of them, slanting eyes briefly blazing in the headlights before he slipped away into a hedge.

Then, to stop herself thinking about Pod, she forced herself to think about Magnus and his proclamation of friendship, and to her surprise she smiled. She wasn't ready to fall in love again, but friendship was much sweeter right now. Friendship was definitely what she needed.

Seeming to read her thoughts, Nell shouted above the music, 'So what's the name of this guy who's putting the band together again?'

'Magnus.'

'Better than "Pod", but still pretty dire.'

'Don't mention the P word.'

'Sorry. On my life. Tell me about Magnus.'

'His mother's Danish.'

'That's no excuse. You fancy him?'

'No!' Dilly stared fiercely out of the side window into the darkness. 'He's just a friend.'

'Gay then?'

'No.'

'Heinously ugly?'

'No. Good looking.'

'So *you're* gay?'

'No!'

'Sexually attractive, heterosexual men and women can't be friends. It's a fact.'

'Magnus and I are friends, and *that's* a fact.'
'There must be something wrong with him.'

As soon as Nell walked into the back room of the New Inn, she
realised that there was nothing wrong with Magnus. Magnus
was quite the most adorable man in existence. The only thing
wrong was that he wasn't already her lover.

He had a louche, easy sensuality that made him irresistible.
The sleepy eyes, sexy smile, distracted air that she was certain
hid a furnace of passion. He was more than just her type. He
was prototype. The mould. The One.

Physically, he was spot on: six feet one or two, broad-
shouldered and slim-bodied, textbook bone structure and
naturally athletic. His face was mesmerising – set with the
biggest blue eyes and the highest cheeks, just lightly stained
with ruddy colour amid a smooth, pale gold skin. And the mop
of golden curls was pure poetry.

What's more, he knew it. When Dilly introduced them, Nell
took his hand, smouldered a kiss on to his cheek, leaned back
and watched that sexy smile stretch into a wider, welcoming,
come-on grin.

Nell felt an immediate connection. As the blue eyes locked
straight on hers, she recognised a kindred spirit that was just far
enough away from incest for safety, close enough to the perfect
DNA match to start a dynasty. Two athletes with nowhere to
run. Two city lovers trapped in a rural idyll. Two sexual
predators forced into unlikely celibacy. Two freeloaders longing for freedom. Two people destined to go to bed together.

And when he played a couple of his old demo tapes to give
them an idea of the sort of music he created, Nell practically
combusted with desire. Raw, angry, sexy lyrics spun their way
through the most bittersweet of tender, rhythmic melodies,
pounded through with drum beats that ripped the words into

high relief. His voice was a lover's, singing of every happy,
agonising, confusing, spiralling, plummeting moment shared
in love and loss. His songs were heartbreaking and uplifting at
the same time – told by someone who truly understood, yet
wasn't afraid to laugh at the stupidity of desire. Self-deprecat-
ing, quirky, sometimes impossibly sad – they were totally
original and catchily familiar. Samples from hip hop to religious vespers to Rat Pack crooners swirled in and out of the
melodic beats. His guitar melodies ate into the heart. And
throughout, his voice, that achingly sexy voice, hypnotised the
listeners completely.

'What d'you think?' he asked afterwards without a glimmer
of self-satisfaction – big blue eyes simply curious and a little bit
nervous.

He stepped back and laughed in genuine amazement as the
little group all whooped, clapped and rolled their fists in
support.

And it was a little group. The Three Disgraces, dressed in
identical long boots, hot-pants and Bardot jumpers had only
gathered a select few to the auditions – Dilly, Nell (who, strictly
speaking, wasn't invited) and a small gang of young New Inn
drinking friends to make up numbers. It was hardly *Pop Idol*.

Lounging against a wall beside her sisters, Hooch in hand,
Sperry narrowed her eyes as Nell – who clearly believed in acting
on instinct and wearing overpoweringly sweet perfume to match
– weaved up to Magnus and kissed him on both cheeks.

'You are brilliant.'

Sperry could tell he was making a real effort not to let his
eyes wander to the plungiest of balcony-bra-enhanced cleavage, resting tantalisingly above the tiniest of little black dresses
which reached down just as far as the start of the longest of long
lacy legs, encased in the shiniest of knee-high patent boots with
the pointiest of heels.

He smiled into the face, but that didn't give Sperry much comfort. It was the sexiest of come-hither faces with parted lips, upturned nose and take-me-home eyes that never blinked.

She glanced across at Dilly, who had followed Nell and was rubbing her nose so furiously that several beads fell off her glasses.

'They're such beautiful songs,' Dilly told Magnus. 'Why the hell did you waste so much time with Roadkill?'

Magnus looked baffled. 'They liked my stuff.'

'They massacred it,' Sperry muttered under her breath, glaring angrily at the Pegasus tattoo on Nell's hip. Magnus would love that.

'I think,' Nell was giving him a slow smile guaranteed to fast-track its way to his groin, 'that you are one of the most talented songwriters, musicians and singers I've ever heard.'

Magnus dipped his head with a modest smile, flipped the CD from the player and decided that he definitely wanted her in the band.

When Dilly sang the Pretenders' track *Hymn to Her* – reluctantly and under pressure – the room fell quiet. Former choir girl she might be, but she sang more like a fallen angel and her martyred, wanton soul was hurting tonight. That husky quality in her pitch-perfect voice came from too many cigarettes and late nights, the throaty growl was too sexy for a cassock-wearer, those haunting know-it-all, been-there notes that tore through her small audience made her impossible to ignore. She knew how to sing about hurt. She was there. It was almost painful, it was so good.

'Bloody hell, she sounds like Joss Stone,' Fe Sixsmith admitted grudgingly.

'She sounds better,' Carry whistled.

Dilly Gently might be looking very odd in thickly beaded

spectacles and a headscarf, but her voice made her the most beautiful woman in the room.

When Dilly sang Patsy Cline's *Crazy*, accompanying herself just with a keyboard, Sperry cried for the first time in years. Her sisters teased her.

'Soft bat.'

'Daft trog.'

It made no difference. Sperry listened to that sweet, lilting, haunting voice and cried. Sometimes it hurt to feel this good about yourself.

'I knew she'd be perfect,' she whispered to no one in particular and looked across at Magnus.

He was sitting at a table with a beer mat in his hands. He must have been flipping it – he flipped them endlessly, driving Sperry and the rest of the Disgraces mad. But this beer mat was utterly, utterly still. It was balanced right on the tips of his finger and thumb, trapped in time, as motionless and suspended in the moment as he was, staring at Dilly.

Beside him, Nell smoked a cigarette. Her body was already curled in a predatory fashion close to Magnus's – quick mover, Sperry realised – but her hands were shaking as she smoked and her eyes were curiously shiny.

Sperry distractedly ran a long fingernail between the two front teeth on her lower jaw, blinking away her own tears. She'd done her job. She'd brought them together just as she promised she would. The rest was up to them. It wasn't her fault Nell was muscling in on the act.

As planned, she texted with a lightning thumb. *Dilly a certainty. Will confirm 18er.*

When Nell sang, it physically hurt to listen.

The Three Disgraces, fighting laughter, tried to catch

Magnus's eye. But he was too busy staring at Nell's long, lean body to notice.

Sitting beside him, munching her way nervously through a packet of salt and vinegar crisps, Dilly tilted her head towards him, knowing she had to put a good word in even though it meant blushing like a menopausal woman in a sauna.

'She's got great rhythm,' she pointed out.

'She can't sing.' He winced, clearly fighting an urge to cover his ears.

'She looks fantastic.'

'She can't sing.'

'She's giving it her all.'

'I can see.'

'She's incredibly sexy.'

'I know.' He watched the disturbingly androgynous figure writhing in a singularly feminine way. 'Is she gay?'

'She's very cheerful, yes.' She grinned. 'And she really wants to be in a band.'

Magnus stole a crisp from her.

'She's in the band.'

'I'm not doing this without her,' Dilly whispered, then realised what he'd just said. 'She *is*?'

He nodded, stealing another crisp.

'Is that because you want to sleep with her?'

Choking on the crisp, he shook his head, nodded, shook his head and nodded again, eyes streaming as he fought for breath and to keep eye contact at the same time. His blue eyes, watering like mad, tried to convey the words his throat couldn't find air for.

Dilly smiled reassuringly. Of course he wanted to sleep with Nell. And at least he was honest.

'Good.' She patted him hard on the back.

'Good?' He looked at her curiously, and then across to Nell who was murdering Coldplay's *Yellow* now.

'You wouldn't be human if you didn't want to sleep with her, would you?'

'Would *you*?'

'You can repeat every last word I say, but it will get quite boring.'

'Boring?'

'Boring.'

'Boring?'

'See?'

The honest blue eyes blinked uncertainly.

'*Are* you two an item?' he checked, suddenly not so sure of himself. 'Because I think I should know if you're both going to be in on this project. Relationships can be tricky things between band members.'

If Dilly had been munching a crisp at the time, she too would have choked. But, empty-mouthed, she had the upper hand.

She lifted her chin and gave him an enigmatic smile, enjoying the confusion on his face. 'You said it. We're friends. And we're girls. We're girlfriends. Just like you and I are going to be friends.'

'Girlfriends?' He didn't blink. She hated the way he could do that. The not blinking thing was weird, as well as a strange, comforting cue to being confessional.

'If you have a sex change, we can be girlfriends.'

'Tempting.' He flipped a beer mat, caught it and tapped it with his chin. 'Don't flirt with me.'

'What?'

'You heard. Don't flirt with me.'

'I'm not.'

'Then God help mankind.' He looked up as Nell finished singing and applauded loudly.

Confused, Dilly remembered to join in, wondering why he had said that.

'That was – unbelievable.' Magnus opened his arms expansively as Nell joined them.

'Fantastic,' Dilly added automatically, blushing all over and unable to look either of them in the eye. 'Excuse me.' She fled to the loo.

'Oh God.' She sat astride a very cold seat a moment later, period pains shredding her belly, one small rectangle of toilet tissue hanging on the roll beside her, no tampon to hand.

Someone swung through the wheezing door and locked themselves in beside her.

'Excuse me?' Dilly addressed the partition apologetically. 'You wouldn't happen to have a spare tampon on you?'

'Yup.'

Even from one syllable, she knew it was one of the Three Disgraces.

'May I have it?'

There was a long pause.

'Please?' she added guiltily.

A tampon was thrust beneath the gap.

As Dilly reached to grab it, the other hand hung on tight.

'Promise me one thing . . .'

'Yes?' Dilly was dangling from the loo seat, in danger of falling off.

'Magnus doesn't get hurt.'

'By a tampon?'

'By the leggy bitch with the pout.'

'I promise.'

The tampon was released.

Dilly clutched its cellophaned little rescue package to her chest and realised she had just traded her soul for a tampon.

She closed her eyes in horror. How was she supposed to stop Magnus getting hurt when his songs already spoke of hurt beyond chords, melodies and lyrics? He knew hurt better than she did.

The New Inn ladies' lavatory door gave another wheeze and the cubicle next to her slammed shut.

'Dilly?'

She leaned her head gratefully against the partition. 'Hi, Nell.'

'He's the most gorgeous man I've ever met in my life.'

'I hoped you'd say that.'

'You did?'

'I thought you'd be perfect together from the start.' Dilly winced. It wasn't quite a lie, but it felt like one.

'He's so fucking fuckable!' Nell giggled throatily.

'Quite.' She looked at the tampon. 'One thing.'

'Yes?' Nell ripped a hunk of loo roll noisily from the spool.

'Don't hurt him.'

'Ha. Ha.'

'I mean it.'

There was a snap of a flint sparking as Nell lit up. A moment later the familiar smell of dope floated across to Dilly.

'I wish Flipper would bloody well hurry up and get here.' Nell handed the spliff under the partition. 'He needs to be in on this. He'll love that guy, too.'

Dilly found this an odd thing to say, but was too busy making sure tampon and spliff didn't get muddled up to comment.

Meanwhile, Magnus was under pressure from the Three Disgraces.

Being male, metrosexual, charming, talented and self-effacing was no match for the Three Disgraces' all-out female wiles. He might have a distance, diffidence and a detachment that fascinated them, but his niceness was a pushover. Even though her sisters secretly thought he should go it alone, Sperry had briefed them to unite for the night and bend him to their will.

'So you have your line-up,' Sperry told him as she handed him a pint of Guinness. 'You're guitar and vocals; Dilly's keyboard and vocals.'

'Nell is backing singer and percussion,' Carry said encouragingly, 'even though she's crap.'

'. . . and Flipper's on drums,' added Fe with a wink, 'even though he's not here.'

Sperry gave her sisters a withering look.

Magnus gave them all an even more withering one. 'I can't create a band from an audition where less people tried out than I want band members.'

'You just have,' Sperry smiled.

'*You* just have.' He flipped a beer mat, trying and failing to think fast.

He looked at their lovely, blank, manipulative faces and laughed in despair. He knew when he'd been had.

He tried, briefly, to be practical.

'Okay. I agree that Dilly's a great singer and musician – mind-blowing – but she doesn't want to do it.' He glanced across at the blonde in the beaded glasses who was munching her way through her third bag of peanuts at the bar as she ordered a round.

'Correction.' Sperry cocked her head. 'Dilly *is* mind-blowingly good, *does* want to do it, and just needs you to encourage her.'

Magnus cleared his throat. 'Okay. Whatever you say. As for this Nell girl, she looks fantastic but she can't sing, can't dance and can't keep time.'

'Correction.' Fe held up her hands. 'She *is* admittedly talentless, but she is so sexy all you have to do is put her on stage to draw a crowd. And you fancy her so much she's in the band whatever.' She drew a W with her thumbs and fore-fingers.

To his credit, Magnus had the grace to blush and look away. 'And whoever "Flipper" is hasn't even turned up.'

'He's good, trust me.' Carry made an appreciative clicking noise.

'The trouble is.' Magnus looked at her seriously. 'I don't. I never have. None of you.' He looked from face to face.

They stared blankly back, beautiful in collaboration.

'Are you my managers or something?'

'Top idea.' Sperry raised her glass. 'I'll start work by break-ing the good news to your new band members. Fe and Carry can massage your ego while I'm gone.'

'What the fuck is she up to?' Magnus sagged back in his chair, looking across the table to Fe and Carry.

They shrugged.

'If it's any consolation, we think this band is going to stink, too.' Fe held up her hands. 'Sperry made us say those things.'

'Even about Dilly?'

'Especially about Dilly. She's better than you. Scary.' Carry pulled a spook face.

'Thanks.'

'You should go it alone,' urged Fe.

Magnus lifted his pint to his mouth and then put it down as a thought struck him. 'Is this what this is all about? A sham audition to persuade me to go it alone?'

The girls shrugged blankly.

'Ask Sperry,' Fe said eventually, exchanging swift elbows in the side with her sister.

'Those two are worse than Godspell and her ghouls,' Carry added between jabbing elbows, nodding at Dilly and Nell at the bar. 'At least Godspell only sleeps with her boy band members.'

'Meaning?'

'Figure it out for yourself.'

Magnus looked across to the bar where the be-scarfed one was exchanging a strangely antiquated high five with her stunning friend, her beaded glasses at a very odd angle.

'Dilly's okay,' Fe muttered, having winded her sister into momentary silence. 'But she has a serious image problem. She used to be really pretty.'

'Gone to pot since Pod dumped her,' Carry gasped as she caught her breath. 'She's running to weight just like her mum.'

'She looks fine to me.' Magnus returned his gaze to his pint. 'And she has a stunning voice – she can pick up a tune right away, vocally and on keys.'

'So hire her and fire the crap one.' Fe glared across at Nell.

Magnus laughed. 'Apparently they come as a package – including this drummer bloke – all or nothing. Like the three musketeers.'

'That's the name!' Carry clapped her hands. 'The band name – Musk and Tears.'

Magnus covered his face in despair. 'Jesus, that's awful.'

'But you *do* need a name,' Fe pointed out. 'What are God-spell's lot calling themselves – Trackmarks? Why not Junkies?'

'Users?' Carry joined in the idea.

'Losers?' Magnus muttered in defeat. Then a voice murmured in his ear:

'How about "Sacked" because that's what you want to do to me?'

Magnus looked up into the verdigris eyes of Nell Cottrell, looked down at her body and felt a depth charge of pure lust detonate, dragging his solar plexus right up to his skull and back down again. 'Sack' took on a whole new meaning in the light of her expression.

'I like "Sacked",' Dilly agreed eagerly as she joined the table.

'Although I was thinking more along the lines of "Only Joking" in case we bomb. Or "Splitting Up Shortly"?'

'Thanks for your faith.' Magnus flipped the beer mat in front of him sullenly.

'Or "The Best Band Ever"?' Dilly spouted hurriedly.

'"We Are All Sleeping Together"?' Nell offered, leaning across him to fetch her cigarettes from the opposite side of the table, her chin sliding on to her upper arm as she did so to give him such an unbridled look of lust that he felt himself lift several inches above the upholstery of his bar stool.

'"Breaking Up"?' Torn between lust and laughter, Magnus sought refuge across the table in Dilly's bright green eyes twinkling cheerfully behind the dreadful beaded glasses.

'Band names are notoriously hard to choose.' He reached for his drink. 'But you're right, we might not last longer than a week, so we'd better choose one quick.'

'As long as a week?' Nell teased as she carefully inserted her stool between Magnus's and Sperry's tightly coupled chairs as skilfully as a housewife steering a Corsa between two white-line hogging 4 × 4s in a supermarket car park.

Close to, she smelled amazing – a classy, honey-sweet scent kicked through with spice.

'Magnus should choose the name.' Dilly was plunging into a pint of Guinness and gave herself a white-tipped nose and a moustache that offset the glasses and gypsy headscarf so that she looked stranger than ever, like Captain Birdseye in drag.

Magnus hastily shelved a smile and looked away. Never had one so pretty looked so gorgeously under-stated.

'Threesome?' he suggested.

'But there are four of us,' Nell pointed out, folding a warm hand over his wrist.

Magnus started, acutely aware of the warm fingers lying idly across his tight sinews. 'The fourth member isn't here. Besides, the Thompson Twins weren't even related and there were three of them.'

'*Hold me now*,' Dilly started singing to herself as she rolled a cigarette – it was one of her mother's favourites. '*Warm my heart. Stay with me. Let loving start . . .*'

A spontaneous smile broke across Magnus's face. 'We should do a cover of that.'

'I love that song,' Sperry rejoined them, fat cigar smouldering, (she was taking her manager role very seriously), eyes immediately checking out the Magnus/Nell situation

'Never heard of the Thomas Twins.' Nell was applying her thumb to the soft underside of his arm to keep his attention.

'Thompson,' Sperry corrected, watching her.

'Our drummer is *my* twin,' Nell pointed out, watching Magnus.

'The drummer I haven't met?' He turned to her.

'He's good,' she smouldered.

Big mistake, mate, Sperry sighed. Don't look her in the eye. But he had.

'So I've heard.' He succumbed, letting his eyes stay with hers too long. Christ, she had sex appeal. Sperry was powerless to stop it happening as she watched him getting sucked in.

'He's a great vet,' Dilly murmured happily to herself as she lit her rollie and drew a smile on her Guinness head. 'Saved my horse's life.'

'And he's very good looking.' Nell gazed into Magnus's eyes, sending the depth charges deeper.

'Think Nell only male.' Dilly nodded thoughtfully.

Magnus struggled with the concept.

'Magnus and Dilly could be twins,' Sperry injected idly. 'You could call the band "Twin Incest".'

Magnus turned and gaped at her across the table.

'I don't think so.'

'Just an idea.' Sperry pursed her lips sardonically. Beside her, Dilly smiled with a sort of sweet apology directed at no one in particular.

'What about calling the band Twin Set!' Nell suggested elatedly.

Magnus baulked, depth charges momentarily stilled.

'Who Dares Twins,' Dilly filled the appalled silence that followed with the first thing that came into her head.

'Twin Towns.' Magnus latched on to the game.

'Twin Beds.'

'Twin Towers?'

'Ugh. Bad taste.'

'Hardly catchy,' Sperry butted in between texting her mates, waiting for her sisters for back-up. But the other Disgraces had already wandered off in boredom, one playing the old pinball machine, the other creating a house of cards from bar mats on a neighbouring table. Then Sperry looked up and smiled through her cigar smoke as she realised what was happening.

Magnus and Dilly were leaning across the table towards each other now, silly ideas running riot.

'Twinny and Susannah?'

'Twin, Lose or Draw.'

'Twin Peaks.'

'Twin Geeks?' Magnus's blue eyes shone with mirth.

'Who are you calling a geek?' Nell withdrew her hand from Magnus's arm and snatched a Marlboro out of her packet. She knew when she'd been upstaged.

'Sorry.' Dilly was immediately apologetic.

'Just playing on words,' Magnus added easily.

'Play fair then.' Nell looked up at him from beneath her lashes and he felt another belly-kick of lust. He didn't even like her very much, but she was having an alarming effect on him.

'Play Four,' Dilly muttered idly to herself as she added dimples to her Guinness face. 'Four Play.'

'Now that I like!' Magnus smiled across at her.

'I hate it.' Nell stole Dilly's lighter from across the table and gave her a withering look.

'Me too.' She looked up from her pint, anxious not to incur her friend's displeasure.

Magnus couldn't work the two out at all.

'Disbanded?' he suggested weakly.

'How about "The Drummer's Always Late"?' suggested a smooth drawl as a shadow fell across the table, followed by an outstretched hand that gripped Magnus's apologetically before shaking it with great warmth. 'Flipper Cottrell. Sorry – local racing stud had a breech birth. Unforgivably late. I take it I've missed out?'

'Not quite,' Magnus assured him, although he was certain that he'd just picked up a note of relief in Flipper's apologetic assumption that he was too late to audition.

'Did the foal survive?' Dilly was asking worriedly.

'Yes! Big filly, still just about alive, thank goodness. Bouncing about now. They've called her Hope. Have we met?' Flipper creased his straight eyebrows at Dilly, a gesture as mesmerising and threatening as hawk wings reshaping from hover to swoop in for the kill.

She nodded. 'You saved my horse's life.'

'I save a lot of horses' lives.'

'Pu-lease,' Magnus muttered under his breath as he studied a face that was, absolutely, the XY of Nell's XX chromosome. It was uncanny. The same sex appeal, without any of the same appeal to Magnus. Like his sister, Flipper Cottrell would pull crowds just by standing on a stage. He certainly lured the younger two Disgraces straight back to the table as soon as he joined them all. He had straw in his short black hair and dust in the long dark lashes around those lichen-green Cottrell eyes.

'Can you really drum?' Magnus demanded.

'I can really drum. Would you like me to buy drinks or show you what I can do?'

'Both?' Dilly suggested.

'I only have a bit of electronic kit here,' Magnus apologised as he took Flipper across to set up.

'Can I beat it with a stick?'

'You can beat it with a stick.'

'In that case, I'll drum first and if I'm crap I'll buy the drinks afterwards.'

Lighting another Marlboro, Nell leaned across to the Three Disgraces. 'You'll love this.'

'We know,' Fe muttered.

'He's good.'

'We know,' Carry smiled thinly.

'He's loads more talented than me.'

Sperry sighed. 'It wouldn't be hard.'

Nell smiled gallantly, let a sharp puff of air escape from her nose and looked from one Disgrace to another.

'Magnus will fall for me before he touches any of you bitches' bony arses.'

'We know,' they chorused dispassionately, turning to watch Flipper.

'Did you hear that?' Nell fumed across the table to Dilly in a whisper.

'No. Sorry. What?' Dilly looked up from replying to a *How's it going?* text from Ellen with an *I'm lead vocals . . . help!* one. She couldn't keep the smile from her face.

Nell gripped her hand, dragging her across the table to whisper in her ear. 'Those Sixsmith bitches just—'

Then a drum beat started, and they forgot what they were talking about.

Nobody had heard anything like it.

Five minutes later, Magnus was buying a round of drinks and Dilly was staring at Flipper adoringly.

'You drum brilliantly. You're wasted as a vet.'

'I'm a brilliant vet.' He had his twin sister's cockiness as well as her looks.

'But that was amazing.'

'I just hit things with a stick.'

When Magnus handed her a fresh pint of Guinness, Dilly gulped back enough to frothily daub her nose again and expand her white foam moustache from prison officer Mackay to Des Lynam.

Nell floated back from the loo fresh from applying lip-gloss, spiking her hair upside down and propping her breasts high on their Wonderbra padding. Settling her long body back on the bar-stool, she looked up radiantly as Magnus brought the rest of the drinks to the table, followed by Sperry bearing big bowls of chips from her mother's kitchen.

'I have the name!' she announced. 'And I won't take no for an answer.'

Sperry groaned.

'*Entwined.*'

'Entwined?'

'It has "twin" in the name.'

When Pheely discovered that her daughter had joined a band, it triggered a massive row.

'What about going back to university?'

'I've already told you. I'm not going back.'

'Well, you can't just hang around here sponging off me.'

'As unpaid nanny, cleaner and cook, you mean?'

'You'll have to get a job.'

'I already have. I'm working at the Gallery. I've been there a week, not that you've noticed.'

'You've done what?' Pheely fumed. 'How could you work for that witch, Pru? She hates me.'

'She sells your sculptures.'

'She still hates me.'

'She rather likes *me*.'

'You could at least have asked me first.'

'You just said I have to get a job.'

'Yes, but I was going to suggest you talk to Pixie. She's crying out for help at the market garden.'

'I'm ahead of you, Mother, as ever. She's given me hours to fit in with the Gallery because she can only afford me part time.'

'Oh.' Faced with such daughterly duty, Pheely couldn't argue.

But she could still disapprove.

'This band. Is there a Wyck in it?'

'No.'

'A Gates?' Pheely named the other notorious family in Oddlode.

'No.'

'Anyone I know?' She was clearly desperate for information.

'Anke's son, Magnus, and the two youngest Cottrells. The twins.'

Pheely pressed her palms to her cheeks and shuddered excitedly.

'Are you joking?'

'No. Why?'

'They are such *lovely* young people. When you said "a band", I assumed you meant some scruffy lot of shoe-gazers, not charming youngsters like the Cottrells.'

Dilly sucked her lips for a moment, uncertain whether to laugh or pick a fight. 'You are *such* a snob.'

'Yes. I am.'

It was the closest mother-and-daughter bonding moment they'd had since Pod had ransacked their lives.

Flipper and Nell didn't bother telling their parents about the band. It was none of their business, although Nell did insinuate that she was at last on the verge of earning big money.

Piggy and Dibs were delighted. Despite Nell's unsuccessful forays into modelling, acting, fashion design and art, they still had tremendous faith in their daughter.

The twins did, however, talk in private about Entwined. Just once. It wasn't good.

'I think I'm going to pull out,' Flipper announced just two days after the auditions, as they rode out to hounds on a sharp January morning with hail lying heavily in the black clouds overhead. 'Magnus seems a nice enough guy, and bloody talented, but I don't have time. I want to get the Thrusters back in training.'

The Thrusters was their team-chasing squad, a sport that involved four brave and foolish souls riding hell for leather across country, attempting to win a competition with the fastest time. In the previous year's Vale of the Wolds Chase he, Nell, Rory Midwinter and Nell's then-boyfriend Jamie had come a close second to elder brother Piers's team, the Galloping Gavels. It was a matter of sibling rivalry to try to reverse the standings this year.

'Now Jamie's off the scene, I thought I might ask Spurs to take his place.'

'You'll have plenty of time for the band *and* the team,' Nell pleaded. '*I'm* doing both.'

'You don't have a job. Besides, I haven't invited you to join the Thrusters again yet.' He trotted away from her along a cover edge, listening for the hounds.

'You know you need me.' She kicked Popeye in pursuit.

It was true. Of all the riders, Nell was the most foolhardy and brave and usually led the way on the invincible Popeye.

A hound breaking and giving tongue postponed the conversation. The pack had drawn the line, now laid by quad bike, but one which the twins pursued no less ruthlessly on horseback behind the racing pack.

Only at its conclusion was Flipper forced to admit the truth and draw his own line as he lit a cigarette. 'I just don't really want to be in a band. It's all a bit teenage.'

'You have to. That was the deal.'

'What deal?'

Not wanting to explain, Nell suddenly hit upon an idea. 'The band could be the team chase squad. We're all riders. It'd be great publicity.'

Flipper laughed incredulously as Olive circled beneath him.

'Think about it.' Nell gave it her all. 'From what I gather, Magnus is only setting this thing up to get back at Godspell and her crew. He's bound to want the hunt ball gig. The VW Chase is just a few days before that, isn't it? Entwined can enter a team.'

He was unmoved. 'Sounds suicidal.'

She slumped back in the saddle.

Flipper eyed her. 'Why is this band so important to you, Nelly? It's hardly big time.'

'You haven't heard his songs.'

'Oh fuck.' He rode alongside her and cupped her face. 'Don't tell me you're in love?'

'I thought you were supposed to sense it?'

He looked up to the sky, blew on his finger, held it up and then shook his head.

'Nope. Nothing.'

'Damn.' She pulled a face. 'I thought it was twin fate.'

'I'm sorry?'

Nell resorted to desperate tactics. 'You *have* to stay in the band. Dilly's mad about you.'

'Dilly?'

'You two could have a lot of fun.'

'Christ. That's all I need.'

Which wasn't quite the reaction Nell had hoped for.

After they had ridden home, she cornered him for another try in the tack room.

'Please stick with the band – just for a few weeks. See what happens.'

'I told you, I'm really not that interested.'

'Dilly's incredibly pretty.'

'And I'm *really* not interested in that, either.'

'You didn't hear her sing. She sings beautifully.'

'Forget it.' He hung his bridle from an overhead hook, ready for groom Titch to clean later. 'You're only trying to pair us up to make yourself feel better about going after her boyfriend.'

'Magnus isn't her boyfriend.'

'You know what I mean.'

'Oh, Dilly's not interested in him – she's only just broken up with someone. Still pretty cut up about it, actually.'

'So she's not exactly "mad" about me then either, is she?' He laughed as he rumbled her.

'She is. I can tell.'

He ruffled her hair and planted a kiss on her forehead. 'Nice try, darling one, but you forget I can always see right through you. And I don't want to be a part of one of your games.'

She ducked away sulkily. 'Just promise me you won't drop out of the band before it's even started?'

'I'll think about it, if you promise to leave him alone.'

'Who?'

'You know who I mean.' His eyes bored into hers.

'I'll think about it.' She headed for the door. 'Meanwhile, I have to get out of here. I'm going to go shopping in London. Anything to get away from Daddy banging on at me to earn my keep.'

'That makes sense,' he grinned. 'Go and spend your allowance instead.'

She ignored the jibe. 'I thought I'd look up some old friends.'

'Good idea. Get it out of your system.'

She paused, studying him for a moment, wishing he didn't understand her quite so well.

5

'Aren't you going to be a bit late?' asked Pheely, who was dying for Dilly to leave her alone with Pixie so that they could talk about her.

'Horribly.' Dilly anxiously checked the time on her mobile phone again. Nell had been supposed to pick her up half an hour ago to take her to the band's first rehearsal. Perhaps she'd forgotten?

She tried calling again now, only to be fed straight through to voice mail.

'I'd give you a lift but I came by bicycle,' Pixie apologised in relief, having already made significant inroads into a bottle of red wine.

Dilly hit upon an idea: 'Maybe I'll take the moped?'

'It can't get up the hill to the Springlodes, you know that,' her mother pointed out. 'Have you tried calling Magnus?'

'No need,' Dilly sighed as her phone started ringing and his name flashed up.

'Okay, so I'm sitting in a recording studio thinking "nothing goes smoothly at a first rehearsal".'

She giggled nervously. 'I'm so sorry. Nell is supposed to be giving me a lift and I can't get hold of her.'

'Have you tried calling Flipper?'

'Isn't he there yet?'

'Nobody is here yet except me. It's all rather Zen. I called you first – give me a couple of minutes to try and get hold of

Flipper and find out what's going on. There's probably some sort of family crisis.'

Dilly perched on the sofa arm as she waited to hear back, watching her mother and Pixie applying thick mud packs.

'If Basil wakes up you're going to give him one hell of a shock leaning over the cot like that,' she pointed out as her mother's face was transformed into the same glossy brown as her hair.

'They recognise their mother's smell and shape more than specific features at that age,' said Pixie, whose own brown face contrasted surprisingly well with her dyed blue hair.

'Like Hamlet?' Dilly grinned as her mother's Great Dane took one look at the two women, yelped and ran to hide behind the kitchen peninsular.

Her phone rang again, flashing *Magnus*.

'Don't go away. I'm coming to pick you up.'

He was in a surprisingly cheerful mood considering two of his band members hadn't bothered turning up for their first rehearsal. Eyes sparkling beneath his woolly hat, he drove her up to the Springlode studio in his mother's immaculate 4 × 4.

'Flipper's apparently somewhere near Cheltenham treating a sick horse,' he explained. 'And he said that Nell's in London having dinner with Milo.'

'Her chihuahua?' Dilly was bewildered.

' "Having dinner with Milo" – that's what he said.'

'How – *weird*.'

'You know, I have a sneaking suspicion we may have lost our drummer and our – rock chick.'

'We can't have. Nell was so keen – much keener than me.'

'I see.'

'At first,' she added hastily, shooting him a guilty look and seeing to her relief that he was smiling.

'Well, Flipper certainly didn't sound bothered. I asked if he could make it on Wednesday instead and he said he'd see what he could do then hung up on me.'

'The cheek!'

'Something's going on they're not telling us about,' he mused as he parked in front of the old agricultural buildings that he and his stepfather were slowly fashioning into recording studios.

Only the smallest of the three buildings was up and running, the other two having been badly fire-damaged the previous year.

Dilly gazed around, zipping her fleece higher up her chin and buttoning up her coat. It was no wonder Magnus wore a woolly hat all the time. The place was freezing. Inside the corrugated shell, it still looked more like a machinery workshop than a studio. The walls had been lined with boards for soundproofing and there were amplifiers and microphones scattered around, along with a tatty old leather sofa and desk covered with sound boards and computer equipment but, with a huge hydraulic winch still dominating the big space, a Portakabin office in one corner and a large pile of quad bike tyres by the door, it wasn't exactly Abbey Road.

'Sorry it's a bit basic.' Magnus went to fill the kettle at a big metal sink in the corner. 'Graham's obsessed with setting up the bookshop for Mum at the moment, so this place is on the back burner.'

'Your grandfather's shop?'

'You know it?'

'I work in the Gallery opposite some days. It's looking really good.'

'Should be open for the summer tourist trade with any luck. Then we can really get cracking with this place. We need good weather to do work here, to be honest. The other buildings haven't even got roofs.'

'So it's all going to be one big studio?' She walked up to the mixing desk, confounded by the number of knobs and buttons.

'Just this building – the others will be rehearsal rooms. I want a sprung floor in one so I can hire it to dancers as well as musicians, but that won't be until I get some money in. Then, perhaps we can even make it into a small venue eventually – there's enough parking, and a pub just a hundred yards away for interval drinks.'

'Can we go there now?' she asked through chattering teeth.

'Don't be such a wimp. Tea or coffee? You have to keep sipping hot drinks here to stay warm – but don't drink too much. The loo is out of order.'

Dilly watched her breath swirling in front of her in a condensed cloud and started to laugh.

'Oh God.' Magnus scratched under his hat, laughing too as he looked around. 'It's no wonder Roadkill wanted to junk it in, is it? Or that the twins didn't turn up? This place is bloody awful.'

'No, it's not,' Dilly assured him, patting him on the back as she passed on the way to try out the keyboard. 'It's going to be the most amazing place ever – and I'm very privileged to be in at the start. Just remind me not to wear mittens next time.' She demonstrated by trying to play a few notes on the keyboard.

Grinning, Magnus pulled off his fingerless gloves and handed them to her. They were lovely and warm when she put them on – and absolutely huge, like bell-bottoms for fingers.

'I'll see if I can borrow some more heaters,' he promised.

'You do that.' Dilly played a few chords. 'I can't see the Cottrell twins hanging around long unless you do.'

'I can't see the Cottrell twins ever turning *up*.' He laughed bitterly.

'Of course they will.'

'Want to bet?' He blew on his hands and rubbed them together as he went to fetch a guitar from its stand.

'Oh ye of little faith. Nell's my friend. She wouldn't let me down.'

He gave her a long, sceptical look.

'She wouldn't!' Dilly threw one of the mittens at him. 'Besides, she's really into the idea of playing at the hunt ball.'

'Not that again.' He gripped his plectrum in his mouth as he hooked the guitar strap around his neck.

'Why not? I think it's perfect – taking on Godspell in the ultimate battle of the bands.'

'At a hunt ball?' He pulled a face, plectrum still in his mouth like a plastic tongue.

'You can just fantasise yourself on the main stage at Glastonbury.'

Plugging his guitar into an amp and plucking the plectrum from his mouth, he started to play the theme from *Black Beauty*, making Dilly laugh. Then, shooting her another of his mocking looks, he started playing it in the style of Hendrix.

Dilly suddenly realised that it would be very easy to stay warm during rehearsals. Magnus's laid-back, jovial, self-effacing friendship made her laugh so much she glowed like a furnace.

She couldn't wait for Nell to be there to enjoy it too.

Unfortunately, Magnus's cynicism seemed set to be proved right. Neither Nell nor Flipper turned up to the next two Entwined rehearsals. The former stayed in London without explanation; the latter seemed to be constantly handling some sort of equine emergency.

Magnus and Dilly muddled through, trying out different songs from Magnus's body of work, plus experimenting with cover versions, chatting constantly and laughing even more.

She introduced him to a lot of the music she loved that he had never heard before, obscure folk and indie bands she had seen over the years.

'My mother was always taking me to gigs and festivals when I was little, so it's her taste really,' she explained, starting to play *Ride On*, a track made famous by Christie Moore. 'They played this at Ellen's and Spurs' wedding, but it's just right for the hunt ball. *You ride the finest horse I've ever seen, standing sixteen one or two with eyes wild and green . . .*'

Magnus listened to that beautiful voice and felt a thud of emotion in his chest.

'*I could never go with you no matter how I wanted to; I could never go with you no matter how I wanted to . . .*' She finished the chorus for the last time and looked up at him. 'So what d'you think?'

Grinning, he pulled his plectrum from beneath his teeth and struck up the *Black Beauty* theme tune again, this time playing it in the style of a diddly-dee Irish folk tune.

Dilly grinned back. She knew he liked the song. He wouldn't have listened all the way through in silence if he hadn't. With the same impatient eagerness that she recognised in herself, he always interrupted if a song didn't capture his imagination. It was why they worked so well together. He'd liked the song; he'd liked listening to her singing it; and if that moment gelled, they always sang well together. That equation fuelled an attraction that neither could see, let alone admit to, but it was what sparked both their creativity and their laughter.

And he was even coming around to the idea of taking on Trackmarks head to head at the hunt ball. To egg him on, Dilly liked to come up with more and more outrageous scenarios involving a battle of the bands surrounded by regimental hunting types foxtrotting around the Eastlode Park basements.

To make him laugh, she also came up with more and more

outlandish outfits to keep warm, layering up in so many coats, hats and scarves that her arms could barely touch her sides and he had to do her seatbelt up for her when he arrived to give her a lift.

The half-finished studio remained bitterly cold even with all the space-heaters blasting out at top notch and halogen heaters directed at their feet.

By the third rehearsal, with no hope of Flipper and Nell coming late this time, they abandoned the old industrial building in favour of the pub's warm function room to be supervised by the Three Disgraces.

'The Cottrell twins are just eye candy,' Sperry told them confidently, lining up the drinks. 'You two are the real talent.'

'But not eye candy?'

She eyed them both critically. 'The image could do with a bit of an overhaul.'

He was wearing his usual woolly hat, over-sized jumper, ancient jeans and desert boots. Dilly, embracing her ugly phase, was wearing a shapeless wool dress and had her hair dragged up in two lopsided bobble buns. Most of the beads had fallen off her glasses, which were at a stranger angle than ever.

But however oddball the duo looked, nobody could deny the quality of the music they were already creating. Their voices sounded wonderful together – Magnus's smoky baritone lifted with Dilly's soft, lilting descant. It was a breathtaking combination.

Sperry put an arm around each of her sisters as they listened, heads tilted to one side.

'Told you they'd be good,' she whispered.

'They are seriously sexy.' Fe whistled under her breath.

'For God's sake don't tell them that,' Sperry muttered. 'They have absolutely no idea. That's why it works.'

Even when they sang a silly, kitsch cover version of *White*

Horses, that they had been jokily playing around with in case they got to the hunt ball, it sounded ridiculously romantic. But it was Magnus's own songs that were pure, scorching, raw emotion. They performed them with all the love and heart-break they knew. In Dilly's case, it was electrifying. Her emotional charge lit up every lyric and chord and riff Magnus sang and played. They were impossible to ignore.

'You understand heartbreak, don't you?' Dilly asked him afterwards as he gave her a lift home in his mother's big off-roader. His car continued refusing to start and Dilly's 2CV was still in a state of collapse.

'What makes you say that?'

'Your songs just sum it up.'

He smiled. 'I guess I'm good at imagining what it must be like.'

'So you've never been there?'

'Not like you have, no.'

There was a pause. Dilly looked out of the window at a big three-quarter moon hanging above the Gunning woods and listened to the engine changing tone as Magnus shifted through the gears around the twisting hairpins to Oddlode. Pod had taken her to the Gunning woods when he'd been doing forestry work there the previous autumn. It was a magical place. She'd told him she loved him there. They'd chased each other through the trees, thrown up great piles of copper leaves, climbed up into high branches like kids and made love up against a huge oak where he'd later carved their initials inside a deep slash of a heart.

'I hope it ends soon,' she sighed.

'You still really miss him, then?'

She felt the familiar stinging twinge behind her eyes and suffocating ball rising in her throat. 'It's the crying that gets to me. I hate crying so much.'

'You can cry. It's good to cry.'

'Men hate women crying in front of them.'

'Not me. Be my guest. Blubber away.'

Dilly let out a couple of satisfying sobs and laughed through her tears. 'So stupid, I know. After all, were hardly together long – I've never been with anyone more than a few weeks.'

'Me neither.'

'Is there something wrong with us?'

'Probably.'

They talked a lot about relationships. Somehow it was easy, and neither of them questioned the fact that it was in any way unusual.

Writing new material gave them an easy excuse. Convinced that most of his songs were too dark and bitter, Magnus was looking to write the ultimate heart-lifting ballad and he quizzed Dilly for ideas.

'Why "fall" in love – like tripping up? Why not "fly" into love?'

'Or "soar"?'

'Could be muddled up with DIY.'

'True. And pain.'

'I've never *fallen* in love,' he pondered. 'I know I've felt pretty high about a few people, and bloody low once it ended. And I've been bloody infatuated – imbecilic about a couple of women.'

'I don't think "loon into love" quite works.'

'Yes, but it is a sort of madness, isn't it? Because when it passes, when you're sane again, you can't wait to get away.'

'You can't.'

He ducked his head with a remorseful smile. 'Maybe it's just me then. I'm better at falling out of love than into it.'

'No, it's not just you. I know I took Rory for granted, as he did me. I guess we just sort of drifted together, and then we drifted apart without even seeing it. I was a lousy girlfriend and he was a lousy boyfriend. We never made an effort for one another. He still drank too much. He still shagged his head girl occasionally, because he always does. He still lived his selfish, luckless Rory life. And I joined in because I loved him for what he was, but I knew somehow, even then, that what he was wasn't enough – and he knew the same about me. And I can look back now and say that I was pretty crap, and I didn't make much effort to keep things going when I went away to Durham, but there was always something a bit distant about him – like he kept a big part of himself separate, if you know what I mean.'

'And I bet you found that wildly attractive?'

'At first, yes, but it started to get to me after a while. And then Pod came along and he was just all there, all out for me – a completely different sort of feeling. He absolutely blew me away. And he was just so . . . damned . . . sexy.'

'Ah, well lust has a lot to answer for.'

'Do you think that's all it was?'

He shrugged. 'I guess my most imbecilic "loons" into love have been the most sexually driven.'

She thought about it. 'I don't think that was it with Pod. I'd behaved pretty badly those first few weeks at Durham – I was horribly promiscuous.'

'You were?' He looked across at her in surprise.

'I got out of control. I just had never had so many people attracted to me; I didn't know how to deal with it. I completely mistook lust for love, and that was very different. I got really hurt, but I was hurting Rory by being unfaithful to him, so I felt I deserved it.'

'But he was unfaithful to you all along. You said so.'

'Only with Sharon.'

'And she doesn't count?'

'I slept with a lot more people,' she confessed, mortified. 'I just thought that was the way to find the answer, you know?'

'I know. I did the same thing once.'

'You did?'

He nodded. 'For different reasons, but with the same result. It's the calculation not the sum that counts. Rory was calculating all along. You just tried to do the sums.'

Dilly took a while to absorb this.

'Nothing added up.'

He shook his head. 'It never does if you run your love-life by maths. You just subtract from yourself all the time.'

'I did.'

'And then?'

'After that, Pod was a total revelation. I thought I'd found my soulmate.'

'Soulmate?'

'I've always believed in them,' she told him earnestly.

'In soulmates.' He hid a smile in his sleeve as he checked right to turn onto the Oddlode road.

'In soulmates,' she whispered. 'I thought I'd found mine in Pod.'

'But he wasn't one?'

She shook her head. 'I was completely obsessed with him. I'd have done anything for him. It hurt being with him, if that makes sense.'

'Complete sense – falling in love. Not flying, looning or drifting or any of that other shit I've done. Really falling. It must hurt.'

'Even before you land.'

'And when you do?'

'Hurts even more. Crazy, huh?'

'Lunatic.'

'Ride on.'

★   ★   ★

They fell into a habit of texting one another – just silly little nonsense messages that cheered each other up. When Dilly was working in the Gallery, Magnus dropped in to see her. His parents were renovating the burned-out bookshop on the opposite side of the little business courtyard that Ely Gates had fashioned from old cider-making buildings, so he had the perfect excuse to while away time on the pretext of helping them.

'He your new boyfriend?' Pru Hornton asked her new assistant the first time Magnus loped in with a cup of coffee to say hi.

'No – just a friend.'

'Gay?'

'Screamingly.' Dilly sighed. Why did everyone assume that she couldn't be friends with a heterosexual man?

6

Unlike his sister, Flipper Cottrell wasn't good at living with guilt, even over relatively minor moral crimes. That he had a reputation for treating women appallingly was a constant source of grievance and worry. He always tried to be honest with them, to make it clear that he was only interested in the most casual of casual flings above the baseline of friendship, yet they had a nasty habit of falling in love with him.

His latest on-off girlfriend, Julia, was a case in point. She had claimed to utterly understand where he was coming from, to be in the same place herself, and yet the messages and texts were getting increasingly hysterical and demanding. If he failed to call her exactly when he had said he would, she was convinced that he was with another woman – ditto if he was ten minutes late to meet her, if he wore any item of clothing she didn't recognise and, most of all, if he was too exhausted to go out on a rare evening off.

Flipper worked incredibly hard and played incredibly hard. He should, he felt, be occasionally forgiven for feeling tired.

But forgiveness was in short supply in Flipper's life.

Tonight, he felt guilty because he was not seeing Julia – even though he had told her exactly what he was doing. And he felt almost more guilty that he was yet again missing a rehearsal for Magnus Olensen's band, even though he'd been as upfront as ever with Magnus when he'd called to explain that he was going to be busy.

'I can't hold out much longer,' he told Spurs and Rory as they gathered at a table by the huge open fire in the Badger at

Great Oddington. 'If my sister doesn't come back soon, I'll just go round there and admit the truth. I should never have tried out for it.'

'Why did you?' asked Spurs.

'Guess.'

'Your bloody sister has you exactly where she wants you,' Rory laughed.

'I know, I know.' He held up his arms in defeat. 'You try growing up with a she-devil as a twin.'

Having all grown up in a very close social group with the Cottrell twins, Spurs and Rory both felt they had. And they adored Nell too. She was something of a little sister to them and, for all her infuriating unreliability and capricious whim, she had two qualities guaranteed to make all three men absolute slaves to her. Her extreme beauty, and her bravery on horseback. To hard-riding men like Spurs and Rory, there was no more admirable quality in a woman than to ride as fast and as skilfully as they did.

And that was also the reason that Flipper had gathered them all together.

'The Thrusters,' he name-checked their old team-chasing squad. 'Are we going to do it?'

Rory and Spurs both looked at one another guiltily, expressions so identical that the family resemblance was uncanny. At first sight, the cousins didn't bear much physical resemblance to one another – tall and athletic, Spurs had a curly dark mop of hair and tawny, speckled skin; Rory was blond, pale-skinned and as wiry as a jump jockey. But both men were Constantine through and through, with the same slanting silver-grey eyes, wide curling mouths and distinctive cleft jaws. And right now, both were sporting identical expressions.

'Can't do it this year,' Spurs apologised. 'I've just got way too much work on.'

'Since when has that stopped you – or me?' Flipper laughed.

Reluctant to admit that Ellen had completely vetoed dangerous sports until after the baby was born – his father, after all, had ridden in the amateurs' chase at Cheltenham the day he was born, so family honour was at stake – Spurs shrugged regretfully and remained silent.

'No can do.' Rory helped himself to more wine. 'I'm competing two youngsters in Somerset that day – staying over. It's their first outing and I have to get some points on them so I can sell them. You have no idea how broke I am.'

'You are always broke. Get Piers to sell them. He'll get you more money than you could hope for yourself.'

'And charge me twenty per cent commission. No thanks,' scoffed Rory, who knew to steer well clear of Flipper's horse-dealing older brother. 'If I pick up a couple of decent places I can ask ten grand apiece. Not bad for hurdling rejects.'

Flipper cocked his jaw irritably. Rory was always buying slow racehorses for meat money in the belief that he could turn them into top-ranking eventers worth tens of thousands. He inevitably ended up with slow eventers worth meat money.

'So you're both wimping out basically?'

It was an accusation guaranteed to get the cousins to change their tune as a matter of pride.

But to his amazement, they both just nodded cheerfully and raised their glasses.

'So you come all this way, accept the twenty quid claret I buy and tell me you're too scared.'

'Yup.'

'Absolutely.'

'Fuck.' Flipper slumped back in his chair.

'You've got Nell,' Rory pointed out. 'All you need is a couple of mad idiots from the hunt. As long as they can stay on board, you and Nell can get them round fore and aft.'

He shook his head. 'She won't do it unless I agree that this bloody band rides as a team.'

'The band you don't want to be a part of?'

'Exactly.'

'Do they ride?'

'As far as I know.'

'Dilly would certainly be game.' Rory lit a cigarette, letting it dangle from his mouth as he talked. 'She rode in the Devil's Marsh Cup last year, when Spurs won.'

'She did?' Flipper was impressed. The race on the Devil's Marsh was an annual kamikaze cavalcade only enjoyed by the bravest of souls.

'Screamed throughout, of course, but who wouldn't on that horse of hers? Absolute fruitcake. Rather like its mistress.'

'You still cut up about that?' Flipper asked cautiously.

'God, no. We're cool. We're friends.'

'Good stuff.' Flipper sighed with relief. Having Rory pour his heart out tonight was not a part of the plan. Having Rory pour his heart out any night wasn't great – he got very maudlin when he was drunk.

And tonight he was set to get drunk as usual. Having drunk two glasses for every one of theirs, he wandered off to the bar to order another bottle and chat up the prettiest of the waitresses while he was there.

'This Dilly girl.' Flipper turned to Spurs while he was gone. 'Is she really as mad as they all say?'

'You've met her.' He shrugged.

'She certainly looked mad as a bag of squirrels.'

'She's a good-looking girl,' Spurs nodded, misunderstanding him.

Flipper scratched his chin, wondering if they were talking about the same person.

'She's not obsessive at all, is she? Betty Blue type?'

'I've no idea.' Spurs leaned across the table at him. 'Why? Want me to put in a good word?'

'God, no. Quite the reverse.' Flipper glanced over his shoulder to check that Rory was still goofing around at the bar. 'Apparently *she's* got the hots for me.'

'Are you sure?' Spurs asked incredulously. He didn't always take in everything that Ellen said when she was talking about her friends and their feelings, but he distinctly remembered her saying that Dilly was absolutely wiped out from being messed around by that scouse jump jockey she'd dropped Rory for.

'I am surprisingly attractive to women,' Flipper said with mock pomposity. 'Sometimes they even talk to me.'

'Really? Do you joust for their favours?'

'As often as possible.'

'But not for young Dilly's?'

'Ah, no.' He picked up his glass and swirled the last inch of wine. 'Not my type.'

'I'm surprised – she's incredibly pretty.' Spurs knew Flipper's taste to be fairly predictable – blonde, bubbly, curvy Kylie types. Dilly was perfect.

Again, Flipper gaped at him as though he was mad.

'Don't let the eccentric mother put you off – she's a hoot. Grows the best hash in the Cotswolds, possibly the western world.'

'I'm really – not – interested,' Flipper said emphatically. 'Nell's already given me the big sell for her "new best friend" and it didn't interest me then. It doesn't now. All I want to know is that she's not going to start hanging round outside the house, boiling my nephews' bunnies or trying to poison Mutt against me.' He reached down to pat the large ball of fluff at his feet.

'Who's this?' Rory sauntered back to the table, a bottle of

claret swinging between his fingers and a pretty waitress's telephone number in his pocket.

Before Flipper could change the subject, Spurs had taken the bottle from his cousin and was filling him in as he poured.

'Dilly – a bunny boiler! God, no,' Rory said cheerfully. 'She's gorgeous – a bit airy-fairy, arty-farty, but basically adorable. Amazing shag.'

Spurs deliberately gave his cousin just half a glass.

'I wish I hadn't said anything now,' Flipper muttered. 'I treated her horse for choke and now she thinks I'm her hero or something. It happens all the time.'

'Dig you!' laughed Rory, who wasn't quite as cool about Dilly as he made out. He tilted back in his chair to wink at the pretty waitress and make himself feel better.

'So that's why you don't want to play in the same band as Dilly?' Spurs was asking Flipper. 'Afraid her "crush" on you will cramp your style with the groupies?'

He shook his head, now in a seriously bad mood and wishing he'd met Julia after all. She made him feel no better about himself, but at least he got to sleep with her afterwards. 'I don't want to be in the band because it's dumb. A dumb thing to do. A dumb band.'

'Instrumental is it?' asked Rory, tipping forward in his chair again.

'What?'

'The band? If it's dumb. No singers. Duh.'

'Stop being facetious, Roar, or we'll make you stand in the corner,' Spurs sighed as Rory helped himself to more wine. 'You've always been in bands, Flipper. Crap bands, admittedly.'

'Thanks.'

'So what's changed?'

'I've grown up.'

'Oh right, of course,' Spurs laughed. 'I forgot you're so close to collecting your pension. Sorry.'

Flipper sneered at him.

'For God's sake,' Spurs rounded. 'Stop taking life so seriously. You're twenty-three. You haven't even started growing up – I'm almost thirty and about to have a kid and I don't feel very grown up. Fuck it, I draw cartoons for a living and go surfing and watch *Dr Who* from behind the sofa with my wife. Doesn't mean I don't knuckle down when I have to, but we all deserve some down time.'

'I have down time. I hunt.'

'You even take that too bloody seriously. You're like bloody Barbara Woodhouse when you whip in.'

'Says who?'

'Most of the field.'

'Dilly,' Rory waggled his finger around, having a totally different conversation, 'has always had this *thing* about men in riding gear. Don't ask me why. She is a sweet, *sweet* girl. She just needs to settle down. She's too fickle.'

Flipper continued glaring at Spurs.

Oblivious, Rory tipped his chair back for another eye meet with his favourite pretty waitress and, with slow inevitable indignity, tipped all the way back until he was lying on the floor, feet in the air, wondering what had happened.

Ignoring his cousin's loud, laughing efforts to cover the gaffe and leap back to his feet, Spurs stared back at Flipper, eyes suddenly intense. 'I've been where you are, Flipper. I've been too regimented and too fuck-off cool to behave like a kid, ever. Thing is, I ended up in prison before I saw the way out. Who's barring your windows and locking your door?'

Draining his glass, Flipper let out a gruff laugh. 'Get a lot of therapy in prison, did you?'.

Spurs shrugged. 'Yes.'

Flipper knew it took a lot of guts to admit that. And he respected guts more than anything.

They'd been friends long enough to call a truce without needing to apologise.

But later, as they both helped manhandle a very drunk Rory to Spurs' car, Flipper looked across at him over the lolling blond head and asked: 'Do you really think the bands I was in were crap?'

'Crap.' Spurs nodded.

'I hear this one's pretty good.'

'So do I,' Spurs grinned.

In Oddlode, Ellen was trying and largely failing to get Dilly to admit who 'bus man' was. For one so totally open, she was being unexpectedly coy.

'He's *got* to be married,' she fished as Dilly painted Ellen's toenails.

'He's not! It's just – nothing is happening, not really.' Dilly waved her free arm around expansively. 'And if I say it is, if I give him a name, it will be happening because you'll think it's happening and I can't deal with that.'

'I don't understand.'

Dilly recapped the bottle of red polish and gave it a shake, looking up at the ceiling in an effort to explain. 'I'm pretty sure he does fancy me a bit – and I feel the same way. But it's *way* too soon. He understands that. We just talk.'

'Talk?'

'Yes. About anything and everything. He likes talking about emotions and love and stuff.'

'Is he gay?'

Dilly rolled her eyes. 'No, he's not gay.'

'And you just talk?'

She nodded. 'We don't flirt, we don't make eyes, we don't

even go there – not even up here.' She tapped her head with the nail polish bottle. 'We both know it's there – but it's like it's in a box, you know, and as long as the box stays shut we can enjoy each other's company without complications.'

'One for the back pocket?' Ellen was starting to see where she was coming from.

Dilly nodded, applying a second scarlet coat to the nails of Ellen's left foot.

'I'm not ready to let my heart out of solitary confinement just yet. It's a bloody hooligan, my heart. Like you said, I have to take it slowly. He knows it, too – he even tells me I'm not ready. I'm so screwed up about Pod. I cry all the time. I'd hate to do to him what I did to Rory because I wasn't sure if it was right. I love being his friend. I think it works.'

'Sounds a good deal to me.' Ellen was impressed, if still slightly confused.

'Being ugly helps.'

'You're not ugly.'

'Ugl*ier*.' Dilly tilted her head to admire her handiwork, beaded specs almost falling off her nose.

Peering at her over her bump, Ellen let this pass. Dilly would always be ravishing, however hard she tried to hide beneath extra layers of clothes and curves, behind thick glasses and under bad hair. It was her low self-esteem that was unattractive, like a wart on the prettiest skin. In a strange way, Ellen recognised that Dilly's 'ugly phase' – which so traumatised Pheely – made her friend feel better about herself. She no longer doubted people's motives for befriending her, especially men – most especially bus man.

'Have you heard from Nell at all?' Dilly asked as she painted Ellen's right foot.

'Nothing. Has she still not turned up at rehearsals?'

'Not yet. I keep texting her.' Dilly tried to hide the tight pip of disappointment in her voice, but Ellen still picked up on it.

'And Flipper?'

'He's still really keen apparently – just bogged down with work, poor man.'

'You know he's meeting Spurs and Rory for a drink tonight?'

'He said he was busy,' she nodded. 'But it doesn't matter – we were only throwing lyric ideas around tonight. Flipper doesn't strike me as the poetic type. Far too down to earth. There!' She leaned back and admired her handiwork. 'I know you can't see them, but they look perfect.'

'Thank you.'

'I'll keep them twinkling up until the big day. Can't have the midwife criticising your pedicure.'

Ellen smiled.

Dilly was painting her thumbnail now, clearly building up to ask something. Ellen recognised the way she chewed at her lower lip and blinked a lot.

'Have you talked to Hell's Bells about us playing at the ball?'

It was the one question Ellen was dreading.

'I've tried. She's pretty adamant that we only need one "youth" band.'

'You mean Ely's got to her?'

'Ely has kind of taken over,' Ellen nodded, reluctant to admit that she was so fed up with the whole hunt ball thing that she was happy to let him.

'But we'll be so much better than Trackmarks.'

'I can believe that.'

'So put your foot down. Demand that we get to share stage time. It means so much to—'

'To?' Ellen fished again, almost certain that Dilly had been about to mention bus man's name; equally certain that she knew who it was, but too cautious of Dilly's fragile ego to say it first.

'To me.' Dilly looked up at her, the green eyes saying it all. Love was like breathing to Dilly. Even when she wasn't aware of doing it, she just carried on.

'I'm working on it,' Ellen promised.

Hours later when Spurs got back home, he found his wife propped up on cushions listening to love ballads and waggling a set of red toenails.

'Very stylish.' He knelt down to kiss them one at a time.

'Courtesy of Dilly.'

'Ah – were her ears burning?'

'What?'

Spurs moved Snorkel, Finns and several cushions so that he could settle beside her.

'Apparently,' he whispered conspiratorially in her ear, 'she has a rather – embarrassing – crush on Flipper Cottrell.'

'Oh, dear. I might have guessed as much,' Ellen sighed, quickly rearranging her mental jigsaw and finding the pieces still fitted.

'I think they'd be rather fun together.'

'God, no. He's a heartbreaker.'

'So's she.' Spurs returned Snorkel's mad blue gaze, which was pressing its nose against his.

'She's really not, Spurs. You've got her all wrong. She's just desperately looking for – well, a male role model, I suppose. She's never really had one in her life and when men only want you for one thing you tend to think that—'

She shut up and turned her head, knowing what she would find. Spurs and Snorkel were cheek to cheek, dozing happily.

'Please be a girl.' She patted her bump. 'Then at least I'll have someone to talk to.'

*   *   *

'Are you sure he's going to come tonight?' Dilly asked as she and Magnus shared the lumpy sofa in the New Inn back room, waiting for Flipper to turn up.

'So he said.'

Dilly found herself feeling unsettled by the idea of the brusque, arrogant Flipper Cottrell in their cosy midst, shifting the dynamic and reminding her far too vividly of Nell and of feeling so let down by her shabby friendship. She didn't want the atmosphere to break. She didn't want anything to change. She needed to sing those songs that meant so much without a drumbeat matching her hearbeat.

To cheer herself up, she decided to bolster Magnus's ego. 'I spoke to Ellen about the hunt ball. I think we're definitely in. She loves the idea.'

'You're kidding?'

'She's going to insist.'

'She hasn't even heard us play.'

'Ah, well, I was going to talk to you about that.'

'Yes?'

'My mother wants to host a naming ceremony for Basil next week.'

'A what?'

'It's like a pagan christening.'

'Isn't he a bit young?'

'No – I think the druids do it when they're practically still attached by the umbilical.'

'Must be good at choosing names.'

'They had less of a range in those days. Anyway, Mum thinks it would be lovely if Entwined played at the ceremony.'

'Right.' Magnus tried not to look too horrified.

'Just a couple of numbers – she's got other friends reciting poetry and playing instruments and stuff, so it'll be like a cabaret.'

'Even better.' He drained half of his pint. 'And where is this "naming ceremony"?'

'Oh, just in the garden at home.'

'In January?'

'We have a patio heater.'

Cupping his chin in his palms, Magnus gazed at her, the smile on his lips waltzing slowly from side to side.

'And as Ellen will be there,' Dilly got to the point at last, 'she will be able to tell Hell's Bells how brilliant we are.'

'Simple.'

'Exactly. We just have to play lots of romantic stuff.'

'Romantic?'

'The ball's on February the twenty-ninth, remember? Women can propose to men in a leap year. Hell's Bells wants loads of proposals.'

'A bit old-fashioned, isn't it?'

'I think it's a lovely idea. I proposed to Pod all the time, but he never accepted.'

'Aren't you a bit young to get married?'

'No. Have you ever proposed to anyone?'

'Kirsty Lewis in the school playground when I was six. Does that count?'

Dilly gave him a pitying look. 'Weren't you a bit young?'

'I wrote a speech. I meant every word.'

'What did you say?'

'Would you like one of my Monster Munches? I like your Dad's car. You have lovely hair. Will you marry me?'

'She was a fool to turn you down.'

'She didn't.'

Dilly baulked. 'You didn't tell me you're divorced?'

'I don't like to talk about it.'

He flicked his beer mat and Dilly caught it.

'I bet you just walked out on her.'

'Like the cad I am.' He picked up another beer mat and spun it around in his fingers. 'During ten-minute break after *Show and Tell.*'

'How long did it last?'

'A fortnight.'

'Was there anyone else involved?'

'Lisa Jenkins. Her dad had a better car.'

She struck his beer mat with hers. 'Bastard.'

'It was an Audi,' he retaliated.

They were play-fighting with beer mats when Flipper walked in, heaving the first of his boxes of drum kit with him, ably assisted by the Three Disgraces.

'Artistic differences?' He dropped a flight case to the floor and smiled across at them.

Having lost her glasses somewhere, Dilly looked up, blurrily saw a tall, male Nell with a big, white toothy smile, and looked quickly away.

'Something like that,' Magnus laughed as he clambered from the sofa to help him set up. 'Glad you could make it. Nell with you?'

'Still in London. She gets back at the weekend.' Flipper glanced across at Dilly who was pink-faced with blonde curls escaping from their crocodile clip as she fished her bent glasses from behind a sofa cushion.

'Hi!' she said brightly and blindly, waving in his general direction.

Dishevelled, pretty and vibrant; perhaps it wasn't so bad that she had a crush on him, he decided.

And when she sang, he almost wondered if he could reciprocate the feeling. Sitting behind her keyboard, hair falling across her face, lost in a happy trance as she belted out those heartbreaking words, she was magical. And for a moment, there was something so hauntingly familiar about her that Flipper stopped drumming.

'Everything okay?' Magnus stopped playing, too.

He nodded, twirling his sticks in his hand and smiling widely. 'I'd forgotten how much I enjoy doing this sort of thing.'

'Good for you!' his sister-in-law Trudy whooped when he told her what he was doing. 'I always said you were a talented little bastard.'

'Less of the little.' He accepted a cup of coffee and sat at the big scrubbed table.

Flipper's older brother Finn and wife Trudy spent their lives living on building sites as they renovated old houses around the Lodes Valley. Wherever they went, the big old kitchen table went with them. It had been a staple of Flipper's childhood, right back to the days when he could hardly see over it.

Now he rested his elbows on its worn surface, sniffed his coffee appreciatively and smiled at Trudy as she gathered a box of biscuits from the larder.

'I know I'm supposed to be on a New Year diet, but these are just too delicious.'

'You don't need to diet. You're perfect as you are.'

'Ha ha.' She settled opposite him, spilling out of her gypsy top in all directions.

Flipper knew that she had become very self-conscious about her appearance since putting on so much weight, but he still just saw Trudy – smiling, reassuring, gregarious Trudy who always cheered him up.

'I'd like you to come and listen to us – see what you think.' She munched on a biscuit and distractedly felt her way up her hair to remove the pencils that were lodged in her loose blonde bun. 'If you really think my opinion counts for anything.'

'C'mon,' he scoffed at her modesty. 'Of course your opinion counts.'

Having penned and performed one of the biggest-selling ballads of the nineties, Trudy knew her stuff. In her time, she had been a pin-up recording artist with a telephone number record deal. A long battle with stage fright may have finally taken her away from the limelight over a decade earlier, but she still wrote songs for a wide range of performers, many of which became big hits. It was an open family secret that her royalty payments were what kept her and the financially hopeless Finn afloat.

'Then I'd be flattered. And Nell's in the band too, you say?'

'In name only.' He rubbed his forehead and looked up at her. 'She's been away partying all week.'

'Ah.' Trudy helped herself to another biscuit. 'Still refusing to settle?'

'You know Nell. We had a row about getting together a team-chasing squad and she naffed off in a huff to spend time with one of her admirers.'

'Not the jet-setting media whizz-kid Finn was talking about?'

'God knows. Your guess is as good as mine. She always has three or four on the go and treats them all like dirt.'

'Rather like you?'

Flipper gave her an offended look.

'How many?'

'Have I got on the go?' He reached for a biscuit. 'One. Part-time.'

'My god. You're on the turn.'

He laughed. 'You make me sound like bad milk.'

She pressed the biscuit to her nose as she looked at him across the table, kind hazel eyes the same golden colour as the chocolate-flecked cookie. 'You know, I am almost tempted to say I can see something different in you.'

'I had my hair cut yesterday.'

'No – you look happier. That's it. Less stressed.' She popped the rest of the biscuit in her mouth.

'You think?' He tried not to stare too fixatedly at the stripe of melted chocolate she had left on the tip of her freckled nose.

'Definitely,' she nodded. 'Playing more music and with fewer women is good for you.'

'Perhaps we should tell Nell the secret formula?'

Trudy lifted her coffee cup to her chin and shot him a knowing look. She was one of the few people who truly understood Flipper's bond with his sister.

'Who else is in this band of yours?'

'A seriously talented song-writer called Magnus Olensen.'

'Dreadful name.'

'He plays guitar like he was born with a plectrum between his digits, and he sings fantastically, too. Bastard.'

'Likeable bastard?'

'Lovable bastard. Bit of a girl's blouse, but a good sort.'

'Good. Anyone else?'

'A friend of Nell's—'

'Nell has a *friend*?'

He took the point. 'Someone Nell was at school with once, apparently – a girl called Dilly Gently.'

'Made-up name.'

'Unfortunately for her not. She's Ophelia's daughter – Norman Gently's grand-daughter.'

'Good grief. The Oddlode artistic dynasty no less. In fact, I know her!' she realised excitedly. 'Pretty blonde thing – works for Pixie Guinness at the market garden?'

'Does she?'

'Mmm.' Trudy nodded, starting on a fresh biscuit. 'Oh, God, *that* Dilly. No wonder she and Nell are friends.'

'Meaning?'

'Dilly's reputation is hardly squeaky clean from what I've heard.'

He laughed disbelievingly. 'You must have that wrong. She's like a Labrador puppy.'

'One that's on a permanent high and on permanent heat, maybe.'

'C'mon!'

'Talk to your friend Rory if you don't believe me.'

'I have – sort of.'

'What did he say?'

'That she was a great lay, that she was fickle, that she needed to settle down. And then he got very drunk and said he loved her.'

'There you go.'

Flipper lopped a biscuit in his mouth. Dilly was starting to get more and more interesting.

Trudy turned up at the next Entwined rehearsal, much to Magnus's excitement. He had always adored her song-writing, however commercial and over-produced the fruits of her labours ultimately became – and he wasted no time in telling her so.

An hour and a half later, she was returning the compliment with eyes ablaze.

'That was breathtaking. You are a very, very clever man. And she,' Trudy nodded towards Dilly, 'is a little gold-mine. Her vocals are amazing. She's a lazy pianist, but she has more than enough talent to see her through. And, God, she sings from the heart.'

'I agree.' Magnus fell in love with Trudy Dew there and then. All men did.

Flipper hugged his sister-in-law gratefully afterwards.

'You really think this isn't a totally arse-wipe, embarrassing exercise?'

She pulled affectionately at his earlobes as she had when he was a kid, shaking her head and laughing incredulously.

'That man is a serious talent.' She nodded towards Magnus. 'If only he knew it. And the girl is the same. They are an amazing team.'

'And me?' He eyed Dilly and Magnus jealously.

'You are a wonderful drummer,' Trudy hugged him truthfully. 'And a huge asset to them. And my favourite brother-in-law.'

'You mean that?'

'I've been saying it for years. Why d'you think I came along to support you tonight, Flips? You're wasted as a vet.'

He ducked away, grinning.

'Worth hanging on in there, then?'

'Absolutely.' She patted his chest. 'You are destined for great things.'

She had been saying it to him all his life, a mantra he needed like a drug. Looking across at Magnus and Dilly, Flipper suddenly believed it at long last.

'Is Nell really a part of this too?' Trudy asked warily.

He nodded.

'Don't let her break this up,' she warned suddenly.

'Break what up?'

She patted him on the chest again. 'This. That.' She added, looking at Magnus and Dilly.

7

'Bastard, bastard, bastard!' Nell howled when she reappeared early the following Sunday morning and crashed her way into Flipper's bedroom during a rare lie-in.

Sitting up groggily, he tried to work out what he'd done so wrong for force-six Nell anger. 'Did Mutt pee on your bedroom carpet again? Did I pee on your bedroom carpet?'

'Not *you*.' She flumped down on his bed, still wearing her long sheepskin coat and Cossack hat. 'Milo. Bastard!'

'Did Milo pee on your bedroom carpet?'

'Not Milo the dog – Milo the ex.'

'Ah.' He took stock for a moment, rubbing his sleep-creased face. 'Don't tell me he dumped you again?'

'Of course he didn't dump me. I dumped *him* for being a bastard.'

'What did he do?'

'Went to Paris on business, left me behind and told me to tidy his flat. Bastard!'

'How ungallant.'

'Quite. So I used his phone to call everyone I know, looked up loads of porn sites on his computer, held a bit of a party to drink his wine collection and emptied the contents of his fridge into his bed.'

'Nice one. So does that mean you're coming to band rehearsal this afternoon?'

She stared at him in shock. 'I thought you didn't want to do that. Too teenage.'

'I changed my mind. We're fucking good. Trudy says Magnus's songs are fantastic.'

'Trudy?'

'She came along to last night's rehearsal.'

'You *were* honoured.'

'Don't be a bitch. She says your friend Dilly has the voice of an angel.'

Nell stared at him furiously for a moment, uncertain where to lash out first. Running away in her customary fashion hadn't improved her life at all. She'd had an awful ten days trying to rekindle a relationship that was well and truly burned out. Throughout that time, she'd been haunted by memories of that wretched convent school and her short time there. She'd also been plagued by disturbingly erotic images of sexy, blond Magnus galloping around on big chestnut chargers. She'd been equally perturbed by sweet dreams of Dilly flapping about in a leafy arbour like some sort of fairy-tale flower fairy.

Flipper lay back in bed and pulled a pillow across his face, saying in a muffled voice. 'We're rehearsing at two.'

'Oh. Well, I guess I'll come along then.'

'Ride your horse first. He's practically exploding.'

'Yessir.' She poked him in the belly, although in truth he was the only person in the world from whom she was willing to take orders.

She was almost at the door when he added a muffled extra. 'I spoke to Rory and Spurs last week – about Thrusters and the team chase.'

'Oh yes?'

'They're both too tied up, so I thought we might give your idea a go.'

Dilly was lying in bed listening to Magnus's demo tracks and trying to figure out the meaning of love, self-hate and ugliness when her phone leaped into life, followed shortly afterwards by her heart.

She read the message greedily.

It was from Nell.

'*Darling little Dilly. Sorry. Went AWOL. Needs must. Back now. Missed you. Missed playing with band. Gather it's terrific. Can't wait to join in. xxx*'

Dilly glowed happily, texting back: '*Missed you too. Band nothing without you. We can all play together now. x*'

'*That's the spirit!*' came the reply. '*The thrill of the chase is half the gameplay. xxx*'

Dilly would have replied, but she was babysitting Basil and he let out a pitiful little bleat beside her as she played with her predictive text. Curling around towards him, Dilly just enjoyed the feeling of looking after him, and of being in touch with Nell again. It was a good morning. She didn't feel remotely ugly. She just felt wanted, needed and – with the right music playing in her ears – deeply content.

'That's brilliant!' Dilly gulped nervously later that day when the Cottrell twins broke the idea of the band on the run – or at least a band at the gallop. 'I'd have to get Otto a bit fitter, and he's not the bravest soul, but I'm game if you are.'

Magnus was shaking his head determinedly, looking strangely pale. 'I'm a shit rider.'

'Nonsense.' Nell had her luminous eyes firmly on target. 'Your parents are both Olympic dressage medallists. You were born to ride.'

'I hate it.'

'We'll get you a good horse,' Flipper offered. 'Something completely idiot-proof.'

'It'd have to be fifty per cent proof and several bottles of it to get this particular idiot to ride again.'

'Please, Mags.' Dilly clutched his arm.

'The answer's still no.'

He'd been in a bad enough mood that afternoon as it was. The long-awaited appearance of Nell had irritated him – the way she swanned in without an apology and then proceeded to wreck the rehearsal by making strange squealing noises in the background, thrashing a tambourine around unnecessarily, and tripping over cables as she danced around in a disturbingly sensual way, pulling out all the amp feeds and knocking over mike stands. Now this idea had darkened that already black mood.

'Let's all ride out together early next week,' Flipper suggested. 'I'm due time off, so I can blag a half day. We can just have a pipe-opener. See how it suits you.'

'Great idea!' Dilly beamed at him. 'I don't work Tuesday mornings.'

'Tuesday it is.' Nell cheered. 'We'll talk to Piers – or Rory – about getting the right confidence-giving armchair ride lined up for Magnus.'

'I don't need confidence,' Magnus said through gritted teeth. 'I need to get it into your thick skulls that the answer is still no.'

'Just give it some thought,' Dilly begged.

He looked at her, his eyes pleading in return to empathise with him. She, of all people, could surely understand him?

But his chatty, broken-hearted mate was just smiling at him hopefully, her green eyes full of a strange bright light, her soft heart protected by an armoured breastplate ready to gallop into battle.

He didn't understand the hold that Nell had over Dilly, but it was as though she had been slipping away from him all day, his sidekick and confidante, kicking him in the sides and telling all his secrets.

'We're not taking no for an answer.' Nell handed him his pint.

Dragging his eyes away from Dilly's, he looked at her beautiful, cruel face and felt his heart and his groin hardening.

'Forget it.'

She smiled easily, grey-green gaze assured and seductive. 'Sure. I have a very bad memory.'

'So that's why you forgot you were in a band that needed to rehearse?' he couldn't resist asking.

'I didn't forget that.'

'Overlook it?'

'I was over-ridden.'

'Sorry?'

'Ride on.'

Magnus blinked in recognition, then creased his eyes into the characteristic smile, saying nothing, but thinking a lot as sexual attraction laced them tighter and tighter together.

'Ride,' she repeated.

'I can't.' He was losing the fight.

'Ride,' she mouthed, knowing he would.

Magnus felt colour and heat leap to his cheeks and groin. Ride. Four letters that seemed so explicit delivered from Nell's lips. Four letters that turned him on.

'Ride on,' he repeated huskily, but she had turned away to talk to Flipper, already certain that she had won him over.

Feeling a sharp, fearful ache in his weak leg, Magnus was less sure.

Dilly tried to talk him around as he drove her home. 'We're just going out for a bit of a ride – see how it feels.'

'It's years since I've been on a horse.'

'All the more reason to get on again. It's easy – foot in stirrup, leg over.'

Magnus punched up a gear, realising that she already sounded like a Cottrell. They were ganging up against him.

He glared out of the windscreen at the frost-hoared verges illuminated in his fog-lights as they descended from the clear, starry ridge into a patchy, frozen mist that was steeping the valley.

'I haven't been on a horse since my leg was smashed up. I haven't even been on a fucking pedal bike.' He knew the excuse was lame – but so was he. It was the first time he'd really spoken to her of his bike crash.

'You won't know until you try.' She still reacted like a Cottrell, not like the compassionate Dilly he knew.

'Hmph.' It was his standard answer when he was under pressure.

'And Nell's right. With parents like Anke and Kurt Willis, you have better riding genes than any of us.'

He went for broke. He wanted his friend Dilly back. He needed Dilly back on side. He needed to know she was still there.

'Kurt isn't my father.'

'He's not?'

There was a long silence. Magnus felt cheap and ashamed and horribly relieved.

His mother Anke had married Kurt Willis in the early eighties when she was a rising Danish dressage star based as a working pupil in the UK, and he had been the darling child of British dressage; a beautiful blond showman with an almost unearthly talent, who added so many trophies and medals to his cabinets that he had more cabinet reshuffles than Thatcher at the time. He and the equally blonde and beautiful Anke had been the golden couple of dressage for over a decade, bringing a new-found popularity and glamour to the sport, as well as Anke's famous Olympic gold medal.

Magnus hated shattering the myth, but every so often he had

to – like de-toxing or repenting his sins. 'Kurt's not my father. He's gay – everyone knows that.'

Dilly was wise enough to know the basics – Kurt Willis had been out and proud longer than Elton John, after all. It was the delicate detail that made her gnaw at her little fingernail and gaze across at him.

'Yes, but I thought . . . when he was in the closet and married to your mum – and you look so like him. Surely . . .?'

'She wanted children so badly, she found fathers elsewhere,' he explained dispassionately. 'Kurt backed her up throughout – he really did love her in his way. Still does, still loves Faith and me. My father is a Swedish riding coach called Stig Jorgen. I've met him – nice enough guy, although he doesn't speak a word of English. Faith's Dad is Irish, but she refuses to meet him.'

Dilly's eyes were wide and unblinking as she took this in. 'Christ, I had no idea.'

'Well, I'd rather you didn't spread it about. I'm cool about it – Mum and I talked it through a lot when she told me. That was years ago. But Faith still has a bit of a—'

'Of course, of course. I'll never tell a soul.'

'Just a soulmate?'

'I tell soulmates everything.'

'I tell you everything.'

'Likewise.'

Magnus glanced across at her gratefully, happy to have her back.

But the Cottrell high was still coursing through her blood. Seconds later the sun-roof was sliding open as she tipped up her face to breathe in the frosty evening mist.

'You do realise this doesn't alter the fact that your riding genes are still as classy as they come?'

Magnus turned up the heater. 'Shame I didn't inherit them.'

'I bet you ride like a Cossack.'

'Hmph.'

'And I bet your father's really good looking?'

He shrugged. 'He just looks like me. Only older.'

'Wow. Don't tell my mother. Thank God he's in Sweden.'

There was another long silence, rudely interrupted by the heater blowing on and off with computerised Japanese efficiency.

Then Dilly closed the sun-roof and all fell silent as she took a deep breath.

'At least your father has an excuse to not see much of you. My father lives in the village – and English is very much his first language.'

Magnus almost drove into a stone wall.

'You're kidding? He lives in Oddlode?'

'Oh yes.'

'Is he . . . do I know . . .?'

'He's Ely Gates. Godspell's father.'

'Godspell Gates is your *sister*?'

'In a manner of speaking. She's adopted. Ely's wife can't have kids. We used to be quite close, but she turned against me when she found out about Ely being my dad.'

They were almost home now, Magnus driving at a snail's pace through a sleepy Sunday evening Oddlode in order to eke this out, but Dilly had fallen strangely quiet.

'Christ. I had no idea.' He shook his head.

'*Touché.*'

Another long silence ensued. Magnus drove at a crawl as he shuffled the car past Goose Cottage into Goose End and towards the big imposing entrance to the old Lodge.

Touché, his head repeated. *Touché, touché, touché.* Soulmates. Prove it.

'I'll ride a bloody horse.'

'Yes!' She hugged him so tightly that, despite his funereal

pace, he almost crashed his mother's car into the big lime tree
in front of the Lodge entrance.

'Just once,' he added quickly. 'To see what it feels like again.'

'You are so fabulous!' She hugged him even tighter and then
pulled away, gazing adoringly up at his face, green eyes alight.

Just for a moment, as her head lifted towards his, he thought
she was going to kiss his mouth and his body started in
response.

But she just planted tens of happy kisses on his cheeks, nose
and forehead. 'Yes, yes, yes, yes, yes. We're going riding.'

Magnus's body lapsed back into trepidation and nausea. 'If I
hate it, I'm never doing it again.'

'Agreed. Absolutely. You are fantastic. I have this massive
fetish for men in riding gear – I can't wait to see you in
breeches!' With a final long, noisy kiss on his forehead, Dilly
jumped out of the car and skipped up the drive, darting left
away from the long-neglected main house and across the
gardens towards the ramshackle cottage.

Watching her disappear from view in his headlights, Magnus
wondered if she had any idea what sort of sacrifice he had just
agreed to make for her.

8

Rory Midwinter slotted the metal bit into his big grey gelding's mouth and hooked the leather bridle-strap over his ears.

'Are you sure he's up to this?' he asked Faith.

Faith Brakespear felt a divided duty. She knew this because she was studying *Othello* for A-level English literature and Desdemona had been in the same boat, although with her it was between a father and a husband. She was also studying *Hamlet* for Theatre Arts and, while designing a set for an outdoor production as she was didn't necessarily require one to empathise with the female lead's loyalties, she had a sudden strong inclination that poor old Ophelia had been equally torn between her great love and her brother Laertes.

'My brother used to ride like a maniac,' she announced theatrically.

Rory looked at her in alarm. 'That's hardly the reassurance I was seeking.'

Faith struggled to figure out how much more to say. Rory was letting Magnus ride White Lies, after all – his best horse, oldest ally, most loyal stalwart. Whitey was a legend under saddle, a testament to the hours of schooling and fittening work Rory put into him. Magnus was a disaster in the saddle.

She loved her brother devotedly. But she was also so madly in love with Rory – despite his singular and stupid inability to recognise the fact – that her divided duty split her in two right now and made her quite tempted to take herself off to a nunnery sniffing into a fine Egyptian silk handkerchief into

which she would have stashed some rosemary for remem-
brance.

'He was never very keen,' she said carefully, 'but he's
talented. And he's got soft hands.'

'Oh joy.'

'Christ, he really can't ride.' Flipper fought giggles as they
hacked through the mist towards the legendary Broken Back
Wood, taking the windswept, rutted bridle-way from Upper
Springlode that ran along Parson's Ridge like a knobbly spine.

'Give him time.' Dilly tried to sound reassuring.

She knew Magnus was struggling, but he had looked so
unbelievably dishy in long boots and breeches when he stepped
out of his car earlier that she was certain there had to be a
natural horseman in there somewhere. He had just the right
long, muscular thighs for stretch cotton. And it was well known
that musicians made good riders; they had the right understanding of rhythm.

Ahead of them, Magnus was clinging on to the grey for
dear life, no longer the laid-back metrosexual guitarist –
just a frightened passenger. After the initial impression of
looking better on a horse than a young guardsman in
mufti, he'd quickly lost points the moment the horse
had moved beneath him and he'd developed rigor mortis
in the saddle. Now he looked like a mortally injured
cowboy tied into the saddle with his cow ropes, carried
along by his trusty steed.

His rapidly dwindling dignity wasn't helped by the fact that
he was wearing a motorcycle helmet covered with graffiti logos.
None of the hard hats at Rory's yard had been big enough to fit
him. He looked ridiculous – like a hit-man making a getaway
on horseback.

Dilly felt waves of sympathy and gratitude extend their way

towards him as he bounced his way uncomfortably between his sister, Faith, and a worried-looking Rory in front.

Riding three abreast behind them with Flipper and Nell, she tried to keep Otto calm as the Cottrell twins leaped and spun about on their brother-and-sister horses Popeye and Olive, delighting in cantering away in fast circles, rearing and bucking like trick ponies and jumping any hedge that took their fancy along the way.

She herself was absolutely terrified and knew Otto well enough to guess that he was on the verge of exploding into the ultimate sulky pink temper tantrum, but Magnus's exhibition of rusty riding was sparing her blushes for now.

But the Cottrell twins were bored. And when the twins were bored, nobody was safe.

'Shall we go a bit faster?' Flipper called out cruelly, kicking his leggy mare Olive into a steady canter.

Standing up in her stirrups, Nell let out a full-blooded whoop and charged past them all.

It was too much for Magnus's long-suffering mount. Whitey was bred and trained for speed. He kicked up his heels and set sail. Magnus didn't.

As the grey thundered into the distance, he left his rider sprawling in a ditch, motorcycle helmet visor steaming up as he spat out expletives.

Dilly missed most of this as Otto performed his own private bronco show for her benefit. Despite thousands of years of in-breeding creating a walnut-brained instinct for fright and flight, Otto had been caught napping when the stampede started. Finding his companions gone, he failed to find the right gear to set off in pursuit. Instead, he squealed, looked around in panic and started to buck, rear and spiral in fury.

Spinning around like a ballet dancer, Dilly fought to control her horse, stay onboard and make sure they didn't stamp on the casualty in the ditch wearing the motorcycle helmet.

By the time she brought Otto to a stop, Magnus had dragged himself on to the bank, lifted his visor and lain back to stare at the sky with criss-crossing blue eyes.

In a panic, Dilly jumped off and stooped down to check he was okay.

'Never again,' he said darkly, his voice muffled by the helmet. 'I fucking hate riding.'

His blue eyes were as honest, straightforward, laconic and amused as ever.

She tried to keep her laughter in check.

'You were so brave.'

'I was so fucking crap.'

'That too.' She knelt down and kissed the mouth vents of his motorcycle helmet.

'Please tell me I don't have to get on again. My mother always bloody made me do that when I fell off.'

'Not much chance of that.' Dilly stood up and scanned the horizon. All the other riders had disappeared from sight. 'Whitey's probably in the next county by now.'

He sat up and dragged the helmet from his head, blond curls springing up as he raked a gloved hand through them and laughed. 'Does this mean I'm excused from the team?'

'I'd imagine so. Are you sure you're all right? No double vision? Headache? Short-term memory loss?'

'My name is Dennis and all three of you are gorgeous.'

'Good.' Dilly swung a leg up to Otto's stirrup.

'You're not going?' He gaped up at her.

'Only to fetch your horse back.' She hopped around as Otto tried to take off straightaway.

'You said I didn't have to ride again?'

'You don't, but your horse is loose. Rory would never forgive you if Whitey hurt himself.'

As she thundered towards Broken Back Wood, heart in her

throat, Dilly doubted Magnus would ever realise what a terrifying gesture she was making. Otto, bit between his teeth and walnut brain seething, was a runaway derailed train, spooking at every gateway, crisp packet and shadow, jumping puddles and pulling her arms from her sockets in his desperation to make up for missing out on the chase.

She finally located the others on the fringes of the misty woods, sharing cigarettes and hip-flasks. None the worse for wear, Whitey was rubbing his big grey cheek against a pine tree and hardly puffing.

'Alive?' Flipper offered Dilly his flask as Otto pulled up with a classic bad-tempered buck, almost jettisoning her into the woods.

'Just,' she nodded breathlessly, taking a swig and gagging. 'Christ, what is that?'

'Mix.'

'Omatosis?' She swallowed reluctantly and handed the flask back, not noticing Flipper's delighted expression at Otto choosing that moment to spin around, rear, squeal and try to make up for his stampede deficit with another bronco show.

Dilly was too wiped out from galloping to put up much of a fight, which was probably in her favour. As loose-limbed as a rag doll, she sat an extraordinary display of equine gymnastics before Otto decided he had made his point and settled all four feet on the ground, head diving down to scratch his nose on a foreleg.

'Right,' Dilly sighed, engulfed in steam from his sweating sides as she looked from face to face. 'Now that's out of his system, can someone hand me Whitey and I'll take him back?'

'Is Mags going to get back on?' Faith asked, uncertain if family honour was about to be upheld or shame entrenched.

Dilly shook her head, taking Whitey's reins from Rory. 'He proved his point – as did this guy.'

Rory gave her a ghost of a wink before turning his horse away.

The Cottrell twins looked petulant.

'Bit lame to wimp out that early.' Flipper screwed the cap on his hip-flask.

'He's bound to get his eye in after a couple more pipe-openers,' Nell insisted, flicking her cigarette butt into a patch of frost-bitten nettles.

'No,' Dilly smiled. 'He said it himself. He's a crap rider. Gifted musician, beautiful singer, God-given songwriter, all-round good-guy – granted. Crap rider too. See you later.'

'Well, I call that wet,' Nell muttered as Dilly trotted away, towing White Lies home.

'I call that steamy,' giggled Faith, watching Otto's hot flanks disappear in a cloud of rising sweat.

'I call that classy.' Rory drained his hip-flask and admired Dilly's bottom rising and falling in the saddle.

Flipper was admiring the same bottom. 'I call that seriously dangerous.'

The others looked at him.

Flipper the vet gave them his most professional worried smile. 'I would never ride and lead from a horse like that roan. Far too jealous of its mistress.'

True enough, in the misty distance, Otto was aiming side-swipes at Whitey with his hind legs.

Magnus was where Dilly had left him, motorcycle helmet at his side, looking groggy.

'Thank God.' She jumped off, throwing Whitey's reins at him. 'Take this one – Otto's been trying to kill him.'

Transferring his anger, Otto bit her arm.

'That's my boy.' She kissed his pink nose, ran up his stirrups and loosened his girth.

He flattened his ears and bit her again, furious that she had not only sat on tightly throughout his sideshow, but had also forced him to lead a far superior model back with her, like a Mini Metro towing a Lamborghini.

'My name is Magnus and you are gorgeous.' Magnus stood up gratefully.

With White Lies in tow, they made their way back to Rory's yard on foot, leading their horses.

Magnus broke the long silence. 'I feel a total and utter twit.'

'Why?'

'Because I can't ride, genes or no genes, breeches or no breeches.'

'You never made a secret of that. It was us lot that forced you into it.'

'I still agreed.'

She shrugged. 'And you still look fantastic in breeches.'

He gave her his best laconic, hang-dog look.

'I'll let you into a secret.' Dilly glanced across at him. 'I hate riding too.'

'You're kidding? You have a horse.'

She hugged Otto's hot neck. 'And I love horses. It's the riding bit I don't like.'

'Just like me.'

'Just like you.'

'*Touché.*'

She squelched through a deep rut of mud. 'Ely wanted me to learn to ride. He bought me a pony when I was three.'

Magnus looked across at her in confusion. 'I thought you said he wanted nothing to do with you?'

'He doesn't – in person, that is. He hardly acknowledges me to my face, but he's written a hell of a lot of cheques over the years, if not any birthday or Christmas cards.'

'How come?'

'Guilt maybe – or maybe he just wants to prove that his genes really are super-gifted? I've had every extra-hours coaching class imaginable, academic and leisure. From maths to ballet to singing to riding to French conversation to piano. You name it, I got it. Mum might have been freezing to death in the big house, but I never wanted for ballet shoes and cooking classes, and attended the sweetest of old-fashioned convent schools where girls are taught to add up the household accounts and charm whole shooting parties. He is unbearably sexist as well as a raging social climber.' She gave him a sad smile.

'And your mother let this happen?'

'She's terrified of him. She backed him up if I resisted, knowing I was getting a better education than she ever had. She's always longed to be better educated. And who was she to deny me anything?'

'But he refused to give you love.'

'Mum gave me more than enough love – oh, I know we fight a lot now. Her pregnancy, the Pod thing, breaking up with Rory, have all served to give us a bad time, but we adore each other. She's amazing.'

He hooked his arm through hers as they trudged through two parallel muddy ruts, horses' heads at their shoulders, mist lingering overhead.

'Have you never rebelled? Against him, I mean?'

She shook her head. 'Godspell was the rebellious daughter. Just think – we were best friends at Pony Club.' She laughed.

'How Oddlode.'

'How odd, you mean. She singled me out long before we knew we had a thing in common – like a homing missile with a mission to be my friend.'

'I singled you out like that.'

'Of course you did. You're a man.'

Magnus let this pass, too curious to hear about Dilly's relationship with Godspell.

'She said she "dug" me,' Dilly remembered happily. 'We were both wimpy riders. She gave me my first cigarette. I adored her.'

'You adore everyone. How can you adore someone who doesn't speak?'

'She used to talk to me – a bit. Enough to realise how bloody awful her childhood was. Enough to know I didn't want my father any closer than he was. In fact I was grateful for his distance.'

'Is he really that bad?'

Every muscle on Dilly's face nudged the other with a painful memory.

'Yes.'

'Poor Godspell. I never knew.'

'She has Saul now.'

Magnus thought back to his cranky, truculent relationship with Godspell, the way she always seemed to communicate through big, strong Saul and live through Saul. 'How come you two fell out?'

'I told you. She found out that we shared a father and that – lucky old me – only one of us shared his gene pool. It freaked her out.'

'Poor kid.'

'Exactly.'

He suddenly looked at her.

'What about you?'

'What about me?'

'Didn't it freak you out?'

Dilly handed him her reins. 'I'm just going to have a pee behind that hedge. Won't be a minute. If Otto acts up, kiss him on the nose. It stops him in his evil tracks.'

Magnus and Otto exchanged boggle-eyed looks as Dilly traipsed off.

When she emerged, Magnus and Otto were cheek to cheek like a pair of old gays at the Proms, with Whitey gazing into the distance, pretending not to be with them.

'Did you kiss him on the nose?'

'Non-stop.'

She grinned, taking Otto's reins and walking on. 'Always works.'

'So,' he delved, having phrased the forthcoming question several times in his head during the unexpected and alarmingly disarming break. 'How did you feel when you found out that Ely Gates is your father?'

Dilly turned to look at him over her shoulder, bright green eyes dancing between his, laced with tears.

Dragging Otto to a halt and waiting for him to catch up, she kissed Magnus on the nose.

Dilly sat in her little room that evening sketching faces. To be specific, she was sketching Magnus, but she couldn't catch his likeness, that intense look in his eyes – quizzical, friendly, analytical, understanding. Again and again she caught the wide jaw, the high cheeks, the flop of curls and the arched roll of his eyebrows, but the eyes defeated her.

She was listening to his demo tracks, although she already knew the songs inside out and could sing them in her sleep. She just liked to hear his voice, that lilting, smoky timbre that ate into her.

They were exchanging the usual lazy nonsense texts.

I ache like hell

You were only in the saddle for twenty minutes

My arse says at least twenty-five

Any bruises yet?

Only where I can't see. Come and admire any time . . .

You were very brave
I was a fool. Did I look a total knob?
Yes
Bitch
A lovely knob
That has been said before
Were you mounted at the time?
Her battery packed up before he could answer.

Dilly pressed finger and thumb to the top of her nose and took a deep breath, recognising flirtation and disliking it intensely. Damn her battery and the fact that she only had a car charger and no convenient car. She wished she could see him face to face. Somehow, she knew he felt the same way too.

She pulled out a fresh sheet of paper and sketched him in profile.

Magnus was at his computer in the Wyck Farm annexe ignoring his mother's calls to table on the intercom.

He had Googled Dilly for the first time that night, for which he felt hugely guilty and slighty smutty, but it was his revenge for her not yet replying to his final text message asking her to meet him for a drink at the Lodes Inn.

She was surprisingly hard to Google. 'Dilly Gently' hardly revealed a thing, and using her full name came up with gardening tips and sermons.

There was a lot of information about her grandfather, the renowned sculptor Norman Gently, and a few links to Pheely via various galleries.

Then Magnus Googled Ely Gates and his eyebrows shot up.

'Dilleeeeeee! Visitor!'

Dilly hid her sketches in a hurry and raced down the tiny stairs to the main body of the cottage, pausing en route to straighten her mad hair and wonky specs. Good old Magnus. She'd known he would feel the same way and want to chat.

But it was Nell, already ensconced on the sofa with a glass of Pheely's favourite supermarket plonk in one hand and Milo held aloft in the other, protecting him from Hamlet, the Great Dane.

'I brought Milo to meet your mother.'

'Is he a chihuahua?' Pheely was sharing the sofa with her daughter's friend, admiring Milo's snarling lips from a distance and Nell's classic profile at shorter range.

'Gift from my ex.' Nell turned Milo around to be admired, while Hamlet salivated greedily over the sofa arm, working out the best angle of approach.

Pheely, who loved all beautiful things, was totally captivated by Nell.

'Have you ever been sculpted?'

Dilly drooped by the wood-burning stove, thankful at least for the chance to warm up.

'I've sat for a few portraits.' Nell was wrinkling her nose. 'Frightfully dull. Milo would make rather a noble dog bust, don't you think?' She more or less threw Milo across the sofa at her friend's mother.

'Divine,' Pheely agreed, gathering the little bundle into her hands. Milo put on his best love-me show – no bigger than a guinea pig, with the sweetest blinking eyes and wriggling body, he knew he'd knocked the Great Dane to the kerb. 'He has a definite grandeur. And Milo's a lovely name.'

'So my ex thinks. It's his name.'

Dilly perched on the clothes-strewn bench opposite the sofa and comforted jealous Hamlet. 'Does that mean you're back together?'

'No. He's a bastard. But I still love the dog. And last week's farewell shag will go down as an all-time favourite.' Her big eyes hit Dilly's full-on, the message clear.

'Good for you!' Pheely kissed Milo's little head, not noticing that he almost bit off her necklace in fury.

'Lovely wine.'

'Isn't it?' Pheely was enthusing. 'CWW – worth remembering. Tremendously good value by the case.'

'Or thousand-litre bowser,' Dilly muttered.

'Is it South African?'

'Hard to tell.' Pheely squinted at the bottle, the label of which simply read Cheap White Wine in large black font.

Lowering her face to the same eye-line, Dilly gave her mother a go-away look.

Pheely ignored her, turning back to Nell. 'I'm so pleased you popped by.'

'I've been meaning to pay a visit for ages,' Nell replied politely. 'Such a sweet cottage. Much cosier than the big house. Do you open that out in summer?'

'No,' Pheely said smoothly, leaning forwards to splash more CWW into her own glass, Milo hanging on to her jumper with his teeth to prevent himself from falling.

Dilly shot her a dark look and went to fetch a glass for herself, glancing worriedly over her shoulder as her mother started interrogating.

'I'm so thrilled you and Dilly are still chums. She adored you at school – spoke about you all the time. She still does.'

'How sweet. We've really only just hooked up again – through this band.'

'Oh yes, Binder Twine.'

'Entwined.'

'Yes, yes. So lovely to be able to have a sing-along with friends.'

Pulling a glass from the cupboard, Dilly silently groaned. Her mother always did this. She might treat Dilly as a cross between a freeloading lodger and an agony aunt, but she treated her friends like toddlers.

Nell didn't seem at all bothered, however, as she held the rim of her glass of CWW to her chin and smiled winningly, now enthralled by Pheely's subject matter.

'We're pretty hot.'

'You are?'

'So my sister-in-law seems to think. Trudy Dew.'

'Our village pop star no less! Well, good for you. I've bumped into Trudy in the post office a few times. Delightfully down to earth. She and your brother are doing up Rectory Cottage, aren't they?'

'Yes.'

'I used to absolutely weep along to that song of hers. What was it?'

'*I Hate Loving You.*'

'Of course. I listened to it non-stop when it came out.'

'I love you but I hate you,' Nell started to sing flatly.

'You are my nadir and my zenith,' Pheely joined in, surprisingly tunefully.

But the harmony was agony.

Give them ten minutes, Dilly decided. I won't get a word in edgeways until then.

She abandoned her wine glass and took Hamlet outside, settling on the frosty edge of the terrace wall and letting him stomp about while she rolled a cigarette and admired Orion overhead.

'Thing is, Magnus,' she muttered quietly, talking to him as she often did these days even when he wasn't there. 'I like Nell a lot. I think she's the most beautiful girl I've ever met. I'd love to be like her. And I like my mother for all her faults. They are great people. I just don't want them to get on. I want to keep them both to myself. Does that make sense?'

'He's in love,' announced Ingmar Olensen as he took up his knife and fork at the Brakespear dining-table. 'The boy Magnus is in love.'

Anke and her husband exchanged long-suffering looks while Faith sniggered with little brother Chad.

Always an outspoken eccentric, Ingmar's regular proclamations had become increasingly obtuse and personal since the onset of Alzheimer's.

'What makes you say that, Fader?' Anke asked eventually, playing along to appease his dementia.

'He's so like me. Both poets. Both heroes. Both fools.'

'You know that about him . . . how?'

'I may have lost my mind, but I will never lose my soul.' He looked up as Magnus finally joined them. 'Isn't that right, boy?'

Magnus dropped a kiss on both of his grandfather's warm, papery cheeks before settling in the empty place beside him and smiling at his family.

'You are in love, eh, boy?' Ingmar pointed his fork accusingly at his grandson, faded blue eyes sharp.

'I'm in love, Morfar,' he nodded.

'Ha!' Ingmar raised his cutlery victoriously.

Anke was gazing at her son in wonder. It was a wonder he was about to turn into total awe.

'I think I'd like to have another crack at riding. Mum. Would you coach me?'

'Oh fuck,' muttered Faith, knowing that she would be sent away from the table but not caring. 'He bloody well must be in love.'

*   *   *

At last, Dilly had Nell to herself in the Lodge cottage as Pheely was forced to attend to a wailing Basil in the bedroom behind the chimney stack.

'I have to go in a minute,' Nell apologised in a whisper, 'but I'm acting as messenger.'

However illogical, Dilly's mind was instantly full of Magnus and the severed text messaging. 'Messenger?'

'My brother has the biggest crush on you.'

'Your brother?'

Nell laughed at her slowness.

Dilly took more than a moment to catch up.

'Flipper has a crush on *me*?'

'Mammoth. Fuck.' She checked her watch. 'I have to go. Family mass in the Abbey chapel tonight – Daddy's annual birthday treat to Mummy. He hires an Irish priest and full backing group especially. They charge massive euros by the hour, so I'll be struck down if I don't get there by the Foremass litany.' She kissed Dilly on the cheek. 'That's when we get to confess. Daddy thinks it's well worth the money. In Flipper's case, it probably is.'

'Still absolutely gagging for you,' Nell announced as she threw her car keys on the side table in the attic flat hidden high in the Oddfield Abbey eaves and flopped on the sofa, extracting a sleeping Milo from her big sack of a handbag.

'Are you sure?' Flipper tightened his tie and grimaced into the mirror, convinced he looked like an estate agent. 'Because I'm really not getting any vibes, and things with Julia are hotting up.' This was a lie, but he sure as hell wasn't going to admit to fancying Dilly Gently.

'Forget Julia. Dilly is *so* into you.'

'Hmm.' Flipper rubbed his face tiredly and shrugged. 'I'll bear it in mind.'

'Don't just bear it in mind. You should be unable to bear it. Eaten up with it. Devoured by it.'

'You can't force me to hit on her, Nell.'

'I can try.'

'She's already pretty much hooked up with Magnus, isn't she?'

'Bollocks!'

'Why so?'

'Because . . .' Nell cast around for inspiration. 'Because he's gay.'

'Jesus. Are you sure?'

'Don't blaspheme.' She smiled sweetly, applying a coat of lip-gloss, teasing out her hair and standing up. 'We're about to go to mass. Armed?'

He tapped the hip-flask in one pocket and iPod in the other. 'You?'

She extracted a ready-rolled joint and a tiny MP3 player from her handbag, slipping them into a bra cup apiece. 'Yup.'

'Let's go.' He offered her his arm gallantly.

Nell held up her palm first.

Grinning, he high-fived it.

'Forgive me, Father, for I have sinned.' Nell chewed her fingernail in agitation. 'It's been – oh, a couple of hangovers and the rest – since my last confession.'

'Are you drunk, my child?'

'Yes, but that's irrevil – irrelel – errivo – that's elephant. Totally elephant.'

'I see.'

'I have done all sorts of awful things, but I have just told an untruth and I think that's pretty bad.'

'You have lied in front of our Lord?'

'I've done a lot more than lie down – oh, right. Your accent's cute. Yes. I've lied. I've told an untruth.'

'Sometimes untruths are truths.'

'Eh?' Nell searched for a lighter.

'Look to the Lord and ask him if you have really lied. Look to him now.'

Nell sparked up, took a deep drag and looked up at the dark wooden ceiling. There were definite signs of worm up there.

She heard a sniff.

'Are you smoking, my child?'

'Yes, Father.'

Another sniff.

'Are you smoking marijuana?'

'Yes, Father.'

'Pass it over here.'

Nell fed the joint through the wooden lattice that divided them. 'Are you really a priest?'

'I am.' He inhaled deeply.

Nell was impressed.

'Okay. Here's the deal. I'm on the rebound. I always am. And I absolutely fancy the arse off this guy. He's nothing special – well he is, but nothing compared to the sort of guy I usually date. But when I met him, wow – I mean WOW. The sexual chemistry is off the gauge. He is divine. Sorry. Not divine in the holy sense, just the smoking one. And I know he's attracted to me, but he really likes somebody else – I mean *really* – I know it, but I just can't stop thinking about him. And I told this fib – just a silly fib – to someone I love. I told them that the person this guy I adore fancies in fact fancies them. And I know that's bad, but I couldn't help myself. And I ran away after that. I always run away. I thought it would go away, this feeling, but now I'm back and it's still here. It's crazy. I mean, he made a complete and total arse of himself today and I *still* adore him. How weird is that? Only he was with this other girl – the one he likes – and she

looked after him and he just adores her and she has no idea
and I was so jealous, and I told the same untruth again in
reverse. I told *her* that this someone I love – the one I fibbed
to – loves her. And what's even worse is I think they bloody
well might, and that means two people who I love love her.
And nobody loves me. Nobody loves *me*.'

She buried her face in her hands.

After a while the priest cleared his throat.

'My child. Would you mind repeating that? You lost me
shortly after you said "arse" . . .'

Nell wiped her eyes.

'Am I forgiven or not?'

'Say twenty rosaries, fifteen Hail—'

'Forget the ransom, am I forgiven?'

'You are forgiven. May the Lord have mercy on you.'

'Thanks. Hide the spliff butt in your shoe otherwise Daddy
will spot it.'

Later, Dibs Cottrell turned to her husband in delight. 'I've
never known such a jolly priest. So full of laughter.'

'I searched far and wide, my love.' Piggy kissed her hand,
thanking Christ for Lastminutepriest.com.

It had got competitive and, now that she was forgiven, Nell was
determined to win as she steamed her way to the Oddlode
Market Garden the following morning.

Pixie, the blue-haired proprietor, was holding the fort behind
serried ranks of onions.

'Dilly?' Nell demanded.

'Cooling things down in the hothouse.'

'That figures.'

Nell stormed in.

'I'm in love with Magnus. I think about him all the time. I
adore him.'

Touché, thought Dilly as she adjusted the pressure on the sprinkling system, feeling amazingly calm – almost numb.

It wasn't that she had really seen it coming. It was a massive shock. But nothing much shocked her at the moment, even massive shocks. Heartbreak made one immune to shock, wrapped in a big suffocating rubber suit, earthed and safe.

'He *is* absolutely lovely,' she agreed artificially brightly, like a WI stalwart admiring a particularly vigorous winter rose.

'Would you have a word?' Nell pleaded. 'I know it's a bit kiddie, but you're like a little sister to him.'

'That's me.'

'I just don't know if he feels the same way I do. I mean, obviously I know he wants to fuck me.'

'You do?'

'God yes, he's been giving me the come-on from the start. It's the love bit I'm stuck on. I've never felt like this.'

'Me neither,' Dilly said hollowly, wondering if she was going to faint.

'I know! Isn't it fantastic? You and Flipper and me and Magnus. Entwined. It's fate.'

'Fate.' Dilly nodded automatically, wishing that she was anywhere else in the world right now.

And yet, when Nell suddenly crunched her into a grateful, bony hug, her slim body trembling, Dilly experienced the same sensation that she had when Hamlet had returned after three weeks away, a starving shell of the big, healthy hound that he'd been – so grateful to see her that he clung on for dear life and followed her around lovingly to this day.

She pulled back and looked into Nell's face.

'You're crying.'

'It's a Catholic thing.' Nell's eyes were downcast.

'I was educated by nuns, remember?' she smiled reassuringly, wiping away her friend's tears.

'We're in this together,' Nell nodded.

'We always have been.'

'You're the best friend I've ever had.' Nell suddenly looked up, the full force of those amazing eyes hitting Dilly. 'I mean it. I don't have friends. Girlfriends.'

'Likewise.' Dilly held up her palm.

Sobbing and laughing at the same time, ashamed and elated at the same time, Nell high-fived it.

9

Dilly phoned Magnus from a gateway halfway between the market garden and the village on her way home. She could see Gunning woods hugging the crest of the distant ridge, a blood-red sun dropping behind it, setting it alight,

'Hi. Can you call me back – I'm a bit busy?'

'This won't take long,' she said brightly, too intent on blurting everything out to notice the strange noises in the background at the other end of the line.

'Right – fire away.' There was a clopping noise and a jingle, followed by a strange snort.

Dilly took a deep breath and fired. 'It's Nell. She absolutely adores you – fancies you like mad. I'm supposed to be subtle about this and sound you out, but that's not my style and I don't think it's your style and she's gorgeous so you're bound to feel the same way anyway. And I know she's free tonight.'

'I see.' There was another snort and more clopping and stamping.

'So you'll take her out tonight then?'

'Woah – steady on!' More snorting and stamping.

'Sorry, sorry – I've got this all wrong haven't I? I should have been subtle.'

'I wasn't talking to – I mean sure. Sure, I'll take her out tonight if you want me to.'

'It's not what I want that counts, Mags.'

'You mean you don't want me to take her out?'

'Of course I do.' She chewed her lip and stared at the horizon, letting the sun blind her. 'She's gorgeous.'

'I'll give her a call then.'

'Good. You do that.'

Later, Dilly drew caricatures of Nell and Magnus twisted into embraces beyond human contortion. They'd be meeting right now.

Good on them.

She switched off her phone and pulled her bedcovers over her head, pencil still scratching across paper.

Having texted Dilly with no reply, Flipper gave up and called Julia. She told him to fuck off.

He drove to Finn's and Trudy's cottage.

'He's out,' Trudy apologised woozily at the door, tousled from napping on the sofa. 'Charity auction of promises near Tetbury. They wanted an authentic auctioneer.'

'What did you offer?' Flipper saw straight through the ruse.

'Signed page of the original score for *Two Hearts*.'

'Fucking hell. Must be a good charity. Or did you really want him to go out for the night that much?'

She rolled her tired eyes at him, but he knew he was on the money.

'Can I drink his whisky and complain that I'll never fall in love?'

'Of course. You always do.'

Magnus was still in a state of shock, but he knew how to host a good date. He was good at dates. It was relationships he sucked at.

He took Nell to the Duck Upstream, Oddlode's much-lauded gourmet pub. But it didn't seem to impress her at all, with its fussy fusion food, over-abundance of duck motifs and smarmy jazz pianist.

She was surprisingly confrontational from the start.

'I remember this old place when it was the Pheasant,' she said as they shared a green silk sofa in the Mallard Drawing-Room, examining the menu. 'Flipper and I used to sneak in through the beer garden entrance and steal drinks when we were about eleven. Of course, it's been ruined now – so pretentious.'

'Would you like to go somewhere else?'

'Well, I hear the Blue Room at Eastlode Park has just won another Michelin star . . .'

Magnus gaped at her. Dinner for two at Eastlode Park was far beyond his budget.

'I'm kidding.' She elbowed him cheerfully in the ribs and winked, looking up as the waitress arrived to take their order.

'I'd like to order at the table,' she told the confused girl. 'I never know what I want to eat until I know where I'm sitting.'

Nell clearly liked to play power games with people and situations. Magnus sensed he was in for a complicated evening.

Heads turned to stare when she passed, he noticed, as he followed her through the dining-room. Her outfit was an understated pair of cream wool trousers and a cashmere polo-neck, her black hair slicked back boyishly, but such was her magnetism, eyes were automatically drawn to her like a Hollywood starlet on a red carpet, to those huge grey-green eyes and the whip-slim body with its hip-swinging walk.

As soon as the waitress had stopped fussing around pulling out chairs and pouring water, Nell unfolded her napkin and leaned across the table conspiratorially.

'What are we like, eh, Magnus? A pair of no-hopers sponging off rich parents. What a pair.'

He was so shocked that he had to fight hard not to spit out the sip of water he'd just taken.

'I love living with my parents.'

'But that's just you, isn't it? So bloody complacent.'

'You think so?'

'I know so. I know men.'

Magnus took another sip of water, trying to figure out why she was tearing strips off him when her eyes and smile kept telling him that she wanted to rip his clothes off. But perhaps that was the point.

'I love my family.'

'Loser.'

'I'm *so* glad I'm buying you dinner.' He cast his eyes over the menu. 'I'll order for you. Plain salad.'

'My favourite.' Nell was scouring the wine menu – specifically the vintage champagnes. 'I loathe food. Flowers I love – being sent them rather than eating them. Salad, at least, has a passing resemblance to an Interflora arrangement.'

Magnus found himself smiling. At least he didn't have to watch her pushing something delicious around her plate for half an hour as he had with so many previous dates. She was strange, but she was honest.

'How come . . .' she debated Krug over Bollinger '. . . someone as complacent as you can write such passionate songs?'

Accustomed to the question – if phrased less brutally as a rule – he replied as always: 'I have a good imagination.'

She lifted her chin and returned his smile. 'Which is why we are going to sleep together later.'

To his shame, Magnus felt a blush singe his cheeks.

'Jesus, you're direct.'

'Family trait.'

'In that case I love your family, too.'

'Believe me, you will never love them. Just me.' Her smile widened even further, totally intoxicating.

Magnus rested his chin on his thumbs and steepled his fingers over his nose, unable to hide his own smile.

'So you think I'm going to fall in love with you then?'

'I know so.'

'I only ever know I'm in love when I'm falling out of it.'

'Did you fall out or were you pushed?'

He laughed. 'Both, I guess.'

Those amazing eyes flashed happily. 'So let's fall into bed and fall out of love together.'

'That sounds like a line from a song.'

'Hey, I may only be able to hang around prettily at the back of the stage and fake playing a pair of maracas, but I'm a shit-hot lyricist.'

He bit his lip and felt the first itch of infatuation burn its way over the dumb-kid blush and scald his skin with a far more lasting scar.

'I hope playing maracas is the only thing you fake?'

She leaned back in her chair. 'Magnus – look at me. I have fake tits, I have fake lips, I have fake lashes and, up until a month ago, I had fake hair extensions; I am the biggest fake you will ever meet, apart from one thing: I am no fucking fake. I never fake fucking.'

And, apart from ordering the most expensive vintage champagne on the wine list, that was the most she revealed about herself and her tastes throughout their meal.

She questioned *him* like Paxman, however.

'How many lovers have you had?'

'Not sure – more than ten, less than twenty.'

'You lost count?'

'I don't think keeping count is appropriate.'

'Ever lived with anyone?'

'Three months at uni, but that was more accident than design. I got together with one of my flatmates.'

'She with you when you had the accident?'

'Not literally, but we were still an item.'

'Dump you at the hospital bedside?'

'Pretty much. Shacked up with my best mate.'

'Break your heart?'

'I was already hooked up with one of the nurses.'

'You fucked in plaster?'

'I fucked in plaster.'

'How fresco.'

He laughed. He couldn't help undressing her with his eyes, like a child guiltily ripping into a gift he knew was his for Christmas, even though he had found it in the back of the wardrobe days beforehand. They were going to sleep together. However fast and furious the questions were being thrown at him, however much this felt like an exchange of fire instead of a seduction, he couldn't stop his mind racing ahead, couldn't stop his eyes eating a dish that he knew would taste better than every plate presented to him beforehand. Nell had offered herself on a plate at the start of the meal. It wiped out his appetite for food, deadened his taste buds and, slowly, loosened his tongue.

When it arrived, he picked his way through the trademark Duck Upstream wild wood duck and brandied cherry parfait. He hardly noticed the way the sweet caramelised pine nuts in the melba toast offset the sharp top notes of juniper and cherry, the rocket salad's bitterness cutting through the sweet succulent duck, the brandy acting on the softest edges of his tongue to melt warmth towards his lips.

In his mind he was already tasting Nell. He was so captivated by the idea of tasting Nell that he no longer tasted food or heard words.

'I *said*, why engineering?' she repeated tetchily.

'Eh?'

'At university. Why study engineering, not music or poetry – English literature, whatever they call it – something you loved? But engineering?'

'How d'you know I studied engineering?'

'Dilly told me.'

Just for a moment, he lost sense of time as well as taste and concentration. Dilly had been talking about him, spreading the truths he had told her about himself. Betrayal lapped against flattery, but his ego won through as Nell's amazing eyes caught his and her eyebrows lifted for an answer.

'Graham encouraged me.'

'Your stepfather?'

'He's a great guy.'

'Who makes you feel guilty?'

'Not at all. He's always encouraged me.'

'Yet you studied engineering for *him*. And now you don't want to go back.'

'He's right behind the studio and the band. It's my mother who wishes I'd go back and get a degree first.'

'She wanted you to study engineering?'

'God, no.'

'I rest my case!'

'Meaning?'

'You rebelled against your mother. Sided with your stepfather.'

'I have never rebelled against my mother.'

'She approved of the motorbike, then? The one that almost killed you?'

'She and Graham bought it for me.'

'You love her?'

'Of course.'

'You love Graham?'

'Totally.'

'Liar.' She stood up. 'I'm going for a cigarette. I hate fascist no-smoking restaurants.'

As he watched her weave away through the candle-lit conservatory, he half-suspected it would be the last he saw of her that night.

Several fingers into one of his brother's finest malts, Flipper studied his sister-in-law over the rim of his crystal glass.

'What first attracted you to Finn?'

She let out an amused breath. 'I don't know. What attracts anyone to anyone? All sorts of things – intelligence, integrity, looks, sense of humour, honesty, outlook, sex appeal.'

'Do you think some people are just predestined to always be attracted to absolutely the wrong partner?'

'I guess so.' She eyed him cagily.

'And what if they get stuck with them for life?'

'Everybody has free will, Flipper.'

He poured himself another glass and sighed. 'What if you meet someone who you know is right, absolutely right for you, but that person loves somebody else?'

'It happens all the time.'

'What would you do?'

'Walk away, Flipper. I'd walk away.'

In the Duck Upstream, Magnus was once again under fire like the proverbial sitting namesake. Invigorated by her nicotine fix, Nell was starting to enjoy herself. Being nervous always made her belligerent, and she'd been certain earlier that she'd put off Magnus completely. Yet he was still being as laid-back and affable as ever. Nothing seemed to rile him. But she had a new tactic up her sleeve.

'Your real father is Swedish, I hear?'

He blinked in surprise. 'Jesus! Dilly's ghosting my auto-biography, it seems.'

It was a knife in the side, but Nell's intense and analytical interest made him feel far too horny and heroic for the pain to really register – just a distant ache.

'Best friends talk.' She shrugged, watching his face closely. 'Betraying other best friends.'

'Meaning you wouldn't have told me about your father anyway?'

He cocked his jaw. 'I'd rather tell you myself. I could kill Dilly.'

'Each man kills the thing he loves,' she quoted idly. 'You fancy her?'

The distant ache closed in, but the throb between his legs was drawing too much sense and blood from his brain to leave enough thought or heart to act upon it.

'No.' He ripped at the bread on his side plate.

'Good. She's crazy about my brother. That's why I'm trying you out.'

Magnus's hand stopped midway to his mouth, the piece of doughy bread crushed between his fingers. Just for a split second his face gave him away completely.

Nell's heart hammered hard in her chest, but her face didn't flicker. She'd proved what she was up against. She wasn't about to stop as a result.

'You're trying me out?' Magnus retreated to laid-back amusement.

She nodded, topping up her glass. He hadn't touched his.

'Think Abba.'

'Abba?'

'Greatest two girl, two boy foursome ever – made more so by the fact they were two real-life couples.'

'Whose relationships ultimately bombed.'

'Dilly believes in true love. She and Flipper could go all the way.'

'I doubt that.'

'They don't.'

'Good for them.'

'So why do you doubt it?'

'Because I am a pessimistic cynic who writes songs about man's inability to stick with woman.'

'Very passionate songs.'

'Cynics can be passionate.'

She grinned, knowing she had finally succeeded in scratching his shiny, happy, laid-back surface. 'You and I will be great in bed.'

This time her directness didn't throw him for a minute. And this time he didn't laugh it off as a joke. 'I hope so.'

'I know so. You have passion. I have passion. Shame the band is such a pile of crap.'

'What?'

'*Entwined.* I ask you! What a shit name!'

'It was *your* idea.'

'I always have shit ideas. You agreed to it. That says a lot.'

'It was better than Twin Set.'

'Not as good as Four Play. I loved Four Play.'

'You said you hated it.'

'Now why would I say a thing like that?' She grinned.

He leaned back as a waitress placed his main course in front of him, his eyes not leaving hers. 'Why are you doing this?'

'I'm undressing you,' she said simply. 'Never heard of foreplay?'

The medallions of lamb stuffed with minted Jerusalem artichoke and glazed with redcurrant jelly were wasted on Magnus. He was in free fall.

'You really think the band is crap?'

'I know the band is crap. We're a bunch of no-hoper trustafarians and mummy-loving stay-at-homes buried in the bosom of the Home Counties. Of course we're crap.'

'You call this foreplay?'

'Nothing like stripping away a few pretensions before we strip off. Think of it as a strip tease.'

'You're not teasing me. You're questioning everything I am.'

'Oh, c'mon – you know the band's crap. You know we'll never make it, and that this poxy hunt ball gig is all we can aspire to. That's why you're doing it in the first place. That's why you were with Roadkill, after almost breaking through to the big time with your last band. You have to attach yourself to crap bands because you think you have no talent.'

'And you disagree?'

'Don't fish for compliments. You're okay.'

'Gee, thanks.'

She propped her chin on the end of her fork handle.

'I have no creative talent. Believe me, I've looked for it. I can't act, can't sing, can't dance. I was even a lousy model, and I know I look good. I just couldn't pose. I can't write "bum" on a wall, play an instrument or draw a perfect circle. Talentless.'

He just stared at her.

'You are allowed to argue with me here,' she laughed.

'You're the one who can argue. And that takes a lot of creative talent.'

'I'm adversarial, true. My father always says I should have trained as a lawyer.'

'You still could.'

'No – just as I no longer have any desire to be a vet like Flipper. I don't want a career.'

'You just want to be famous?'

'I did,' she admitted quite openly. 'And maybe I still do – by association. You see, I've decided to marry someone famous.'

'Phew! I'm safe then. I'm only in a crap tinpot local band.'

'For now.' She smiled at him wickedly.

Going to bed with Nell was unlike any other sexual encounter Magnus had ever experienced, and he was no novice.

She knew what she wanted and she demanded it loudly and cheerfully. She was very, very loud.

'Shhh,' he tried to quieten her down. 'My parents are just next door.'

The Wyck Farm annexe was completely separate from the main house, with its own front door, but a party wall separated it from the main living quarters.

'Good for them,' Nell laughed cheerfully. 'Now suck my nipples – *hard*.'

What she lacked in creative talent, she more than made up for in sheer athleticism, enthusiasm and encouraging vocals.

'Yes, yes! That's it! Oh, yes! Lower, lower – harder, faster. YESSSSS!'

'I can't figure her out at all,' Magnus told Dilly the next day, 'but I like that. She's just the most amazing person.'

It was mid-morning and he had wandered into the Gallery with a cup of coffee steaming in his hand and a goofy smile on his face.

'I agree. She is amazing.'

'So bright.'

'I agree.'

'And funny.'

'I agree.'

'And feisty.'

'I agree.'

'And she is amazing in bed.'

'I ag— oh. Right.'

'Like no other woman on earth. Totally wild.'

'I'm glad for you.'

'I could seriously get into her, Dilly.'

'I thought you already had?'

He gave her a withering look and then smiled deliciously, his blue eyes lighting up. 'I'm talking falling here, you know?'

'Falling?'

'Not flying, soaring or looning. Falling. Big time.' Whooping, he kissed her on the cheek and started dancing around the sculpture plinths.

Watching him, Dilly chewed her lip and thought about the tears she had shed the previous night. Agonising, soul-sucking tears of self-hatred and despair. She cried because she had lost her broken heart again, sharing the two halves equally between two people who would never know it was theirs.

'Don't get hurt, Magnus,' she whispered as he do-si-doed a large raku ceramic of a bulldog. 'I couldn't bear it if you got hurt.'

Suddenly he stopped dancing and looked at her over his shoulder. It was a curious look. She couldn't figure it out at all.

They both jumped as the door let out a loud ping and a customer came into the Gallery, browsing around, changing the atmosphere with cheery complaints about the cold and the prospect of snow.

'Call me later.' Magnus kissed her on the cheek again and wandered back towards the bookshop, leaving his half-drunk coffee on the counter in a mug made to look like a Penguin Classic book jacket.

Dilly picked it up and took a sip, curling her hands around the warm words *Women in Love*.

Nell called her at midday, yawning happily into her mobile.

'My parents are seriously pissed off because they were looking after Milo last night and he chased my nephew's hamster into the upright piano in the breakfast room where it's now stuck and squeaking a lot.' She giggled.

'Good night?'

'It was okay. I didn't get back until three. Flipper went ballistic when I fell over his drum kit and woke him up. Did you two meet up?'

'No.'

'Why ever not?' She sounded furious.

'I wasn't in the mood.'

'But he's mad about you.'

Dilly thought about the two odd texts she'd found from Flipper when she'd switched on her phone that morning. One, sent the previous evening, had said *Drink?* The other, timed a couple of hours later, *Drunk.*

'I've already told you,' she sighed. 'I'm still really cut up about my ex.'

'So go out on the rebound. Flipper won't mind.'

'I'll bear it in mind. Anyway, tell me more about your night with Magnus.'

'What does he say about it?'

'How d'you mean?'

'C'mon, Dilly. I know he'll already have called you with all the lowdown. You are my interpreter.'

'I wasn't aware you needed one any more.'

'More than ever! He plays it so cool.'

'But you two slept together.'

'There! I knew he'd have told you already.' There was an accusing tightness in her voice, despite the laugh.

Dilly cursed herself. 'He's *really* into you.'

'Good.' Nell sounded instantly cheerier. 'Because I'm rather into him. He's pretty eloquent when you get him going – and funny. And he's hung like a—'

'Must go. Customer!'

Dilly rang off and threw a till roll at the wall.

Much later that day, Magnus sent her a text. *If I fall too far, will you catch me?*

She felt stupid tears pricking at her eyes and smiled as she texted back: *Wear a parachute and goggles just in case.*

10

In the week leading up to Entwined's first 'gig', Magnus fell further and further for Nell. Yet his friendship with Dilly didn't diminish. He still texted her, popped into the Gallery and sometimes the market garden to chat, joined her for walks with Basil and Hamlet, and arrived early to give her a lift to band practice so that they could catch up on their days. But the friendship changed. Magnus rarely talked about anything but Nell. Childhood nostalgia and secret confessionals were quickly replaced by an endless analysis of Nell. To Dilly, who found Nell fascinating and alluring, this was a topic she was happy to embrace, but she missed the silly side of Magnus. And, secretly, she missed talking about herself as she had before. She was more confused than ever and desperate for advice.

The cosy post-rehearsal natters in the pub went too, of course. He was always sequestered on the tatty sofa with Nell, laughing and kissing. This was where they seemed happiest to play out their blossoming addiction to one another. Nell the exhibitionist loved the roar of the crowd. In the Three Disgraces' case it was more of a snarl, a growl and a hiss. They didn't approve of Magnus's new playmate at all. Sperry was particularly poisonous.

'Why don't they just go ahead and have sex here? Why wait?' she would mutter acidly as their hands delved into one another's clothes.

'I hate bloody exhibitionists,' Fe complained.

'It won't last,' Carry predicted darkly.

The younger two Disgraces consoled themselves by vying for Flipper's affections. He seldom stayed for more than a quick pint but, when he did, he was the centre of attention.

Dilly was grateful to take a back seat. She saw no evidence that he was as mad about her as Nell insisted he was, and she was relieved.

She felt very low, and exhausted from working long hours at the Gallery and market garden, interspersed with endless Basil nannying and nightly rehearsals to perfect the three songs they had chosen to play at the christening party. What little time she slept was plagued by menacing dreams. Food was her great comforter, along with anonymity. Her ugly campaign had stepped up accordingly. She couldn't blame Flipper for his short-lived interest in her never bearing fruit. She was as unpalatable as she could make herself.

By the day of Basil's 'naming ceremony', she was at her all-time fattest and hadn't brushed or washed her hair in a week.

'You,' Pheely cornered her that morning, 'are going to wear a very pretty dress today. But first you're having a bath.'

'Have we got any razors?' she muttered darkly, glaring at her feet.

'What?' her mother yelped. 'I know you're very unhappy at the moment and I know you refuse to talk to me about it, but Dilly darling, you mustn't ever feel—'

'I want to shave my legs.'

'Oh – right. There are some Bics in the cupboard under the basin.'

'I will be clean for Basil's big day,' Dilly promised, 'but I will not be pretty.'

While Dilly was locked in the bathroom listening to a turgid opera on Radio Three, Pheely hunted for her daughter's phone and looked up Nell Cottrell's number.

'Nell! Pheely Gently. I have a little favour to ask you . . .'

She knew that Dilly would do anything Nell asked her to. She wouldn't do it for her own mother, nor lovely Ellen, but she would do it for Nell.

'I don't know what's got into her,' Pheely complained to 'Godless Mothers' Ellen and Pixie as they laid out plates of devilled turkey and glazed ham ready for the buffet.

'She's not her usual bubbly self at all,' Pixie agreed. 'At the market garden, she works like a Trojan, bless her, but I can hardly get a word out of her.'

'And I've barely seen her lately,' Ellen admitted guiltily. 'She used to pop in most days, but I think Nell has rather taken over from me as her sounding board.' She contemplated mentioning that Dilly reportedly had a crush on Flipper Cottrell, but decided it was disloyal. She wasn't even supposed to know his name.

'She's still so upset about what that wretched Liverpudlian did to her.' Pheely sighed angrily at the thought of Pod, whom she had welcomed so open-heartedly into her home, despite harbouring grave doubts. 'She loved him so completely. I hear her crying in her room late at night sometimes when I get up to feed Basil. It's heartbreaking. Both my beloved children crying – one simply because he is hungry, the other . . .' She shook her head. 'I wish she wouldn't take it out on me so much. She seems to hate me.'

'She loves you more than the world,' Ellen reassured her.

'And she worships Basil,' Pixie pointed out, arranging king prawns in a big fan on a serving plate. 'She'll make an effort for his big day, you wait and see. It might just cheer her up.'

'I do hope so. I even asked that band of hers to play to make her feel extra special.'

'I'm looking forward to hearing them.' Ellen helped herself to a piece of ham. 'Don't tell Dilly yet, but I've almost talked my mother-in-law into letting them play at the Look Before You Leap ball.'

Upstairs, Nell was helping Dilly paint her face.

'I really don't get on with eyeliner.' Dilly tried to swipe her hand away.

'Trust me – it's very subtle.' Nell drew a thick kohl line along the lid and smudged it with a Q tip. 'You have to look the part for our first performance. I've already chosen an outfit especially for you.'

'So have I. The one I'll be wearing.' Dilly pointed towards the back of the door from which was hanging a shapeless brown tweed skirt and a baggy green jumper.

Nell, who was already dressed to perform in a fur-collared floor-length clingy cardigan and black leather trousers, eyed the choice in horror.

Dilly usually loved being painted and pampered, but today was different. The fact that Nell, who was so beautiful, was trying so hard to recapture her lost prettiness made her squirm with self-conscious inadequacy.

But for almost an hour, the long delicate fingers worked on her face like butterfly kisses, painting and dusting and blending. The intense grey-green eyes, so beautifully painted themselves, focused closely, darting left and right, checking that beauty was emerging, covering up ugliness in their own image.

Nell chattered happily as she worked, not noticing that Dilly was unusually subdued.

'Magnus has this amazing way of looking at me when we're lying in bed, like I'm so precious, and he can do it for just hours, you know? He loves writing on me with his fingers, making me guess what he's tracing out just from feel' . . . 'then

he just picked me up and carried me into the shower and' . . .
'says I'm the most beautiful woman that he's ever met and that
I am talented and . . .'

Magnus this, Magnus that. Dilly zoned out.

A make-up brush tapped her sharply on the nose. 'Are you
listening to me? I said Flipper's really looking forward to today.
He told me last night.'

'That's nice.'

'He's still mad about you.'

'I don't think so.'

Nell narrowed her eyes at Dilly's double chin.

'You're not helping, you know.'

'Huh?'

'He has a very fragile ego. You keep ignoring him.'

'I'm always perfectly friendly to him. Besides, he's hardly at
rehearsals long enough to talk to – he's always late and buggers
off early if he's not being surrounded by Disgraces.'

'He thinks they're awful. You have to rescue him.'

'Isn't he man enough to rescue himself?'

'He's a man; he's weak. Take this ex-girlfriend of his, Julia.
She's still hanging about and she's *such* a blank, but he hasn't
got the heart to tell her to get lost, and anybody in their right
mind would have got the message by now' . . . 'always been the
same . . . crazy blonde called Zoe who was forever turning up
in the middle of the night' . . . 'then Camilla told him she'd kill
herself if he didn't . . .'

Flipper this, Flipper that. Dilly zoned out again.

'Pod.'

She jerked her head back so suddenly that the mascara wand
Nell had been holding up to her lashes daubed her chin.

'What did you say?'

'Nothing.'

'You said the P word!'

'I didn't.' Nell started dabbing at Dilly's chin with a cleansing wipe.

'I heard it.'

'Must have been dreaming it. You did look as though you were drifting off into a daze. Shit. Don't cry. You'll ruin everything I've just done.'

> *My heart is like a singing bird*
> *Whose nest is in a watered shoot;*
> *My heart is like an apple tree*
> *Whose boughs are bent with thickset fruit;*
> *My heart is like a rainbow shell*
> *That paddles in a halcyon sea;*
> *My heart is gladder than all these*
> *Because my love is come to me.*
>
> *Raise me a dais of silk and down;*
> *Hang it with vair and purple dyes;*
> *Carve it in doves, and pomegranates,*
> *And peacocks with a hundred eyes;*
> *Work it in gold and silver grapes,*
> *In leaves, and silver fleurs-de-lys;*
> *Because the birthday of my life*
> *Is come, my love is come to me.'*

Dilly finished reading and retreated to the fringes of the garden, snuggling deep into her fake fur hat. That Nell had bullishly got her way by dressing Dilly in a long velvet skirt and frilly shirt hardly seemed to matter given that both were hidden under an ankle-length coat. She could have been naked underneath for all anyone knew. She certainly felt it – naked and vulnerable and raw.

It was snowing, which matched her mood perfectly and provided the prettiest of backdrops for Basil's naming ceremony. He certainly seemed to appreciate the weather as he gurgled pink-cheeked in his tie-dyed robes and fleece cap, waving his mittens around.

The overgrown garden was transformed magically by the white icing, its rambling shrubs and hedgerows curving fluffily and protectively around the gathering, the broken sculptures rendered into ghostly sentries and well-wishers – a snow-fleeced hare here, a pure white dancing group there, all uniform in their frosted purity.

Two of Pheely's friends were playing harp and flute together as she danced around her enchanted white garden with her son.

Magnus signalled for Dilly to join him on the terrace where he'd set up the amps, instruments and mikes.

'Don't panic,' he whispered, 'but we're still missing Flipper and his drum kit.'

'Still?' Dilly took his wrist and checked the time on his watch. 'We're supposed to be playing in ten minutes.'

'I've set up the drum machine as a back-up – and he can still play that if he gets here in time, but we're too late to try to set his skins up so it's going to sound pretty rough whatever happens.' He pulled his woolly hat lower over his ears. 'Whose idea was it to do this in the garden?'

'I think it's rather beautiful.' Dilly watched her mother catching snowflakes and showing them to Basil. Behind her, the tall yews, already bent low with snow, seemed to be leaning against one another and sighing contentedly.

'It's colder out here than playing in my studio,' he grumbled.

'Nothing's colder than playing in your studio,' Dilly sighed, glancing at him again. 'Where's Nell?'

'She's just gone to try and raise Flipper by phone again and to fetch another coat from her car.'

'Seems to have found a Red Coat,' Dilly gasped when she turned back to the garden.

Nell was making her way through the white-covered path from the lane gates swathed in floor-length sheepskin. At her side was a mud-splattered Flipper, who was dressed in a red hunt coat, white breeches and long black boots, his stock unravelling and his beautiful face flecked with dirt from galloping across wet turf.

'What the—' Magnus was slack jawed.

Dilly tried and failed not to find the sight incredibly uplifting. All her life she had adored the sight of men dressed to ride, and none more so than the traditional hunting pinks, especially when modelled by lean-shanked, broad-shouldered men with smouldering eyes and wicked smiles.

'Sorry I'm late,' he said as he joined them, rubbing his cold hands together. 'Couldn't find the place.'

'Interesting wardrobe choice,' Magnus hissed sardonically.

'Just been on hound exercise,' he explained in an undertone, shooting the gathered party in the garden a suspicious look. 'I whip in occasionally when I get free time – thought I'd take advantage of a morning off to fit half a day in. What *is* going on here?'

'Our first bloody gig. You were supposed to be here an hour ago to set up your kit.'

'Christ.' Flipper caught sight of Pheely who was holding Basil aloft and chanting good luck spells. 'Who the fuck is that?'

'My mother,' Dilly said flatly, handing him his drum sticks.

'Isn't she wonderful?' Nell giggled, pulling Milo from her deep coat and kissing the top of his poppy-eyed head. He appeared to be wearing a matching sheepskin gilet. 'It's an adorable baby-naming ceremony. Everybody lit a candle and joined in a chant welcoming Basil to the world and then Dilly read a sweet poem.'

'God help us.' Flipper took up position behind the electronic drum pads.

'Well, that was shameful,' Magnus groaned afterwards as they buried their blushes and shame in CWW as far from the party as they could secrete themselves.

'We were under-rehearsed.' Dilly tried to be encouraging despite her melancholic mood.

Nell was giggling too much to speak.

Nothing had gone right. The snow had played havoc with the acoustics. They might have looked like the ultimate Christmas romantic ballad video, but they had sounded more like turkeys. Magnus's guitar had gone hopelessly out of tune as he played because of the cold tightening his strings, the amp from Dilly's keyboard had blown up halfway through the first number and Milo had howled throughout, later joined by Hamlet and most of the neighbouring dogs in the village.

'We were abysmal,' Flipper had been the only one who'd performed his part without a hitch.

'Well, you didn't fucking help, turning up late,' Magnus fumed.

'I was busy.'

'Chasing poor bloody foxes.'

'We were line hunting – chasing a pre-laid scent.'

'Yeah, and the rest.'

'Now, now – calm down,' Nell mocked. 'I didn't think we were that bad.'

'How would you know?' her brother sniped. 'You just jiggle around in the background.'

'And Dilly's poem was lovely,' she sighed, refusing to rise. 'All about love.'

Dilly glowered into her CWW.

'Shame I missed it,' Flipper muttered insincerely.

'Recite it again, Dilly!' Nell urged, taking Magnus's hand in hers and looking up at his sullen face with a big, possessive smile. 'It's beautiful.'

Suddenly, Magnus smiled back at her, his irritation forgotten.

Dilly shook her head. 'Not on your Nelly.'

Flipper found this hugely funny.

'Please!' Nell pleaded.

Dilly looked at her and Magnus, holding hands, faces glowing from the fire and wine, framed together in a little window-seat, a snowy backdrop behind them. 'No.'

'But it's so romantic. It sums up love.'

Dilly chewed at her thumbnail, eyes narrowed.

'You know, I used to think so too,' she murmured. 'When I believed love to be this great overwhelming emotion that makes people feel safe. Only it doesn't make you feel safe at all. You can't trust it – just as you can't touch it, smell it, taste it or see it. It's just there, this intangible feeling that takes everything in your life and throws it upside down, and then it robs you blind. It's cruel. It frightens me. It really bloody frightens me.'

They all gaped at her.

'That poem isn't a beautiful poem. It's a fallacy.'

With that, she grabbed her glass and raced out into the snowy garden.

'Still cut up about her ex,' Nell sighed, snuggling up to Magnus. 'She was having a bit of a cry earlier, poor thing.'

Magnus's arm tightened instinctively around Nell, and she curled every sinew into him for a moment.

There was an indignant squeak as Milo popped up from the collar of her coat, panting hotly in his gilet.

Dilly sought sanctuary in her grandfather's old glasshouse, amid the long-neglected growbags and dead geraniums.

Perching on an old bench, she rolled a cigarette.

'You okay?' Magnus appeared at the door after a few minutes. He had Nell's lipstick all over his lips and cheeks.

'Fine,' she snapped.

'Want to be alone?'

'That's the idea.'

'What a shame. You're stuck with me.' He came and perched beside her, pulling her cigarette from her fingers before she could light it and crumbling it up. 'You have to give up. How else are we going to sing together when we're old?'

She shot him a furious look.

'Hey, don't take it out on me. I didn't break your heart.'

'You broke my fag.'

'Saving your life.'

Still she glowered. 'What about Nell's life? She smokes ten times as much as me.'

'She can't sing.'

Dilly thumped him.

Magnus cuffed her.

She threw her tobacco pouch at him.

He threw it back at her.

They were lobbing the contents of two ancient growbags at one another when Nell and Flipper walked in.

'There you are,' Nell said tightly. 'What *are* you doing?'

'Propagating,' Dilly laughed breathlessly, aiming a handful at her.

'Don't you dare!' Nell screamed, backing hysterically away. 'This coat is Joseph.'

She threw it at Flipper instead. She aimed at his chest, which was already pretty muddy and covered in horse scurf, but she was a lousy shot and Nell had made her leave her glasses off so she couldn't see a thing. A great mulchy lump of dirt hit him square in the chiselled jaw.

'Oh shit,' Dilly squeaked apologetically.

Those intense, arrogant Cottrell eyes blinked in indignant shock. It was the first time that Dilly sensed he wasn't looking straight through her. He was looking right at her. Short-sighted she might be, but she knew when she'd got someone's attention.

Slowly, he pulled a large, crumpled handkerchief from his pocket and wiped away the debris.

Then, to her surprise, he smiled widely. 'Mud never sticks to me.' As Magnus and Nell went off in search of fresh CWW supplies to drown the group's sorrows, Flipper lingered with Dilly in the glasshouse.

She knew he was waiting for an apology, but something bloody-minded stopped her. She felt immensely cheered up landing a mud-cake on handsome, haughty Flipper. She didn't want to spoil the moment.

'I don't get it.' Flipper looked at her seriously. 'Why throw compost when there's two inches of snow outside?'

She smiled delightedly, realising there was no need for an apology if he had his chance to enact revenge. 'You want a snowball fight?'

'Not particularly.'

'Shame.' She tipped her head up to look at the thick white pelt of snow covering the glass roof.

There was an awkward silence. Dilly hoped he'd just go away if she ignored him long enough.

'Dilly, I have to say something.'

'Uh huh?' Having edged closer to the glass, she was picking out individual snowflakes now, admiring their perfection with myopic focus.

'My sister's told me how you – er – feel about me, and I have to just come out with it and admit that I really wish I could feel the same way, but I don't. I am what I am and I rarely change my mind once it's made up. I do, however, appreciate your honesty.'

She smiled with relief.

'Thank God for that.'

'I'm sorry?'

'I'm just glad you can see where I'm coming from, Flipper.' She looked at him with new-found respect. 'And I don't want to hurt your feelings. I really wish I *could* fancy you. I mean, you're gorgeous, but I'm—'

'Hang on a minute . . .' He scratched his head. 'You're supposed to be the one fixated on *me*.'

'Like hell. I'm heartbroken.'

'Me too.'

'You are?'

Flipper looked startled for a moment, realising what he had just said. He squinted up at the white overhead, pulled a grimace and then shook his head. 'No, just kidding. You're simply not my type.'

Dilly hugged herself happily, knowing that the ugly plan was well and truly working.

'Same here,' she nodded earnestly. 'You are just too – geeky.'

'Geeky?' he snorted.

She kept on nodding. 'And boffish.'

'Boffish?'

'Mmm – and New Age.'

Suddenly he got what she was doing, and grinned.

'It's the sandals and cardigans, isn't it?' he asked apologetically.

'And the pipe.'

'Well, your pipe puts me off too – along with all that rubber fetish gear.'

'I love my fetish gear.'

'It's all right on its own, but matching it with deerstalker and gumboots is going too far. I could never take you home to my parents.'

'Let's face it, it's never going to happen for us.'

'Not unless we both took the date rape drug.'

To his amazement, Dilly laughed so much she had to clutch her knees. 'Now that does call for a snowball fight!' She dashed past him to fetch a great scoop of snow from the paving stones outside.

'No Dilly – I'm warning you! I really don't want to – ugh!' A wodge of white flakes landed in his open mouth. 'You bitch!'

He retaliated with a mammoth double handful.

Soon they resembled a pair of giggling Yetis.

'Shit.' Flipper laughed through chattering teeth. 'I am fucking frozen and soaked through. You really are like a cold shower to my bloody libido. I was going to have another crack at Pixie Guinness later.'

'Come.' Dilly grabbed his numb hand with her gloved one and dragged him into the wooded side of the garden, through great heavy snow-laden pine drapes until they reached a clearing. 'Lie down.'

'What the?'

She was already spreadeagled on the unblemished snowy carpet.

'Hurry up before we freeze.'

Flipper started backing away. 'I've told you, I'm really not interested in you—'

'Oh, just bloody well lie down. I'm not going to jump on you.'

Baffled, Flipper grudgingly obliged.

'Now sweep your arms and legs up and down like this.' Dilly showed him.

'Is this something to do with your mother's hippy birthing ceremony?'

'Naming ceremony, and no. It's something I did as a kid, and it's worth it. Hurry up.'

Flipper swept. 'This hunt coat is ruined.'

When Dilly jumped up, he clambered upright beside her and they both looked down.

'Snow angels,' Dilly said brightly.

And there beneath them in the whiteness were, indeed, the silhouettes of two angel-like figures swept out of the snow.

Flipper looked across at her again, at the pink cheeks, upturned freckled nose and bright eyes, the blonde hair escaping from her fluffy hat. She reminded him so vividly of someone that he had to look away.

'Christ, you're weird.'

'Come inside to warm up by the fire. I'll find you a towel to dry yourself.'

'This is your room?'

'It's where I sleep.'

'It's a bit Brothers Grimm.' He admired her sketches. 'These are good.'

'You're dripping on them.' Dilly snatched them away and handed him an orange towel. She hadn't expected him to follow her upstairs and now the room seemed terribly small and vulnerable with him in it, like an Action Man thrust into a doll's house.

'You're seriously good.' He spotted some more loose sketches on her little desk.

'It's in the genes. I come from a long line of impoverished artists.'

He peered around the tiny fairy-tale attic room, breathing in the unfamiliar scents of essential oils and lavender bags, noticing more sketches on the floor and dressing-table. 'They're all of the same man, aren't they?'

'My ex.'

'The jump jockey?'

'Yup.'

'Funny, he looks like Magnus.'

'No, he doesn't.'

Casting his damp jacket to one side, he sat on the narrow cast-iron bed and studied all the framed paintings and drawings on the wall, slung low because of the steeply sloped ceiling under the eaves.

'Did you do all these?'

She shook her head. 'They're mostly my grandfather's.'

'Norman Gently? I thought he was a sculptor?'

'That was his main living, but he painted a lot – especially for me, when I was a little girl.'

'Most of them are of you, aren't they?'

'He liked to cast me as characters from fairy tales and stuff.'

Flipper whistled as he scrutinised them. 'My brothers would kill to have these through the sales room.'

'Yeah, they'd have to kill me first.'

He rubbed his tufty black hair with the towel and settled back on the bed, leafing through her bedside reading.

'Take your boots off if you're going to do that,' she snapped, picking up his wet jacket and draping it over the oil heater.

'Don't be so suburban.'

'I'm not – the washing machine's bust and that's the last clean duvet cover.'

He swung around so that his feet dangled from the side. 'Can't get them off without pulls. Sorry. Unless you care to pull me off . . .'

Dilly glared at him, heart slamming uncomfortably because, having told her he didn't fancy her one bit, he was now taking over her room, teasing her, making innuendos and wearing an outfit guaranteed to get her pulses racing. Some sort of reverse psychology was at play here and she knew it, but the lashings of CWW that she'd guzzled made understanding what was going on impossible. She just had to try to enjoy it.

'Who comes to a christening dressed for a day's hunting?'

'I do. Patently.'

'If you did it to wind up my mother, you're on a hiding to nothing. She's as pro as they come.'

'Good for her.'

Dilly tilted her head to one side. 'You are *so* like your sister.'

The familiar sea-green eyes returned her gaze just as intensely. 'We swapped a lot of notes when we shared a womb.'

'I always wanted a brother – or a sister.' She sighed. 'Now I've got Basil, I feel more like his bloody mother sometimes.'

'How . . . dull for you.'

She snorted, realising that he was no Magnus. Magnus would have made something of this – even if it was only a silly joke. Flipper just found the statement inaccessible and boring.

'Do you sense things as twins?' she asked. 'That symbiosis thing, you know?'

'Feel her pain, know when she's in trouble?' He cast her favourite reading to one side and sat up.

'Yes, do you?'

'Sometimes. Mind you, she screams so loudly whenever she hurts herself, you could hear it in Cairo.'

Dilly laughed.

He picked up her old, dog-eared comforter. 'What is this?'

'It was a toy donkey, but its ears and legs fell off years ago.'

'Shame I wasn't around then. Just needed a good vet.'

'Any hope for it now?'

'Best put out of its misery.'

She snatched it back.

'Funniest thing.' He undid his stock pin and pulled the muddy silk scarf from his throat. 'I know when Nell's in love.'

'You do?'

He nodded. 'I almost feel it too.'

'You *do*?'

He smiled slowly, loosening his top button, looking up at her through those long dark lashes.

Dilly hesitated. 'And . . . is she?'

Nodding, he leaned forwards and brushed a finger along her cheek.

'She is. And she's right. Actually, you *are* quite cute.'

Gathering his steaming jacket from the oil heater, he left her reeling as he bounded downstairs.

'There you are!'

Half an hour later, Nell tracked down Dilly as she emerged from the bathroom downstairs. 'Magnus and I have been freezing our butts off in that greenhouse waiting for you to come back. Where's Flipper?'

'Gone. Had calls to make, I think.'

'In this weather? Isn't he just the *best*?' Nell hooked her arm through Dilly's and swept her back into the bathroom. 'You two seemed to be getting on famously.'

'We don't fancy each other, Nell.'

'Bollocks to that.' Nell checked her reflection in the mirror. 'You're both mad about each other – anyone can see the chemistry.'

'Funny *we* can't.' Dilly tried not to think about the alarming intimacy of having him in her room, lounging on her bed.

'So where did you two get to for so long?'

'We just came into the house to warm up.'

'Maybe it's a good job you didn't come back out. Mags and I just had the most fabulous fuck in the snow.'

'Wasn't it rather cold?'

'Not in this coat, although poor Milo wasn't best pleased when he got squashed. Did I mention that Magnus is incredibly well hu—'

'Euaghhh!' Dilly screamed as she caught sight of herself in the mirror. She had a thick coating of compost in her eyebrows, up one nostril and on her top lip like a moustache. She must have looked like this for the past hour.

'Don't tell me you hadn't noticed?' Nell giggled. 'I just thought you were sporting it as a part of your child of nature look. You didn't seem to like my makeover much.'

'I am, I was – I didn't,' Dilly said through gritted teeth as she splashed water on her face. 'It's just suddenly gone out of fashion, and I hate to be behind the times.'

When she looked up from drying her face, Nell was taking a pee and lighting a joint.

Dilly hastily diverted her gaze, staring at her reflection again, Flipper's words still ringing in her ears.

'You *are* rather cute.'

She smiled. He'd been lying on her bed dressed in riding gear. She'd found it hard to breathe. Who was she trying to kid? It would make Nell very happy, and she loved making Nell happy.

'You know,' she said suddenly. 'I think I do fancy your brother a little bit.'

'You do?' Nell blew on the end of the joint and crinkled her eyes delightedly as it sparked. 'I *knew* you did.'

'He really doesn't fancy me.'

'Of course he does.' Nell handed her the joint and pulled a hunk of loo roll from the holder. 'Just wait and see.'

'He told me so.'

'He's a compulsive liar.' She pulled up her knickers and flushed. 'You're just his type.'

Remembering the patter about the fetish gear and deerstalker, Dilly took a couple of hasty drags from the spliff and giggled, then jumped out of her skin as there was a hammering on the door.

'Fuck.' She started to lever open the window to throw out the guilty evidence, but Nell stopped her with a hand on her arm.

'I'd recognise that sexy rhythm anywhere.' She laughed, letting Magnus in.

'Oh, you're *both* in here,' he grinned, leaning against the door, obviously quite tight. 'I am officially hiding from a woman in a kaftan called Yolande who wants to rebirth me.'

His blond curls were flopping wildly and he had red stains on his cheeks. Too much CWW tended to have that effect on the complexion. Dilly knew because it had an identical effect on hers.

As he perched on the edge of the bath, Milo on his lap, Dilly felt herself sprout great hairy green gooseberry sides.

'I'd better – er – check Mum's okay.'

'Put that out.' He was staring at the spliff in her fingers.

'So much for Mr Rock and Roll,' Nell teased, taking it from Dilly and offering it to him.

'No thanks.'

'Sure.' She inhaled a deep drag and lowered her lips to his, curls of sweet dope smoke entering his mouth at the same time as her tongue.

Dilly's hairy green sides bulged.

'Bye!' She escaped.

The last remnants of the naming ceremony guests were staggering around in various states of drunkenness, mostly her mother's old stalwarts. Pixie was holding court on a sofa, tearfully cursing wayward husband Sexton. Anke and Ellen were washing up and talking babies. Someone was playing the guitar.

Pheely was sprawled in an armchair, fast asleep, with Basil curled contentedly to her chest.

Dilly dashed guiltily past them all and back up into her bedroom. It smelled of wet hunting coat and turf.

She picked up her sketchpad and leafed through to a clean page.

Flipper's good-looking face was easy to capture. It had such classic symmetry, it was a Grecian bust.

She drew Nell alongside, trying to avoid the cruel, jealous caricature she had recently perfected.

The similarity was eerie. Reflections in a mirror.

She hastily hid her sketchbook as she heard Magnus and Nell crashing around at the base of the stairs to her room, but they were only calling up to say goodbye. Magnus started drunkenly singing, but Nell dragged him away

Later, Dilly headed outside at twilight and crunched her way through the snow to the clearing in the woods. The snow angels were almost covered over – just two shallow indentations in fresh fall. Dilly lay in the shorter of the two and spread her wings.

Then, without knowing why she was doing it, she rolled over to the longer dip and flapped and high kicked for all she was worth.

He texted her at two in the morning.

Come riding with me, little snow angel. We need to talk. Meet up by the River Folly. 9am.

II

Dilly was almost an hour late to meet Flipper, despite setting out in plenty of time to head for the River Folly, which was less than a mile from Otto's field.

Otto resolutely refused to go there forwards. Unridden for several days, hating the snow and freaked out by the wind that had whipped up to blow it into monster sculptures overnight, he took his own curious path to the Oddlode folly. Mostly on two legs, backwards, sideways or spiralling, he and Dilly jinked and crabbed their way from one side of the icy bridle-way to the other as they headed towards the grassy bridge over the Odd.

But Flipper was waiting for her, his long waxed coat draped over Olive's quarters, a fag dangling from his mouth.

There was more than a dash of the Regency cad about him, especially back-dropped by the classical Aphrodite temple of a folly with its ornate, uniform arches and its buxom domed roof that was wearing a puffed snowy mop-cap. Behind it, the virginal white bridle-path stretched up through the hills to the ridge like an ancient unmade road, destined to break carriage wheels as it spirited a fiery-hearted young orphan to her Gothic new abode in midwinter, ready to be greeted by a misogynist uncle with a secret. And waiting en route, with a beetled brow and a dancing steed to catch her eye and her heart, was this handsome, dark-haired stranger.

You really *must* fancy him, Dilly told herself as she took in the amazing verdigris eyes flashing above the high-zipped fleece collar, the rich colour in his cheeks, the wide shoulders and the longest of muscular legs.

'Hi!' she called out through chattering teeth as Otto bounced and boggled the last fifty yards. 'Sorry I'm late – horse is a bit fresh.' She smiled apologetically as Otto let out an excited squeal and danced sideways.

Without a word, he pulled his coat back on and remounted while Otto was still napping and baulking on the bridge.

Then he and Olive took off at breakneck speed along the iced track.

'You bloody idio-ooooooooooh!' Dilly wailed as Otto bolted in pursuit.

After a hundred yards, she closed her eyes.

'God help me.'

They finally pulled up by Shad's Barn, an old Cotswold stone heap halfway along the hill to Broken Back Wood.

'You bastard!' she screamed as she slithered to the ground to check Otto's legs. 'Call yourself a vet? You could have killed these animals. The ground is frozen solid – there are ruts as deep as a man's leg in that track, not to mention the snow balling in their hooves. You utter, utter bastard.'

'You could have pulled up.'

'No I couldn't.'

'Not my fault you're a shit rider. Old Olive knows how to pick the ground. We've hunted in far worse than this.'

Breathless, red-faced and bursting with indignation, Dilly opened and closed her mouth several times before patting her sweating horse apologetically and starting to lead him away.

'I'm glad we talked,' she called over her shoulder. 'Thank you for the ride. Remind me never to attempt to do either with you again.'

He called after her. 'You're right. Love is cruel.'

'Isn't it just? Goodbye, Flipper.'

'Why did you come today?'

She paused. 'I was curious.'

'About me? Or about Nell?'

'Both.' She didn't look around. 'Why did you wait?'

'Because I knew you'd come.'

'And now I'm going.'

She could hear him crunching through the snow after her, Olive's jangling bit getting louder.

'Don't. Please don't. I'm fucking humiliating myself here.'

'How?'

'I'm being – *emotional*.'

It was such an odd thing to say that her anger dissipated.

She turned to look at him, and the expression on his face made her hold her breath in surprise. It was so open, it changed his whole face, widening the beautiful eyes, softening the mouth, drawing the dark eyebrows together beneath deep, honest furrows.

'I don't want to fall in love. I never want to go there again. My girlfriends can't get that, but it's a fact. I won't go there. Not again.'

She nodded, uncertain what to say.

'I flirt, fuck and forget.'

'Bully for you.'

'I bully, too.'

'Am I your confessor then?'

'You're my avenging angel.'

She laughed. 'I'm just a soppy romantic, Flipper.'

'A heartbroken soppy romantic.'

'True.'

'Who believes in soulmates?'

She nodded. 'Please don't tell me you think you're my soulmate?'

'God, no.'

'What then?'

He looked down at his feet, the black boots disappearing into two snowy footprints.

'I think we could help each other out.'

She raised her eyebrows enquiringly.

'Let's make like we're a couple.'

Dilly laughed incredulously. 'You mean *pretend*?'

'Yes.'

Dilly pressed her nose into Otto's hot, solid neck, shrouding her disbelief.

'I don't need to pretend anything, Flipper.'

'I do.'

'Why?'

'I just do.'

'Then find someone else.'

She gathered up her reins and lifted her foot to the stirrup but, before she could mount, he'd gathered her up and was carrying her towards a pile of old straw bales in the corner of the barn.

'Get off! Who d'you think you are? Fucking Heathcliff?'

Otto, quite cheered by events, wandered off to forage around the barn as his mistress flailed around furiously, screaming as loudly as she could.

Dropping her on the bales, Flipper backed away pretty sharpish. 'I am not going to fucking well rape you, okay? I'm a vet.'

'Since when did that preclude you from perversity?'

'Perverse, yes. Rapist, no.' He backed away with his arms up. 'Okay, no pretending. Absolutely no pretending. I'm planning to love you.'

'*What*?' Dilly sat up.

'I'm prepared to be in love with you.'

'*Prepared?*'

'Just say the word.'

'Love me.'

'I do.'

She laughed incredulously. 'Just like that?'

'You told me to do it.'

'I was joking.'

'Back-fired. Now you have my love.' The steely green eyes wouldn't let hers go.

'You can't be.'

'I think I know my own mind.' He rubbed his hands through his hair before dropping his arms back to his sides.

'Bugger off.' Dilly scrabbled upright, dusting herself down.

'Let me kiss you, and tell me if I don't love you.'

'Completely and utterly bugger off.'

He crossed his arms irritably. 'I don't *want* to love you.'

'Then don't.'

'It's not that simple. You're so like – you're so . . .'

'Lovable?' she suggested sarcastically

'You're so like someone I know. Someone I loved.' He added the d on to love a fraction too late. Not that Dilly cared to notice. She was far too outraged.

'Great! So, let me get this right. You say you love me – even though you don't want to – because I remind you of someone else you loved but presumably lost. And now you want me to be your pretend girlfriend because you don't really "do" love. And I thought I was screwed up.'

'You know, I never took you to be such a cross-patch. I always heard you were such a sweet thing. So trusting. So full of joy.'

'I've changed. Joy dumped me, just like all the others. Now fuck off.'

He walked towards her. 'I still love you. I've loved you since the moment I held your limbless donkey.'

'Don't you dare bring Donk into this!' He was standing close enough to slap now and she was sorely tempted to defend her donkey's honour.

'You can't trust it, you said. You can't trust love. You can't taste it, smell it, hear it.'

Dilly stared at him in amazement as he repeated her words to her, those turbulent, dark-lashed eyes no longer looking through her or at her but into her, into her broken heart. He knew exactly what she'd meant.

He leaned down to speak into her ear, his voice low. 'I love you, I love you, I love you – see? It means nothing. You can only *feel* it.'

Before she knew what was happening, his lips touched hers – just for a second, barely more than a breath.

She ran a shaking tongue across them to check that they were still there. They'd gone curiously numb.

'That's just lust,' she mumbled, lips now in desperate need of being kissed again.

He shook his head. 'This is lust.'

His tongue hit hers before his lips – muscular, twisting and yet soft as it curled alongside hers. And then his mouth closed over hers and the kiss that followed dissolved every last spark of fight from Dilly's body as fireworks exploded through her belly and chest. Staying upright had never been so hard.

And, as suddenly as he had kissed her, he stopped.

'That,' he smiled, stepping back, 'was lust.'

Dilly was too excited to speak.

He licked his lips with that enticing tongue. 'Believe me, I love you more than I lust after you.'

She swallowed, took a couple of deep breaths and nodded. 'I see.'

'You see what?'

'I see . . .' She was still fighting to regulate her heartbeat and breathing, let alone think straight, '. . . that we are – that we have – that there's – a problem.'

He looked up, rubbed a hand through his hair and laughed. 'I think that's pretty obvious.'

Dilly winced, and chewed at her lips to stop their overwhelming urge to go in search of his again.

She looked up at him guiltily. 'The thing is, you say you love me but don't lust after me—'

'I didn't say that exactly. I meant—'

'And I think I just lust after you, to be honest.'

To his credit, he laughed.

'Now that,' he backed away to the open doors, 'calls for another snowball fight.'

Looking up, the horses watched in confusion as their two riders hurled powdery white balls at one another.

Dilly came off worse, but she got her reward when he kissed her again, making her so horny that she would have been perfectly happy to get naked there and then, despite the cold.

'I love you,' he insisted between kisses.

'I lust you,' she kissed him back, not understanding what was going on, but enjoying it far too much to care.

When they finally rode home, he didn't say much, but he didn't gallop off into the distance, either. He saw her back as far as the River Folly and promised to call.

'For a pretend date?' she joked.

'I hate dates.'

'I hate all dried fruit,' she agreed.

Smiling, he stepped up in his stirrups and leaned out of the saddle to kiss her cheek before trotting away.

There were two texts from Magnus when she remembered to check her phone after rubbing Otto down. The first complained that she hadn't been doing her usual morning shift at the market garden when he'd popped in for a Brakespear Sunday lunch vegetable top-up. The second was clearly after chatting to Nell.

How goes with Flipper? Together at last, I hear?

Dilly analysed this for a moment, longing for more of an angle.

She hedged her bets. *Think so.*

It took less than five minutes to hear back. *Think?*

He says he loves me. She went for all out honest.

He texted back within seconds. *Good for him. Happy?*

Think so. That'd fox him.

But he didn't reply.

Nell was on the phone moments later.

'Ohmygod, Flipper is *so* all over the place. I've never seen him this wired and excited. You two must be electric together.'

'Well it's early da—'

'I'm coming round.'

In the time it took Nell to drive from home to Oddlode, Pheely had already cornered her daughter on the sofa.

'Phillip Cottrell is gorgeous! Why didn't you tell me you were seeing him?'

'I wasn't aware that I was,' she fudged.

'Glad Tidings told Hell's Bells that you were spotted kissing on horseback by the River Folly this morning.'

'God. Really?' Dilly gulped. News travelled fast in Oddlode. Village gossip Gladys 'Glad Tidings' Gates had spies everywhere. No doubt the Old Bat-phones had been ringing all morning.

'Hell's Bells says that Flipper Cottrell is one of *the* most eligible young bloods in the county. I am thrilled!'

'Mum, we just went for a ride together.'

But Pheely was on a roll, her raging snobbery as inflamed as her vicarious passion. 'It will do you so much good to stop moping around over that dreadful low-life louse—'

'I loved Pod!'

'– and have fun with someone of your own class. And he is *so* dishy and charming.'

'We've only just started to get it together, Mum,' Dilly warned. 'Please don't ruin it by getting over-excited. I'm not even sure I really want to see more—'

'The family is loaded!' Pheely clapped her hands, looking around her tatty little cottage, no doubt thinking of the improvements that could be made by acquiring a wealthy son-in-law.

'The family is broke.'

'But he's a vet. He's got a future.'

Dilly sighed, 'I don't think I could ever love him.'

'You don't? You always love your boyfriends at first sight. You're like me.'

'I lust after him. That's all. I don't think I even like him very much.'

'Oh, dear God. Don't tell me you're taking after your grandfather now?'

Nell whisked Dilly straight to the Lodes Inn snug, Milo stashed in her moleskin Puffa game pocket.

'I am *so* thrilled! Tell me all. You got down and dirty in Shad's Barn, am I right?'

'Flipper told you that?' Horrified, Dilly looked up from painting a confused face on her pint of Guinness.

'I read between the lines.'

'We kissed.'

'How romantic.'

'Not very.' She took a big swig of her drink.

'Is he a good kisser?'

Dilly felt her Guinness waver midway down her throat as it contemplated coming back up. It somehow didn't seem right to be discussing Flipper's kissing technique with his twin sister.

'Is he?'

By the time she had finally swilled the mouthful of stout in to her system, Nell's restless mind was racing ahead.

'This is so thrilling. I just *know* you're going to propose to him at the hunt ball, and he'll snap you up like a shot.'

Dilly looked at her curiously, suddenly wondering if this was what her friend had been planning all along.

'Nell, we've only kissed. He doesn't even want to go out for a date. And he knows I'm not ready to fall in love with anybody yet.'

'But he fascinates you, doesn't he?'

'Yes,' she admitted.

'By the end of next month, you'll be proposing. Believe me. He's the loveliest man alive.' Nell fed a crisp to Milo.

Dilly looked at the face she had drawn in her Guinness foam, the S-shaped mouth of which had transformed into an O since she'd taken a sip, like Munch's *The Scream*.

'Who broke Flipper's heart?' she asked suddenly.

'What?' Nell scoffed, almost choking on a crisp.

'He says I remind him of someone. Someone he loved. I think it's the only reason he's into me.'

Nell shook her head. 'You must have that wrong. Flipper's never been in love. Not properly.'

'Are you saying he was lying?'

'Of course not. Flipper never lies.'

'So he loved someone he can't forget?'

'Maybe he thinks he did. He stayed up all last night thinking about you. It twists any head.'

'Do any of his exes look like me?' Dilly asked.

'Darling, they all look like you. I've always said you're just his type.'

'Overweight dizzy blondes with bad glasses?'

'You're not overweight,' Nell insisted. 'But he does like curvy, pretty girls, which is strange because I read this article in a mag recently that claimed we're all naturally more attracted to people who physically resemble us, our siblings or our parents. And I *do* find men who look like my brothers attractive.'

'That's because all your brothers look like male models and movie stars,' said Dilly, hoping she wasn't programmed to seek a partner who looked like Ely – bearded and evil.

'No – no, listen, it's called self-resembling attraction and we are genetically programmed to seek out a mate of a similar stamp. It's fascinating.'

'So I should find men who look like Basil attractive?' Dilly laughed uncertainly.

'Ah! You're not actually far off the mark, because the other thing this article said is that we're all really attracted to baby faces. I think Flipper has the baby-face thing big time.'

Slightly miffed to be called baby-faced, Dilly slurped her pint and looked around the snug, trying to figure out which faces she found most attractive. Given that it was full of the Wyck family, who all shared the same low-browed, bull-chinned expression and lack of teeth, she didn't get very far.

'Now *Magnus* is a different matter,' Nell was saying as she leaned back and lit a cigarette, studying Dilly's face. 'Magnus is attracted to androgyny.'

'Oh yes?' Dilly tried not to react.

'He's very in touch with his feminine side, you see.'

'Are you saying that he's a closet gay?'

'No, but he likes to play with the boundaries. He's always liked dominant, boyish girls who know what they want. That's why he's so absolutely fixated on me.'

Dilly played with a beer mat. 'But he doesn't look like your brothers, so why are you so attracted to him?'

'Magnus is incredibly good looking.'

'I know, but he doesn't look anything like you.'

'I think he does. Straighten his hair and dye it black and we could pass for brother and sister any day.'

Dilly, who found this image highly disturbing, said nothing.

'You know, I might just propose to him at the ball. Especially as you're going to propose to Flipper. We have to honour the pact.'

'I'm not going to propose to Flipper.'

'You will. You wait and see.'

12

There was a curious atmosphere at the next band rehearsal. Flipper insisted that he give Dilly a lift, even though it meant a big detour and Magnus would be driving past anyway. To her immense disappointment, he didn't kiss her when he arrived to pick her up. Unlike Magnus, he didn't chat en route either. He simply drove incredibly fast with his stereo belting out *Green Day* at full blast.

Hanging on to her seatbelt, Dilly stared at his profile, trying to work out why she was suddenly so wildly attracted to him. Like Nell's his features were perfect – the straight nose, chiselled jaw-line, noble brow. He was almost too good looking, too clichéd. She had always been attracted to quirky imperfection – loving Rory's lop-sided, slightly over-crowded smile, Pod's scarred eyebrows and broken nose from so many racing falls. Yet her belly squirmed excitedly looking at his movie star beauty, longing to be kissed again, amazed that he had shown her such emotion. She felt strangely intimidated by him, too. The next move was firmly his, and waiting was slightly scary.

When they arrived, Magnus and Nell were already there. They had spent the day shopping in Cheltenham and were sporting his and hers woolly hats. They couldn't leave one another alone. Dilly was amazed that she hadn't spotted the similarity before. Unlike Nell, his nose had a slight upward curve to it and his cheeks were more apple-shaped than high-angled, but they had the same smile, the same bone structure and the same leggy playfulness.

The Three Disgraces were conspicuously absent.

'Checking out the opposition,' Magnus explained. 'Trackmarks are playing at the Lodes Inn tonight.'

'Can we go too?' Nell suggested.

'No?'

'Why not?' she pleaded, hanging on to his fleece collar and staring up at him.

'Because,' he kissed her on the nose, 'we'd be too bloody obvious.'

'We can go in disguise.'

He rolled his eyes. 'No arguments. We seriously need to rehearse.'

'I like arguments.'

'I know you do,' he laughed, sliding his hands into her back jeans pockets and kissing her properly.

Dilly couldn't stop herself glancing longingly from them to Flipper, only to find that he was already staring straight at her. He looked furious, a muscle slamming in his cheek.

True to her word, Nell disrupted proceedings with her usual arguments. As usual, she led an argument about the band's name.

'I just hate Entwined,' she complained. 'I know I thought it up, but it makes us sound trapped somehow. Can't we change it to Four Play?'

'No.' Magnus was resolute. 'We have far more important things to concentrate on. Like the fact we were so lousy at Basil's christening.'

'Jesus, christenings and bar mitzvahs.' Flipper covered his face. 'What am I doing here?'

'Ogling Dilly,' Nell teased him, shooting Dilly a cheerful wink.

'Drumming out of synch, mostly,' Magnus muttered.

'Fuck off,' hissed Flipper, only half-jokingly. 'I think we should call ourselves "Bollocks", because we are, and the hunting lot will assume we've just cut the "to Blair" bit out of the slogan.'

Magnus groaned. 'Do you know how many times I've sat in band rehearsal rooms listening to arguments about the bloody name?' he wailed in frustration. 'We're called Entwined. It's not great, but it's fine. Now let's play some music.' He picked up his guitar.

'You tell them, baby.' Nell blew a kiss at him, conveniently forgetting it was she who had started the debate. 'Let's play sweet music.'

'Nothing sweet about the din Nell makes,' Flipper muttered.

Magnus slid his fingers up and down his strings irritably, setting all their teeth on edge.

'Nell is getting a lot better.' He smiled at her. 'It's you who isn't putting the effort in, Flipper. You don't know the songs, you don't practise, you're persistently late at rehearsals if you turn up at all.'

'I do work for a living unlike you bloody layabouts.'

'I work too!' Dilly wailed.

'Now "Layabouts" is a good name . . .' Nell mused idly.

And so it went on. They scrapped, teased, taunted, occasionally laughed, and got very little music played. Magnus and Nell took every opportunity to touch one another and share private, whispered words that made them groan and giggle. Dilly kept catching Flipper's grey-green eyes looking at her, but every time she did, he looked away, refusing to hold her gaze. She couldn't figure out the expression on his face at all.

When the Disgraces came back from the Lodes Inn to report worriedly that Trackmarks were, in fact, 'not bad' and were playing again the following weekend at the Young Farmers' Valentine's drag party, nothing could stop Nell planning an excursion.

'We can *definitely* go in disguise!' she announced. 'We'll dress the boys in wigs and dresses.'

'Oh Christ,' Flipper almost wept. 'Going to Young Farmers' bollock. I'll be lampooned. I can already feel the shame.'

'Not if you're wearing a false nose, you won't,' Nell reassured her brother 'Nobody will recognise you.'

'*The prize for the best cross-dresser is a day out with the Cotswold Drag Hounds,*' Flipper read out the party flyer that the Disgraces had brought back. 'It gets better,' he snorted, laughing. 'Vegetarian hunting and cross-dressing. Have the Young Farmers been infiltrated by a load of Islington lefties or something?'

Dilly, who had been admiring his profile again, decided his politics left a lot to be desired. She caught Magnus's eye and tried not to giggle.

'I've always rather fancied going drag-hunting,' she pointed out, having long laboured under the misconception that it was slower and safer than following foxhounds.

'Oh, it's great fun,' Nell assured her, taking the flyer from her brother and cuffing him with it. 'We should all go.'

'Count me out,' Magnus muttered.

'I'll take you next weekend as a birthday treat if you like,' she promised Dilly as she read the flyer. 'This is on Friday night, so we'll go on the Saturday if there's a meet. Best cure for a hangover.'

'It's your birthday next weekend?' Magnus asked Dilly in surprise.

She nodded.

'You didn't say anything.' He looked miffed.

'I've got past the age when I start announcing it in advance in the hope of surprise trips to Disneyland,' she joked.

'It's my birthday in July and I'd like to go to Disneyland.' Nell put her arm round Magnus's waist and then smiled wickedly. 'Or better still Vegas.'

*   *   *

In the week building up to their covert surveillance trip to the Young Farmers' party, the band rehearsed just once. Magnus and Nell were on too hectic a loving schedule to fit in any more. Nell was convinced that Trackmarks would be terrible, and Magnus was so deeply under her spell that he was happy to be led by the groin away from his guitar stand. Together, they went clubbing, clay-pigeon shooting, walking, drinking and most of all they made love. Both texted Dilly regularly to let her know what they had been doing – Magnus referring to the shooting and wildlife-spotting, Nell to more nefarious activities. For two people falling in love, they were unexpectedly happy to share, and invited Dilly – and Flipper – to join them to eat out and go dancing, but Dilly didn't want to be a gooseberry and Flipper always refused.

For a man who claimed to be in love with her, he wasn't showing much enthusiasm to adopt boyfriend status. He never called her, or texted. She kept far more regular contact with Magnus and Nell.

Eventually, he just turned up, shocking Pheely who, dressed in just a towel and rollers, was sculpting a clay cast for a nude elfin figure.

'Are you coming out for a drink or what?' he called up to Dilly, who was in her room, listening to embarrassingly naff music while she sketched ugly self-portraits.

They ended up in the New Inn. The Three Disgraces and their friends joined them, all texting happily to one another. Flipper started texting too. Soon, several of his friends rolled up to join them. Loud, drawling horsy types, they all proceeded to get drunk and discuss Flipper's sex life, most specifically how many of his female clients he had slept with.

'Did you know why Flipper's known as "King Gorgeous" at the clinic?' one of his vet colleagues asked Dilly.

She shook her head.

'Because every time he meets a female client for the first time, she comes away saying "Ohmygod, he is fucKING gorgeous"!'

Dilly sent just one text. To Magnus.

Please let your twin be more romantic than mine.

He didn't reply. She took that to mean he was having a much better time. At least he stood an outside chance of exchanging a few words with Nell – better still body fluids.

'Hey, Flipper!' a voice whooped from the door as Rory wandered in, cheeks pink from the cold and from the half bottle of scotch he'd downed at home. 'What are you doing here – hi, Trist – Holly! Gordon – Cal – Hamish! Fancy finding you all lined up waiting for me in my local.' He started kissing cheeks and shaking hands as he reeled happily around a table like a loose hound reunited with his pack, until he reached Dilly. 'Shit! Dilly Dally my darling! What the devil are you doing with this disreputable lot?'

Dilly beamed up at him, thrilled to see a familiar and very friendly face. 'Just having a drink.'

'Then let me get you another!' He ruffled her hair and bounded up to the bar.

Beside her, Flipper turned his back conspicuously on her and started talking to Tristan about Defra subsidies.

When Rory joined them again, he had drawn an arrow in her Guinness top which he carefully swivelled around as he placed it in front of her so that it pointed at Flipper.

'Thanks,' she smiled up at him.

He raised his sandy eyebrows questioningly.

She nodded.

The eyebrows shot up further and he looked impressed, holding up his palms in respect and going to fetch himself a chair.

Dilly perked up a bit more.

Rory might be so drunk that he told her twice that she looked different, three times he was thinking of switching from eventing to dressage and once accidentally called her 'Mo', but he still knew her well enough to recognise something close to infatuation.

'You've got good taste,' he whispered in her ear. 'After me, Flipper Cottrell's one of the best riders in the county. Of women as well as horses.'

Dilly burst out laughing and then blushed as Flipper's friends shot her curious looks. Rory's mouth was still pressed to her ear.

'Okay, he rides women better,' his voice slurred slightly, 'but I've beaten him in the Vale point-to-point amateur's plate three times.'

She gently shifted her ear away as he lolled against her shoulder and set him upright again.

And when Flipper, still nose to nose with Tristan, chose that moment to lay a warm hand on her thigh, Dilly almost expired with excitement.

This was the old Dilly, she realised, as that familiar mask gladly overtook her. Rory had helped her rekindle her safe, dilly-dallying and passive alter ego. The ugly camouflage slipped. She felt attractive again, and feeling attractive was dangerous. It meant she no longer saw herself as others did. It meant she no longer cared to protect herself. She was an open target once again.

'I'm in this for lust,' Dilly reminded herself in the loo. 'He doesn't have to talk to me. Just kiss me again.'

Dilly was aware that she was being equally uncommunicative and lax, but as someone accustomed to being pursued, wooed and chased all over the county by men, she was having difficulty adjusting to this silent treatment.

Flipper, similarly accustomed, couldn't get a handle on Dilly at all. He didn't understand what had happened to the chatty, cheerful, belligerent spirit with whom he'd drawn angels in the snow. She had been noisy, entertaining and impossible to ignore any longer. Now she had fallen quiet.

'I don't get you two.' Sperry Sixsmith cornered him in timely fashion, settling herself in Dilly's empty chair and waggling her Hooch bottle in his face. Sperry had never been shy of speaking her mind.

He blanked her.

'She's too soft for you.'

'Could have fooled me.'

'Don't you fucking dare hurt her, buster.'

'Who are you? Her pimp?'

'Her guardian angel.'

He blinked, missing a beat. 'Her what?'

'Guardian angel,' she repeated, tapping the bottle neck against her chin and regarding him with those mistrustful, slanting eyes.

Flipper ignored the fact that Tristan and Rory were having a loud conversation about farriers over their heads and held her gaze.

'Did she put you up to this?'

'Absolutely not, mate. I don't think she even likes me very much.'

'Even though you're her *Guardian* reader?'

'Guardian angel.'

'You're not very angelic,' he pointed out bluntly. 'You're not even her friend.'

'I agree. People rarely like their guardian angels. They make them do things they don't want, even if it's for their own good. Dilly's particularly stubborn and rebellious.'

'Now that I can believe.'

The cat-like eyes didn't blink.

'Are you warning me off?'

She shrugged.

'I don't back down that easily.'

One plucked eyebrow lifted.

'I don't have to justify myself to you.'

The other eyebrow arched.

'I'll fight for her,' he hissed, completely wound up now.

'Wouldn't it be easier,' she rolled the rim of the Hooch bottle on her lower lip, 'just to get to know her?'

Flipper stared at her.

Sperry winked and returned her gaze to its usual resting place – the little screen of her little phone.

Just as she was coming out of the loo, Dilly received a text from an unlisted number. It read *Kiss him before you say another word.*

Hanging fire in the corridor, she texted back. *Why?*

Because he's f**King Gorgeous!

Dilly grinned. Old Dilly was heaven-sent tonight. Even strangers were egging her on.

As soon as she was back at the table, she pressed her forehead to Flipper's, then her nose, her chin and finally her lips.

He kept his eyes open. So did Dilly.

Around the table, Flipper's friends cheered and jeered with sporting, bloodlusty approval.

Ignoring them, Flipper kept on kissing that amazing kiss which made Dilly forget where she was, who she was and whether or not it mattered being in love if it felt this good.

'You scare me fucking rigid,' he breathed as they surfaced for air.

She blinked in amazement, licking her kissed, numbed and blissfully slippery lips.

'You scare *me*,' she whispered.

'I love you.'

'I lust you.'

When they kissed again, neither could bring themselves to surface for air until their red, hollow cheeks were aching, lungs bursting and heads spinning.

'Did I just hear Flipper declaring love?' Rory asked them cheerfully afterwards, customary fag dangling from his lips, sleepy eyes smiling.

Still rowdily applauding at the table, the gathered friends all started stamping on the ground and chanting raucously. Despite this, most of them looked astonished.

Flipper held up his hands to silence them.

'I'd like to officially announce that Dilly and I are very much,' he shot her a ghost of a wink, 'in lust.'

The friends, palpably relieved, stamped harder and raised their glasses.

Dilly glowed happily and drew a love heart around the fading arrow in the top of her pint. Old Dilly was love-sick and officially no longer feeling in an ugly mood. She was in lust. And dangerously close to love, too.

And yet, later, Flipper drove her home without a word, stereo blaring, dropping her at her garden gate without a farewell kiss.

'He has left broken hearts all over Oddlode.' Ellen warned Dilly the following day as they shared a Galaxy bar on the sofa in Goose Cottage.

'And I haven't?'

'You believe in love.'

'I don't love him.'

'That's what worries me most.'

Dilly wriggled down into the cushions. 'Mum thinks I'm turning into my grandfather, who turned to lust after his wife died young and broke his heart. Mum thinks that now that I've had my heart broken, I'm set to become a hardened man-eater.'

'Please tell me you're not?'

'What's wrong with turning the tables?' Dilly pressed an ear to the big, warm, bump on the sofa beside her.

'Tables are where we all gather to feel safe. Turning them just confuses.'

'We should all change periodically.'

'Periodic tables are even more confusing.'

'I love you, Ellen.'

'I love you too. Now fess up to the truth behind this.'

Dilly shook her head. 'No point. Nothing to fess. As Nell says, you have to live first and confess afterwards.'

'That's just Catholicism. You shouldn't listen to Nell.'

'I should. She's the best. And she says it like it is, sees through things. I can't see like she does, so I haven't found out the truth yet. All I've found out is that Flipper says he loves me and that I really want it to be true.'

'You do?' Ellen asked worriedly, knowing how vulnerable that dilly-dallying heart could be, and at the same time stupidly resentful that Nell had such a big share of its trust.

'I think so,' Dilly was dallying. 'What does Heshee think?'

'Heshee agrees with me, of course.'

'Spurs had a terrible reputation when you fell in love with him. He's an ex-con and an ex-womaniser. He even slept with my mother.'

'Heshee's father and I fell in love the moment we met,' Ellen said sanctimoniously, and then laughed. 'Actually, if I'd known the truth about Spurs when we met, I'd probably never have let him near me. But I fell in love with him – with *him* – before I heard the potted, unauthorised biography and the unabridged, honest autobiography.' She stroked Dilly's hair, feeling impossibly soppy. 'And now we're writing the rest of that book together.'

'Maybe I'll fall in love with Flipper after I hear his auto-biography?'

'Write your own first, Dilly.'

'Mum wants me to fall in love with him.'

'How can you while you're in love with someone else?'

'I'm not in love with anyone else.'

'You sure?'

Dilly said nothing, letting Ellen tease her hair away from her face and gently finger her way through the tangles as they sat in companionable silence for a moment.

'I know,' Ellen said eventually, 'that you've had a huge Dilly crush on someone lately. Your "bus man". And when Spurs said it was Flipper, it all made sense. But it's not him, is it? I know you and it's not him.'

'Flipper would never travel by bus,' Dilly agreed quietly.

She retreated to make another pot of tea, trying hard not to cry or think or make sense of her muddled mind.

'Please let's talk about something else,' she said brightly as she carried it back through.

Ellen sighed in tired defeat, knowing Dilly too well to probe further. 'Like what?'

'The hunt ball?'

'Don't ask,' Ellen groaned.

'We've been rehearsing like mad,' she lied as she slopped out more tea. 'We can't wait to knock them dead.'

Ellen heaved herself upright and reached for the milk carton, looking shifty.

'You're not telling me something?' Dilly realised.

'I don't want to worry you.'

'But?'

'Nothing.'

'Tell me or the stereo gets it.' Dilly held the teapot over Spurs' beloved Bang and Olufsen.

'Your father wants to pull the plug on Entwined playing.'

'Why?' she wailed, pot rattling.

'I really don't know.' Ellen nervously eyed the teapot wobbling above the stereo.

'Tell me!'

Ellen cupped her hands around her nose, watching her with tearful eyes, not knowing how to stop this happening.

'Shall I tell you why?' Dilly hugged the pot to her chest, nodding frantically. 'I can tell you why Ely wants to stop us. Because of me. Because of *me*.' She breathed deeply to stop herself sobbing, looking up. 'He hates me. He absolutely hates me. He wishes I'd never been born.'

A pot of tea crashed to the floor.

Rushing across a room was hard to do when heavily pregnant and treading on broken crockery swimming in hot tea, but Ellen would have gained the world record if it had been timed. Hugging someone was equally hard with Heshee in the way, but she still enfolded Dilly in the tightest of crossed arms.

'You have to stop thinking that, Dilly. You have to. You'll destroy yourself.'

For the first time in her life, Dilly wriggled out of a hug.

'Tell him that. Tell your friend to stop me doing just that.' She wrenched away and ran, stopping by the door with her head in her hands. A couple of sniffs and a deep breath later, she disappeared around the corner, reappeared with a dustpan and brush and a roll of kitchen paper, cleared away the broken pot and tea and then left without a word.

Ellen watched her throughout, eyes troubled, guilt gnawing at her bones.

She had let Dilly down. She hadn't put up a fight. She'd heard Entwined play last week and thought they were a discordant, decadent mess. She had heard Dilly recite her beloved Christina Rossetti poem and realised she was in a state. She had thought that by not putting up a fight she was being protective. Instead she had compromised a friendship.

And now she was absolutely frozen in panic, realising the bitter truth. If she couldn't even act as a surrogate mother to Dilly – her joyful, enchanting daughter-friend – how could she possibly be a good mother to Heshee?

Sitting up in bed in the early hours, her face illuminated only by the little LCD screen, Dilly contemplated the text she had just written.

She pressed send.

The screen asked her which destination.

She scrolled through her address book.

FLIPPER

MAGS

NELL

MAGS

NELL

ELLEN

MAGS

RORY

MAGS

POD

Up and down she scrolled indecisively until she finally punched a button, threw her phone to the end of the bed and curled up with Donk, who lasted twenty seconds at her cheek before joining the Nokia. It lit up his asinine face as it buzzed and vibrated excitedly.

But Dilly had dragged her pillow over her head. At her feet, the phone and Donk acted like flash photographer and model a few more times before falling off the end of the mattress.

13

The following morning, at the market garden, Magnus loped into the main greenhouse and hugged her tightly. Dilly pressed her face into the soft cashmere shoulder and felt sobs rise and fall in her throat. To her surprise, she didn't actually break down and cry, but he always managed to lift her back to safety by making her think and talk and laugh rather than simply weep.

'King Lear had a similarly blind spot,' he told her now.

'Am I Goneril or Regan?' She wriggled away from the hug – a new power-tool at her disposal. Leave hugs half-finished.

'Cordelia, of course.' He plunged his hands awkwardly in his pockets and cast out a kind smile, blue eyes crinkling uncertainly.

'That means I die at the end.' She forced her hands into her pockets too, although her trousers were so tight she could only slot in a couple of fingers.

At this point, Pixie drifted casually past with a trug heaped with an orgy of twisted carrots.

'I've always rather liked Goneril since playing her at school.'

'She was always a gonner,' Magnus agreed.

'And very ill.'

In the face of such lack of sympathy, Dilly dragged her fingers from her pockets with some difficulty and punched the delayed tears away from her eyes with the balls of her hands.

Let thy loveliness fade as it will,
And around the dear ruin each wish of my heart

Would entwine itself verdantly still.'

'Is that from Lear?' Pixie asked, entranced.

'Thomas More,' Dilly said hoarsely. 'It was the only mention of "entwine" in my dictionary of quotations.'

'You looked that up?'

'I looked it up.' She shrugged.

Faced with her weird mood, Magnus didn't know whether to smile or not, so he hovered somewhere in between, the soft lines alongside his eyes crinkling in and out like bellows, and the fire in Dilly's eyes burning all the more as a result.

'My father is a ruin – a moral, physical, paternal ruin.'

'Yet you're still trying to win his heart?'

'Verdantly,' she vowed.

Magnus closed his eyes and remembered a quote from exams gone by: *I have no way and therefore want no eyes.*

'Why did you text me last night?' he asked.

'I was upset.'

'It was three in the morning.'

'You must have been awake to text me right back.'

'And then you didn't reply.'

'I was asleep.'

Pixie took her carrots to a more discreet spot to listen in.

'And why "*Methinks I was enamour'd of an ass*"?'

'You're the Shakespeare buff.'

'In that case, let me first point out that the quote is me*thought* not me*thinks I was enamoured.* She's over it by that point.'

'Lucky her.'

'Who's the ass?' he asked bluntly.

Her green eyes still darted from place to place, fervent and verdant.

'Your father?'

'Hee haw.'

'Flipper?'

'Hee haw.'

She looked up at him, her gaze fixing at last, and he knew exactly who the ass was.

But he couldn't admit it.

Neither of them could admit it.

When Nell texted Magnus her usual list of new band name suggestions that afternoon, he hardly even looked at them. His response was emphatic.

We are Entwined. Until this madness ends, we are Entwined.

Nell called Dilly straightaway.

'I think he's going to tell me he loves me tonight!'

'That's . . . great.'

'Get you! My brother has already declared undying love.'

'Funny way of showing it.'

'Fucked-up childhood. Believe me, I know. I was there.'

'I had one of those.'

'So treat him with a bit more respect. He's shy.'

Dilly was about to complain that Flipper was the one who alternated between ignoring her and kissing her like it was his last hour on earth, but Nell launched into a long description of what she was planning to dress Magnus in for that night's party.

'I want to avoid the pantomime dame look, especially if he's going to tell me he loves me. He needs something much more subtle. That drag queen thing is so off-putting. I'm thinking The Crying Game meets Eddie Izzard – sexy and mysterious as well as funny. I've banned him from wearing fishnet stockings – *so* tarts and vicars. And it's not black tie, after all, so we can really go to town with the boy-girl thing. What are you wearing? I'm thinking maybe gangland homeboy with a hoodie and lots of gold bling. Or sleazy pimp in a tux, perhaps.'

'I haven't really thought it through yet,' she admitted.

'What about Flipper?'

'What about him?'

'Aren't you lending him something of yours to wear?'

'I thought you were.'

Nell laughed impatiently. 'For God's sake, Dilly, he's dying to get into your knickers. Don't you see, this is the perfect opportunity to help him out?'

But when Dilly texted Flipper to suggest that she help him drag up later, his reply was blunt and to the point: *Will pick you up at 7pm. Wear a dress or you stay at home.*

Dilly was in full-on ugly mode for the Young Farmers' party. Her fingers were gritty and black from potting up seedlings all afternoon, a new spot had sprouted on her chin and she'd received no Valentine's cards.

Her mother, meanwhile, had received three and was obnoxiously, lovingly maternal as she reigned it large on the sofa that evening in a self-satisfied glow of CWW.

'You look beautiful!' she told Dilly as she scuttled through the main body of the cottage towards the door and Flipper's distant horn beep.

'I look horrible.' Dilly flew past.

'You look like a princess!'

The door slammed.

For a brief moment, Pheely chastised herself for her lies. Dilly had looked bloody awful, spilling out of a too-tight corset, swathed in a great, loose tutu of a skirt, her hair clipped tightly to her head like a swimming cap and sequins glued to the rims of her lopsided glasses. But Ellen had been on Pheely's case lately, telling her that she was worried about Dilly, making her feel guilty. Pheely did feel guilty. Guilty enough to lie and tell her daughter that she looked lovely, although her motivation was far less noble than Ellen's entreaties beggared.

Two of Pheely's three cards that day had been for her daughter. 'D' and 'O' being fairly easy to misread on the envelope, Pheely had ripped them open before putting in her contact lenses, and her rose-tinted spectacles were several prescriptions out of date.

The cards were hardly romantic. Both featured donkeys. One featured a cartoon of a donkey sunbathing on a beach with the catch-line 'Look at the ass on that'. The other was an old-fashioned sepia shot of two Blackpool donkeys sharing an ice-cream.

Both cards contained the same line – one in neat black writing, the other in slanted blue.

I love you

Dressed in a dark suit and white T-shirt, Flipper pecked her demurely on the cheek at the Lodge gates and opened his passenger door. 'You look—'

'Don't say beautiful!' She stopped him, feeling far too ugly for more insincerity. 'I'm going for the comedy look.'

'I was going to say you look like a girl.'

'Oh, thanks. You look like a boy.'

For once he was quite chatty as he drove her towards the party, making her laugh by telling her about a particularly quarrelsome Shetland pony he had treated that day, and then asking her if she was looking forward to going drag-hunting. 'I think there'll be quite a crowd of us. My sister's been rallying the troops to come out and wish you a happy birthday.'

When Nell had found out that the Cotswold Bloodhounds were meeting in Oddlode on Dilly's birthday, she'd got thoroughly over-excited, nagging her brother until he agreed to be there too, and then starting to get to work on Magnus. After twenty-four hours of persistent begging and pleading, he was reportedly showing signs of cracking.

'Think Mags'll brave it?' Flipper asked now.

She laughed. 'Nell's plan is to get him incredibly drunk tonight and keep him that way until he finds himself on a horse tomorrow morning.'

'He wouldn't last five minutes.'

'I might not either,' she warned him.

'Of course you will. And if you last all day, you're definitely on the team.'

'What team?'

'The band is going team-chasing in a fortnight, remember?'

Dilly removed a sequin from her nose. 'But I thought Magnus and me were too hopeless.'

'Magnus is. You're okay.'

'Okay?'

'Your horse could be fitter.'

'I'm not really up to team chasing.'

'Not even for the sake of the band?'

'It won't be for the band without Magnus.'

'What *are* you two,' he snapped, 'joined at the hip?'

There was an awkward pause. It turned out talking to Flipper wasn't so nice, after all, Dilly realised. Smouldering at him in silence was better.

She plunged her hands into her coat pockets and smouldered silently for a bit, wondering why he was so impossibly hard to have a normal conversation with. He was so pompous and superior and male. If he wasn't so utterly sexy, she'd tell him to turn the car around and take her home. Then her fingers closed around something small and fluffy in her pocket and she had an idea.

'Stop the car.'

He pulled up in a gateway, engine running.

She reached forward and silenced the stereo.

'I think we should swap clothes.'

'I've already said I prefer you as a girl.'

Dilly fingered the false beard in her pocket.

'I want to see *you* dressed as a girl.'

'No way.'

'Why not?'

'I just don't *do* girly.'

Suddenly, Dilly screamed and pointed out of the window in horror. 'Dragon!'

He ducked so fast he hit his head on the steering wheel.

'You see . . .' She turned to smile at him. 'You *do* do girly. Drag on.'

He laughed his first belly laugh with her. To Dilly that was a whole new declaration of love.

Beside her, laugh subsiding into a smile, Flipper relaxed enough to test the idea.

'How can a six-foot man swap clothes with a five-foot woman?'

'Five foot four!' she protested. 'Easily. Let me show you.'

Yet even when they stripped to their underwear behind a hedge, swapping clothes in a chilly tangle of lycra, limbs and bare naked flesh, Flipper didn't lay a finger on her.

Nell swaggered out of the mêlée towards Dilly as soon as she and Flipper arrived in the crowded, noisy tithe barn – a Freddy Mercury vision of white smile, white tux and black moustache. Her pupils were so huge that her Cottrell eyes were barely recognisable – black halos of lashes around big, black pools of high. She looked disturbingly like Flipper.

'Great beard,' she greeted her friend, stroking her own tache. 'Gay love.'

She planted a long kiss on Dilly's lips, lifting both their fake facial hair up into their noses.

Dilly reeled back in alarm. 'What have you taken, Nell?'

'Joke!' Nell laughed at her reaction, her eyes sparkling black holes. 'Kiss Magnus now.'

Dilly still gaped at her worriedly. 'What *have* you taken?'

'Kiss Magnus,' Nell instructed, black eyes impregnable.

Magnus was frighteningly convincing as a woman. His curly blond hair tumbled seductively around his heart-shaped face, his blue eyes were luminous in their high relief war-paint, and his made-up lips were plump and glistening. Nell had dressed him well, disguising the harder edges of his body not with transvestite frills, but with tight corsetry, his waist nipped in, his hips jutting out. From his glazed expression, he was obviously already pretty drunk.

'Kiss!' Nell demanded, stroking her moustache.

Dilly angled her head on command, studied Magnus's shiny lips and – holding on to her beard – kissed them jokily.

They tasted of fruity lip-gloss. And they moved deliciously against hers as they smiled, starting to part.

Heart suddenly hammering, Dilly hastily stepped back and straightened her beard, determined to stay jokey in the face of such debauchery.

'With a snogging technique like that, you saucy minx, I'd like to mark your dance card,' she said in as butch a voice as she could muster – something between Orville and Joe Pasquali.

He was hopeless at camp, his voice as gruff as a navvy. 'You got my card?'

But Dilly was looking around for Flipper, needing his back-up. The place was heaving with big-boned, horsy girls in suits and ties, and red-faced, broad-shouldered country lads in their mother's party frocks. But Flipper, and her favourite corset that contained him, had vanished.

As her gaze passed Magnus again, she couldn't help but stop and stare. He was watching her with big, troubled blue eyes, swaying slightly. He really did look beautiful, and strangely

vulnerable too. Whatever Nell had taken to make her so wired
and out of it, she appeared to have slipped some to Magnus
too.

And Nell, who was screeching with laughter at the bagginess
of Dilly's suit, was completely out of control.

'Let's go!' she ordered, hooking her arms beneath both theirs
as she strutted her way to the dance floor, so disturbingly
androgynous that hot looks came from every side and both
sexes as she passed by with her pretty blonde consorts.

Her beard at a jaunty angle along with her specs, Dilly
allowed herself to be towed along, still looking desperately
around for Flipper.

But, as her ears and then eyes took in something close to heaven
performing on the minstrels' gallery, she forgot all about him.

The Three Disgraces had been right. Trackmarks were
good. They were better than good.

They were angrier than Magnus's ensemble, but that antagonism lent them a more sensual and complex resonance. Their
songs had a better backbeat. Godspell's screaming voice
echoed through every frustrated young libido out there, along
with the thrumming club anthem of a beat and the chill-out
mid-sections. It was incredible stuff.

'Oh shit, shit, shit,' Magnus complained as he, Nell and Dilly
camped it up around the dance floor. Dazed and confused he
might be, but he could still recognise sensational music when
he heard it.

Nell absolutely loved it. She danced her way through the
crowd around them, happy and wired, a completely loose
cannon who wanted to dance with everybody.

Abandoned together, Dilly and Magnus distractedly kept up
their camp boogie as they listened carefully to the music.
Around them, couples were close dancing, bumping and
grinding to the sexiest of rhythms.

'Whoever came up with these mixes is a genius.' Magnus put his forearms on her shoulders and danced her back from the minstrels' gallery so that they could see who was on the decks behind the band. He looked up at the figure in the dark glasses and hoodie, listening as Trackmarks melded one thrumming rhythm into another, the sensual, stolen samples symbiotic, the melodies unique. 'The beat is phenomenal. Godspell's voice sounds fantastic with it. Fuck, we need new songs.'

'Your songs are great,' Dilly assured him as she shimmied and grinded to the beat.

'The hunt ball is less than a fortnight away,' he pointed out, hips moving against hers, hands dropping from her shoulders to her waist. 'This sounds way better than we do. More original. Sexier.'

As Magnus pulled her closer, Dilly's beard attached itself to his necklace.

When she tried to detach it, it came away from her face and fell down his cleavage. She fished around for it.

'This music is so fucking sexy.' Magnus tipped his forehead against hers.

She stopped fishing for a moment, gaze swivelling up to his face.

Laced with mascara, lined with kohl, shadowed with green and highlighted with glitter, his true blue eyes stared into hers. She could feel his breath quicken against her cheek.

'This lot will make fools of us,' he muttered.

His mouth was inches away from hers, the sweet gloss all kissed and talked away so that his lips stood out naked and male in his painted, feminised face.

Dilly suddenly wanted to taste them again more than any-thing. And, like a body rush from falling too fast, she knew he felt the same.

'*We'll* make fools of us, Magnus,' she gulped, trying to pull away.

Just for a moment, he wouldn't let her go.

'I used to think you were like my little sister.' His eyes stayed with hers. 'Now I'm not so sure.'

Reaching up, she delicately wiped away the black smudges from beneath his lashes.

'We're best friends.'

'Please tell me you're only saying that because I'm dressed as a woman?'

She shook her head. 'I'm saying that because you're my best friend and I love you.' She kissed him hard on both blushered cheeks, adding in her best Jerry Springer trailer trash accent, 'girl*friend.*'

Magnus licked his masculine lips and batted his feminine eyes before hugging her so tightly to him that she thought she might pop.

As she buried her face into his chest, squeezing him back, breathing in his lovely familiar smell, she reacquainted herself with her beard.

'I love you too,' he whispered in her ear.

Then he let her go.

Swaying at a discreet distance, suddenly unable to look at one another, they gazed awkwardly around the room.

'Dancing from womb to tomb,' Magnus muttered to himself.

Following his gaze, Dilly spotted Nell dancing with a very reluctant-looking Flipper.

Then she laughed as she realised Flipper was now wearing the old jeans and sweater he kept in his car boot in case he needed a change of clothes when he was working.

And, as Flipper caught her eye, she experienced the now-familiar tight grip of lust between her legs.

'What do you see in him?' Magnus asked.

'Same thing you see in Nell, I guess.'

'Great legs, lovely tits?'

She thumped him.

'Ow. That was my boob, you brute.'

'Be more ladylike then, you tart.'

Grateful that the awkward moment between them had passed, Dilly smiled across at Flipper.

'Kissing him is heaven,' she sighed.

As the music thrummed on, Dilly and Magnus danced their way to the twins' sides. On a strange sort of a high that she didn't understand, Dilly looked from face to face adoringly.

All were smiling at her.

Nell, her moustache still perfectly symmetrical, her eyes all-black, mouthed 'I am *so* out of it.'

At her side, Magnus, decidedly cross-eyed and drunk again now, grinned as he swayed.

Dilly smiled joyfully back. She hadn't drunk a sip of anything all night, smoked a puff, sniffed a line or even chomped on a square of chocolate, and yet every pulse point and nerve end thrummed.

Flipper, who appeared to have already sipped, smoked, sniffed and possibly freebased every narcotic in the building along with his sister, removed her beard and held a lighter to it. There was a smoky flash and it combusted to nothing.

'Was that supposed to impress me?' Dilly burst out laughing.

'No. This is.' He flicked a wrist and produced it from his palm by her ear.

'You do magic!' Dilly took the beard and stuck it back on upside down.

'I do.' He pulled it back off and kissed her.

Nobody on earth kissed like that. When Dilly breathed

again, she felt as though she had taken every drug in the building.

Smiling, he unpinned her hair so that it fell around her face in a cloud.

'There. You're a girl again.'

'But am I a girlfriend?'

His intense eyes didn't blink. 'I love you.'

'I lust you.'

Beside them, Nell wrapped her arms around Magnus, too wired to notice that his mascara was running.

Flipper deposited Dilly at the Oddlode Lodge gates just before midnight like Cinders from her carriage. And, although Dilly only saw the prince in all his finery, he was still behaving as a perplexing love rat, losing his fairy godmother makeover sparkle by the second.

He didn't kiss her again, or look at her as he bade her farewell, just raced away in a plume of exhaust fumes with her fishnet stockings still around his ankles and her corset in his car boot.

Dilly trailed through the gardens to the cottage, kissing her grandfather's frost-covered statues as she passed, and humming mindlessly. Magnus's songs. Those beautiful songs.

And then *Ride On* rang from her lips.

'*I could never go with you no matter how I wanted to.*'

She stopped herself and heard the words, as though for the first time, looking up sharply as an owl hooted overhead, its shadow crossing the moon.

'*I could never go with you no matter how I wanted to,*' she sang again.

It set her mind racing. That butterfly mind, which had been on a self-induced high all night, wouldn't rest.

★   ★   ★

'I love you more than I love myself.'

'And?'

'I love your hands.'

'And?'

'Your face, your lips, your wife.'

'That doesn't work.'

'It does if your lover's married,' Dilly told Magnus as they composed lyrics by phone in the early hours, exchanging yawns at twenty-second intervals.

'This *is* the hunt ball we're writing for.'

'Exactly.'

'*Your lips, your wife,*' he spoke each word carefully as he wrote them down.

Dilly could imagine his left hand curled far around the page so that he could monitor the words.

'*I am so in love that I am blind,*' she dictated, curling up into her pillow and eyeing Donk. '*I want your bed, body and your mind.*'

'Naff?'

'Slightly.'

'Deeply.'

'Think we'll get more proposals than Trackmarks' *Love me Legless*?' She rolled over.

'It's hunt ball, Dilly. Toffs reeling around, admiring one another's in-breeding and horse-breeding? Nobody will propose. They'll just mate according to class.'

'I'll be proposing during our new song if it's good enough,' she said encouragingly.

'I'll hold you to that.'

'I won't be proposing to *you*, Mags.'

'Natch.'

'Just thought I'd point it out.'

'No need. "*I want your bed, body*—" and what?'

'*Mind.*'

'Of course.'

'It *is* naff, isn't it?'

'It's naff truth.'

'You want those things, too?'

'I have them.'

'All hail Magnus.'

'You have them too – look around you,' he pointed out with a yawn.

'I haven't got my glasses on and it's dark. I can't see a thing.' She looked up blindly at her dark bedroom ceiling. 'Do you *really* not mind me calling you at this time of night?'

'I said so, didn't I?'

'It's just the lines for the song came to me when I was cleaning my teeth and I knew I wouldn't be able to sleep until I told you.'

'I said, it's cool, I'm still up. We haven't been back long. Nell's out for the count already. It's good to have someone to talk to, girl*friend.*'

'Girl*friend,*' she giggled happily. 'It was such a great party.'

There was a pause. 'Did you fuck him tonight?'

'No.'

There was another long pause. Dilly hugged the phone to her ear and rolled over in bed, her cheek pressed to the pillows.

'Are you still there?' he asked.

'Yes.'

'Happy birthday.'

'Thanks.' She chewed her lip, listening to him breathing.

At the other end of the line, he listened too.

She closed her eyes, falling too fast again, her heart racing, adrenaline peaking.

'I have to go,' she said eventually. 'It's going to be a great song.'

'It is.'

There was another pause as they breathed at network rates.

'Don't ride tomorrow,' she suddenly blurted.

'I won't,' he promised without question.

'Night.'

'Good night.'

She waited for him to hang up, but he didn't.

Forcing herself, Dilly snapped her phone shut, knowing she had to sleep. It was already past two in the morning and she and Otto had a big day ahead.

And yet she lay awake waiting.

Later, he texted her, as she had prayed he would.

Wordsworth more than actions.

When she didn't reply, he texted again:

And a single small cottage, a nest like a dove's,
The one only dwelling on earth that she loves.

Dilly was fumbling around with her predictive text when another text flew through.

Through love, through hope, and faith's transcendent dower,
We feel that we are greater than we know

Finally she fumbled her way to Send:

Ten thousand saw I at a glance,
Tossing their heads in sprightly dance

He replied in moments:

And then my heart with pleasure fills,
And dances with the daffodils.

She lay awake all night after that, tasting cherry lip-gloss, dancing every dance again, freefalling and flying and longing to be kissed, and this time saying what she really wanted to say in her head.

14

After a sleepless night spent listening to her mother getting up to feed Basil, to the dawn chorus, and most of all to her own blood pumping through her ears, Dilly went out at first light to get Otto fed and groomed ready for his fun day out, returning an hour later to share a huge birthday fry-up with Hamlet just as the rest of the village was waking up. Twenty felt a strange and uncomfortable age to reach. Yet losing her teenage status was long overdue.

The occasion cheered her enough to cast off a little of the ugly mask for a day, however. Practicality dictated that she wear the contact lenses that her mother had bought her as a birthday present, vanity added a dab of mascara, even if self-preservation strapped on her hefty old sports bra and padded knickers. Far too plump to fit into her own hacking jacket, she had borrowed Nell's sister-in-law's which was cut like a fifties starlet's and had such a fabulously nipped-in waist that she looked slimmer than she had before putting on weight.

'Trudy once pulled minor royalty wearing that,' Nell had told her when she dropped it off. 'Finn's hip-flask is still stashed in the pocket. He gave it to her the day he proposed. Probably full of the Mix.'

'The Mix?'

'Sloe gin and cherry brandy.'

And so it was, embossed with the initials PLC, which made Dilly feel a part of the great Cottrell family corporation some-how. She filled it with her own mix before setting out – three parts vodka to one part tequila. She sensed she was going to need its anaesthetic qualities to keep out the butterflies as well as the cold.

Her mother was on the phone to Pixie as she left, waving her off distractedly: '. . . I am *so* there, my darling. It takes a hell of a lot to get over these things. Men can be so destructive, so haplessly cruel. I am comfortable living in my own body and my head, but whether or not I'll ever let a man back into either is debatable. Basil could be the last male to ever make contact with the sides of this gorgeous woman's vag—'

Dilly slammed the door and headed off to tack up Otto.

He was at his maddest as she hacked him the short distance through the village to the meet, trying his hardest to thrust his twitching pink ears up her nose as he poked his head in the air and crabbed along sideways.

It was a drab day, the last of the snowy slush melting away beneath clouds that hung in low rows overhead like greying underwear clustered on serried backyard lines

The Lodes Inn car park was full of horseboxes and trailers shuddering under the impact of kicking hooves as drivers and riders lined up at the bar inside for Dutch courage.

The Cottrells' small red-haired Irish groom, Titch, was hanging on to Popeye and Olive as the twins stood inside, having their own hip-flasks filled with the Mix.

'I love the Oddlode meet,' she said excitedly as she spotted Dilly. 'The lines are always seriously fast here.'

'Are you not riding?' Dilly asked, accustomed to seeing Titch on various different horses that Piers Cottrell was trying to sell.

She shook her head. 'The third place in the lorry was going to be taken up by a horse for Nell's boyfriend, but he went lame this morning and it was too late to get anything else ready.'

'Magnus was really going to ride?' Dilly checked anxiously, trying to stop Otto from bolting.

'So she thinks.' Titch glanced towards the pub to check that the twins weren't on their way out and dropped her voice. 'Truth is, I'm pretty sure he'd have bottled it. He's a nice enough guy, but he's not a great rider and today's country takes serious riding. You need a lot of stickability and luck. Good thing the horse went lame if you ask me.' She couldn't hide the blush that was stealing across her freckled face, giving away the fact that she and Magnus were in cahoots. Dilly couldn't blame her for turning pink; he had exactly the same effect on her. She was only grateful that he was saved from what looked likely to be equestrian carnage.

She took an anxious swig of her Mix and searched for familiar faces.

The first she spotted was the scowling one of Magnus's sister Faith as she pranced into the car park on her flashy black horse with only marginally more control than Dilly had over Otto.

The twins emerged from the pub at the same time, looking glorious in tweed jackets, cream breeches and long boots, white silk stocks against their tanned, laughing faces.

Dilly looked around hopefully for Magnus. He would surely have come on foot to support both Nell and his sister, she thought. She needed him to make her laugh and assure her that she was going to be safe.

Nell was shouting at her from across the car park.

'Dildo! You're here! Happy birthday! Did you hear Magnus wimped out?' She laughed as she made her way through horses towards her

'I thought his horse went lame?'

'So Titch says.' Nell took Popeye from the groom who was rapidly turning as red as her hair. 'Looked sound enough to me.'

Titch cleared her throat and stared at her feet.

'We could have found him a spare horse if he'd been that keen,' Flipper muttered. 'He was more than happy to back out.'

Dilly looked down at Flipper as he took his own reins.

'Hi!'

'Hi.' He looked up at her, unsmiling.

She waited, but he pulled down his stirrups, checked his girth and mounted without another word. She wanted to scream, but instead she looked away determinedly and watched as Faith trotted over to join them, no longer scowling quite so much as she halted her over-excited stallion alongside her brother's pretty girlfriend.

'Hi, Nell.'

'Faith! How're you doing? Steady on!' Nell laughed as the horse reared up and span around before trying to lash out at Otto.

'Bit nervous,' Faith admitted, shooting Dilly a dirty look as though the incident had been her fault. 'It's Rio's first drag hunt. Magnus said you'd nanny us.'

'He did?' Nell looked appalled. 'I like to gallop, you know.'

'So do I.' Faith lifted her chin proudly as her horse backed up and tried to kick out at Olive this time.

'You can tuck in behind me if you like,' Nell offered cheerfully, 'but I won't wait for you.'

'Cool.' Faith grinned, fighting to stop Rio sitting on poor Olive.

'Is Magnus coming to see us off?' asked Dilly, watching miserably as Flipper rode away from danger to join some of his braying friends.

'He's busy,' Faith muttered, shooting Dilly another dirty look.

Dilly had never been able to get much out of Faith, who

adored Rory so slavishly that she'd loathed her when Dilly was
his girlfriend and now couldn't forgive her for hurting him.

'Mags made me promise to wish you a happy birthday,' she
told Dilly reluctantly.

Dilly beamed at her. 'Thanks.'

'You're welcome.' Faith shrugged.

'You look lovely in your smart riding gear, by the way,' Dilly
told her, suddenly wishing she would like her a bit more. She'd
always hated knowing anyone disliked her.

'Thanks.'

'I wish I had long, slim legs like yours. Cream is bloody
unforgiving for tree-trunk thighs like mine.'

Surprised, Faith suddenly let a tiny smile flicker across her
usually stern features.

'It's my first drag hunt,' Dilly confessed. 'I'm terrified too.'

Otto proved her point as the bloodhounds were let out of a
nearby horsebox and he almost expired on the spot.

'I used to go a lot on my pony in Essex,' Faith said, feigning
cool, despite the fact Rio was sharing Otto's panic-stricken
reaction to the hounds.

'Is it really as fast as they say?'

Faith nodded. 'It's pretty fast.'

'Oh, Christ.'

'Has your horse hunted before?'

Beneath them, Otto and Rio were now bonding like mad as
they shared a mutual terror of the waggy-flagged hounds
milling close by. If they could have held hooves in fear, they
would.

'Believe it or not, yes,' Dilly laughed nervously. 'We bought
him from an MFH.'

'Then he'll be fine once we get going. They know their job.
This one won't have a clue what he's doing. That's why he
needs a nanny who knows what's what.'

'Otto can nanny Rio if you nanny me,' Dilly joked desperately.

'Nell's my chaperone,' Faith reminded her tersely.

Dilly, who was too proud to ask Flipper to nanny her, realised she was on her own.

In the end, she and Faith were destined to be glued together throughout the afternoon as the twins out-raced them along every line.

By the second break between lines, Flipper had still barely acknowledged Dilly, let alone wished her a happy birthday. The strong spirits in Dilly's hip-flask had not only given her the courage to ride hard and fast, they also made her feel surprisingly tough and headstrong about Flipper – as well as unusually indiscreet.

'I am going to dump him,' she told Faith as they waited together, letting sweaty horses catch their breath and the Mix sink in. 'We're hardly happening.'

'He's seriously sexy.'

'No he's not.'

Dilly had never been particularly good at getting on with girls of her own age and younger, but was surprised to find Faith much easier to talk to than most. At sixteen, she was refreshingly starry-eyed and curious about love and sex. After a few swigs of the Mix, Faith loosened up.

'Is Flipper better than Rory?'

'Better than Rory how?'

Faith blushed puce. 'In bed.'

Unwilling to admit that she didn't know, Dilly said. 'Not as romantic.'

Faith's blush deepened.

'Rory was the loveliest boyfriend I've ever had.' Dilly drained the last of her Mix, now feeling delicious and warm and decidedly tight.

Faith paled. 'D'you want him back?'

Dilly shook her head. 'God no. We were all wrong together. Perhaps we're too similar. He needs somebody much stronger.'

'Stronger?'

Faith was agog, desperate for the secret formula to Rory's heart.

'She'd have to be able to defend him better than me.'

'From what?'

'From himself, of course.' Dilly smiled, lighting a cigarette. 'And predatory women.'

'Women always throw themselves at him, don't they?'

'Yes, but the ones who throw themselves at him aren't the ones he really wants.'

'They're not?'

'He's lazy, so he's happy to work his way through them without having to make the effort to seek out something better; and he's romantic so he's a sucker for big gestures and declarations of undying adoration; and he's egotistical so he loves to feel attractive and dynamic and sexually desired. But most of them aren't even his type,' Dilly finished, having basically described herself.

'What is his type?'

'Well, he's got a thing about big—' Dilly stopped herself just in time as she remembered Faith was flat-chested. 'About big hair.'

'Hair?' Faith had a huge frizzy helmet of hair.

'Yes, and noses.'

'Really?' She looked thrilled.

'And blue eyes.'

'Wow.'

'And he's definitely a leg man,' she announced euphorically. 'He used to tease me about my fat thighs.'

Faith glanced down at her own slim legs excitedly.

'But most of all,' Dilly realised she had to be truthful for Rory's sake as well as Faith's, 'he needs someone who can look after him and look out for him without him really knowing you're doing it.'

'Oh, I agree!'

'And sooner or later that big, soft heart of his will fall in love good and proper and stay that way.' Dilly looked across to Flipper sadly. 'And she'll be a lucky girl because he's such fun and so affectionate and so *damned* cuddly.'

Faith sighed dreamily, and then shot her a suspicious look. 'And you're sure you don't want him back?'

'He wouldn't have me even if I did,' she lied.

'True,' Faith muttered jealously, kicking Rio into action as the next line was drawn.

Bouncing around behind her on a hysterical Otto, Dilly gritted her teeth and glared at Flipper's distant tweed back.

On the final line of the day, Nell reined back and joined Dilly at the rear of the field, so that they were cantering together towards a huge hedge that Flipper's horse's heels were currently clearing with a glint of crescent metal.

'Don't dump him.'

'What makes you think I'll do that?' Dilly gritted her teeth, starting to feel sick from so much Mix

'He does.'

'He deserves it.'

'For what?'

'Ignoring me all day.'

'You've ignored him!'

Dilly grabbed a hunk of pink mane as Otto decided to take the hedge from his own unique angle – sideways and at full pelt. Forced to swerve at the last minute to avoid him, Popeye scrambled his way over a narrow gap between two trees.

On the other side, Dilly and Nell continued arguing.

'He loves you.' Nell was spitting twigs from her mouth.

'He loves himself.' Dilly had most of a bramble bush hanging from one shoulder.

'So he should. He's fucking lovely.'

Dilly felt the Mix churning around in her stomach. 'He hasn't wished me a happy birthday.'

'Maybe he was planning to do that later?'

'What – next year?'

'If it's any consolation, he never wishes me a happy birthday either.' Nell gathered Popeye ready to jump some post and rails. 'He hates birthdays because he's always had to share them. He loathes sharing things.'

'You see?' Dilly wailed as they flew over the rails side by side. 'He's so *spoiled.*' As Otto landed on the other side, she felt the Mix starting to bubble noxiously in her throat.

'Complex,' Nell corrected, reaching into her pocket 'He's complex. Here.' She held out her own hip-flask. 'Top up before you throw up.'

Something about Nell's devil-may-care attitude made Dilly perk up despite herself. Topped up with Mix, she laughed as they pelted towards a Cotswold stone wall on a hill brow that divided a high field from a low one, making it seem like a leap into space.

'You're much easier to like than Flipper.' Dilly closed her eyes as she felt Otto square up to the task ahead.

'Like is much easier than love,' Nell called across to her as she swung Popeye to one side for a better approach.

'I don't particularly like your brother.' Dilly opened her eyes and suddenly saw two walls dancing around one another ahead of her.

'You don't?' Nell turned to stare at her.

Otto, confused that he appeared to be seeing a different wall from his rider, faltered a few strides in front of it.

'I am in love with somebody, though,' Dilly said drunkenly and, as Otto took off a stride too soon, she promptly fell off.

Faith caught Otto while Nell pulled up and jumped off to stoop over Dilly.

'Are you drunk?'

Dilly nodded. 'I'm also twenty.'

'Many happy returns.'

'I love . . .' She giggled too much to go on.

Nell and Faith exchanged baffled looks as Dilly shrieked and wept with laughter.

'It must be someone hilarious,' Faith said seriously as they watched her rolling around at the base of the wall.

'C'mon Dilly – pull yourself together.' Nell leaned over her. 'The field's getting away.'

For a moment or two, the laughter died and the tears continued, just a few quiet sobs, before Dilly mopped herself up, got to her feet and apologised.

'Are you okay to carry on?' asked Nell.

She nodded, embarrassed at her display.

Faith gave her a leg-up. Reunited with Otto and hanging on to his mane, she cantered him between Rio and Popeye to catch up with the field, aware that she was acutely pissed.

'So who do you love, Dilly?' Nell turned to ask her. 'Who is this somebody you are in love with?'

Dilly looked dizzily between the two pink ears in front of her.

'Otto. I'm in love with Otto. He always brings me down to earth.'

Looking over Otto's sweaty neck, Nell aimed an amused look at Faith. But Faith was beaming at Dilly. Now that Dilly had loved and lost Rory, she loved her horse more than anything in the world. That, to Faith, was almost heroic. She looked at Dilly with new-found respect.

★   ★   ★

The drag hunt concluded with another pub gathering, this time at the Duck Upstream.

Dilly's Mix had almost worn off, and she felt too ashen and shamefaced and humiliated by Flipper to stage an appearance. She just wanted to text Magnus, at home, alone, and try to see the funny side.

But Otto had other ideas. Having hunted side by side with his sweaty compatriots all day, he lined up beside them outside the pub and refused to budge.

'Let Titch look after him for a minute,' Nell insisted. 'He deserves to debrief with his chums.'

Dilly reluctantly let Nell drag her into the duck-decked main bar, the tables of which were laid out with trays of hot toddies and food.

Of course Flipper was waiting, lounging back against the bar in his muddy breeches, the most desirable and dislikeable figure imaginable. He had a bottle of champagne on ice beside him.

Nell propelled Dilly towards him.

'I owe you an apology.' He looked up through his lashes, grey-green eyes intense.

Dilly wasn't going to fall for that one. 'You owe me more.'

'Happy birthday.'

'Thanks.'

'I love you.' He reached a warm hand out to cup her cheek, his little finger sliding around her ear, his thumb tracing her lower lip.

She wasn't about to fall for that one either. 'So you say. Prove it.'

And, as he kissed her full-force for the second time in twenty-four hours, he gave it his best shot. This kiss was phenomenal. Flipper had kissing off to a fine art. He kissed like his life depended on it. Then he whispered in her ear:

'I'm going to give you me. You get me for your birthday. All of me.'

And he kissed her again.

Just for that moment in time, it was the sexiest thing Dilly had ever heard in her life, matched with the horniest kiss. She could almost love him back for it.

When Nell clambered into the horsebox cab alongside Titch, Flipper stayed on the verge with Dilly and Otto.

'Don't you want to come back and change?' Nell called out of the window at him.

He shook his head. 'You can bring me a change of clothes.'

'What about the *you-know-what*?' Nell looked infuriated.

'You can bring that, too.'

'*What!*'

'Titch'll help you.'

'Thanks a bunch.' Titch started the engine.

'Flipper, tonight's been carefully planned,' Nell shouted. 'We have to fit in with other people.'

'Well, I'm re-planning it,' Flipper shouted, tapping his watch. 'Seven o'clock did we say?'

Nell poked her tongue out at him as they drove away.

'Are you and Nell going out somewhere nice?' Dilly asked him as they started walking towards Giles's cottage, trying not to feel miffed that they were obviously going elsewhere on her birthday. Her champagne-and-kissing high was too euphoric to lose.

'Just some friends getting together,' he muttered, not looking at her.

'Where?'

'Nowhere special.'

Okay, so he's not good at talking, Dilly reminded herself as she licked her recently kissed lips and weaved along beside

Otto. But he bought me champagne and told me he loved me, so I'll give him a chance. She glanced across at him and hiccoughed happily. And he is so *king* gorgeous.

He helped her bed Otto down, sharing the last of their second bottle of champagne.

'Where's Uncle Giles?' he asked as he surveyed the distant cottage in darkness.

'Topping up his tan in Thailand I gather.' Dilly's mother had been weeping about it all week.

'You have a key to the house?'

'No – but I do know where he keeps his dope—'

His lips hit hers before she could suggest a bolstering spliff.

His fingers were already feeling their way inside her while she was still figuring out his belt clip. Dilly was surprised by the sweet, foaming warmth that welcomed them. That killer kiss had a lot to answer for.

He was a very quick worker. Where his fingertips had flicked only sweetly and briefly, his cock soon followed and filled her up so tightly that Dilly squealed in alarm as well as delight, caught between pleasure and pain.

He fucked as fast as he rode to hounds, and he lasted as long. This was three miles of fast galloping with no break. On and on and on, faster and faster, louder and louder. He made a lot of noise and, when he came, he howled with delight. It was a breathtaking adrenaline rush, a huge turn-on and a great antidote to the cold.

Afterwards, he kissed her ears and eyes and nose and throat and mouth, and told her he loved her again, a faint breath of a whisper.

She couldn't see his face in the darkness, but she knew he was lying. It took fucking to know that. And she had enjoyed sharing that. It was lying she hated.

To prove her point, he was out of her and upright in a shot, pulling his breeches back up over his bare arse and dusting straw from his hair.

'You don't have to pretend any more just because you want to bed me,' she laughed softly. 'Consider me bedded. And very much pleasured.'

'And loved.'

She shook her head incredulously, laughing, although a curious part of her wanted to cry.

'Do you still lust after me?' His grey eyes glinted in the half light.

'Yes. I lust you very much.'

'And I love you very much. That's the deal.'

'You're weird. And a great lay.'

'Not as weird as you. Although I agree, I'm a great – ow, get off!' He dodged away as a great lump of straw came flying at him.

'How many women have you bedded in stables?'

'Loads.'

'Do you prefer straw or shavings?'

'I like shredded paper. Very clean. Better for wiping off, too.'

She laughed as she started to button up her shirt. 'You're so bloody callous. I wish you'd admit you're just a no-good heartbreaker. It'd make you so much easier to deal with.'

'I'll admit it if you do.' He tied a neat knot in his discarded condom and dropped it in Giles's composter.

'But I'm not. I'm . . . just . . . not.'

'How many men have you slept with?'

'A few.' She shrugged. Admitting to her slut weeks in Durham the previous summer was always shameful.

'How many?'

'Not as many as you.'

'I haven't slept with any men. You know what I mean. How many, Dilly?'

'Guess.'

His eyes glinted at her in the dark again. 'Oh, fuck. What *is* it about you?'

The script didn't alter. Tongue against hers, body slamming her back into the straw, lips, unbuckling, fingers, then that fantastic cock. Hammer-drill action, fast and furious, riding her home across miles of jumping country.

It was blissfully simple and strangely invigorating. He groaned and moaned and yelled and laughed and howled. He made more noise fucking than he ever did in conversation, showed more emotion, and had more fun. This beautiful, aloof, arrogant man who intimidated her was a friend inside her body. It felt great.

Dilly laughed and squealed along, too, loving the ride.

Afterwards, wrapped up in a horse blanket, they drained the last sips of champagne as they lay back in the straw, and he told her that he loved her again. Dilly didn't believe him any more than she had before, but she no longer cared.

'Okay, I'm twenty and I've reached double figures,' she said drunkenly as Flipper walked her home, sharing the contents of his hip-flask with her.

'Isn't that ten?'

'Go to the top of the class. I've slept with ten men by the age of twenty. Is that bad?' She cannoned against him as she fought to walk in a straight line.

'Better than sleeping with twenty men by the age of ten.'

Laughing and tripping along, she deliberately cannoned against him again, hoping he'd put his arm around her. But he didn't.

'I'm chuffed I was your double figure,' he said, handing her the flask.

'I'm certainly *seeing* double.' Still laughing, she swigged back some more of the sweet Mix. 'Double trouble.'

She kissed him all the way through the overgrown garden to the Lodge. He was heaven to kiss.

'There's a bit – of a – surprise waiting – for you,' he told her between mouthfuls of Mix, lips and tongue.

'Oh yes?'

'A birthday surprise.'

'You've just given me my best birthday present.' She giggled, pulling him behind one of her grandfather's sculptures by the front door. 'In fact, it was so good, I think I might just have to unwrap my present again.' She dropped down to her knees and started to unclip his belt.

'Dilly – I'm not sure you . . . it's bloody cold out here and . . . Christ. Don't stop.'

As she slipped her lips around his ever-expanding cock, Dilly experienced a brief, unexpected moment of self-hatred that almost made her gag. She wanted to please him, and she was doing this to please him – just as she had for Pod. It was Pod who had taught her to give head properly, training her tongue to lick so expertly along the vein at the back of the cock, to butterfly across the tip, roll its way around the head, slide wide and soft across the length of the shaft and then draw back in a tight snake-flick that teased the last creases from the foreskin. But as she performed every little intricacy, just as she had been taught, all the booze and galloping and nostalgia and self-doubt and newness of the day started rising up her throat.

'That is fucking amazing,' Flipper groaned, his fingers raking through her hair. 'Oh God, you're lovely. So fucking lovely. I love you.'

Pod had said things like that, too. Perhaps all men did, Dilly wondered, feeling more and more detached as she sucked him off. She also felt more and more nauseous.

And then, just as Flipper started shouting out that he was going to come, and she was wondering if she could carry on long enough to let him without being sick, a shaft of light fell across the statue beside them.

The door was thrown open.

'HAPPY BIRTHDAY DILLY!'

Flipper hastily dived into the shadows, breeches around his knees.

Still crouching at groin level, Dilly looked up and reeled in surprise. The Lodge cottage was full of people. And they were all staring at her.

'SURPRISE!'

Thankfully, the statue had totally obliterated Flipper from view throughout, so that all that the assembled guests could see was Dilly on her knees, seemingly nose to nose with an elfin foot.

'What *are* you doing?' demanded her mother, holding a party popper aloft.

'Er – just – lost my contact lens,' she spluttered, wiping her mouth.

'Not your birthday present?' Pheely bustled forward to help look. 'They cost a fort—'

'Found it!' Dilly hastily pretended to snatch something up from beside her feet, aware that Flipper's shiny black boots were twitching just a few inches away as he tried hard not to make a noise, despite landing erection-down in an ornamental box hedge.

Dilly jumped up and forced a bright smile as she peered into the house to be greeted by the loveliest sight. Nell, Ellen, Spurs, Pixie, Faith and all the Brakespears, Rory, Titch, the Three Disgraces and a raucous group of other family friends fired off party poppers and cheered.

'HAPPY BIRTHDAY DILLY!' they chorused with even more vigour after the false start.

At their forefront, Magnus smiled his usual smile, making her heart bounce around happily.

'Happy birthday.' He walked forwards to hug and kiss her in welcome.

Dilly ducked her head away, meaning that he kissed her hair. She couldn't possibly let him near her mouth just at the moment.

'Thank you,' she muttered into his armpit. 'You organised all this, didn't you?'

'Everyone mucked in.'

'It's why you didn't come out drag hunting?'

'I didn't come out hunting because I'm bloody terrified of riding,' he laughed, but his hug tightened and she realised gratefully that this lovely surprise had saved his dignity that day as well as making her day. As proof, he whispered in her ear, 'And you told me not to, didn't you? I thought I might as well keep busy.'

She held him as long as she could, feeling the sharp corners of love rake at her belly.

'Where's Flipper?' Nell was at their side, looking unusually agitated.

'Oh, he's just – coming.' Dilly pulled reluctantly away from Magnus's comforting chest.

'He was supposed to bring you here over an hour ago,' she complained, peering out into the garden. 'And I could have sworn I heard him just now. I need to talk to him urgently.'

'He won't be long.' Dilly hastily closed the door.

Magnus's amiable blue eyes were noticing a fretful edge to Dilly that everyone else had missed. As the rest of the guests turned back into the main body of the cottage, he held her back a moment. 'Are you all right? You look a bit flustered.'

'Fine!' She couldn't hold his gaze. Then she suddenly remembered her alibi. 'Just going to pop to the bathroom to put this back in before I lose it.' She held up her clenched hand and waggled it, like something out of a coffee commercial.

'Your contact lens?'

She nodded.

'The one you picked up with your other hand?'

'That's the one.' She scuttled off.

In the bathroom, she buried her hot face in her hands and groaned.

The Mix and champagne high was finally wearing off, taking with it the sudden high that came from Flipper's seduction. For all his beauty and enthusiasm – and impressive size – he didn't have what it took, and she knew it. He hardly knew how to talk to her, so how could she expect him to fire her imaginative libido for long? Her lust for him was as shallow as a puddle, a way of communicating and feeling wanted where words failed them. Strong enough to have her dropping to her knees to pleasure him, but nothing compared to the other feelings that were marching around her confused head in ever-decreasing circles. She felt soiled and trapped – old Dilly with new tricks.

Simply hugging Magnus made her knees give way. In her heart, she had wanted Magnus to be her double figure, and she knew it. Flipper made her feel far more bad than good, far more horny than happy and far more unloved than all his 'I love you's put together. Magnus just made her whole being, body and dizzy head, light up every time she saw him.

15

When Dilly emerged from the bathroom, Flipper was standing in his breeches and boots in the rear lobby, having a frantic, hissy scrap with Nell.

'There you are!' Nell span around as soon as she saw Dilly and flashed a big, shifty smile. 'I'll fetch the others.' She dashed away, shooting Flipper a warning look over her shoulder.

'Why is she fetching the others?'

'I have something to show you.' Flipper didn't look her in the face. 'Outside.'

'What is it?'

'A present.'

'But you've already given me a birthday present,' she reminded him as she curled up against him, willing him to look at her, longing for that warm, intimate connection again.

He flicked his eyes briefly across to hers. 'It's not *for* you.'

'Oh.' She pulled away. 'I see.'

But his hand closed tightly around hers and he lifted it to his mouth to press his lips to it. 'It's for the love of your life.' The grey-green eyes trapped hers this time, ruthless and challenging.

'Sorry?'

The eyes narrowed. 'I'm seriously fucking jealous to hear that you love someone else, but I'm being big about it, so I've decided to give him a present, too.'

Dilly's heart filled with cold dread and started slamming itself against the bars of her ribcage as he led her towards the door.

Then, out in the cold and darkness, with just Flipper's warm guiding hand to lead her, she had a near-biblical moment of relief and gratitude.

Tethered to a statue of two boxing hares in a far corner of the garden – illuminated just by the bright silver moon and golden light spilling from the cottage – was a small, brown donkey wearing a shiny pink bow around its neck and another around its tail. It looked extremely put out.

'This,' Flipper led Dilly up to it, 'is Bottom. He's for Otto. I thought he might keep him company.'

Dilly laughed, then stifled a sob, then laughed again. Then she jumped up to hug Flipper in an excited, laughing, sobbing vice of trembling emotion, arms and legs wrapped around him.

'Thank you, thank you, thank you!' She kissed his face all over before jumping down to turn and meet the bad-tempered Bottom. 'I love him, I love him, I love him!'

'I'm glad you love *him*,' Flipper muttered, but he couldn't keep the smile from his face.

'Oh, I do!' Dilly touched the long ears and mealy muzzle, tears dropping happily from her eyes. 'This is the most wonderful present anyone has ever given me.'

'You mean given Otto.' He ducked his head and smiled wider.

Dilly gazed into his grey-green eyes, registering that while he couldn't talk easily, hold hands, play kiss or hug her, Flipper was capable of affection nonetheless. Looking at his smiling face led to a spasm of emotion that ran right through her – partly lust, and partly something that was suspiciously close to love.

Behind him, Nell had just arrived, arm in arm with Magnus, the other party guests filtering into the garden behind them amid much tittering because they were under strict instructions to stay quiet and not alarm Bottom.

And at their fore, Magnus had just heard Dilly thanking Flipper for her best-ever birthday treat. He scratched his forehead and glanced around at the little group who had been so hard to rally and orchestrate, but had worked so hard to help him organise food and booze and decorations. Yet, even after all that, he had got it wrong. He should have just bought her an ass.

'Bottom's from me, too,' Nell was telling Dilly, having begged her brother to be added to his gift because as always she had forgotten to get one. 'Titch and I brought him here for you, which took *ages*. We couldn't get him to go in the sheep trailer until Titch doped him, blindfolded him and got me to prod a pitchfork into his backside. He's a grumpy sod.'

Magnus exchanged a look of empathy with Bottom, now understanding his bad temper.

'I love him,' Dilly sighed as she wrapped an arm around each twin and stretched up to kiss them in turn. 'He might be a grumpy sod, but I just love him.'

Flipper rested his chin on her head and looked across at Magnus briefly and victoriously before dropping a kiss into Dilly's blonde curls.

Magnus turned and walked away, leaving them to it, hands thrust deep in his pockets and chin buried in his collar. He kicked a bronze stag as he passed it, fracturing a toe in the process and almost taking his lip off as he bit it hard to stop himself yelping.

When Dilly came downstairs after changing into a pair of cream trousers and a floaty white shirt that made her feel prettier than she had in weeks, Flipper was working his way through a bottle of scotch beside the kiln with Spurs and Rory, laughing uproariously. He had changed, too, his baggy, soft grey fleece playing house to Milo, who was wearing a birthday bow and snarling at nobody in particular.

She faltered, wondering whether to approach the tight-knit little group.

'What else did Flipper give you for your birthday?' Nell bounded up, passing her a brimming vodka and coke. 'Is it something you can wear?'

Dilly thought about it. 'Only in private.'

'How thrilling.' Nell narrowed her eyes decadently.

Dilly took a swig from the spilling glass and winced. It was mostly vodka.

'Magnus and I have something special for you, too.'

'You do?'

'Mmm – he'll pass it on later.' Nell didn't like to admit that she hadn't actually bothered to find out what it was. Getting herself added to two of Dilly's birthday presents had been a coup. 'Are you going to change?'

Dilly looked down at her outfit.

'Flipper's made the effort,' Nell pointed out.

Dilly stomped back upstairs. Perhaps wearing trousers the colour of breeches and a shirt not dissimilar to her riding one had been a mistake, but she no longer felt remotely pretty – just invisibly bland.

If 'making the effort' like Flipper meant jeans and a fleece, Dilly decided to match him. But her fleece was currently underneath the snoring Hamlet on the end of her bed and her jeans still wouldn't do up, so she settled for a hoodie and trackie bottoms, teasing out her hair to a wild blonde cloud, applying lip-gloss and dousing herself in the last dregs of Coco left in the bottle she had pilfered from her mother's dressing-table weeks ago.

Nell, who was swathed in a turquoise suede dress that set off her eyes and knee-high cream boots that showed off her slim brown knees, shook her head and laughed when Dilly stomped back down.

'Call that dressing up?'

'It's my birthday.'

'True. You'll have to do. The boys have agreed we'll play a couple of songs.'

'What?'

'We're on in five, so do your voice exercises, Madge.'

'Entwined's performing here?'

'Everyone's agog.'

'Didn't they hear enough at Basil's party?' Dilly complained in vain as Nell dragged her to the hearthrug in front of the wood-burning stove, where Magnus had set up a minimal keyboard and drum machine, and was already perched on a stool, guitar on his knee, tuning up.

'Flipper!' Nell shrieked, and a moment later her brother was pushed towards them by Spurs and Rory, exchanging a look of horror with Dilly.

They sang their two best-rehearsed original songs, *Kissing Your Shadow* and *You Make Me High*, along with their cover of *Hold Me Now*.

And this time, they held it together. This time, they performed. This time, Dilly felt tears spring to her eyes as she harmonised with Magnus's beautiful, smoky voice and belted out his amazing lyrics, loving his talent and his kindness. Flipper was drumming away behind her, that familiar, sexy rhythm that she had felt between her legs just an hour ago. Nell looked beautiful beside her, black hair gleaming, hips swaying, backing vocals muted by the fact she had no microphone.

The very partisan little audience went so wild that deaf Hamlet fell off Dilly's bed upstairs, came thundering down to join them and howled along.

Then Flipper struck a drumroll at the end of the third

number, and Magnus and the twins launched straight into a drum'n'bass rendition of *Happy Birthday*, everybody joining in. Dilly clapped her hands to her burning cheeks and laughed in amazement and delight.

Magnus cleared his throat several times afterwards, waiting for the cheering to drop enough for him to be heard. 'Just before we hand the stage over to anyone here who has a song or a party piece they want to perform for Dilly's birthday, I have a new song I'd like to sing for you, if that's okay. It's dedicated to somebody very special.'

He struck a chord on his guitar, one of those haunting minor sevenths that always augur melancholy.

'You said that you loved me more than you love yourself
Well that's no fucking good to me
You don't love yourself you see
You said you love my hands, my face, my lips
Pieces of my skin
Not the soul within
You said you want my bed, my body and my mind
You want my kind
Not me. Not fucking me.'

The hoarse passion in his voice had silenced them all, singing out above the simplest of chord changes, the slowest of tempos.

Now his guitar strings hummed and bounced as he slid his fingers from fret to fret and thrust the plectrum across them, changing to an angry, sexy tempo. The chorus kicked in, blue eyes looking through them all.

'We have been loved. Inside out. You and me.
We have been fucked. Inside out. You and me.
We have been kicked. Far and wide. You and me.
We have been hurt. Deep inside. You and me.
Now we have each other.
Jealousy.

Each other. Sweet jealousy.'

Hairs lifted on backs of necks as there was a hushed silence before the minor seventh stroked its gentle, bittersweet way back into the room.

'*You know you need love just to keep you sane*
I'm the same
Such sweet shame
Your heart is a place where I can never live
Ten thousand deep
Where no one sleeps
Through love, through hope, we'll keep alive
A nest of doves
Day-dreaming loves.'

He belted out the chorus again, making skin prickle beneath those upstanding hairs, tears reluctantly dance behind eyes. As he dropped his voice to sing the last three lines, Pheely started to audibly snivel.

'*. . . have each other.*
Jealousy.
Each other. Sweet jealousy.'

For the final verse, his plectrum barely touched the strings of the minor seventh and its melancholy allies, his voice just a little more than a whisper.

'*You are the woman that I love*
Pleasure fills
My heart
Tossing your head as I walk past
Pleasure fills
My heart
Dance with me in my mind
Pleasure fills
My heart.'

He dropped his chin and fell silent, leaving them all prickly-skinned with excitement and wet-eyed. Because they knew that they'd heard something special. Something raw and beautiful and honest.

As the little party crowd started to clap and whoop, Nell thrust her way past Dilly and jumped straight into Magnus's arms, crushing his guitar to his chest with a screech of feedback from the amp.

'Thank you. Thank you, darling man.' She kissed him until he couldn't breathe. 'You wrote that for me.' Her face was streaked with rivulets of mascara and salt water.

And Dilly's own eyes were suddenly so full of tears that when she turned away, she didn't see Flipper looking at her until he walked up and wiped the wet splashes from beneath her lashes with his thumbs. He gave her a half smile.

'She's a thief. Always has been.'

'Sorry?' Dilly cocked her head, ears still ringing with Magnus's words.

He leaned his mouth down to her ear. 'My sister steals things – hearts, songs, minds, souls. Anything she can get her hands on. Don't let her steal you as well, Dilly. She can take everything from you, but she can't take you.'

'Needs toning down a bit for the hunt ball,' Pheely was raving to Ellen. 'But all there, you've got to admit.'

Ellen shook her head, looking across at Magnus and Nell. 'That man's talent is wasted on a hunt ball.'

'That's what he wants, though,' Pheely assured her. 'He wants to play there.'

'Why?'

'Maybe he wants his girlfriend to propose?'

Ellen caught Dilly, pale and panic-eyed, dashing out through the French windows on to the terrace.

And it suddenly struck her. 'What if Dilly proposes too?'

'Why would she?'

'Because,' Ellen realised in fear, 'she believes in happy ever afters.'

'I told you to give up.' Magnus reached around her and plucked the spliff from her fingers, tossing it into the slushy undergrowth.

Taken by surprise, Dilly stepped sharply away and almost slipped. 'Where's Nell?'

'Talking to friends. We're not tied by the ankle, you know.'

'Oh.'

'Everything okay with Flipper?'

'Of course. We're not tied by the ankle either.'

'I worry about you, that's all.'

'Stop being so sanctimonious and lording it over my relationship. We're fine.'

'Fine!' He backed away, blue eyes hurt.

They stared at one another, neither fully understanding where the antagonism had come from.

Dilly rubbed her forehead and laughed first. 'Sorry.'

'What's up?'

'I'm just – older,' she laughed. 'No longer a teenager. Trying to work out where to bury the angst, y'know?'

'I know.' He nodded and stepped forward to hug her, tousling her hair and cuffing her arms for good measure.

'I loved the song.' She pulled reluctantly away to stop herself squeezing him to death.

He nodded again, ran his fingers through his curly mop and looked away.

'And I love my party. Thank you.'

His lips twisted in a half smile and he lifted his hands to her cheeks. 'God, you're freezing.'

Dilly felt his fingers imprint themselves exactly where

Flipper's had been just a few minutes earlier. One set had branded her with shame, the other warmed and comforted her.

She shrugged. 'Hell's frozen over.'

'What's that supposed to mean?'

Unable to look at him, she let out a sigh that plumed steamily between their faces.

'Eh?' he persisted.

'. . . *the birthday of my life is come, my love is come to me*,' she murmured so quietly that she wasn't sure he even heard.

Cupping her hands over his and gently squeezing them before prising them away, Dilly wandered back to her party. She didn't see Nell standing in the shadow of the doors as she passed.

Flipper was back in his corner with Spurs and Rory. She grabbed a wine bottle and joined them.

'We've just been talking about the team.' Flipper took the bottle and drank directly from it.

'The team?'

'Thrusters Entwined. The squad we're fielding for the VW team chase next week. You're in.'

'Oh yes?' She gaped at him, uncertain whether to whoop or cry.

'You, me, Rory and Spurs.'

'What about Nell?'

Flipper's eyes hardened. 'Out.'

'Why?'

'She's unreliable.' His face was a mask of grey-eyed Cottrell cool, the classic marble bust of hard beauty.

Spurs and Rory shrugged and pulled amused faces when she looked at them. The latter gave her the ghost of a wink with a wide almond eye, reminding her that life had been much simpler once, when she'd been with him and only had to worry about giggling so much during sex that she propelled him back out again. He was drunk as a skunk as usual.

'Bit of a liability across country is Nell,' he reminisced, eyes crossing. 'Once jumped a fence judge's car and two picnics taking a short cut at Springhill trials.'

Dilly patted his knee affectionately.

'Where *is* Nell?' She gazed around the room.

'Gone home, I guess,' Flipper muttered, eyes narrowed as he watched Dilly's face. 'Looks like she's taken your birthday present boy with her.'

'She took Bottom back?' Dilly gulped.

'No – Titch took him to Giles's paddock earlier,' Rory slurred. 'Lovely girl. Lovely Bottom.'

'What birthday present boy?' Dilly asked Flipper, genuinely confused.

'You are the woman that I love. Pleasure fills. My heart.'

'God, Flipper's gone soft in old age,' Rory hiccoughed and slid off his chair.

Dilly looked around. Nell was nowhere. Magnus had disappeared too.

Her mother was at the keyboard, belting out *It's My Party*, accompanied by Pixie on the maracas.

But Dilly hardly heard a word or note. All she could hear in her head was Magnus's amazing song. Every note coursed through her veins. But pleasure didn't fill her heart. Teenage angst did. A day too late, she felt her full teenage rebellion strike. And a lover too late, she realised that reaching double figures had halved her fragile self-esteem.

'I'm going to bed,' she announced suddenly.

'I'll see you safely there.' Flipper took her hand and led the way.

Tripping dejectedly behind him, it drunkenly occurred to Dilly that he might want her to finish what she had started earlier – the doorstep blow-job that had almost blown their cover. The thought made her drag her heels and run a dry tongue around her lips.

But in her tiny cot of a room, he did the strangest of things. He undressed her to her underwear, laid her down on the bed and tucked her in, kissing her on the forehead.

'I love you.'

'I lust you,' she murmured automatically, although she was already drifting off to sleep and towards lovely, erotic dreams of Magnus that knew no shame while her unconscious mind was in control.

Flipper studied the drawings her grandfather had sketched of a little princess in an enchanted garden. Then, taking one last, long look at her sleeping, he patted Hamlet, switched off the light and wandered downstairs.

16

For a girl who had slept with ten men, Dilly knew surprisingly little about them. All her boyfriends had seemed incredibly unreliable and difficult to read. That she might be, too, had never occurred to her.

Flipper was the worst of the lot. He hardly spoke to her, never called her – and yet he kissed her like no other boyfriend had, made love with boundless enthusiasm and looked at her with such searing intensity she couldn't think straight.

After her birthday, their strange relationship enjoyed a brief purple patch. With intense rehearsals underway to get Entwined ready for the ball, plus concentrated fittening work to get Otto ready for the team chase, they saw each other every day. It didn't matter that Flipper never called. He was always around – as were Nell and Magnus.

The relationships overlapped. They would meet early before rehearsals to get some food, spill into the pub together after rehearsals for a drink and then all end up back in Magnus's annexe at his parents' farm or the twins' attic flat, talking and smoking dope until the early hours.

As a foursome they worked far better than they did as two pairs. Dilly and Magnus did the talking and dreaming while Flipper and Nell did the arguing and joking. Dilly felt more relaxed with Magnus around. Despite their intimacy, Flipper made her nervous. There was something detached about him, almost to the point of cruelty.

Out riding together, he would think nothing of galloping off and leaving her far behind, jumping fences that she was too terrified to attempt, ploughing through rough ground that left Otto bogged down and exhausted.

'He has to get fitter and braver,' he would explain unsympathetically. 'You both do.'

They would meet up just before it got light, riding across country as dawn broke. Nell always promised to come too, but usually overslept. Once or twice, Rory and Spurs joined them, but they were more usually alone. On these occasions, Dilly longed for Magnus's easy chatter, but he still absolutely refused to have anything to do with riding.

Dilly grew to look forward to the end of the ride when they would stop off at Rectory Cottage in Oddlode to have porridge with Flipper's sister-in-law, Trudy. She would either be dressed in her nightie, looking bleary-eyed and groggy from being woken, or still wearing the clothes from the day before, having stayed up all night working on songs and lyrics. But she always welcomed them with warmth and excitement.

'I'm so thrilled Flipper has found a lovely girlfriend,' she told Dilly with a guilty smile. 'And I'm terribly sorry to admit that I tried to put him off when he first went after you.'

'You did?'

'I'd heard – well – a pack of lies. You suit him perfectly.'

Dilly wished she could be so sure.

But there was no denying that their sex life was off the scale in terms of adrenaline and adventure. He was an al fresco addict – not easy in the bleakest months of winter, and yet he knew every cosy, deserted barn in the valley and just how to keep warm in them.

'A lifetime's hunting,' he explained. 'It's called blue-cock sex.'

And so Dilly found herself stripped and straddled in pheasant coops and sheep shelters, Dutch barns and hay stores on a daily basis.

Her mother complained as the muddy clothes piled up beside the broken washing machine.

'You were just like this as a little girl. That man's turning you into a tomboy.'

Dilly thought there was very little tomboyish about being ravished by a known cad in an old Cotswold stone barn, but said nothing.

While her sex life took off, her text life remained wonderfully comforting, too, as she and Magnus exchanged the usual nonsenses, quotes and lyric ideas day and night, a creative habit they couldn't break.

Yet being in a foursome so often meant that the two could no longer analyse and dissect their relationships as often as they had. They were mostly reduced to meaningful glances of empathy or amusement. Magnus was good at administering lovely split-second hugs when the twins were out of the room, but these felt strangely guilty, the unspoken sub-text between them too close to the surface when their hearts were beating just a few layers of ribs, muscle, skin and clothes apart. Texts were easier than sub-texts.

Nell dominated him totally, but he didn't seem to mind. He didn't tell her off for drinking and smoking too much as he did Dilly. He also refused to take the constant bait she fed him for fights. His easy-going humour was the perfect complement to her reckless *joie de vivre* and spikiness.

Dilly, who generally avoided confrontation, apart from with her mother, was astonished by how far Nell was prepared to push it to try to get a rise out of him.

'You know I'll dump you straight after the ball,' she said one night after he'd told her off for putting a full wine glass on top of an amp.

'If that's what you want.'

'Wouldn't it bother you?'

'Of course it would. I'd be devastated.'

'Would you write a song about it?'

'Probably.'

'I hope it'll be called *She Was Too Good For Me*.'

'Absolutely.'

'I am, you know.'

'You are.'

'Face it – I'm better looking, better in bed, better connected, better educated, better dressed, better at partying . . .'

'You are better by far.'

Magnus would never rise, driving Nell demented with the effort of trying to get him to snap.

'Why d'you do it?' Dilly asked her when they were alone.

'It makes for amazing sex. That's when he gets his own back.'

'But don't you think it gets him down?'

'Why should it?'

'I'd hate being put down all the time like that.'

'Of course you would. You're a girl. It only works our way around, tackling that great male ego. You should try it with Flipper – put him in his place more.'

'I don't think so.'

'He'd love it, believe me. It'll make the sex fantastic.'

'Fantastic sex is the least of our problems. Fantastic conversations is where we fall short.'

'Oh God, you don't want to actually *talk* to him, do you? Forget it. That's a girl thing, too. *We* can do that.'

And Dilly and Nell talked a lot. But not as Dilly longed to talk. Nell was great at anecdotes. 'I once had a boyfriend who . . .' was a common first line. She was equally good at doling out her extreme form of advice. But she didn't really listen, and she never empathised.

As the days passed and rehearsals went on later and later into the night, Dilly exchanged more and more meaningful, happy-sad looks with Magnus.

She was secretly certain that the way Nell treated him wasn't the best way to his heart, however smitten he seemed. She started to wonder if he was just in lust too. But the amazing song that he had written, a song they now rehearsed as a group every day, was a constant reminder that he had to love Nell. Only love could write chords that passionate and could sing with such meaning.

And because Nell had claimed it so emphatically as her own, Dilly never dared dally with the truth behind the words that she now sang alongside Magnus, their voices harmonising so perfectly despite the howling discord in their love-lives.

She sought advice, as ever, from Ellen.

'If Flipper intimidates you and you can't talk to him, he's not really making you happy, is he?'

'None of my boyfriends has ever made me happy exactly.'

'I thought Rory did?'

'For a bit. He's a genuinely nice guy, but he's still one of Flipper's gang and they have a lot in common – the drinking and fast living and treating sex as a sport. Isn't Spurs the same?'

Ellen laughed. 'Maybe. But he's not like that with me.'

'You've tamed him then?'

'God, no. He can never be tamed. I think when we fell in love, we both landed up somewhere we wanted to stay.'

'Falling not flying,' Dilly murmured cryptically. 'Landing not looning.'

'Are they song lyrics?'

She shook her head. 'Flipper says he loves me.'

'And do you think he means it?'

'Not for a moment; not the way I understand love.'

'And do you love him?'

Dilly rubbed her face. 'I didn't think so, but right now I feel – so full of . . . something. Hard to explain. Like having head-rush and heart-spin and this crazy high all the time.'

'Could be love.' Ellen looked down at her uncomfortable bump. 'Could be indigestion.'

'I don't think it's indigestion. I can't eat.'

'Then it sounds suspiciously like love. Or at least infatuation.'

'Why do they call it in*fatu*ation when it makes you thin?'

Ellen laughed and then cocked her head as she studied Dilly properly with her sports therapist's hat on. 'You are looking much better. Fitter.'

'Not according to Flipper although getting fitter was his idea in the first place. He actually likes the extra weight. He keeps complaining that my boobs are shrinking.'

'Wow. Forget everything I've said. That man is one in a million.'

Dilly grinned.

'Okay, here's the plan.' Ellen narrowed her eyes as she pondered Dilly's problem in hand. 'Get him to take you out to dinner in a fabulous restaurant. That way, he fattens you up a bit and you might be able to get him to talk to you, too – away from practical distractions like music and horses.'

'He doesn't do dates,' Dilly remembered.

'So? You do. Make *him* do too. For you.' Ellen had been reading too many books on simple logic for babies.

Simple logic for babies didn't work on Dilly.

'Even better!' She laughed, clapping her hands. 'I could cook a romantic meal for him. I *love* cooking!'

'Where would you host it?' Ellen asked gently, knowing full well that, however much Dilly loved cooking lavish meals, she was hopeless at it.

'I can get rid of Mum for the night.'

'And Basil?'

'You're right,' she nodded excitedly. 'I'll have to suggest his place. I'm sure Nell can make herself scarce – she practically lives in the Wyck Farm annexe with Magnus now anyway. I'll have a word.'

At the mention of Magnus's name, Ellen couldn't contain herself any longer. She'd been playing good fairy far too long.

'That amazing song.' She tried to be subtle. 'The one Magnus wrote for your birthday . . .'

'He didn't write it for my birthday. He just performed it there.'

'Okay, but you know the song I mean?' Ellen sighed. 'That beautiful song.'

'*Jealousy.*'

'Is that what it's called?'

'Yes – it was originally called something else apparently, but Mags changed the name because it was too "flowery".' She giggled as she remembered him saying it, all gruff and manly for once.

'It quotes a poem,' Ellen went on, trying to keep Dilly focused, knowing that when she chattered inanely she was hiding the truth from herself and everybody else.

'Wordsworth poems – several, I think.' Dilly nodded. 'He was throwing all sorts of ideas and quotes around when he first looked for this particular song. We both were. In fact at one point—'

'*Which* Wordsworth poems?' Ellen interrupted.

Dilly scratched her head, muttering her way through the lyrics.

'Only, Spurs and I can't agree where one particular line comes from.' Ellen pressed her thumbs to her mouth and crossed her forefingers over her nose. 'The one about a heart filling with pleasure.'

'Oh, that's from *I Wandered Lonely as a Cloud*!' Dilly explained.

'And what does Wordsworth find when he wanders lonely as a cloud?' Ellen laboured the point, knowing that Dilly already knew, already lost sleep over it and cried over it and delighted over it, but didn't trust herself enough to ever admit it out loud.

'Daffodils,' she said quietly. 'He finds daffodils.'

'That's flowery.' Ellen opened her arms and Dilly gratefully curled up into them, cheek resting on Heshee.

'I'm not going to tell you what to do.' Ellen kissed the top of her head. 'But I am going to tell you to do *something*.'

'I am. I'm cooking a romantic meal for Flipper,' Dilly said in a small voice.

'You don't love him, Dilly.'

'I love Bottom.'

'You love Magnus.'

Dilly didn't deny it.

17

The romantic meal – AKA Dilly's covert mission to uncover some truths – was hijacked from her grasp as soon as she mentioned the idea of dinner in the annexe to Nell, who immediately took the plan to include her and Magnus. Nell hated missing out. And, despite Ellen's wise advice to talk to Flipper alone, Dilly secretly wanted them there so much too that she couldn't bring herself to suggest it should just be *à deux* when Nell was already offering to help with the catering and writing a list to take to Waitrose. She seemed almost more excited by the whole idea than Dilly had been.

'I'll do starters and pud, you can do the main course. We can prep it in advance in Mummy's kitchen and just heat it up again up in the attic flat. We'll raid Daddy's wine cellar – he never notices as long as we don't touch the clarets – and we'll light a fire and loads of candles. I know it's a bit cold up there, but it can be seriously atmospheric. The boys will love it.'

Dilly caved in, as always.

Cooking under the long, noble nose of Dibs Cottrell was terrifying. The twins' mother was a whip-thin Irish matriarch with a white lightning stripe through her black hair and contrasting thundery black streaks through her grey eyes. Dilly found her Mrs Danvers gothic.

In truth, Dibs was a kind-hearted stalwart whose only weakness was total impatience with dithering. And Dilly was the queen of dithering, particularly when she was cooking. A clash was inevitable.

'Oh, for God's sake, girl, you can't expect the meat to stay tender if you brown it that slowly! Let me.'

Dilly felt like a gauche six-year-old who had messed up making flapjacks as Dibs took over, creating the most tender wined beef stew imaginable.

Giggling at the vast refectory table while she decorated her poached pears with sugared rosemary sprigs, Nell said nothing. Her own mushroom soup, swimming with cream and Madeira, was a triumph, largely because she'd bought it ready-made, as she had the poached pears. The only extra ingredient she had added to both was lashings of Pheely's home-grown sensimilla, but her mother and Dilly were blissfully unaware of this.

When Flipper covered his glass as they sat down to eat later, Dilly and Nell both looked at him in horror.

He raised his eyebrows innocently.

'I thought you knew I'm on call tonight?'

Dilly's heart sank. If Flipper was the vet on call, his female clients always seemed to get wind of it and he was called out endlessly, as every equine in the county swooned unexpectedly late at night and needed King Gorgeous to save it.

She had compromised like mad, planned endlessly, cooked what she could under Dibs's beady eyes, pampered herself silly and spent a fortune on the food. Now it was all in vain. Flipper would no doubt disappear in moments to deal with a colic that could last all night.

Across the table, Magnus cupped his wine glass and watched them over it. Even though she had her head turned away from him so that her face was hidden, he knew just from the way Dilly had it angled, from the line of her shoulders and the curve of her back that she was close to tears.

'I told you I was cooking a special meal tonight, Flipper.' She swallowed down the lump in her throat. 'Thursday night.'

'I know, and I told you I'd be on call.'

She shook her head emphatically, too upset to speak, remembering the conversation exactly.

Flipper shrugged unapologetically.

'This soup looks fantastic.' He lifted his spoon.

'You can't have any!' Nell whisked his bowl away.

'Give that back!'

'No.'

The twins glared at one another for a moment.

Dilly gazed up at Nell in wonder and appreciation, proud to be avenged so righteously.

Magnus watched Nell suspiciously.

Flipper just looked highly indignant.

'I'm on call.' He raised his palms. 'I'm sorry I obviously forgot to mention it. I save horses' lives for a living. Please don't punish me by taking my food away.'

Nell shook her head stubbornly. 'It's got tons of Madeira in it. Practically ten per cent proof. Too risky.'

'I'm sure I'll be okay with a bowl of soup.'

'No you won't!'

As they started scrapping across the table at one another in traditional fashion, Dilly and Magnus caught one another's eyes in just as customary a fashion. Dilly took the silent hug his eyes were offering her across the table and sent back a hug in return.

Nell had obviously told him to dress up, she realised. He was wearing a black cashmere sweater and snug honey-coloured cords. His blond mop flopped, freshly washed, into his eyes and he'd even shaved.

'You look nice.' She smiled.

'Sorry?' He cupped his hand to his ear as the twins yelled more loudly at one another, now wrestling with the soup bowl.

'You look nice!' She raised her voice.

To her surprise, he flushed. 'You too. I love—'

'Let go of the soup bowl, you bastard!'

'Give it to me, you little bitch!'

'– the hair.' Magnus finished.

It was Dilly's turn to flush. Flipper hadn't even noticed the way that her hair was piled up on her head with a small, decorative swarm of glittering butterfly clips. Nell had done it for her, easing out her blonde tresses to fall seductively across her face and throat. It was pure pre-Raphaelite heaven and quite the most sophisticated Dilly could remember looking, especially matched with the little blue velvet dress Nell had lent her which she had been amazed she could fit into, until Nell pointed out that it belonged to her plump sister Phoney. Nell loved dressing up Dilly, like a doll. She could spend hours playing with her hair and making up her face. Dilly found it embarrassing, but the end effect was undeniably amazing and far better than she could ever hope to achieve.

Such a shame it was wasted on its target, who seemed far more obsessed with mushroom soup.

'I am fucking hungry!' Flipper was yelling as they continued wrestling the bowl. 'I haven't eaten all day.'

'I'll fetch you some cheese!'

Dilly and Magnus tangled gazes and laughed as they tucked into the soup, which was delicious, admittedly very boozy and laced with a curious earthy top-note.

They exchanged appreciative looks now.

'Truffles?' Magnus mouthed across the table at Dilly, still pointedly ignoring the screaming.

Dilly glanced down at the little brown flakes which peppered the creamy concoction and recognised the taste straightaway. The soup was absolutely laced with the stuff. It was no wonder Nell didn't want Flipper to eat it. He'd be totally stoned within the hour.

She chewed her lip as she caught Magnus's eye again and then nodded vaguely. It was delicious soup. If she told him it was packed with dope, he'd probably whip *her* bowl away too. She needed comfort food right now. And she needed the lovely, euphoric anaesthesia of dope. She glanced up at Flipper just in time to see a bowl of soup fly across the room and splat against a skirting board

'Now look what you've done!' Flipper howled, as the soupy mess was eagerly addressed by his hairy grey mongrel Mutt and poor, poppy-eyed Milo, who was wearing a miniature superman outfit.

Now in such a sanctimonious male strop that he was even prepared to do housework to prove his martyred status, Flipper ordered the dogs away and cleared up the shattered crockery himself.

'Problem solved.' Nell settled back in her chair, flapped her napkin back across her lap and, smiling widely, started sipping her own soup. 'I once had a boyfriend who got banned from driving after a particularly alcoholic bortsch, so I am very vigilant now. Enjoying?' Her incandescent eyes twinkled between Magnus and Dilly.

'Delicious.' Magnus gazed at her in open admiration.

'Yummy,' Dilly muttered guiltily, watching Flipper throwing the crockery into the waste-paper basket before stalking back to the table and ripping into the bread.

'What's the main course?' he asked her tetchily.

'Boeuf Bourguignon.'

'With pears poached in spiced red wine for pud,' Nell added.

'Great! I guess I'm on bread and cheese all night then.'

His phone rang.

'Cottrell . . . yes . . . how long? I'll be there in twenty minutes.' Without further explanation or a farewell kiss for Dilly, he was gone.

Deflated beyond belief, back in gooseberry mode, her night ruined, Dilly picked her way through the main course.

'This is the most tender beef I've ever eaten.' Magnus tried to cheer her up.

'Nell's mum cooked it.'

'C'mon, Dills, you did most of it.' Nell joined in the bolstering.

She shrugged, snorted, and started to see the funny side, realising the doped soup was starting to kick in.

'Doesn't Dilly look gorgeous tonight, Mags?' Nell continued on the ego-boosting mission.

'Beautiful.' Magnus nodded. 'As always.' He smiled across at Dilly and then remembered to add, 'You both look beautiful.'

'Aren't you the lucky one?' Nell laughed, watching him closely. 'You have us both to yourself.'

'My beautiful laydees.' He adopted a smarmy Essex accent as he shrugged and opened his hands. 'My gels.' He was frighteningly convincing as a pimp.

Dilly burst into laughter.

'We'll give you a good time, little laydee,' Nell joined in the joke, running a finger along Dilly's cheek. 'We'll rob you blind and send you out on the streets, but we'll never leave you, sweetheart.'

'I'm touched.' She looked at them both, the tears in her eyes grateful as well as mirthful.

'We know you're a bit touched.' Nell leaned against her and they collapsed into more laughter.

Pretty soon they were all laughing at anything. The dope took them over. Topped up with vast quantities of Piggy Cottrell's finest burgundy, they didn't take long to reach the point of no return. The poached pears were a killer.

'Don't tell me you've put truffles in this too?' Magnus ate his greedily.

Nell and Dilly collapsed into laughter.

Afterwards, backs propped against the sofa as they lined up in front of the fire with dogs on laps and brandies in hand, the three stared contentedly and dizzily at the flames, laughter almost unbridled.

When Dilly realised that she was the only one still laughing, she turned to see Magnus and Nell kissing. For a moment she was transfixed by how beautiful they looked together in the firelight, her own live porn movie.

Then she looked away guiltily, trying to stumble to her feet to discreetly head off and clear up the supper débris. But she was far too drunk to make it upright in one and, after flopping around like a fish for a moment or two, she realised that somebody was holding her arm.

'Where're you going?' Nell pulled her back down beside her.

'I thought I'd just wash—'

'Stay.' Magnus waved his arms around expansively, looking blue-sky-eyed and completely out of it, his lovely wide smile wider than ever. 'We were all having such a great chat.' He sagged back against the base of the sofa and patted Dilly's leg companionably. Or was it Nell's?

When Nell crawled away to change the CD, leaving a gap in the middle of the sofa, Magnus bowed sideways against Dilly and, finding he couldn't straighten up again, nestled his head into her velvet belly, looking up at her.

'You're beautiful,' he mouthed.

Dilly gazed down at him light-headedly.

His wide smile widened wider than she had ever seen it. 'I love you.'

Suddenly Damien Rice's voice filled the room, impossibly sexy, impossibly wise.

Nell settled back down in front of them with her back to the fire, folding her legs over Magnus's, snuggling up to Dilly too and refilling their glasses.

Afterwards, Dilly couldn't pinpoint the moment it started. She remembered her head spinning and her heart thumping, the music that surrounded her filling her up with emotion of such equal happiness and sadness that she felt poised at the centre of a great set of glimmering copper scales like the ones in Dibs Cottrell's kitchen, with Magnus and Nell balanced on either side, her perfect complements. The magic ingredients, combining to make her feel loved and relaxed and high. Her recipe for disaster.

She remembered a hand stroking her cheek. Was it Magnus's or Nell's? Then another hand had danced along her thigh, searching its way to the hollow of her hip. When a third hand joined in, tracing the line of her collarbone, nothing much added up.

She remembered feeling so turned on that she had flushed a deep red, felt her breath failing her, felt a beat thrumming between her legs like an electric current.

She remembered being kissed; a strangely familiar kiss. A wonderful kiss. Tongue then lips then laughter. A Flipper kiss.

But Flipper hadn't been there. His eyes had looked into hers, the same sportsmanship, mirth and cruelty. But Flipper hadn't been there.

She remembered kissing another set of lips. They had tasted so sweet, the tongue that had danced alongside hers so succulent she'd wanted it to stay in her mouth for ever as a thirst-quenching treat.

Afterwards, as those recipe for disaster scales slowly fell from her eyes, other memories flashed back to haunt her.

Still kissing those sweet, heavenly lips and dancing two happy tongues together while her legs were parted and another soft tongue drew circles and spirals from thigh to thigh to hip to pip.

Later, her own mouth tasting and exploring a whole new

landscape of delicious little folds and slippery crevices while her back arched against a hand that ran down her spine, her buttocks rose to meet another's hips and her legs parted to let in a friend and lover and fantasy. A new body inside hers, a new joy. Long fingers cupping her breasts, wide palms against her hard nipples, a smoky voice saying her name over and over again. A sugar rush of physical feeling had exploded through her, an all-consuming sensation like no other.

Afterwards, that feeling echoed through her for days. It drew a tight line from her groin to her chest. She would never forget it.

At the time, she remembered groaning, groaning and laughing and groaning and crying out with pleasure and squeals.

Afterwards, she groaned just as much, but not with pleasure. She groaned and cried out with shame. And she groaned and cried with loss.

That night, Flipper had found them all curled up together in front of a dying fire, naked and satiated, his fellow dinner guests who had not only enjoyed the soup denied him, but also the main course, dessert, cognac and post-prandial orgy.

They'd all awoken as he leaned over them to pluck a very contented Mutt from their midst. It was, as Nell would later joke, a very x-rated Abba moment.

'How dare you do this in front of my dog?' was all he had said.

Thinking back on it afterwards, Dilly suspected that Flipper would have left them sleeping had it not been for Milo wagging his stumpy little tail against Magnus's foot and then yapping so shrilly in Nell's ear that she had shrieked and woken them all. And every red-rimmed, groggy eye that opened had looked straight up at Flipper. Of them all, Dilly's had been the most inconsolable and contrite.

Dilly remembered reeling around gathering her clothes,

remembered crashing foreheads with Magnus, treading on Milo, almost falling in the fire. She remembered Flipper screaming at her and Magnus to get out, over and over again.

And she remembered the worst thing. The absolute worst thing. Flipper had taken off his coat as she flailed around naked and frightened and dazed. Like a matador, he had swept forwards and she had stumbled towards him, tearful and terrified. Then he had knocked her flying as he gathered up a giggling Nell, covered her as best he could and carried her to her room.

She'd heard his words to his sister.

'My Nelly. My crazy little elephant. Please don't do this to yourself. You know I will always love you. Don't do this to me. To either of us.'

Dilly and Magnus had stumbled from the house in incoherent shock to his car, parked so companionably alongside the Cottrell line-up. Damien Rice had been on the stereo when he started the engine, Dilly recalled. They'd both tried and failed to get the CD out or cut the power button, still too stoned to know what they were doing. How Magnus had driven was beyond her. She seemed to remember he'd been crying, but she could have imagined it. Somehow, he'd manoeuvred the big, borrowed car out of the Abbey's drive and as far as a passing space on the edge of the village before beaching it up against a high hedge, cutting the engine and sinking his head into his hands.

For the first time ever, they had nothing to say to each other.

Damien Rice had sung on. Magnus had lifted his head and looked across at her, his face so stricken that she'd looked away.

Hands shaking, Dilly had started to obsessively pick the jewelled clips from her hair.

Afterwards, she vividly remembered the only thing Magnus said to her, his voice cracking.

'Please don't let down your hair.'

Side by side in silence, they'd stared out of the windscreen into darkness for hours. She must have passed out into sleep at some point, because when she awoke they were driving home through a blinding red dawn.

Magnus dropped her at the Lodge gates.

She couldn't even look at him, jewelled clips scattering as she ran back to her little fairy-tale room to cry wretchedly.

Later, numb and shaking, she had looked at the paintings her grandfather had made, depicting an innocent little girl with angel wings and endless hope. Pinned between them were her sketches of Pod and Flipper.

Dilly ripped them from the wall and stared at them.

Flipper had been right when he'd said they all looked like Magnus.

Even her grandfather's paintings of Dilly looked like Magnus.

Everything looked like Magnus.

The following day, Dilly received her first text from Flipper since *drink?/drunk* all those weeks ago. It read, '*You are incorrigible. Wish I'd got back earlier, but perhaps best not – double entries should be domain of dodgy accountants and Magnus not my type, nor categorically is incest my bag. You are my bag. Speak soon. Ride out together sooner.*'

Dilly reread it several times and still completely failed to understand him. It was the most he had said to her in weeks. Despite herself, she felt a very slight spark of cheer lift her.

Nell texted later. '*Am in dog-house, although you and I made great bitch couple. What fun. Must chat soon. Magnus doesn't remember a thing, bless. Love that boy.*'

Dilly agonised a long time over texting Magnus. In the end, after about a hundred false starts, she just sent '*R U OK?*'

He took twenty-four hours to reply. And then it wasn't even with words.

11

It seemed they could no longer talk as they once had so easily. They couldn't even text except with abbreviations and numbers.

Dilly ached with loss. Her eleventh lover was her only true love. Sending him a dozen red roses wouldn't win his respect back any more than sending him a text could. Smoking thirteen cigarettes in a row didn't bring any comfort. Nor did those fourteen-line Shakespeare sonnets, fifteen of which she managed to read before she was crying too much to focus any more.

She didn't emerge from her room for sixteen hours. When that happened, it took seventeen repetitions of 'The house is on fire!' from her mother to elicit it. She locked herself in the bathroom afterwards, counting every tile on the wall with a crack through it. Eighteen.

Then she catatonically spooned nineteen teaspoons of sugar into the mug of tea her mother lined up for her at their tiny kitchen table before Pheely whipped it away and made a fresh one, hiding the sugar and sitting across the table to take her daughter's hands.

'I'm twenty,' she realised out loud. 'And I haven't ever told a man what I really think of him. What I really *think*, feel, want.'

'I'm thirty-five and I haven't either.' Pheely squeezed her hands, desperately worried.

Dilly's dull, dark-rimmed eyes stared at her.

'I'm going to talk to him.'

'You do that, darling.'

'Tell him why I can't ever love normally or happily or functionally until he accepts me for who I am. And what I feel.'

27

'Speak from the heart.' Proud tears sprang to Pheely's eyes.

'I'm not afraid to lose him.'

'No.'

'I never really had him, after all.'

'Quite. We never do.'

'I really want to love him, Mum.'

'I know.' Pheely squeezed her hands tighter around the small, shaking fists.

'I'm sure he wants to love me, too – I think I've always known that – but now I see I can't let him until he's prepared to love my weaknesses as much as my strengths.'

'Good for you,' Pheely rallied, impressed that she had raised a daughter with more guts than she could ever hope for.

'I'm going to talk to him now.'

'Go for it.'

Dilly nodded, fists unfurling as her hands twisted around to take her mother's palms in hers and raise them to her cheeks. 'I'm going to talk to Ely.'

'You're what?' Pheely gasped.

'I'm going to talk to my father.'

18

The lights were on in River Cottage when Dilly did her evening
stables check, and Giles's stash had disappeared from its hiding
place. He was obviously back from Thailand and enjoying a
mellow evening.

She watched the orange glow behind the lowered roman blinds,
imagining the roaring fire and a few shaded table lamps as a tanned,
smug Giles puffed on his weed-stacked clay pipe and listened to
jazz. He was no less of a heartbreaker than her own father, and yet
suddenly she found herself envying Basil his paternity. Giles, for all
his philandering and wife-seducing antics, was a straightforward hedonist with a mission to pleasure women – especially
unhappily married ones. He made no secret of his passions, and
that, at least, made him straightforward and easy to read.

Letting her eyes follow the trail of smoke emerging from the
chimney above the steely, moonlit tiled cottage roof, Dilly
studied the distant crescent of Parson's Ridge in the darkness,
just a few sparse lights on view from the hamlets clustered
between swathes of marl grazing, crop fields and black woods.
Above it, the sky was far more crowded with lights as another
clear, frosty night made for spectacular star-gazing, with every
heavenly body parading their glittering bling like body pier-
cings flaunted in a darkened nightclub.

Dilly gazed for ages, wishing that she could have a little toke
of blow to stop her heart thumping quite so uncomfortably.
She felt as though she had swallowed Flipper's drum kit
complete with drummer performing a solo.

She then fussed about, checking on Otto and Bottom, filling up haynets and drinking buckets, putting off the moment that she would set off back along the drive and turn left instead of right, heading towards Manor Farm.

She supposed that planning to get mildly stoned on pilfered dope before confronting Ely had never been a great idea, but just knowing that the little stash was there had been a comfort, and now that it had gone she could feel her nerves jangling alarmingly. She should have brought the Cottrell 'PLC' hip-flask from Trudy Dew's hacking jacket that was still hanging on the back of her bedroom door. She could do with a little Cottrell family fire in her belly right now. Nell would have no qualms about tackling Oddlode's hypocritical, puritanical patriarch.

But Nell wasn't Ely's daughter. Nell belonged to a big, comforting, squabbling pack of a family who had a shared faith and a big, beating heart and collective passions. It was a support network that gave her a magical confidence, the confidence to say what she wanted, go after what she wanted and do as she wished without the guilt and self-loathing so familiar to Dilly.

Dilly had never rebelled against Ely. She had never rebelled against anything in her life. Not even Otto, who now took advantage of her current fussy distraction to bite her on the bottom and try to hustle her out of his stable.

She kissed him hard on the nose and set off along the drive, her heart racing so far ahead of her dragging feet that it was beating against Ely's glossy black door long before she stepped beneath the Georgian portico and held a shaking hand up to the bell-pull.

As she did so, the noise of a roaring, high horse-powered engine made her turn to look over her shoulder, only to be blinded by halogen headlights as a huge car pulled into the drive behind her, gravel spitting from its tyres.

Frozen uncertainly on the doorstep, Dilly squinted into the white light, wondering if it was Ely, a lofty-shouldered mountain of indignant parental denial, ready to strike her from his door.

But when the engine was cut and the lights extinguished, she saw Godspell framed behind the windscreen of her father's Range Rover, pale-faced, black-eyed and as expressionless as ever.

Godspell licked her narrow, dark-painted lips and regarded her for a long, silent minute before stepping out on to the drive. When she locked the car with an electronic bleep and a flash of hazards and walked towards Dilly, she said nothing and kept her eyes glued to her feet. But she jerked her head as she let herself into the house, indicating for Dilly to follow.

The farmhouse was in darkness, a backdrop with which Godspell seemed comfortable. She led the way through the pitch-black hallway and on through shadowy corridors at speed, like a small, bony-shouldered bat in search of her favourite perch.

They ended up in a large kitchen, lit only by the cool glow of the neon strips beneath the wall cabinets and the dim flicker of standby lights.

Dilly tried and failed to strike up a polite patter, but commenting on the weather, asking after Saul and admiring the dark kitchen all raised no response.

Silently, Godspell removed a bottle of vodka from the freezer and went in search of two shot glasses.

'He's not here,' she said from the depths of a Welsh dresser. 'He's taken Mum to tour the churches of Norfolk. They get back next Tuesday.'

'Right.'

'Give you a better chance to think up what you're going to say, anyway.'

'How d'you mean?'

'I can help you work out how to get through to him. I've lived with him for twenty-two years after all. Sit.'

Dilly sat.

Still not looking at her, her face shadowy in the half light, Godspell poured out two shots and joined her at the table.

'You have to be cool-headed to talk to him. Any hint of tears or tantrums and he'll dismiss everything you say as female hormones on the rampage.'

'I see.'

'If you really want to get him where it hurts, quote the Bible at him.'

'I'll bear it in mind.'

'And look him in the eye throughout. That's very important,' muttered Godspell, who hadn't looked Dilly in the eye once. She downed her shot and nodded for Dilly to do the same.

Dilly took a sip and winced as the cold hit her teeth then the alcohol hit her bloodstream.

'How do you know that's why I came here?' she asked eventually.

Godspell stared at her empty glass for a long time. 'I've been expecting you for weeks.'

'Why?'

She beetled her dark eyebrows together and continued gazing at her glass.

Dilly sighed in frustration. It was admittedly the longest conversation they'd exchanged in years, but it wasn't getting her very far.

'You don't mind?' she asked now.

'It's about time you had it out with him. He's had it coming for a long time.'

'I don't want to pick a fight with him. I just want him to help me understand a few things.'

'That means picking a fight with him.' Godspell reached for the bottle. 'Dad doesn't *do* understanding.'

'He's accepted Saul, though, hasn't he?'

Godspell let out a hollow laugh and refilled her glass. 'Never. He'll never accept Saul. He won't let him over the threshold.'

'So why do you stay here?'

'My bugs.'

'Ah.'

Godspell had one of the largest collections of rare insects and moths in the country, housed in amazing purpose-built insectariums and lepidopteries behind the farmhouse as well as in her rooms upstairs. Dilly thought they were a deeply creepy sight, but knew that Godspell was devoted to them.

'I love Saul more than my bugs,' she said quietly, 'but I could never abandon them.'

Dilly nodded, trying to look understanding. She supposed she would feel the same way about Otto, despite his nastiness.

'Saul understands,' she went on. 'He even wrote a song about them – *Skin Crawl*. It's pretty sexy as it goes.'

Dilly nodded, jumping on the bonding opportunity. 'I heard the band play at the Young Farmers' party. You sound amazing – really, really good.'

'Thanks.'

'Magnus says that whoever is mixing on the decks for you is quite brilliant.'

She nodded silently, black fingernails tapping lightly on the table.

'Considering you've only been together a few weeks, you're seriously slick. It's a great sound. Really sexy.'

'Better than Magnus's soppy stuff.'

'I love Magnus's soppy stuff, too.'

'Yeah. Girls love Magnus's stuff.'

Dilly tried not to react. The mention of Magnus made her

heart ache so much she had to press her hand to her chest, and she was suddenly paranoid that Godspell could see right into her guilt-riddled head

Instead, she struggled to be conciliatory. 'There's no bad feeling, you know. Between Entwined and Trackmarks.'

'Yes there is,' Godspell hissed, her small face pinched with anger.

'Honestly not. I think this whole "battle of the bands" thing at the hunt ball has been blown up out of all proportion. We're hardly the Oasis and Blur of Oddlode, after all.'

'Trackmarks hate Entwined. We hate you.'

Dilly laughed. 'Don't be daft.'

'We don't want to play the fucking hunt ball anyway. We never asked for the gig. We want out.' She glared at her glass. 'We wouldn't share the same stage as you lot.'

Dilly swallowed awkwardly and cast her eyes around the dark room, suddenly feeling very vulnerable.

'Why do you hate us?' she asked in a low voice. 'Is it me?'

Godspell let out a snarl that made her jump. But then she shook her head and snapped. 'Of course not.'

'Magnus?' Her heart pinched again.

Godspell's small spiky head continued to shake. 'Nobody hates Magnus, even if his music *is* fucking soppy.' She suddenly glanced up briefly at Dilly, her dark eyes gleaming in the dim light.

'What then?'

Staring fixedly at her hands again, Godspell picked at the cuticles around her black nail polish. 'You do the maths. Take two away from two pairs and you're left with . . .'

'The Cottrell twins? What about them?'

'We hate them.'

'Why?'

'They're poison. They steal souls, you know.'

Dilly recalled that Godspell liked to hang around in graveyards, but stealing souls sounded rather far-fetched, even
coming from her. Then, with an uncomfortable lurch of her
battered heart, she remembered Flipper calling his sister a thief
on the night of her birthday party, the night Magnus had sung
about dancing with daffodils.

'Do they steal soulmates, too?' she asked hoarsely.

'Oh yes.' Godspell clicked the rim of her glass against
Dilly's, at last raising her eyes, two black spiders of thickly
crusted lashes, pale bodies jewelled with anger. 'That's their
speciality. They're the ultimate soulmates you see. Ulti*mates*.
And they can't stand anyone else having what they can't show.
They have to hide their love.'

'How do you mean?'

'Think about it, Dilly. Think about it while you're thinking
what to say to my – to *our* – father. You could start with Our
Father . . . Praying might be the only way to save yourself this
time.'

Dilly swallowed a dry husk in her throat. 'Are you saying that
Nell and Flipper are . . . what . . . *lovers?*' The word stuck
awkwardly on her tongue, dangling there obscenely.

Godspell shrugged. 'I didn't say that. You did.'

Dilly hugged herself tightly, trying to make the idea go away,
stop tormenting her, making her feel sullied and smutty just for
suggesting it.

'Well, I take it back. It's a horrible, impossible idea.'

'If you say so.'

'I do.'

'Fair enough.' Godspell refilled their glasses. 'Calling anyone
lovers is a pile of crap, anyway. Love doesn't exist, so lovers
don't exist. We want to fuck someone, we care about someone,
we want to be with someone. End of. All three together is a
pretty good deal, but calling it love is just packaging.'

'You really think that?'

The spider eyes curled their lashes together.

'Why do you think I look the way I do, Dilly?'

'What?'

'The way I look? Do you like it?'

'It's your own unique style.'

'Oh yeah – self-expression. All that bollocks.'

'Isn't it?'

'Partly. Mostly it's to put off gold-diggers.'

'Gold-diggers?'

'My father's rich. I'm a good catch. The weirder and freakier I look, the easier it is to weed out the ones on the make. How do you think I know Saul isn't after me for my inheritance?'

'I suppose you don't.'

'I do. King hell, I do!' She banged her shot glass against the table.

Dilly flinched nervously. 'So how?'

'First – he's a Wyck. His family hate mine too much to ever touch Dad's money. Second, he's a Goth. Through and through.'

'Isn't that a bit old-fashioned?' Dilly seemed to remember her mother talking about being a Goth in the eighties.

'And being the local landowner's daughter isn't?' Godspell sneered.

'Point taken.'

'Being his bastard daughter is just as hard.'

Dilly froze. 'Meaning?'

'Dad's never seen you wanting. He never will. Everyone knows that.'

She felt her veins tighten. 'I never asked for his help. I work two jobs. I'm not here to ask for *money*.'

Godspell's dark, spider eyes tightened disbelievingly, but she seemed to concede the point. 'Still, you're at a disadvantage.

You're pretty, unlike me. You put out, unlike me. You look like him, unlike me. Jesus, you must doubt every man who claims to "love" you. Saul wants to hold me – day and night. Wants to be with me. Cares about me. I feel the same. We're together despite my father, despite my money, despite my looks.'

'And *to* spite your father?'

She shrugged. 'Maybe there's an element of that.'

'And you're saying I can't get that?'

'What do men want out of you, Dilly? Ask yourself that. As well as that beautiful body of yours, you can bet your inheritance comes into it. There's Our Father for a start.' She placed her palms together in mock prayer. 'And, of course, there's that big house that your grandfather left for you in trust . . .'

Dilly pressed her ragged fingernails to her lips and felt sharp edges dig in as she fought tears.

'No wonder you love the twins,' Godspell went on. 'They're playing ball with you because they're way too wealthy, pretty and self-obsessed to think you're a real catch. And they'll drop you like a stone as soon as they get bored.'

'And Magnus?' Dilly asked without thinking.

'You just gave your game away.'

Dilly gaped at her.

But Godspell remained silent as she cleared away the shot glasses and vodka bottle and saw Dilly to the door, only resuming her new-found chatter on the threshold, her dark gaze once again glued to her feet.

'I have to check on my bugs. Dad's back next week. Come here again then. And in the meantime, pray. Like I said. Pray.'

Dilly did say a prayer as she walked home. She prayed that Magnus would make contact.

But he didn't, and her shame raged on. Alone in her room that evening, she tortured herself with guilty memories and utter confusion. Her head throbbed with muddled attempts to self-analyse as she tried to fit her relationships with her mother, Ely, Godspell, her new baby brother, Magnus and the twins into a big, clear diagram. But all she ended up with was a spirograph resembling a spider's web. And at the centre was Ely, the great spider whose religious fervour hid a black soul. Perhaps that was why her own was so tarnished? She had inherited his hypocrisy as well as his looks.

She fingered the buttons on her mobile phone, longing to call Magnus. Talking to him always helped her find a way through the chaos of her thoughts. But they'd ruined that now. Her heart pounded crazily just tracing his number across the key-pad. Godspell was right. She'd given her game away. Her heart and soul belonged to Magnus, and she needed to hear his voice so much right now it hurt.

Instead she called Ellen.

'How are you?' she stammered gratefully as soon as the familiar Somerset burr greeted her. 'How's Heshee? Not kicking too much, I hope? Ankles still giving you hell?'

'I'm fine. Now tell me what's wrong, Dilly?'

Dilly rubbed her knuckle against her forehead, guiltily grateful that Ellen had seen straight through her. Much as she did genuinely care about her friend – and Ellen knew it – she always gave herself away by asking too many questions in short succession when she was upset.

Taking a deep breath, she asked Ellen if she had ever done anything that she really regretted, or found just too embarrassing to cope with.

'Like what? Wee myself?'

'No – more sexual than that . . .'

'Ah.' There was a thoughtful pause before Ellen admitted, 'I did fart very loudly during sex with my ex-boyfriend once or twice.'

'Worse than that.'

'Worse. Oh, right. I . . . um, oh God, I can't believe I'm admitting this. I got caught playing with myself by an estate agent and some prospective buyers.'

'Worse than that . . .'

Ellen let out a small whistle. 'Are we talking S and M here or something?'

'No, not that.'

'Right.' There was another long pause as Ellen waited for more, eventually saying: 'Are you going to spit it out?'

Dilly closed her eyes. 'Unfortunate way of putting it.'

'Sorry. Just slipped out. Sorry! That did too. Oh, God. What are we talking about here, Dilly?'

'I c-can't tell you,' she whispered. 'It's too embarrassing.'

'Nothing is too embarrassing to cope with,' Ellen said firmly. 'We all try lots of odd things in and out of bed, and if we don't then we wish we had. Some work, some don't – it's a fact. But you should never be ashamed of trying. We're all a little bit kinky one way or another, you know.'

'But what if someone gets hurt? Really hurt.'

'Oh, Christ, don't tell me you've hospitalised someone?'

'No – I mean hurt emotionally.' She started to cry.

'Oh, Dilly,' Ellen sighed gently. 'Tell me what's happened?'

'Can't,' she spluttered. 'Sorry. C-can't. Don't tell Mum I called you. P-please.'

Hanging up on Ellen after such a cryptic and abbreviated conversation didn't make her feel a whole lot better. Nor did a text message from Flipper that read: *Is my favourite sandwich filling free for a bite to eat one night this week?* She knew that he was trying to joke it off – a fact that still amazed and impressed her – but she wasn't in a laughing mood and was still slightly suspicious that Nell was behind the Flipper texts. Tellingly, she called just a few minutes later.

'Darling Dilly, how are you?'

'Ish.' Dilly picked at her bedclothes.

'Got a bug? Oh, poor you. I wish I'd caught it from you, then I could have cried off sick from the bloody Cottrells' board meeting. It lasted all bloody day and now we have to endure dinner together – I'm just getting changed. Family has to be there on pain of death – not that Flips has turned up yet, but then again he does have a proper job. Is he with you?'

'No – no. I haven't seen him since . . .' Dilly's voice wobbled.

'He must still be working, poor sod. I know he's dying to see you. After his little tantrum about us all getting a bit carried away that night, he displayed distinct signs of jealousy. Accused me of leading you astray.'

'But I thought—'

'He is *completely* smitten. You know, I actually think you frighten him a little bit too.'

'Me?' Dilly felt her blood pump faster through her veins at the prospect of shameful conduct being re-branded as boho cool. What Flipper thought counted a lot right now. He was suddenly her moral judge as well as her sometime dictatorial lover.

'You're just *such* a wild child. He loves that, but he's had a lifelong battle with his reactionary side and so his taste in women creates the most frightful inner turmoil.'

Dilly absorbed this as best she could. She did feel fairly childish – and she had certainly behaved wildly lately, although she really couldn't see herself as a wild child. She'd grown up far too fast.

'I hate to see one man fighting over me,' she joked lamely, happy to embrace forgiveness for now.

Yet it didn't hang well with her. Afterwards, she had to ask herself why somebody so supposedly smitten – even frightened

– had made no contact beyond a text or two that could have easily been forged by his sister.

'I guess he doesn't love me, after all,' she told Donk, who was resting leglessly on her chest as she lay in bed. 'Which is okay, because I never believed he did anyway. Real love takes ages to admit. Real love takes ages to spot. Real love is usually gone before you ever knew it was there.'

Donk toppled sideways as Dilly let out a long sigh and blinked away a few stupid tears.

'Why am I crying over a twisted, selfish rugger bugger of a vet?' she wailed furiously, although she already knew the answer.

In kamikaze fashion, she texted '12' to Flipper to prove her point. Then, even more suicidally, she texted it to Magnus, too, so desperate for contact that she was beyond caring.

'I am so self-obsessed,' she bawled, grabbing Donk and disappearing shamefully beneath her duvet.

Magnus replied first. At two that morning, he called her mobile.

Dilly was fast asleep, trapped by a nightmare in which Ely Gates was a high priest forcing her to stay in a silent order.

She was awoken at eight by a text from Flipper. '*Can't meet at midday. Sorry. Take you out to dinner instead. Be ready at eight.*'

Dilly read the text in a flash and then scrolled hurriedly back to Missed Calls, staring at Magnus's name with a pounding heart. She dialled immediately. His voice, calm and reassuring, husky and familiar, made a sob crack in her throat as he told her to leave a message and that he would get back to her as soon as he could.

She hung up without speaking.

Instead she texted '*13*'.

Unlucky for some. Unlucky for Dilly. He didn't reply this time.

19

Later that day, Dilly held the fort at the market garden while Pixie took her kids for a half-term treat to London.

She stared at her phone for a long time. She buried it in with some potted hyacinths and then dug it up again to wrap it in frost fleece and green wire before burying it in amongst the new potatoes. It was exhumed twenty minutes later to be un-wrapped like a Christmas gift as a text beeped.

It was Nell, announcing that she was going to bring her some lunch.

Guiltily, Dilly texted Magnus again. '*14.*'

After half an hour, she texted again. '*15.*'

She was up to eighteen when he finally replied. '*We can both count.*'

Dilly slumped to the floor among the tubs of daffodils, mortified. She had got the reaction she wanted, but at what cost?

'*3*' she texted.

'*3 what?*'

'*Magpies.*'

'*For a girl?*' he replied.

Call me, call me, call me, she begged in silence as she read the message and replied.

'*7*'

'*For a secret never to be told?*'

'*666*'

'*Now you're getting weird.*'

She sobbed and laughed, at last hearing his voice however muffled by predictive text.

Her phone rang and she snapped it open without looking at the display, certain it would be him and that her gamble had paid off.

'I think Mags is having phone sex with one of the Disgraces again,' Nell giggled conspiratorially at the other end. 'He's so busy with his thumb, I can't get a word in edgeways. Are you ready for lunch? Promise I won't spike it.'

'Is Magnus coming too?' she managed to croak fearfully.

'No. Says he's busy all afternoon. He's being so cagey yet loving at the moment; I think he might be planning another romantic surprise. He's so damned sweet and saucy like that. He's just eating me with his eyes all the time. I'm sure all these texts are just to make me jealous, the dear heart.'

Dilly cowered guiltily on the floor, listening to the daffodils creaking open around her, knowing what she had been doing was bad, mad and sad. She was giving her game away and counting the cost; two's company; three's a crowd and the four that had played together had lost the game.

Yet, over a girly lunch of Oddlode Stores' pork pies followed by Mars bars, it was Nell who was instrumental in making Dilly accept that a threesome was a completely normal rock and roll thing that bands do from time to time.

'I once had a boyfriend who invited two Filipinos, a Bengal cat and a roadie into our bed.'

Somehow, Nell could make everything seem all right. She simply refused to countenance awkwardness, and Dilly was happy to follow her lead as always.

'I gather you're going out with Flips tonight?'

'I am?'

'I thought you asked him?' Nell fed the jelly from her pie to

Milo as they all huddled together beneath Pixie's ex-display bargain patio heater.

Remembering Flipper's reply to the '12' text, Dilly nodded vaguely.

'It means the world to him, you know. He adores you. We both do.'

'He does? You do?' Dilly was ashamed by her need for reassurance.

Nell's turquoise eyes flicked between hers with the sparkling, welcoming warmth of an exotic ocean.

'You are the sweetest, sexiest girl in the world.'

Dilly flushed.

'And you're already a part of the family. Our triplet.'

From a twin, that was the best testimony Dilly could desire.

Flipper's reaction was even more heart-lifting. Nell was right – he suddenly did seem incredibly smitten. That night, he took her out to dinner as promised – a full candles, champagne and three-course extravaganza at the Terrier in Idcote-under-Fox-rush – and bedded her in his own king-size afterwards. They made no mention of what he had stumbled upon that dreaded night, nor of his furious reaction. Magnus's and Nell's names were conspicuous in their absence. He didn't talk much at all, in fact, but they made love all night and he even cooked her breakfast. She felt cherished.

When they rode out together the following morning, he kept pace with her, chose a route that was guaranteed to give her confidence, and told her that she and Otto were more than ready to go team chasing.

'You're in the Thrusters, darling. You have more balls than the rest of us put together.'

'You mean that?'

'We'll trounce the opposition,' he promised. 'You just focus on this beautiful arse,' he reached around to pat Olive on the rump, 'and this one,' lifting his rear out of the saddle and slapping his tight buttocks, 'and we can't go wrong.'

Dilly was so high on forgiveness and rock-and-roll lifestyle that she spun Otto around, tapped her own backside with her crop and said, 'You'll be the one chasing this across country, mate!' before thundering away to lead the gallop for once.

When she and Flipper finally pulled up at the River Folly, they were hardly out of the saddle by the time he was inside her.

It was the first time Dilly climaxed with him, and it was a divine, breathless, chilly charge that sliced right through her and warmed her tingling toes and grateful heart. When he told her he loved her, she was almost tempted to repeat the words back to him in happy gratitude.

Later, Nell texted her to excitedly report that, for the first time ever, she'd heard Flipper singing in the bath – '*that soppy old love song of Trudy's!*'

'*I hate loving you?*' Dilly texted back.

'*He's wildly jealous that you were so naughty without him. He'd be hopeless in a threesome. He's a one-girl guy. And you, beautiful one, are his girl.*'

Dilly thought about the big, Cottrell pack slumbering together in the old Abbey and truly felt a part of it.

Maybe threesomes weren't so bad, she reflected. They were very rock and roll. She was a triplet.

Flipper duly texted her too. '*I love you.*'

'*I lust you,*' she texted back happily.

Then, unable to stop herself, she texted Magnus again. '*376616*'.

'*What's there to laugh about?*' he replied, knowing the numbers read 'giggle' upside down.

Dilly flinched, her happy bubble of threesome triplet acceptance threatened. She needed her fourth dimension.

'*Please be my friend again.*'

'*I never stopped. You have been my greatest friend. My greatest.*'

Dilly's fingers hovered over the buttons. Without warning, she remembered the hips against her buttocks, the hands cupping her breasts, the soft, smoky voice calling her name, the shameful, stoned guilt and love. Her whole body coiled in reaction, pulses leaping between her legs, at her wrists and temples, behind her knees and through her nipples.

I love you. I love you. I love you. You are my best friend. I love you. Talk to me again. Call me.

But trying to tap out a message that conveyed all this without threatening him defeated her. Instead she sent '*There is no greater than 11. There never will be.*' She was sure he would understand.

His reply wasn't what she wanted to read.

'*Nell's here. Don't text again.*'

With their friendship intensifying again, Dilly and Nell had yet another secret pact – and only Nell could make it feel like such a good thing. The threesome was officially cool. The friendship was on fire again. Dilly's secret, rejected texts to Magnus, meanwhile, were a cause of such guilt that Dilly had permanent heartburn.

'You did it – we did it,' Nell told her the next day when she called into the gallery. 'Flipper is finally kicked into base, darling Dills. You have him absolutely where you want him.'

Dilly longed to believe it, but her heart ruled her mouth as always. 'You didn't plan this all along did you?'

'Of course not! I didn't plan anything – I just enjoyed everything. Happenstance.'

She braced herself to ask the question pounding through her head. 'And Magnus?'

'He adores me. We both enjoyed it.'

She felt a confused pip of hope, guilt and betrayal lodge in her throat as she croaked, 'I thought he might blame me.'

'Oh, that's because he does,' Nell said simply.

Dilly tried not to react

'Eleven,' she muttered flatly.

'What?'

'Eleven.'

Nell raised her eyebrow enquiringly.

Dilly looked at the exquisite face, the amazing eyes, at the sheer joy and vibrancy, and found a sob turning into a laugh.

'Eleven days to the ball.'

'Holy shit. We need another rehearsal.' Nell headed towards the door. 'I'll hoof across and tell Magnus he has to pull his finger out. You free tonight?'

Dilly nodded, silenced completely by the sudden realisation that Magnus must be in the little bookshop just across the courtyard.

'Flipper's on call, I think, but we can work around that. I'll pick you up around six.'

'Magnus could pick me up,' Dilly suggested before she could edit herself.

'He could.' Nell nodded, reaching out to ruffle Dilly's hair. 'But he won't. Let him recover in his own time, hey? You scare him even more than you do Flips now. Mags just wants to make music with you – and seduce me. He's Danish. Go figure! I thought they liked group sex. My stupid idea. Forgive me?'

Dilly nodded, the pact tightening, along with her heart-strings.

She didn't need to ask why Magnus couldn't even bring himself to give her a lift. How they were going to sing together, she had no idea. He undoubtedly couldn't even look her in the face, let alone talk to her. He must blame her for everything.

One by one, she read through his recent texts. In isolation, they seemed cold, dispassionate, humouring. They were divorced from the man she thought she knew.

Nell's boyfriend.

She read them again, embarrassment mounting.

He's Nell's boyfriend, she reminded herself.

When Pru Horntoń arrived back at her Gallery after a jolly visit to her parents to drop off her tearaway children for a mini-break, she was concerned to find Dilly systematically wrapping her mobile phone in Sellotape.

'It's art,' Dilly told her simply. 'I'm calling it "Con-text".'

Increasingly concerned about her daughter's mental health, Pheely had called in the troops. Ellen, Pixie and Anke all had strong opinions on the matter as they gathered on the Lodge cottage sofa awaiting Dilly's return from work.

'Something obviously happened between her and that new boyfriend,' Pixie pointed out the obvious. 'Why else lock herself in her room for hours and then announce that she's going to confront Ely?'

'I think it has more to do with Nell Cottrell. She's very manipulative,' Ellen worried. 'Both the twins are.'

'I hope she goes off this idea of talking with Ely,' Pheely fretted. 'It will only end in tears. Thank goodness he's away. With any luck she'll cool off, and I can get to the bottom of all this.'

'What does Magnus have to say about it?' Pixie asked Anke. 'They're great chums, aren't they?'

'He's a son,' Anke apologised. 'I haven't really been able to draw him out about anything for twenty years.'

Ellen chewed on her lip, battling a moral dilemma.

'The Three Disgraces have been calling in a lot,' Anke was saying. 'They do like to fuss over him. I wonder Nell doesn't get jealous.'

'Oh, I don't think Nell's the jealous sort,' Pheely sighed. 'Lovely girl. So full of *joie de vivre*. So good for Dilly. She's really cheered her up in the past day or two.'

'She has a spell over her,' Ellen said darkly.

'Dilly's always been spellbound by older girls.'

'Godspell-bound?' Pixie giggled.

Pheely smiled worriedly. 'She was in a terribly black mood after speaking with Godspell, I have to say. That girl is weird. I always worry when she and Dilly get together.'

'I thought they hardly ever spoke these days?' asked Ellen.

'They don't.'

'So she can't have been the one to upset Dilly.'

'I still say it's Flipper,' Pixie maintained.

Pheely shook her head. 'He's been rather dashing – took her out to dinner. She was very bucked up and bubbly afterwards. Didn't come home all night.'

'Perhaps it's you, Pheely?' Anke suggested with her customary Danish frankness and lack of tact. 'Have you done something to upset her?'

Pheely's big green eyes filled with tears.

'Oh for God's sake,' Ellen snapped tiredly, her swollen ankles throbbing with irritation. 'It's Magnus. He and Dilly are absolutely mad about one another – Nell knows that and Flipper knows that, but they won't let them get on with it because they are both playing some sort of ridiculous childish game to keep them apart.'

'Magnus?' Anke gaped at her. 'My Magnus?'

'Who has, we gather, women hanging from every available limb?' Pixie giggled, and then remembered excitedly, 'Actually, I have thought the two of them looked rather cosy and lovely together when he pops in to see her.'

'Oh God, it all makes sense!' Pheely was staring at Ellen.

She nodded. 'And I suggest you have a very firm mother to

daughter chat with her about it, because Dilly is on self-destruct.' Then she turned to Anke. 'And you should have a firm mother to son chat about it.'

'You tell 'em,' Pixie gurgled happily, patting Ellen's bump. 'Heshee's in for a damned good upbringing.'

'I hope so,' Ellen gulped nervously.

Anke was not one to hang about. As soon as she got home, she rounded on Magnus in the annexe. No matter that the Three Disgraces were lounging around on his sofas playing with their mobile telephones; Anke had always been very upfront with all of them.

'Pheely is worried about Dilly. She thinks you might know something, Magnus.'

'Like what?'

'Like what is bothering her. Ellen says that you two might be hiding feelings for one another.'

Sperry Sixsmith looked up from her telephone with interest.

Horrified, Magnus blanked his mother. 'I'm flattered to be the source of such intense conversation, but I really would rather you and your friends restricted yourself to talking about the romances that you read for the Literary Circle.'

Anke huffed at him, hands on hips. 'This is your life that we are talking about here, *kaereste*. You only have one chance at it. Dilly is a very special girl.'

'Don't get deep on me, Mother,' he snapped, retreating deeper into the sofa and the comforting surroundings of the Three Disgraces.

Anke was undeterred. 'Surely you and Nell talk about her? You are all so close.'

'No.' Magnus shifted uncomfortably amid the scatter cushions.

'But she is your girlfriend, isn't she?'

'Hmph,' said Magnus, who had been contemplating that status all week.

The Three Disgraces now all looked up with interest.

'Dilly is terribly overwrought,' Anke sighed, peering critically down at him slouching on his sofa. 'It seems she will do absolutely anything those twins ask of her.'

'If she's happy with that, who am I to stop her?'

'Her friend, perhaps? In the same boat, perhaps?' Anke suggested wisely.

He narrowed his eyes.

'They've fallen out,' Sperry told her brightly. 'He won't tell us why, but we're working on it.'

'Surely not?' Anke was appalled, stooping to take her son's shoulders in her broad, capable hands. 'You two were such close friends. Is that the problem? Is Ellen right? You and Dilly have feelings for one another?'

Magnus scuffed his shoes.

'I think you're on the money there, Mrs B.' Sperry watched his reaction with interest.

'For God's sake, *do* something about it, Magnus,' Anke huffed. 'Don't keep letting life happen without exerting some sort of influence over it. You and Dilly are both as bad as each other.'

At the far end of the sofa, Sperry smiled with quiet relief. If even his mother was on his case, perhaps Magnus would show some backbone at last?

He certainly seemed to show early promise. 'Perhaps you're right.' He stood up. 'Yes, you're right. I have to say something.'

'Of *course* I'm right,' Anke rallied proudly, patting him on the back as she gave him a hug before marching out of the annexe.

The Three Disgraces turned six luminous, kohled eyes on Magnus.

He held up his palms.

'She only does it once or twice a year,' he explained apologetically.

'I hope you listen.' Sperry cocked her chin.

'For God's sake.' He pulled a tragi-comic face. 'She's my mother.'

'Meaning?'

A broad hand swept through his blond curls and he flashed his easy-going smile.

Sperry sighed irritably, recognising his head disappearing beneath the sand again.

'As something of a self-styled guardian angel to the often ungrateful and extremely stubborn pair of you,' she said theatrically, 'I would like to back your mother up and suggest that you get off your arse and sort this situation out. Because if you don't,' she cast around for ideas, 'I shall personally burn every single one of your jumpers.'

Fe whistled, not looking up from her phone. 'Deep.'

Beside her, Carry nodded. 'Intense.'

Pheely was, like her daughter, a great prevaricator.

She had known that Giles was back in the country for three days now and longed to take Basil along to River Cottage for a catch-up with his father.

She had known that Dilly was in love with Magnus for half an hour, and longed to talk to her about it. The latter revelation spurred the former action. It was the way Pheely worked.

Nell shared a two-minute phone conversation with her brother as he raced between calls, but it was enough to split any atom of shared molecular structure.

He had called her from his hands-free, but the reception was terrible and the line continually broke up. 'I forgot to po . . .

team-chasing entry – it needs to be . . . tomorrow. It's on the
table. Can you . . . a stamp on it and fling it . . . box?'

Nell pinched her wide lower lip between thumb and ring
finger as she read the form in question.

'Hang on! My name's not on it.'

'You know why.'

'C'mon, Flips. I said sorry. I shared him with her. I thought
that's what you wanted?'

'I want a nephew – or niece – in one piece,' he exaggerated
the rhyme.

She held her breath.

'I share a bathroom with you, sister . . . ling,' he reminded
her, his voice breaking up with interference on the line again.
'You shouldn't leave your mess lying around, particularly on
the shelf above the bog. We chaps face that way, you know.'

Face burning, Nell dashed into the bathroom with the phone
under the crook of her neck and cursed as she realised that the
package she had stuffed between a jar of face cream and an old
aftershave of Flipper's was clearly identifiable from its label.

Picking it up, she tapped it against her chin. 'I haven't taken
it yet.'

'Well, I suggest you do.' He sounded frighteningly like their
father.

'I'll do it after the chase.'

'You're not taking part.'

'I always ride the chase,' she insisted.

'Not this year.'

'So I won't send the entry.'

'Fine. I'll call Magnus and tell him what's going on.'

'Bollocks you will.'

'Try me.'

She listened as he changed gears, Mutt barking from the
back of his car.

He was as bloody minded as she was, and she knew it.

'Great.' She saved face. 'I'll just post it then.'

'You do that.'

She counted to ten. He was still there.

'Do you love me?'

'More than life.'

'That means nothing to someone who drives like you.'

He laughed as the car rattled over a cattle-grid.

'More than Mutt?' she checked.

'A fraction.'

'More than Mummy and Daddy?'

'A tad.'

'More than Olive?'

'A lot.'

'More than Dilly?'

'You know the answer to that.'

'More than . . .'

The line cut out as he ran out of reception.

Nell carefully laid her phone down on the table, picked up the long cardboard box again and read the instructions. Then she picked up the entry form and re-read it as she headed for the loo.

20

'My brother is such a shit!' Nell fumed as she paced around the Lodge cottage lobby, waiting for Dilly to gather her coat, gloves and hat for the rehearsal that evening.

'I agree,' muttered Dilly, who'd had a text that evening from Flipper reading: '*I love you. What's between your legs far out-weighs the imbalance of your mind.*' He was getting far too arrogant and snide for her sanity. Her insecurities were already pulling teeth and hair. She desperately needed to talk to him, to seek reassurance, but when she had texted back '*Call me*', he'd made no further contact.

Nell faced her from the doorway. 'He's dropped me from the Thrusters just to spite me. No disrespect, but he knows I'm a far better rider than you.'

'I agree.'

'And he's practically blackmailing Rory and Spurs to be a part of it. Neither wants to. I swear he's spiting me. The shit.'

'The shit.'

'After all, he doesn't even know for certain that I'm—' Nell stopped herself.

'You're what?'

'Nothing. Let's go.'

There was a strange, wild edge to Nell's mood that Dilly had never seen before, and she was ashamed to find that it fright-ened her. She needed Nell on full charm overload to keep her in her happy place, Dilly-dallying with the truth. She needed her to fill her head with the usual effervescent chatter that would stop the great ball of fear and anticipation from strangling her completely as she faced the prospect of seeing Magnus at last.

In the car, Nell thrust Milo on to Dilly's lap and drove like a maniac through Oddlode and on towards Upper Springlode.

'Know why I called Milo Milo?' she shouted over the din of her stereo.

'After your ex, you said?' Dilly looked across at her.

'Nope. Milo arrived during my biggest low. My low. See?'

'So your ex wasn't called Milo then?'

'Yes he is, but that's immaterial.'

Dilly almost lost her chin in the glove box as Nell slammed on the brakes. Winded from her seatbelt, she looked down in a panic to find Milo upside down between her knees, boggle-eyed.

Nell reversed sharply into a gateway, cut the lights and flipped down her sunvisor.

'What are you doing?' Dilly asked warily.

'You're going to enjoy this.' A lighter glowed in the darkness as Nell sparked up the spliff she'd pulled from the visor.

'We'll be late for rehearsal,' Dilly pointed out. 'And I really don't want to get stoned again for a bit – not after what happened last time.' Magnus would be furious if she turned up high. She was already in enough trouble.

'Don't be so goody-goody.' Nell handed her the spliff. 'Want to know why Flipper won't call you?'

Dilly took a couple of drags before nodding.

Their eyes were growing accustomed to the dark, a half moon gleaming through the glass sun-roof.

'Because you won't call him.' Nell snorted with laughter.

Dilly closed one eye. 'Makes sense.'

'You two are so crap. Unlike me and Mags.'

Dilly said nothing because the big ball in her throat had just inflated to ridiculous proportions. Thinking about Flipper made her dyspeptic with irritation and guilt; any mention of Magnus made her wretched with jealousy and confusion.

They sat in silence for a bit, Dilly puffing awkwardly on the dope, trying hard not to inhale too much, but too frightened of Nell's strange mood to stub it out. Nell opened the sun-roof to the stars, letting in the frosty night air and the owl hoots. Milo, having recovered his composure on Dilly's lap, settled in the coin well between the two front seats and gazed upwards.

'Jesus, this is strong,' Dilly realised as her head started to spin. 'Where d'you get it from?'

'Your mother.'

'Figures.' Dilly looked unhappily up at the black sky.

'C'mon, Dilly – cheer me up for a change.' Nell turned towards her.

'What's wrong?'

'I didn't say I wanted to talk. I said I needed cheering up.' The huge grey-green eyes watched Dilly through the darkness.

Dilly let the heady dope take a grip of her, pushing thoughts of Magnus as far from her head as she was able.

'What's long and hard and pink in parts and sometimes used to put in tarts?' She told one of her mother's favourite silly jokes.

'Dunno.'

'Rhubarb.'

Nell snorted with mild amusement.

'Two asparagus are walking down the road when one gets hit by a car. His friend goes to hospital with him and finally gets to speak with the doctor who says "There's good news and bad news. The good news is, he'll make a full recovery" . . .'

'And the bad news?'

' "He'll be a vegetable for life." '

'God, your jokes are appalling,' Nell groaned. 'Are they all themed around fruit and vegetables?'

'Knock knock.'

'Who's there?'

'Lettuce.'

'Lettuce who?'

'Lettuce in and we'll tell you.'

Dilly tipped forwards in spasms of laughter, doubling up as a fox screeched nearby and Milo barked a camp reply.

Beside her, Nell didn't move, her face frozen.

'Okay.' She stared at the steering wheel in front of her. 'You fuck my brother around. You steal my place on the team. You play with Magnus's poor fucking head. You freeload off me. Just where do you get *off*, Dilly?'

It was a moment before Dilly realised that this was all directed at her.

'I – I – I –' She was so dumbfounded, she didn't know where to start.

'I thought you were my friend, Dilly.'

'I – am!' At least she could start there.

'Funny way of showing it.'

'I'm sorry,' she bleated, although she still wasn't sure what she was apologising for. 'I adore you.'

'I adore you too.'

'Good.' Dilly took a nervous puff at the spliff and offered it back, but Nell batted it away.

'Cool.' Nell stared out of the windscreen. 'We adore each other.'

As the dope stole away the awkwardness of the moment, there was a pause that Dilly took to be almost companionable.

'Aren't we supposed to drive over a cliff at this point or something? Like Thelma and Louise?' she suggested.

Nell ran her tongue along her teeth and kissed her lips together. 'Show me you adore me.'

'What?'

Without warning, she burst into noisy sobs. 'Show – me – you – ad-d-dore me. Please. D-do something for me.'

'Oh, Christ, Nell.' Dilly reached across to hug her and squashed Milo, who let out an indignant squeak. 'I'm sorry. What can I do?'

Nell shrugged her away. 'You know I don't do hugs. Finish the spliff first. Where is it? Have you dropped it?'

'Shit!' Dilly retrieved it from her lap where it had burnt an unfortunate hole in the baggy crotch of her trackie bottoms. 'Shit! That's all I need – crotchless joggers.'

At last, she succeeded in cheering up Nell. The sight made Nell laugh delightedly through her tears, although she still refused to explain why she was crying or to accept any sort of touch of comfort. And the tears kept coming.

They shared the last inch of the potent mix, although because Nell was still sniffing and battling down tears, she made Dilly smoke the lion's share. 'I'm d-driving – you k-kick on.'

'I won't be able to sing,' said Dilly, whose head was already so jumbled and woozy she felt suddenly detached and skittish.

'You'll always be able to sing.'

As Dilly got higher, Nell got lower, tears streaming down her face and into her mouth while unstoppable hiccups coursed upwards to meet them. Every time Dilly tried to hug her, she batted her away, just lifting Milo to her face to lick her tears and crying on silently.

Soon cocooned in a small, swirling whirl of worldly loveliness, Dilly felt a distant twitch of worry float around in the back of her mind, far beyond her reach, as she turned to Nell and smiled, certain it was just PMS or the fact that Flipper had dropped her from the team.

'So c'mon. Tell me what's up? You want . . .?'

Nell wiped her wet face with the backs of her shaking hands and shuddered as a great wrench of tears was forced back down long enough to speak.

'I'm going to ask something very – very special of you, Dilly.'

'Fire away.' Dilly's head was spinning far out of the sun-roof, up into the starry sky, dancing around the half moon and her starry friends.

'I'm pregnant.'

As she said it, Dilly swore she saw a shooting star skip across the sky, but then all the stars started to jumble together as her eyes filled with tears. A great, cold crashing wave of *déjà vu* and fear splashed the colour from her cheeks and punched the air from her lungs.

'Are you sure?'

'My period should have come a fortnight ago. I took a test today. It was positive.'

'Does Magnus know?'

'God, no.'

Dilly tried to stay focused as her stoned mind raced wildly. 'What can I do to help?'

'I want you to talk to Mags. Tell him.'

'No way!' Dilly's jumbled head was in free fall.

'I just can't talk to him about that sort of stuff.'

'You're his girlfriend, Nell!'

'But you are so much better at talking to him.'

'No way.'

'He'll just be all loving and supportive and I can't cope with that right now.'

'That's exactly what you need.'

'No I don't. I need you to talk to him.'

'No way.'

'Please Dilly.'

'No way. This is between the two of you.'

'But I thought we were a threesome?' Nell said in a small voice.

Dilly rubbed her face with her hands. Think straight, Dilly, she told herself firmly. C'mon, girlfriend. Think straight. No – don't giggle just because Nell mentioned the threesome and that wasn't very straight girlfriend at all. Think *straight*. This is serious. What would Ellen say? Ellen always knows what to say. Imagine you're Ellen.

'I think you should call Magnus now and arrange to meet up away from his studio,' she managed to suggest without either giggling or crying. 'I'll get out and find my own way home. If you need to talk to me come and see me or phone me, anytime, I'll be there for you. But *you* have to talk to him, Nell. Not me.'

'No!' Nell set her lip petulantly. 'I need to know how Magnus will react first.'

'Why?'

'Because he'll tell you the truth in a "what if" situation. In an absolute fact situation, he'll just act.'

Dilly rubbed her knuckle against her nose. 'That's just Irish, Nell.'

'My mother is Irish, remember?'

'There is no "what if" about pregnancy.' Dilly heard Ellen in her head. 'You either are or you aren't pregnant – and you are.'

'These tests aren't always one hundred per cent, are they?'

'I think they're pretty good these days,' Dilly nodded. 'Mum did three with Basil just to make sure and they all came out positive – even the one she accidentally flushed down the loo and we had to fish out of the U bend.'

'What if Magnus doesn't know I've taken a test?' Nell asked in a small voice.

'This is crazy.' Dilly sank her head into her hands, still trying hard to think like Ellen, to stop her stoned mind spinning.

'Let's you and me talk "what if" then. What if you are pregnant? You'll keep the baby, yes?'

'I'm Catholic.'

For some reason, this made Dilly start to giggle again. With mortifying impropriety, she snorted and cackled until her chest ached. The awful, uncanny *déjà vu* and parallels to another time in her life should have made her cry, but the amount of dope in her bloodstream had changed the system settings and was all going horribly wrong.

'Have you finished?' Nell asked eventually, as the laughter started to ebb.

'Almost.' Dilly wiped her eyes, aware that she had to make up for her behaviour. 'Sorry, sorry, sorry. Magnus will stand by you, you know that.'

'Will he?'

'Absolutely. He's very honourable.'

Nell pulled at her jacket collar and cranked up the heater as she stared at the stars through the sun-roof. 'Would he marry me?'

The sudden blast of hot air in her face made Dilly feel sick. 'How do I know?'

'That's what I need you to ask him.'

Dilly's muddled mind wasn't up to this. She could no longer think like Ellen. She could only think like stoned, confused, love-lost Dilly.

'You want me to ask Magnus if he'll marry you?' she bleated.

'In principle,' Nell nodded.

'No way.'

'Oh, don't start that again.'

'No way.'

'Please.'

'No way. We're hardly even on talking terms at the moment. *You* tell him you might be pregnant and *you* ask him if he'll marry you if you are. I'm out of here.'

Her head was spinning everywhere now. She wanted to get out of the car, but she didn't know where the handle was. Groping madly around for it, all she encountered was something squishy and then a sharp little bite on her wrist as Milo took umbrage at her unwanted grope.

Nell turned to her, grabbing her arm. 'How much?'

'What?'

'How much d'you want to bet?'

'What bet? Bet on what?'

'That you can persuade him to marry me? How much?'

'Nothing. I'm just not talking to him.' The thought of talking to Magnus about anything right now made her feel sick with nerves and self-loathing. To talk about this was insane.

'A thousand,' Nell offered.

Dilly made another grab for the door handle and this time found herself clutching Nell's knee. Oh. Christ, she was high. Far too high. She started to giggle.

Nell covered her hand with her own. 'Prove you adore me.'

Dilly gazed up at her, so overrun with bewildered emotion she just wanted comfort. 'I don't need to prove that.'

'Please don't make me beg. You're the only one who knows what I went through when I was fourteen. You have to understand what that's done to me; why I'm asking you this; why I trust you more than anyone in my life. More than Magnus. More than Flipper.'

Dilly closed her eyes, knowing that she had to do it.

As she fired up the car engine, Nell added, 'More than myself'.

Magnus was determined. He would make his feelings known. He would be strong.

He watched the headlights turn into the yard through the window, clicked his knuckles, felt his heart lurch as Nell spilled

from the driver's door, then spiral out of control as Dilly tipped
from the passenger's, followed by such a cramping fear in his
belly that he bent double.

Behind him, the Three Disgraces exchanged knowing looks.

But when the two girls rolled into the studio, it was obvious
that there was something wrong with Dilly. She could hardly
walk in a straight line.

'You're late,' he complained half-heartedly, heart thumping
in his ears. 'Where's Flipper?' His worried gaze tracked Dilly
who was tripping over everything and giggling to herself.

'On call – emergency,' Nell said smoothly, planting a long
kiss on his mouth and noticing the way that he still watched
Dilly over her shoulder.

'Got to do it now,' Dilly was muttering to herself. 'Get it over
with.'

'What's she on about?' Magnus's worried look intensified.

'Got to ask him.' Dilly was rubbing her face frantically,
blonde curls on end.

Which was when Nell realised that the Three Disgraces were
lined up on the far wall, like hookers on Rue St Denis, hips at a
louche angle, cigarettes dangling from mouths, Hooches in hand.

'Shit.'

'You all right, Dilly mate?' called Sperry.

'Mmm,' Dilly nodded emphatically, eyes sparkling. 'Just got
to do something. Don't go away. Magnus, can I have a word?'
Her green eyes twinkled at his face, but still didn't look him in
the eye.

'Sure,' he nodded, heart hammering all the more as he
glanced awkwardly at Nell.

'In private,' she muttered, glancing at Nell, too.

'Be my guest.' Nell beckoned towards the Portakabin 'office'
that still lived in the corner of the big space, its windows
obscured by broken Venetian blinds.

Dilly scuttled inside, muttering, 'This is crazy, but I have to do it. Have to do it now.'

Following her, Magnus closed the door behind them. 'Have to do what, Dilly?'

'Talk to you.' She kept her face turned away from him, hugging herself and pacing the little room, bumping into the walls.

'If it's about the other night, I really think it's best forgotten and not men—'

'It's not. It's about – something else.'

'Okay.' He perched against an old desk. 'What "something else"?'

'It's complicated.'

'I do complicated.'

'I don't.' She screwed up her face in concentration and suddenly giggled.

'Dilly, look at me.'

'Can't.'

'Look at me.'

'Won't.'

Magnus watched her for a moment, an exotic caged animal driven mad by its surroundings – and by something else . . .

'Are you stoned?'

'Just a little bit – Nell and I had a quick toot on the way here.'

'For God's sake, Dilly!' He stood up angrily and turned towards the door.

'It's all right – I'm not going to join you in a nefarious sex act,' she said without thinking and then giggled even more.

Magnus waited a few beats, desire dancing inappropriately close to his loins. But he fought it down, his anger with himself compounding his anger with her.

'Quite the reverse,' Dilly was saying as she waved her arms around over-dramatically, laughing delightedly.

'The reverse?'

'I want to talk to you about moral upstanding.'

He let out a long sigh, looking at the door, uncertain which side of it he'd rather be. All week he had longed to be alone with Dilly, to talk about what had happened, to find their easy friendship and mutual adoration again, but he hadn't had the guts to try to go there. He had rehearsed their seeing one another again with as much repetitious dedication as he rehearsed his guitar solos and lyrics. But nothing had prepared him for this. Here they were, thrown together in a metal box in the corner of his studio with a small audience gathered outside and a rehearsal to get on with. And on top of it all, Dilly was stoned.

'The thing is,' she wiped her eyes, 'I need to talk to you about fatherhood.'

Magnus froze.

'I know we've chatted about all sorts of things, but I don't remember ever sounding you out about that one.'

Slowly, he turned towards her, his blue eyes huge.

She was still pacing the cabin, arms windmilling

'Funnily enough it's been on my mind recently – what with what happened, and how I just fuck up everything, or fuck everything I love one way or another. My father is, after all, hardly a good role model and I wanted to talk to him about it but he was visiting churches so I didn't.' She finally took a breath, having run out of air and giggles, her arms by her sides and head bowed: 'And now I need to talk to you about it.'

He walked towards her and put his hands on her shoulders. 'Dilly, what are you trying to tell me?'

'Just supposing,' she peered up at him nervously, eyes red-rimmed, 'you were to become a father now, unexpectedly, what would you do?'

His eyes danced between hers, big blue windows to his soul

and to his soulmate. Then, without a word, he crushed her into a tight hug, his face buried in her curls as he let out a smoky laugh of confusion and relief.

'I'd say some things are meant to be,' he breathed into her hair, 'however fucked up and messy. Some things are just meant to be.'

Hugging him tightly in return, Dilly realised that just for that brief moment in time, she had never felt so safe.

'Do you think it's necessary, in this day and age, to marry the mother?' she asked.

He tilted his head back and cupped her face in his hands. 'If it made her happy, I would. I'd do anything for her.'

'Because she's going to be the mother of your child?'

'Because I love her,' he said simply, his gaze holding hers, body wrapped around her, his fingers sliding from her cheeks to the back of her neck.

Dilly might be stoned, but she knew that she had got something very, very wrong here. Her leading conversation had veered wildly off course and her moral standing had gone seriously weak at the knees.

And to her shame, she couldn't stop herself straightaway. As his lips dropped to hers, she had to taste them, had to feel them just once, had to know if Flipper really was the best kisser in the world.

There was no comparison. Kissing Magnus was everything – love, shame, desire, guilt, longing and safety pressed into a brief second of mouth against mouth. Kissing Flipper was just foreplay. Kissing Magnus was a lifetime's commitment.

'Dilly, why are you crying?' he asked as she pulled violently away, her tears splashed across his own cheek.

She covered her face in disgrace, hating herself for her duplicity, turning to a wall and cracking her forehead against it.

'You have to talk to Nell.'

'I know, I know – I have to end it.'

'No! Talk to her about the baby you're both going to have.'
She peered at him miserably over her shoulder.

He took a step back, his face bewildered. 'But I thought . . .?'

She shook her head and then, as it began to spin and muddle
itself again, she slapped herself quite hard on the forehead. 'I'm
just a silly bitch. A silly, selfish little bitch. I'm sorry, Magnus.
Truly I am. I've really fucked this up. I'm the world's worst
friend. I can't be in your band any more. I can't—'

She turned and fled.

Sperry caught up with her halfway across the steeply sloping
Springlode village green, a bleak strip of marsh, rabbit hole and
molehill known as the Prattle.

'Where are you going?' she demanded, catching Dilly on
such a sharp incline that one tug at her hood halted her dead.

'Rory.' She blustered mindlessly.

'I wouldn't.'

'He'll give me a lift home.'

'He's cooking a new girlfriend dinner for the first time. The
last thing he wants is his crazed ex reeling in.'

Crying and laughing and stumbling around on the edge of
the frozen dew pond, Dilly was far too stoned to take much in.
'Oh, how lovely. How do you know?'

'I know everything.'

'Really. Wow. You are truly cool.'

She smirked, trying out a favourite old tactic. 'I even know
what happened the other night . . .'

Dilly baulked. 'Magnus told you about the threesome?'

As her tactic paid off with the most unlikely piece of
information she'd been expecting to hear, Sperry lost a beat
– a rare moment.

'Are we talking about the same Magnus here?'

Dilly nodded, giggled and sobbed all at once, too over-wrought to realise that she had been duped.

It wasn't long before Sperry regained her cool. 'Well, he likes the Three Disgraces, and he is part Danish, so I guess . . .'

'Oh, I don't think he liked it very much. Flipper certainly didn't.'

Sperry whistled. 'You, Flipper and Magnus . . .?'

'No – me, Magnus and Nell. Flipper found us. Now every-thing's a mess and we're acting like nothing happened, but it did, and Nell's all over the place. She cried for ages earlier.'

'Now you *do* surprise me.' Sperry was genuinely gob-smacked. 'Nell can *cry?*'

'A lot. She's pregnant.' Dilly had no discretion when stoned.

Sperry whistled. 'Is it Mags?'

'Of course. Who else?'

'I could suggest a small field.'

But Dilly was too upset and stoned to take this in either.

Sperry changed tack. 'And you thought you'd make things better by laying a kiss on Magnus just now?'

'You saw?' Dilly gasped in horror.

Sperry put an arm around her. 'Only me. The others were on the opposite side of the room.' As she started leading Dilly away from the pond, she switched off her mobile for the first time in known history. 'Come and have a drink.'

Which was basic first aid for a Disgrace, but perhaps not the best solution for stoned, tear-stained Dilly.

Parked in a corner table of the New Inn, far from the regulars, Dilly accepted endless brandies and coke from Sperry.

'Tell me everything,' she urged. 'About you, Flipper, Magnus, Nell – the lot . . .'

*   *   *

When Dilly weaved her way cheerfully into rehearsal two hours later, Magnus and Nell were watching *Celebrity Big Brother* on the tiny portable television. From the defensive smirk on Nell's face and the depressed glower on Magnus's one, it was obvious that they hadn't done much talking, but Dilly was too pissed to care.

'Where the fuck did you get to?' Nell rounded on her.

She held up half a bottle of cognac, eyes criss-crossing. 'I've been disgraced.'

'Ah.' Magnus rubbed a blond eyebrow tetchily. 'Fine. Are you too pissed to play?'

'Depends what you mean by "play"?'

'Keyboard,' Nell snapped.

Dilly weaved across to the keyboard, propped up her cognac bottle on a speaker, switched on the power and hit a few chords – remarkably accurately. Getting into her swing, she played a scale of gothic, minor improvised arpeggios in Vincent Price manner.

'I don't want to play any more.' She turned to look at them, realised that she was facing quite the wrong way, turned again and fell over a speaker. 'I want to talk.'

'Talk?' Both Magnus and Nell repeated in horror.

She nodded guiltily.

'You're pregnant, Nell. You're the father, Magnus. And I'm sorry if I've behaved inappropriately in any way, but I promise I won't do it again. And I will never smoke dope again, although avoiding alcoholism is unlikely. That's my talk over.' She picked up her bottle again, delighted that she had done as she had promised Sperry she would. 'Now, if it's all right with you, I might just pass out.' Her head span.

'Need to lie down?' Magnus was already at her side, stopping her from falling.

She nodded, shooting Nell a shamefaced look as she tripped towards the big pile of sag bags and cushions in one corner, did an about turn, handed Magnus the brandy and then pitched into her den.

'I told you.' Nell unstoppered the bottle and gave it an appreciative sniff. 'Absolutely devastated that Flipper isn't here. Where she got this pregnancy idea from is anyone's guess. I think she's having a breakdown.'

Magnus snatched the bottle away from her and then pressed his lips to the neck, tasting Dilly there, swallowing back the same false oblivion to make up for his cowardice.

When Dilly woke the next morning, her mouth furred, she felt a great weight on her neck and panicked that she was buried alive. Screaming quickly disillusioned her as the weight was whipped away.

It had been somebody's arm, or leg. Hard to tell. When she peeked out through bleary lashes that were almost glued together with dry contact lenses, all she spotted was a sprawl of limbs.

She closed her eyes, dozed for five minutes and then screamed again as reality hit.

'Nothing happened!' Magnus leaped up. 'Nothing whatso-ever happened. You were too comatose to move, and I got really pissed and Nell was knackered and we just crashed alongside you.'

'Flipper?' she asked groggily.

'Didn't turn up.'

Taking the silence that followed as sadness, Magnus folded a comforting arm around her. But then he looked into her face and saw that she'd fallen asleep again.

Gazing down at her smooth, freckled cheek, he was cut through with such an aching feeling of sadness and loss that he would willingly have ripped out his own heart if it would stop it hurting.

Curled into the small of his back, Nell slowly opened her eyes and looked into Milo's expectant, poppy gaze as he licked her nose. She heard the kiss behind her – just the lightest of lips and breath touching a forehead, but it still scorched her soul.

21

Ely Gates kept half an eye on the time-delay CCTV playback of the front entrance to Manor Farm as he spoke to Hell's Bells on the telephone. He wanted to check that Godspell had been good to her word during his absence and hadn't allowed Saul Wyck over the threshold.

'We really must make a decision, Ely,' she was barking at him in her baritone boom. 'I told Ellen that this second band can play, but you still veto me. And now you say that God-spell's ensemble may not play either?'

'That's just a childish threat.' He watched with interest as the footage showed Glad Tidings delivering the parish magazine and having a good snoop through the windows as she did so. 'Of course they'll play.'

'They *must*. Uptake in tickets has already been far better from the teens and twenties this year, particularly after the Young Farmers' ball. I gather Trackmarks went down frightfully well – such an apt name for a hunting shindig.'

'Quite.' Ely cleared his throat and watched as Godspell came and went on screen at comedy speed without Saul in sight. Good girl.

'But I do think we should finally agree to the other lot backing them up – belts and braces and all that. Awful for the young 'uns not to have anything to dance to.'

Ely let out a great sigh as he fast-forwarded through footage of the early hours, knowing he would have to cave in for the sake of diplomacy.

'Perhaps they could understudy?'

'I don't think this live music stuff quite works like a pro-vincial production of *The Merry Widow*, Ely.'

Ely paused and rewound as something caught his eye.

'Ely?'

It was Daffodil Gently at his front door. Moments later, she was let in by Godspell. The time stamp put it at four days ago.

'Ely?'

'Whatever you say, Lady Belling.' He fast-forwarded until Daffodil re-emerged some twenty minutes later. 'Most odd.'

'What?'

'I must clear the line, I'm afraid. I'll leave it with you.'

'In that case, I'll give this other lot the go-ahead.'

'By all means.' He was already hanging up and redialling the internal intercom to raise Godspell from her lair.

'What,' he asked as soon as she picked up, 'was Daffodil Gently doing here during the week?'

'She came to see you, of course,' Godspell replied in a monotone.

Ely replaced the receiver and smiled. At last.

As a dress rehearsal for the team chase, Flipper, Spurs, Rory and Dilly took their horses to a local cross-country course to have a fine-tuning blast around together and select a final running order.

Still chronically hungover from the disastrous band rehearsal the night before and deeply ashamed of what little of her behaviour she could remember, Dilly was unusually quiet.

This suited Flipper who, as usual, said practically nothing to her. But as soon as they were out on course, he wanted her to sneak away to one of his favourite haunts – a derelict farm-house cupped in the haunch of a steep hill, with a perfect seduction spot hidden in its draughty depths.

The dry, wind-proof cellar was even equipped with a hurricane lamp and a mattress.

'Come here a lot?' Dilly asked him.

Flipper just smiled.

She felt dirty and unwilling. The room smelled musty and dank, and hinted at previous encounters.

He was already lounging back on the mattress, a willing bulge in his breeches.

'Flipper, we need to talk about something,' she said urgently.

He looked up sulkily. 'Must we?'

'Last night, Nell told me something – and I can't tell you what it is, that's for her to tell you – but it made me think and—'

'I know she's got herself banged up, if that's what you mean.'

She gaped at him. 'You do?'

He nodded. 'Stupid bloody idiot. She's done it deliberately, of course.'

'I'm sure she didn't plan it like this.'

'I know her better than you do,' he snapped. 'And I know exactly why she's doing this – to herself, to poor bloody Magnus, to us.'

'It's nothing to do with us.'

'We have everything to do with it,' he glared. 'She's playing games with us, Dilly. She always has.'

'By setting us up in the first place?'

He shrugged. 'We were the ones who decided to get it together.'

At last Dilly had arrived at the point that she'd come in. 'And now what are we doing?'

'You,' he smiled slowly, returning to his original intentions, 'are going to strip for me.'

'Strip?'

'Strip.' He nodded, smiling again.

'There's no music.'

'Here.' He picked up his phone and flicked it open.

A moment later a state-of-the-art ring-tone was grinding out the latest raunchy dance track.

To her shame, she danced to it.

Dilly danced to make him happy. Her hips swung. Her shoulders rolled. Her belly jutted. Her butt jabbed. Her chest jiggled. Her clothes came off.

She stripped a layer at a time – fleece flying, T-shirt spinning, socks swirling, jeans flinging, bra twirling, knickers propelling, mind numbed to a thoughtless drone. She stripped like a pro – or so she thought. It was only laid bare that she heard his laughter. No matter that he was already stripped for action himself – and in possession of an all-action hard-on – he was laughing at her, and those beautiful crinkling eyes were more arrogant than ever.

'I love you,' he laughed happily.

Hands on hips, spinning slowly, Dilly shook her head. She no longer lusted after him, she realised. She had no idea what she was doing with him at all. And suddenly it occurred to her that he was like Pod. He had been like Pod all along – the same intensity, sexual drive, cruel streak and unbridgeable distance. Not falling in love with Flipper – no longer even fancying him – was a final dawning realisation that she really had now fallen out of love with Pod once and for ever. Her heart only had one home.

Another ring-tone joined the dancing *mêlée*.

Gathering her fleece and jeans, she walked out of the barn, answering her own phone, leaving Flipper and his laughter and his erection behind her.

She walked past Rory and Spurs who were puffing cigarettes and sharing a small thermos. Both tried and failed to divert their gaze as a naked Dilly clambered back into her clothes, climbed back on to Otto and trotted away, talking earnestly all the while.

'Yes . . . I understand – uh huh . . . absolutely . . . I'll come and see you tonight. Yes, absolutely. Of course I won't tell Mum.'

Otto was most put out to find himself hacking the ten miles back to Oddlode instead of being chauffeured in the lorry in which he had arrived.

Dilly received a text from Flipper as she trotted home.

'*Last-minute nerves?*'

Texting on horseback was not an art she had perfected. She started to write '*I don't think I know you at all. If you really want a relationship, you have to talk to me about how you feel,*' but managed somehow to just send '*I don't think I know*'. Which said it all.

Magnus had driven the same circuit from Oddlode to Morrell-on-the-Moor to Idcote-under-Foxrush three times before he changed the CDs in his mother's six-stack. Fed up with Anke's beloved hits from West End musicals that had finally started to pierce his conscience, he loaded up a succession of singer-songwriter classics and drove up to Broken Back Wood to look back down across the Oddlode valley and watch his future descending into dusk.

Dilly watched Giles Hornton nervously pouring two glasses of white wine. It was an unexpected sight. Giles did nothing nervously in her experience. And yet he was undeniably nervy. His hands shook. His moustache positively twitched. His tan faded visibly by the second, and his much-admired tight buttocks were knitted together at waist-height.

'Thank you for agreeing to come and see me.'

'No worries.'

'I have to start this off by laying it bare that I know you hate me.'

Dilly cocked her head, accepting a glass of wine.

'Says who?'

'Your mother – and Pru, too.'

'They've got it all wrong. I don't hate you.'

'You don't?'

'I'd like you to acknowledge Basil, but apart from that . . .'

'I acknowledge Basil.'

'Since when?'

'Your mother and I have had a talk.'

Dilly looked at him askance, not liking his tone.

The moustache tightened beneath the flared nostrils. 'Talk to me, Dilly. I know you have more to say.'

'Has Mum put you up to this?'

'In a manner of speaking. She seems to think I am an unmitigated shit. Then she started banging on about you falling for the same dreadful tricks that had robbed her of her own childhood. Then she accused me of ruining both your lives. I took it to mean she was worried about you.'

At least he was honest enough to broach the subject without prevarication. The sexist serial shagger and lothario of Odd-lode – with a famously one-track knack for transforming neurotic housewives into exotic adulteresses – had a life outside seduction. He had soul.

Dilly raised her glass to his.

'Okay, you asked for it, Giles. The deal is, I love this man who I think loves me too, but now we can never admit that because his girlfriend's pregnant, and I know that he loves her – for different reasons. They're not friends, but they are lovers. And he'll stand by her, but they'll be bloody unhappy. Because he can't make her happy; she can't make him happy. They can't even bloody well talk. They just fuck and argue. I have a similar thing going on and I'm starting to wonder if I'm the only one who can see it. We have friends – full stop. We have lovers – full stop. Mixing the two is a no-no.'

Giles downed his wine and poured another with shaking hands.

'That's all very – traumatic. But it's not quite what I had in mind.'

'It isn't?'

He shook his head apologetically. 'It's pertinent – and very tricky for you, obviously – but essentially off topic. I asked you here to talk about your *mother*, Dilly. And me, of course.'

Dilly sighed, swigged her wine and eyed him thoughtfully, aware that she had just confessed the darkest working of her innermost soul to an uninterested party. In a funny way, it helped enormously, lifting her spirits from the depths of self-pity to a 'what-the-hell' recklessness. She suddenly wanted to laugh, to share the joke. Her silly teenage preoccupations meant nothing to Giles, yet they were both in the same boat – confused, anxious and boxed in to awkward corners.

'Go on then – you shoot,' she urged.

'Well, I was hoping to sound *you* out.'

'As a potential step-daughter?'

'Woah – steady on!' he laughed nervously

'I thought you said Mum put you up to this?'

'She said you were unhappy,' he cleared his throat. 'Not sleeping, crying a lot. She seemed to think it might be something to do with Basil – and me. Feeling threatened.'

'It isn't. I love Basil. I like you.'

'You do?'

'You let my horse stay here for peanuts.'

'Such simple logic.' He couldn't resist a supercilious smile.

Dilly let it pass. 'I think Mum still likes you, despite all the anger.'

'You do?'

'You are the father of her child.'

'I'm the father of many children. None of their mothers like me.'

'Good point.' Dilly wondered how much her mother would want her to say. Pheely had always brought her up to be unwaveringly honest, but also fiercely loyal – and the two were at odds right now.

She watched him closely. 'In my opinion, she has every right to feel let down.'

'Why?'

'You're far from a model father. You didn't acknowledge the pregnancy; you hardly dashed around to see Basil after he was born. But she was cool about it – I mean, you were her lover, not her partner. She knows that. And if that's all she gets from you, that's enough. She's a tough cookie. She's done it before, after all, and she can do it again.'

'I'm not like Ely.'

'I know that. At least you're up front about your inability to keep your dick in your trousers and your reluctance to embrace fatherhood.'

He laughed in shock.

'I admire that honesty,' she assured him.

Giles nodded, gaze fixed on hers, a moustached epiphany taking place as he no longer saw her as a teenage irritation, but as a younger version of her mother.

'How do *you* feel about her?' she asked suddenly.

Giles's dissipated blue eyes didn't waver. 'I think she's bloody marvellous.'

Dilly nodded, burying her smile on her shoulder as she rubbed her chin against her over-sized polo neck and then eyed him above its fluffy rim, amazed by his open-hearted admiration. She hadn't expected such candour.

'Don't quote me,' she smiled into the mohair, 'but I suspect she feels the same way about you too.'

'Really?' His voice broke through several pitches like a pubescent teenager.

She nodded. 'She just needs to learn to trust again. And you're not very trustworthy, Giles. You don't have to slay a dragon for her, but if you really do want to get the love affair back on course, some semblance of fidelity would help.'

'Understood, oh wise one.' He stroked his moustache and lay back on his leather Chesterfield, starting to laugh. 'And to think she's worried about *you*.'

'Oh, I'm tough, too.' Dilly cupped her cold wine glass in her hands, instantly feeling very small and alone and a big, fat liar.

Giles laughed on, shaking his head. 'You're a lot tougher than your mother. In fact, you are truly your father's daughter, aren't you?'

'What's that supposed to mean?'

'Straight-talking like him. Single-minded like him. Moral like him, yet such a creature of flesh and blood that you can't resist mortal temptation.' His eyes traced her body admiringly.

'Giles,' she chastised him witheringly. 'Please pick your eyes back out of my chest and remember why you asked me here.'

'Of course! Apologies – force of habit.' Giles leaped up gallantly and pulled a thick envelope from his back pocket. 'This is for Basil. Your mother refused to take it earlier. Please find a way of making her use it.'

Nodding, Dilly thrust the wad into the depths of her coat and marched out, too furious that his eyes had wandered to say anything in acknowledgement.

'About what you said earlier.' He saw her to the door, racing to courteously keep up. 'Your – er, love complications. Trust me, you're far too young to worry about these things. It'll all be water under the bridge soon.'

'Whatever you say.'

'I do. I can fairly wisely vouch for the other side – I was a hot-blooded chap of your age once, after all, and believe me – she won't bag him by getting pregnant, silly girl. He'll feel bad for a bit, but he will go on to sow his oats far and wide for a long time hence.'

At the door, Dilly nodded slowly, taking this in, repeating it in her head, hearing the echoes and parallels create a strange discordant melody like a maddened wind chime in her mind.

'I'll tell Mum you said that,' she nodded, bidding him farewell.

Left on his doorstep, Giles admired her retreating rump and then, at last, his brain processed what he had just said and lined it up against what he had been trying to achieve with Dilly – and more importantly – Pheely. He closed the door abruptly and banged his head against it.

'Bugger.'

It was only after she had kissed Otto on the nose and scratched Bottom on the rump that she thought to examine the big paper lump Giles had handed her.

It was almost seven thousand pounds in fifty pound notes.

The following morning, Dilly caught the Maddington bus and asked for a single fare for the first time ever.

'What is it?' demanded Pheely.

'A car. Duh!' Dilly showed off the showroom shiny monster that she had just driven home.

'I can see that. I mean, whose is it?'

'Yours.'

'I don't like the colour.'

'Tough.'

'It's fearfully ugly.'

'It's the safest car on the road today as voted by readers of *Which* or something.'

'Are they blind?'

'Here.' Dilly thrust the keys at her mother. 'Enjoy.'

'But where did you get it from?'

'I hot-wired it, used it as a getaway in a building society raid and then ran over all my enemies in it.'

'In that case . . . is it diesel or petrol?'

22

'*Are you a team player?*' The text was deliberately obtuse.

Dilly's heart hammered. However far away Flipper was when he had sent it, it felt as though he was sitting on her shoulder.

The urge to roll over like a performing dog was ever-present. She wanted to reply, to soothe him, to apologise for walking out on him, but she stopped herself.

'*Call me,*' she replied.

He didn't.

The battle was still raging. The war was far from won. Dilly felt she had gained an enemy without ever losing a friend, simply sacrificing a lover.

Pixie, on full alert, watched her closely as Dilly cut and bound early, forced daffodil posies, but her namesakes were as tightly closed as she was.

'Team chase tomorrow, huh?' she tried to draw her out.

Dilly nodded.

'Excited?'

Dilly shrugged.

'Nervous?'

Dilly shook her head.

Back in the market garden office an emergency call went through to Anke.

'Send your eldest boy out for carrots – now.'

'It's Friday. I'm cooking a salmon tonight – with new

potatoes, fennel, chicory and spinach.' The answer was as pragmatic as ever with Anke. 'I have no need for carrots.'

'Start with carrot soup.'

'I—'

'You need carrots! Magnus must buy them. I have the best!'

After which, Pixie, her children and her dogs made themselves scarce.

Dilly chose the freshest, sweetest and neatest carrots as lovingly as she would have chosen daisies for a chain.

All the time she avoided Magnus's gaze.

All the time he avoided hers.

Shop girl and customer, she placed the carrots in a brown paper bag, twirled the top with limited aplomb, gave him change for a fiver and returned her gaze to last week's *News of the World* magazine that had been amongst the recycled paper used for lining the veg boxes.

'Where did Mystic Meg say your treasure was going to be hidden?' he asked as he pocketed his change.

'*Fortune is in an old jewellery box,*' she read flatly.

'Did you find it?'

'No.' She smiled at up at him awkwardly and their eyes tangled together before both looked quickly away.

'And mine?'

'*Behind a black door.*'

'That figures.'

He headed for the exit and stopped, not looking around, waiting and knowing.

'Are you okay?' she blurted.

Magnus nodded, not moving, carrots in hand.

Then he let out a shaking breath. 'Help me, Dilly.'

Longing to dive-bomb her way over the counter and rugby tackle him into the mother of all hugs, she held her heart hard and looked at the back of his head, the way his hair curled across his collar, the unruly tuft at the crest of his head that couldn't decide which way to go. Her heart exploded like the early daffodil heads finding the first touch of heat.

Finally, she managed to squeak. 'How?'

'Walk with me.' He didn't look around as he turned left and marched into the long seedlings glasshouse.

They toured the greenhouses and then lapped the poly-tunnels at alarming speed, a respectable arm's length apart, a hothouse of warmth between them.

They talked, yet there was still a strained politeness between them that neither seemed capable of crossing.

'What do I do?' Magnus asked, hands buried in pockets, head buried in his high collar. 'How do I embrace fatherhood?'

'You go with the flow.' Dilly trotted alongside. 'You always go with the flow.'

'What if I'm swimming against the tide?'

'Are you?'

'I don't know. I truly don't know.'

'Do you love her?'

'I think so – yes. She's the most amazing girl I've ever met.'

The blow hit Dilly by the winter raspberry canes. She kept pace as her heart exploded inside.

'So you must want the baby?'

'It doesn't work like that.'

'I know. I know, it doesn't, but . . .'

'But what? It does for you?'

'No – I mean, I wouldn't get pregnant, at least I hope I wouldn't, until we were both ready – I mean me and whatever man I fell in love with. And then I've always thought it would be the most beautiful, amazing moment of connection, you know? Who can imagine a more perfect way of validating your love for one another than to share the ultimate gift to one another, creating a little life fused out of both your bodies – bodies that love one another so much they can create a whole new being from their two halves.'

He turned to stare at her, his expression unreadable, the big blue eyes so intense it was impossible to make out what he was thinking. He seemed to be thinking about so much, he couldn't even focus on her face properly.

'But it doesn't always work like that, of course – I know that,' she went on as they continued marching between the raised beds. 'I mean, I didn't come along that way – and neither did you. I mean . . . what happens happens, doesn't it . . .' she trailed off lamely.

'And it's happening.' He nodded behind his tall collar, his breath rising in a plume of steam.

At that moment, hearing the crack in his voice, Dilly's urge to touch him overruled her head. Her hand flew through the great divide towards his arm, then stalled, dangling around in a strange balletic half-pose, inches from target

Beside her, Magnus trudged on, face beneath his collar, carrot bag under his arm, hands still buried deep in his pockets.

'At six weeks, the embryo is the size of a plum,' he announced matter of factly. 'With a primitive heart and little limb buds that will one day become arms that reach out and . . .'

Dilly could resist no longer. She grabbed his arm and hugged him tight. He folded instinctively around her, engulfing her impulsive gesture with such gratitude that he claimed it for himself.

The bag of carrots fell to the gravel pathway between their feet.

Then Magnus pulled away, cupped her face, kissed her forehead and focused two blue eyes on hers. The open, honest expression was back in them – innately good and kind and trustworthy.

'I'm going to make this work. We both are. Nell and me. We did this – this amazing thing. We've started this amazing process. I'm going to be a father, Dilly. Imagine that?'

'Imagine that,' Dilly smiled, reaching up to cup his face too. 'Fatherhood.'

'Think I'll be any good?'

'Blinding.' Her heart lifted, knowing that she had him back as her friend. And friendship was everything.

Arm in arm, they wandered through arched plastic aisles, talking about his child's future.

'I worry a bit about your in-laws. They are *very* reactionary.'

'Oh, I'll override them.'

'Sure? They'll want the baby to grow up to be an archbishop or prime minister at least.'

'Why not? As long as he's free thinking . . . state-educated . . . creative . . . humanist . . . non-sexist . . .'

'Hunting-mad . . . shooting . . . fishing . . . public school . . . confirmed . . .'

'Feminist if it's a girl – feminist if it's a boy . . . poetic . . . broad-minded . . .'

'Sent away to board at eight, buggered by ten, entrenched in old snobbery by fifteen . . .'

But he was as impregnable as Nell was pregnable.

'You'll be a godmother of course.' He shouldered her affectionately.

'Godless mother. I'm an atheist.' She shouldered him back jokily.

'Whatever you want to be. You mean everything to Nell and me.'

Dilly picked up on the formality as they tripped past the pallets of compost.

'Can I be bridesmaid then?'

'We're not marrying.'

'But . . .'

'But what?'

'Nothing.'

'Don't you believe in marriage?' She realised she had never asked him.

He shook his head. 'Neither do you.'

'I do!'

He smiled at her, still shaking his head. 'You believe in settling down with a soulmate and creating the perfect fusion of love by having lots of little babies melded from your two halves.'

'You're right,' she grinned back. 'And one day I will do just that.'

'With your soulmate?'

'With my soulmate,' she nodded and their smiles – still slightly too polite, uncertain and awkward – stayed firmly in place as they looked at one another.

Pixie, who had just returned from buying a packet of cigarettes, quickly hid behind a large potted bay as she caught them gazing into one another's eyes like a pair of love-struck teenagers.

'I miss your texts,' Magnus told her suddenly.

'It just doesn't seem right any more. And you didn't seem to like the number ones.'

'Nothing added up then. But there's nothing wrong with friendship. We both know that.'

'Wouldn't Nell mind?'

'Of course not. Look at the Three Disgraces. They text me all the time.'

'Will they be godmothers, too?'

He laughed. 'I somehow can't see the Cottrells letting that one past.'

'You're a part of the PLC now,' she agreed.

'I am,' he sighed, looking away and burying his hands in his pockets once more.

They returned to the tills and, selecting a fresh batch of carrots, preparing to part as formally and politely as they had joined up. Only their hearts stayed together.

'Good luck.' It was all Dilly could think of to say.

Magnus picked up the *News of the World* magazine and studied Mystic Meg again.

'Tell me . . .' his eyes remained on the print. 'Will we be friends until we're old buggers?'

'Till death us do part.' Dilly handed him his carrots.

'I'll hold you to that.'

That afternoon, there was a package waiting for Dilly on the Cider Court Art Gallery's counter – a small red battered velvet ring-case. Inside, slotted where a ring would fit, was a mobile phone sim card.

She clicked it into her phone and waited for a network to register.

There was a text message waiting from 'FGM'.

'*Help.*'

The number assigned to 'FGM' didn't match any she knew, but as she rushed to the Gallery's window and looked across to the old bookshop, she knew it had to be Magnus. For the first time, she noticed that the shop had a black door.

'*How?*' she replied hurriedly.

Network busy came the reply.

She re-sent the message.

Network busy.

Howling, Dilly tried and tried without response.

Too impatient to think, Dilly selected a card from the stand by the till and wrote 'Never doubt me'.

She raced across the courtyard to thread it through the

brass-rimmed slot in the black door, driven by immediacy, proof and truth rather than words spinning through a satellite sea of air and masts.

After posting it, she replied to the text.

'*How?*'

When it came at last, the response baffled her.

'*Just be.*'

Dilly texted back. '*Be what?*'

'*True.*'

As soon as she had finished work, she took the ailing moped along the valley road to the equine clinic, knowing that – barring emergencies – Flipper would be there finishing off for the day.

His car was outside. On the back seat, Mutt wagged his tail and tried to lick Dilly through the gap in the window as she drew the moped alongside.

She blew him a guilty kiss, unable to look him in the eye as she pulled off her helmet and scuttled by, slipping into the clinic by the side entrance.

Thankfully, Flipper was alone in the smaller of the two offices, tapping details of his day's calls into the computer.

'Lo.' She hovered in the door, head hanging.

'Hi.' He looked across at her, eyes narrowed and suspicious. 'I've been trying to call you. You missed the course walk. We all went at lunchtime.'

'I was working. My mobile's on the blink.'

He nodded, unsmiling. 'Are you still going to ride tomorrow?'

'Do you want me to?'

'Yes.'

'Then I'll ride.'

There was a long, awkward pause. Having promised herself

that she was going to be utterly truthful, Dilly found herself biting back the apologies and platitudes that were her usual stock in trade and would only lead to misunderstandings.

'And us?' he asked eventually, not looking up from his computer screen. 'Are we through, then?'

She shrugged, glancing over her shoulder as two of the veterinary nurses giggled their way along the corridor, nudging each other excitedly until they spotted her talking to their intended target, stopping in their tracks and eyeing her irritably as she barred the way between them and King Gorgeous.

'Got time to take a walk?' she asked.

He nodded again, still stony-faced as he saved his work on disk and gathered his coat.

Sleet was dirtying the air as they trudged alongside the clinic's neatly railed paddocks and fetched Mutt from the car.

'Don't tell me you're sorry,' he muttered, heading along the tarmac drive with giant's strides and across the lane to a mulchy, tree-lined footpath.

Dilly trotted in his wake, gritting her teeth and hoping this was worth it.

'I loved kissing you – fucking with you – flirting with you,' she called after him as she hoofed in pursuit. 'I even quite liked waiting for you to say something, do something, *make* something of *us*. There's nothing so enticing as anticipation. But it's never going to happen, is it?'

'That's what I *do*. I love you. If that's not enough . . .'

'No you don't *love* me!' she yelled, racing to catch up with him. 'For once and for all, stop bandying that word around like you know what it means.'

'I do know what it means!' he roared, turning back to her. 'Christ, I know!'

'Then tell me who you love so much, because it sure as hell isn't me!'

He turned a circle on the spot, looking to the sky with desolate eyes before losing his dignity somewhat as Mutt excitedly thrust a stick into his crotch.

'I thought if I said it enough it might happen.' He took the stick and hurled it along the path.

'It doesn't work like that,' she sighed.

'I fell for you,' he admitted. 'Really fell, the first time you played piano and sang. Then we made snow angels and the *déjà vu* became too much to bear. You are so like her. Even she says so.'

'Who says so? I'm like who?' Dilly pressed. She suddenly heard Godspell dropping poison in her ear, telling her that the twins were hiding a shameful secret.

'You don't need to know.'

'Like who?' she persisted.

'You have no right to know.'

'I have no right to know why you said you loved me all the time?'

'Love isn't a possession. It's a verb.'

Dilly shook her head. 'It's a shared noun.'

Flipper's hands flew to her face and stilled it from shaking, every knuckle jumping in the cold.

'I loved you a little bit – I still do,' he assured her. 'Nell said it. You are too fucking lovable for your own good.'

At the mention of Nell, Dilly's hands dropped away from his face, but he kept his gripped on her cheeks and pulled her nose against his.

'She loves you, too.'

As her eyes caught up with his, Dilly tried and failed to lose them. Tears brimmed.

'Is that who you love?'

'I love her, yes. I love you. I love all my family.'

'I'm not family.'

'You are. Bad luck. You *are* family.'

Dilly threw herself into a hug so tight that the hip-flask in Flipper's pocket bruised a rib. But he didn't complain as he hugged her back.

'Of course, I'll have to pretend to be terribly hurt and embittered because you have dumped me,' he pointed out.

'Of course.'

'But this love affair was only ever pretend, so you and I will understand it's an act.'

'*Was* it only pretend?'

'You've just thrown me out of bed. You tell me.'

Dilly hung her head. 'I guess we both wanted it to be real, but knew it would never get there.'

He kissed her on the forehead. 'Now shove off.'

They would never be able to talk, but they could always kiss and make up, even through a break-up.

'Fuck off and die, diligently!' he yelled after her when they parted.

'Screw you too, flippantly!' she retorted, flicking v-signs behind her back.

'I love you.'

'I love you.'

'Bollocks! And don't be late tomorrow! You've still got to walk the course.'

As evening drew a shadowy cloak over Oddlode, Dilly tried and failed to find a comfortable stance on Ely Gates's leaden drawing-room sofa as she took her new, sudden quest for truth to even greater heights.

'To what do I owe this honour?' he asked with frosty hospitality.

'I don't want money or paternal recognition,' she told him shakily. 'I just want the truth.'

'Namely?'

'Did you ever love my mother?'

'No.'

'Have you ever loved me?'

'No.'

'Are you proud of me?'

'I hardly know you.'

'Would you like to know me?'

'No.'

'What do you think of me?'

'You're passably pretty and I hear you're moderately bright.'

'I see. Anything else?'

'No.'

Staring at his feet, tears clustering in her eyes, Dilly saw the shiny toes of his brogues jerk. It was that which saved her.

'Well, I'd like you to know that I am proud of *you*,' she breathed, daring herself to say it. 'I'm proud of you because, while you have never acknowledged me, you have tried very hard to do well by me. And while I'm sorry that hasn't always worked, that I have let you down, that I am a disappointment, I have never been unaware of your influence. You have always sought to improve me, to make me a better person in your eyes – educated, accomplished, classy. And I thank you for that.'

Ely shifted uncomfortably as he listened, brogues twitching, but he said nothing as Dilly went on.

'The trouble is . . .' She stared at her fingers, folding them down one at a time. 'I didn't want any of it. I'm like my mother – a clever girl, a free spirit. I resented most of the perks you offered because they came without interest. I couldn't stop my ingratitude, although I know it was churlish. All I ever bloody well wanted was a hug. A big hug; to let me know I'm looked after; and cared for. It takes three fingers of one hand to hold a pen and sign a school fees cheque.' She held them up. 'It takes a lot more than that to be a father. You have only ever held up two fingers to me.' She demonstrated this happily.

Ely sighed, diverting his eyes. 'I expected more from you . . .'

'Like what? Gratitude?'

'Negotiation.'

'For what? Genes?'

With a half smile, Ely rose grandly and stalked to the leather-covered desk in the corner, uncapping a fountain pen and writing out a cheque with a flourish before handing it to her, hands unshaking.

It was a six-figure sum.

Dilly looked at it for a long time. Her name; all that money. A little rectangular contract promising her a lifestyle she – her mother, Basil – could never have dreamed of.

Shaking her head, as much because she couldn't believe her own stupidity as because she refused his money, she ripped up the piece of paper and deposited it neatly in her coffee cup saucer.

'Sorry. I know you mean well, but that really wasn't the point.'

Long, bony fingers pressed to his nose, Ely nodded. Just for a moment his blue eyes fixed upon hers with respect.

Then, very calmly, he turned back to his desk and wrote her another cheque for the same amount, which he folded up and returned to tuck into her jeans pocket as carefully as a laboratory assistant inserting a radioactive cell into a reactor. After which, he closed his eyes, opened his arms like a messiah and fell forward to hug her.

Dilly felt the bone and sinew and muscle against hers, felt her gratitude explode outward, felt nothing in return.

He was quick to regroup, towering above her, dusting himself off.

'I think you should go now, don't you?'

She was ejected from the house at such speed, it was only when she was halfway home that Dilly realised she had left her coat behind.

Late that night, she drove the new vile-coloured people carrier to the bank of the Odd river by the folly, let off the handbrake and pushed it into the reeds.

'What the hell did you do that for?' wailed Pheely, who was starting to grow to love the car – if only because she had discovered it had eight cup holders and two dark glasses caddies.

'Basil will never exist off guilt money,' Dilly raged, kicking the sinking car for good measure. 'Here – buy yourself a fucking Ferrari.' She handed Pheely Ely's cheque.

Pheely sat on the banks of the Odd and stared at the amount in amazement.

'Love has no price,' Dilly went on as she gathered her little brother from his buggy and hugged him tight. 'Love is hard to earn, but ultimately it's worth nothing. That's the whole point. You have nothing to lose by taking it. Nothing. It's too priceless to have any value. Only men think they can buy it. We know different. I love you, Mum.'

Pheely stared at the cheque.

'I love you too.' She crumpled it in her hands and looked at her sinking, vile-coloured car.

As she threw the little ball of paper in after the car, Pheely muttered 'Bugger'. She muttered it again and again, but Dilly didn't hear. She and Basil danced along the banks of the Odd celebrating the value – priceless value – of being too precious to be bought.

23

Flipper drove straight from the clinic to Rectory Cottage, where Finn and Trudy lined him up with a huge scotch and a big hug respectively,

'You *will* pick them, Flips,' Finn laughed, but not unkindly. He knew enough of his brother's tortuous love-life – most related through Trudy – to recognise yet another classic blow-out. 'And the day before the team chase. There's no way you'll beat the Gavels now.'

'She's still riding.'

'Top girl!' Finn was impressed. 'You sure you can't win her back?'

'No point.' He smiled sadly at Trudy. 'She's in love with someone else.'

'Oh, that old chestnut.' She patted his shoulder comfortingly and invited him to stay for supper.

Sitting opposite her at the scrubbed kitchen table, chopping onions laboriously while she gutted mackerel with expert skill, Flipper waited until Finn drifted out to top up his whisky before asking:

'You liked her didn't you?'

'Dilly?' She nodded. 'Of course. Amazing singing voice. It's such a shame her heart's taken. I thought you had found someone worthy of you at long last.'

'I'm unworthy of anyone.'

'You are wonderful, Flipper. My bestest little brother out-law.'

He grinned at the old joke, although the onions were making his eyes smart like mad.

'Looking forward to being an uncle again?' she asked, looking up brightly from pulling out bony spines.

'One loses count.'

'Not with Nell.' Her eyes stayed fixed on his.

'Maybe not,' he conceded, although he knew he was on eggshells. Nell's pregnancy – any pregnancy – was a subject close to Trudy's heart because it was an open family secret that she had been trying to conceive for several years.

'I guess it gets her out of having to work for a living,' he said mock-bitterly. 'She's throwing her life away if you ask me.'

'And the Magnus is sticking by her?'

'Stoically.'

'Think he's up to the job?'

'Likeable enough bloke. Bloody talented, as you know. But too wet if you ask me.'

'Oh dear.' Trudy pulled a face. 'I can't see him making Nell happy.'

'Nothing makes Nell happy,' Flipper pointed out.

'You do. You make everyone happy, Flips.'

He grinned almost bashfully across the table at her. 'She wants to marry someone rich and famous. Go figure.'

It didn't take wise Trudy long to figure this one out. 'What if we made him rich and famous?'

He cocked his chin thoughtfully. 'As rich and famous as you?'

'I'm neither any more.' She flipped a mackerel spine into the scraps bowl. 'I just know the ropes better than any ancient mariner; I know how to encourage anyone to tie the knot.'

Just a few fields away, Nell was reaching breaking point.

The argument had started while Magnus was cooking a

special meal for her in the Wyck Farm annexe, desperate to create some sort of comfortable, relaxed atmosphere in which to sit her down and start talking properly about the pregnancy. But Nell had been in fight-picking mood from the start, criticising everything from the way he chopped vegetables to the amount of cheese he added to the sauce, to his taste in music and his choice of sweater. By the time the lasagne was in the oven, she was in full-scale self-destruct.

'I'm bloody cracking up and you do nothing to help,' she wept.

'I'm here for you.' Magnus took her long, slim hands in his.

They were pulled away a finger at a time.

'You are so fucking gutless.'

'How?'

'You should walk away.'

'I'm not going anywhere.'

'And if I wasn't having your baby?'

'You fascinate me.'

'Thanks.'

'I love you.'

'Liar.'

'I'll never let you down.'

'The truth at last!'

Magnus pressed his fingers to his temples. 'What can I say to make you happy?'

'Say goodbye.'

'Never.'

She leaped to him with such gratitude and relief that he felt his body clamp around her in response. Yet as he pressed his lips to the top of her head, he knew his heart was absent.

'You're going to be a father,' she breathed into his chest.

'Help me out here,' he hugged her tighter. 'Where do I start?'

'Prove that you've got some guts.'

'How?'

'If you have to ask me that, you're already proving you have none.'

Sometimes Magnus thought there was no way of winning with Nell.

She continued to scrap and bicker for the rest of the evening, hardly touching her food and stomping off to bed early. When Magnus climbed in behind her, trying to comfort her, she curled her spine away and tucked her knees up to her elbows.

He lay awake for hours, heart hammering, knowing that she was right. He was gutless. He felt totally hollow, his heart and guts both missing. Soon it would be his mind.

'*Tell me a truth?*' Dilly texted FGM that night.

'*You are in love.*'

'*With who?*'

'*Your heart knows.*'

She felt a delicious shiver of hope scale her spine, knocking a little heartbeat hammer against each vertebra, tracing a long finger across every rib.

'*And who are you?*'

'*Your mate with soul.*'

She pressed the cold phone face against her hot cheek and sank down beside Hamlet on her bed, kissing his big nose happily.

Dilly dallied, re-reading the texts, loving Magnus. She dallied so long that she lost real time.

Her old sim card was lying on her dressing-table. Had she inserted it, she would have found several messages from Nell, demanding to know where she was and why she hadn't walked the team chase course. Instead she thought only of love and its escape from mistakes.

Unable to sleep, she visited a surprised Otto and Bottom in

the early hours, kissing their noses over their stable doors before twirling around beneath the stars watching her breath cloud in front of her face.

There was a strange car parked outside River Cottage, tucked companionably alongside Giles's. Dilly's heart went out to her mother.

At least her own love was more reliable. A forever friend that couldn't let go. Fatherhood would hold his heart, but so would she. They would be friends until they were old buggers.

She ran along the dark Oddlode lanes, texting as she went, '*On way! Please be awake. Need to talk/hug/understand.*'

As she left the village behind on the station road and ran beneath the wooded verges towards Wyck Farm, the reply spurred her on.

'*Hurry!*'

She crunched along the gravel drive, ignoring the security lights and guard dog Evig's furious barks as she ran around the back of the house to the annexe's door, reaching for the key that was hidden in the hanging basket Anke had stuffed with hopeful snowdrops, primroses and frost-defying daffodils.

Dilly leaped up the stairs, through the open-plan kitchen/sitting-room, through the double doors and came face-to-face with two sets of butt cheeks spooned together on a vast bed.

Guilt and shame drenched her like a cold shower.

They were beyond beautiful, gold and silver intertwined, ripples of caramel and white chocolate, leggy and tumbled, bronze and pale skin tangled sleepily.

She backed away in horror, out of the bedroom door, into the discarded comfort of the sitting-room.

A baby book was spread open on the coffee table.

Beside it, a mobile phone was flashing a text message

Dilly felt deeper indignity engulf her as she picked up the phone.

It was from FGM.

'*Be true.*'

Dilly checked out the number for FGM. It matched the one that had been pre-stored on her new sim card too. It couldn't be Magnus.

She used his phone to reply.

'*Who are you?*'

'*Your mate with soul.*'

As she stood in the half dark absorbing the message, she spotted an arty card lodged in the frame of the mirror over the fireplace. 'Never doubt me' read her own hand inside.

She had never questioned anything as much.

Finding a pen, she added 'as much as I doubt myself . . .'

Tucking it back into the mirror, she let herself silently out of the annexe and trailed back home, only remembering to check her phone as she clambered into bed. It was flashing loyally with a text message, but Dilly now knew that the sender wasn't Magnus, so it hardly mattered.

'*Your love is true.*'

Dilly pressed Call sender. What the hell.

Of course no one answered. A recorded network message told her that she couldn't leave a voice mail at this time.

A text came flying through afterwards. '*Don't call. FGM has no voice.*'

'*Who are you?*'

'*Your mate.*'

'*What are you playing at?*'

'*Speaking your mind. Speaking his mind.*'

'*Who?*'

'*Your soulmate.*'

Dilly stifled a confused laugh. A threesome of soulmates this time. She really was having a strange start to the year.

'*You can't bear to be apart,*' came another message. '*Truth.*'

Dilly felt that tight pip of love strangle her as she texted back: '*Truth.*'

'*So tell him.*'

'*What is FGM?*'

'*Fairy God Mother. Here's a magic spell . . .*' And there followed a mobile phone number.

Dilly called it.

'Who is this?' he answered curtly.

It was Magnus. She hung up hurriedly, knowing Nell was with him.

He rang straight back. 'I don't know what game you're playing at, but—'

'It's me,' she replied in a small voice.

His tone changed to hushed wonder. 'Dilly?'

'Yes.'

'Why do you have this number?'

'FGM just texted it to me.'

'Who is FGM?'

'I don't know. I got a sim card in a ring-case, earlier today at the Gallery. You?'

'Waiting for me in the bookshop when I got back from seeing you. What the hell is going on?'

'I don't know. Whoever it is says they're a mate and that FGM stands for Fairy God Mother.'

There was an ominous pause.

'I promise I'm not behind it,' she bleated. 'I'm just as confused as you are. I came to see you tonight but . . . Nell's there and you were both asleep. Sorry. Then I came home and FGM texted this number, but she just said it was a magic spell. I should have guessed, but . . . this is just too weird.'

There was another long pause. She could hear him breathing.

'Nell's still asleep.'

'Sorry – did I wake you?'

'Not when you came here. I wish you had.'

'I'm not up to any more threesomes, especially not . . .'

'To talk. God, I need to talk to you. I need my friend.'

Hearing this, Dilly found that there was such a large lump in her throat she couldn't actually talk at all for a few seconds.

'What about you? What are you doing?' he asked eventually.

'I went to see my father earlier. All I w-w-wanted was a hug. He g-g-gave me a big cheque instead.'

'The bastard.'

'It's the only c-c-currency he knows. Mum and I ripped it up.'

'Good for you.'

'I think he's the reason I'm so hopeless with men, you know?'

'You're not hopeless with men, Dilly. Men are hopeless with you.'

She let out a teary snort of grateful laughter. 'You'll be a g-good father.'

'Will I?'

'Yes. I'd like you as a father, or a brother, or just a best friend again.' Her nose made a horrible squelching noise as the sobs ripped through her. 'Sorry – c-c-crying again.'

This was classic bunny-boiler behaviour, she realised to her shame.

Magnus said something, but Dilly was stifling too many snorts to hear his words properly.

'What?'

'Cry,' he repeated hoarsely.

'Sorry, what?' She pressed Donk to her wet eyes.

'Me too.'

'Me too, what?'

'Cry.'

'Did you say cry?'

'I said sorry. I said I wish I could cry too. I'll say anything if it makes you happier right now.'

She couldn't stop the strangled sob escaping her lips. 'Sorry. I'm so uncool.'

'Me too.'

Dilly hugged the phone to her ear. 'Is that really you?'

'I think so. You?'

'I'm here.'

'I've missed you.'

'Same here.'

To her surprise, Dilly found a yawn ripping at her smiling mouth.

'I haven't been able to sleep.'

'Nor me.'

'I might have a kip now.'

'Me too.'

'Night.'

'Night.'

Linked live on gifted sim cards, they slept, breathing and snoring on an open line – one sprawled on the sofa in the room next to his pregnant girlfriend; the other in her little fairy-tale bedroom on the opposite side of the sleeping, frost-nipped village.

The connection was only cut when Hamlet chewed Dilly's little flip phone to shreds at three in the morning, waking her in the process.

'He's not mine,' Dilly agreed with the big dog as she picked shards of metal and circuitry from her hair. 'But that doesn't stop me loving him.'

Less than an hour later, Nell arrived before any of the Lodge cottage residents – including Basil – had awoken. She threw stones at Dilly's tiny casement window to get her out of bed.

Peering out in the darkness, fighting ludicrous hope that it was Magnus, Dilly felt a great shard of shame cut through her side like a blade, certain that Nell was about to confront her with the fact that Dilly had just slept with her boyfriend – albeit down the phone.

But Nell had far more pressing matters on her mind.

'I am going to ride the team chase,' she told Dilly defiantly as she marched inside. 'And if you don't help me, God help you.'

'I don't believe in God.'

'I do. That's enough.'

And such was Nell's determination, it seemed it was.

Dilly – who hadn't slept properly for days – was too groggy to argue straightaway.

'Women have ridden around Badminton while five months pregnant,' she went on as she watched Dilly dress. 'And I've borrowed a side-saddle.'

'How's that supposed to help?'

'Practically impossible to fall off. Plus the outfit's sexier. C'mon. We're going to walk the course.'

24

The Vale of The Wolds Hunt Team Chase was held across the ancient turf of Oddthrop Hall, high on the marl hills above Market Addington.

Dawn had only just broken when Nell and Dilly arrived to walk the course, trudging into a violent, scudding wind that was dragging black clouds on to the ridge, pulling dead wood from trees and howling through the hedges and grass like a pack of wolves with laryngitis.

'The others checked it out yesterday afternoon,' Nell explained, shouting to be heard above the gale, 'but they couldn't get hold of you so I said I'd bring you here first thing.'

'My mobile was – er – playing up,' Dilly explained as she caught her first sight of the fences and gasped. 'They're *huge*!'

'It's certainly not for wimps.'

'I still won't let you take my place.'

'We'll see about that. I have Titch on side, and Jade.'

'Who's Jade?'

'Rory's new groom. They both agree I should ride, not you.'

'They don't even know me!'

'They know Otto.'

As Dilly and Nell walked the course, they argued all the way.

'You'll never get round this alive on that nutty horse, Dills.'

'I'll be fine. Otto likes following.'

'He won't keep up. Popeye's much fitter.'

'You can't ride in your state.'

'I feel fantastic. The baby's hardly bigger than a pea.'

'You might fall off.'

'It's almost impossible to fall off a side-saddle, besides which Pop is as safe as houses.'

'We'll be disqualified if we field a new team member.'

'No we won't. I'm already entered. I added my name to the form as reserve. And Magnus's.'

'You did what?'

They were still arguing as they arrived at Fox Oddfield Abbey for the team breakfast that Flipper had insisted upon, although neither girl could stomach the piles of fried food he and Spurs were amassing on the huge kitchen table.

'Tell her she can't take my place.' Dilly begged their help.

'You can't take her place,' Spurs obliged.

'Absolutely not,' Flipper backed him up.

But their words were wasted on Nell.

'I am and I will and you can't stop me.'

Nor was Rory much help when he arrived with Twitch the terrier at his heels.

'You can take *my* place, Nell.' He sank down at the table and started creating a bacon sandwich. 'Jesus, I'm hungover. Or am I still pissed? Hard to tell. I cycled here and fell off in to a ditch twice. I hope that's not an omen.'

'Jade's taking your horses straight to Oddthrop in your lorry, yes?' Flipper checked.

'If it starts.'

'Titch will load up Olive and collect Otto on the way,' Flipper told Dilly.

'Olive *and* Popeye,' Nell muttered.

Flipper ignored her.

But Popeye was already in the lorry when Dilly headed outside to travel to Oddlode with Titch.

'Olive won't load unless he goes in first,' the red-haired groom explained guiltily, not looking Flipper in the eye.

Nell smirked, hopping into the back seat of Flipper's car beside Rory. Titch was easily bought.

'We'll see you there,' she called out of the window at Dilly.

'She'll find a way to ride one way or another.' Titch shook her head in wonder as she manoeuvred the big lorry out of the gates, already left far behind by the Audi.

'We won't let her.'

'Don't be so sure.'

'Okay,' Dilly hissed into Titch's mobile at Nell twenty minutes later. '*Where* have you hidden my horse?'

'Maybe he just wandered off?'

'The gate's padlocked – you're one of the only people who knows the combination.'

'Jumped out?'

'The donkey's gone, too.'

'Stolen?'

'Don't be flippant.'

'In that case I'll be Flipper – he says – what's that?' She covered the mouthpiece as her brother shouted in the background. 'Get your arse in gear. Rory is throwing up bacon sandwiches and turning green. He might not be able to ride.'

'How can I, without a horse?'

'Not my problem. Can't you borrow one?'

'*Please* tell me where Otto is?'

'I'm sure he and his little chum will be back safely this evening,' Nell giggled.

When she still couldn't get a straight answer from her headstrong friend, Dilly insisted that Titch drive around to Wyck Farm. Even if Magnus hadn't lent a hand in kidnapping Otto and Bottom, Dilly was pretty sure his younger sister might have.

'I think Magnus is still in bed,' Anke greeted her at the farmhouse door when she could get no answer from the annexe. 'Are you all right, Dilly?' She glanced anxiously across at the horsebox waiting in her drive, where Evig had his big paws up against the cab door, terrifying poor Titch inside.

'I'm fine – is Faith here? Are Otto and Bottom here?'

'Who?' asked Anke, calling over her shoulder for her daughter.

But Faith had no idea what had happened to Otto.

'Hang on – I'll come along and help.'

Dilly ran around to the annexe again while Faith fetched her coat, and hammered on the door. It had started raining – a cold, lashing downpour that, from the black clouds still gathering ominously overhead, looked fixed to set in for the day.

'Mum's car's gone,' Faith pointed out, appearing at her shoulder. 'Magnus must have taken it to Oddthrop already.'

Dilly started to panic as they drove hopelessly around the Oddlode lanes, peering over hedges from the high vantage-point of the lorry cab, desperately looking for a rain-sodden strawberry roan and a donkey.

'Maybe they have been stolen, after all?' she fretted. 'Should I call the police?'

'Nell's behind this,' Titch reassured her. 'I'm certain of it. She's desperate enough to ride that race to try anything.'

'But why? It's just a team chase.'

'I don't know, but she and Flipper had such a screaming row about it a couple of days ago that you could hear them for miles. I think there's a lot more to this than just the team.'

'But Nell's . . .' Dilly stopped herself, glancing at Faith.

'It's okay, I know she's up the duff,' Faith told her matter of factly. 'We all know. Mum's been crying about it all week. She thinks his world's about to end.'

'And you?'

'I think so, too. So does Magnus.'

'Maybe that's why she's racing?' suggested Titch.

'How do you mean?'

'Well, I'm from Irish racing stock and there's long been a tradition of sending any unmarried young girl fool enough to get herself pregnant for a hard day's hunting in the hope the Lord will see fit to reclaim the unborn child. All that sloe gin and galloping, you know? It takes a brave girl to try it, but some fools still do.'

'That's just awful!' Dilly wailed, heart hammering as she thought about the secret she and Nell shared.

'I didn't say I approved, did I?' Titch sniffed as she turned the lorry on to the Maddington road. 'Now what are we going to do about this missing horse? The others can't take much more of this.'

Behind them, Popeye and Olive were kicking merry hell out of the container panels.

'Let's go to Oddthrop,' Dilly sighed. 'I need to talk to Nell face to face.'

The rain was positively hammering down by the time they arrived at the event, parking in a big, sloping field beside the course in which a dozen or so rain-lashed horseboxes were already lined up and a few bedraggled competitors were warming up.

Rory's ancient, rusting horsebox was at the far end of the line with everyone huddled in the living compartment, apart from Rory.

'Locked in one of the thunder-boxes being sick,' Spurs explained. 'Thank God you're here. He's way too ill to ride. You can take his horse round.'

'D'you think he'll mind me riding Whitey?' Dilly asked nervously.

'No choice. Safer than your monster any day.'

He had a point. If she wasn't so panic-stricken that Otto and Bottom were in peril somewhere, she might even have perked up at the idea of taking the reins of one of the classiest, safest and fastest horses in the county.

'But it does mean you'll have to trail-blaze,' Flipper reminded her. 'Whitey's lead horse.'

She gulped and cornered Nell by the tiny wardrobe. 'Why are you doing this?'

'Doing what?'

'You've hidden my horse!'

'Says who?'

'You know it!'

'Whitey's better than Otto, anyway. And Rory's too ill to ride now . . .'

Dilly gaped at her, suspicion inflamed to paranoid proportions as it occurred to her that Nell had planned this all along with Machiavellian ambition and gall.

'Don't tell me you've also poisoned Rory!'

Nell laughed in astonishment. 'How could you say that?'

But Dilly was too panic-stricken by the implications to be rational. Nell was on a suicide mission – she was certain of it. 'I know why you're doing it, Nell. I know you think it's brave and noble, but it doesn't have to be like this.'

'I'm riding because I want to, Dilly.' Nell snatched her jacket from the wardrobe, elbowing Dilly out of the way.

'Think of the baby,' she pleaded desperately.

'It'll enjoy the ride.' Nell's smile was pure self-denial as she jabbed Dilly in the chest with a coat-hanger, part playful, part threatening, her grey-green eyes blazing with determination.

They were schoolchildren again, the charming bully and her frightened, adoring sidekick pleading with her.

'Pack it in!' Flipper fumed. 'I'm going to declare a change of

rider. I want you to be ready to warm up by the time I get back.'
Pulling up his collar, he headed out into the rain, leaving them
still scrapping.

Faith helped the grooms unload the horses while Spurs tried
to pacify the girls.

'Now kiss and make up, both of you,' he joked affably, with
no idea what was at stake. 'We're supposed to be a team. I
don't want you two horse-whipping each other as we go
around the course. Save that for the party afterwards.'

But he soon had a fight of his own on his hands when the
door to the groom's compartment was flung open and a very
wet, very pregnant and very mad Ellen stood framed in it.

'How *could* you lie to me!' she screamed tearfully. 'You
promised you wouldn't ride today. You said you were going to
Cheltenham. You *lied* to me.'

Which at least shut up Dilly and Nell.

'Who told you?' Spurs asked, appalled.

'Me,' a voice apologised from behind Ellen's shoulder as
Magnus appeared. He was wearing long boots and breeches
beneath his big oiled coat. 'Sorry, mate. I'm going to take your
place.'

Dilly caught her breath. He looked spell binding – all rain-
soaked, windswept blond hair, broad-shouldered, long-
shanked heroism and blue-eyed bravery and grit. He had never
looked more masculine, or intimidating, or sexy, and he
seemed to fill the entire lorry as he stepped inside and towered
over them all, raising his sandy eyebrows, unsmiling, as if
daring them to challenge him. Her heart flipped over and over
with love, like an out-of-control wind-up yapping toy dog.

Nell couldn't stop laughing. 'Is this your way of proving
you've got guts?'

He gritted his teeth and said nothing.

'Darling, brave Magnus,' she laughed happily. 'I'll go and

tell Flipper. The secretary will have a fit, but they'll have to lump it. The band is going to ride together after all!' Kissing Magnus on the nose as she passed, she danced off into the rain.

Dilly was still staring at him open-mouthed, heart flipping. 'But you can't ride well enough.'

'I've been practising. I've even bought a proper helmet. Look. It has a bobble.' He held it up, smiling reassuringly, happy to be the butt of the joke.

Her crazed, flipping heart speeded up at a dangerous rate as fear drenched it with adrenaline as well as pride. She was suddenly so worried about how badly he could get hurt, she felt physically sick. 'You really don't have to do it.'

The easy Magnus smile slipped away and his blue eyes bored into hers. 'Believe me, I do. I have to do this for the woman I love.'

The Entwined team were amongst the last to go in a packed class.

'Going's seriously slippy but still fast,' Flipper told them when he returned from the secretary's tent. 'Lots of accidents already in the novice section – two blood wagons dispatched and more lined up waiting. We'll need some bloody big studs and serious glue. Are you sure about this?' he asked Magnus, who nodded, although he was looking very pale.

Dilly had pinched herself so hard – several times – to try to wake herself up from this surreal dream that she was quite tempted to get herself checked out by one of the ambulances before mounting. Any excuse to avoid setting out in the monsoon conditions would be gratefully embraced. She could feel her own nail indentations still biting into her skin. Some had drawn blood.

'Nell can't possibly ride.' She grabbed Magnus's arm to bury her nails elsewhere.

He winced. 'I can't stop her.'

'You have to. It's your baby we're talking about here.'

'Face it, Dilly, she's a better rider than both of us. She'll be fine.'

There was something curiously detached about him. Dilly knew how pumped up he had to be, that fear was hardening every artery in his body as it was hers, knitting her muscles together and chilling her bones. Yet as she stared desperately into his eyes to seek out the old friend whom she had talked sleepily to on the phone just a few hours earlier, she found that he was hiding from her, refusing to acknowledge just how crazy it was for Nell to be riding.

'Don't you care?'

'Of course I care. That's why I'm going to be riding right alongside.' His eyes bored into hers. 'Now will you please let go of my arm? My fingers are starting to go numb.'

Dilly wanted to tell him what Titch had said in the lorry but, before she had a chance, they were distracted by the noisy and chaotic influx of her supporters. Pheely and Pixie, with children and dogs in tow, had just arrived crammed into Pixie's ancient Land Rover. Trotting loyally behind them with a vast picnic hamper came Anke and sulking younger son, Chad.

'Aren't your family coming?' Dilly asked Flipper.

'Most of them are competing against us,' he reminded her snappily before going to check on Rory again.

It was only then that Dilly realised she had no idea how any of the Cottrells had taken the news of Nell's pregnancy – if, indeed, any of them knew.

Nell looked simply amazing in a black riding habit, mounted side-saddle on the impatiently pawing Popeye. She could have ridden in from another century, were it not for the fact she was talking on her mobile phone.

'I'm going to bloody well do it. Yes, well, you should have

thought of that before. Fuck you!' she screamed into it before throwing it at Titch and trotting away.

'Who was she talking to?' Dilly asked.

Titch shrugged.

Dilly glanced in the direction that Flipper had left and wondered for a moment before shaking her head. No, it was ridiculous – why talk on mobile phones when they were within real life shouting distance? It didn't make sense. Yet everything about the day was turning out so weirdly, she couldn't entirely dismiss the suspicion.

Rory finally appeared from the thunder-box looking very grey and out of it, just in time to see the Thrusters Entwined team mounted and checking their girths.

'You look great together,' he told Dilly, swaying wanly at knee level. 'Take care of him for me.'

'Any tips?' she asked anxiously, feeling very high up and unaccustomed to having such pale ears twitching in front of her.

'If you stay on, he'll do the rest.' Rory smiled palely, patted White Lies and then turned around to retch again. 'Jesus,' he gagged. 'I really have to quit drinking. I didn't even have that – ugh – much. Thought I'd go easy as I was riding today. Could it be gastric flu?'

'Actually, I think Nell poisoned you,' Dilly told him, but he was too busy throwing up to hear.

The course was already almost underwater, and only a small clutch of stalwart supporters braved the elements to walk around it with cowering dogs and watch their loved ones compete amid an oil slick of rising mud. The rain was slashing sideways, making visibility practically impossible. Hoods whipped from heads, golfing umbrellas turned inside out and, deep inside his plastic-wrapped off-roader baby buggy, Basil started taking on water.

The horse that Rory had originally lined up for Spurs was no armchair. One of his ex-racehorse bargains that he was trying to turn into an eventer, it had no brakes, little steering and just one gear. Magnus looked both huge and vulnerable on it, and yet he made a surprisingly good job of staying aboard and keeping it from boiling over as the team all found a quiet corner of the lorry field to have a trot and canter around, loosening up tight muscles, warming up and shaking off the worst of their nerves. The twins looked like a flashy pair of old pros. Dilly and Magnus pulled frightened, silly faces at one another as they careered this way and that, uncertain what they were supposed to be doing.

'You've improved so much!' she told him as they passed one another at speed.

'Thanks,' he managed to reply when they next whizzed close by.

'I thought you hated riding,' she laughed as they hurtled within earshot.

'I did.' He fell in step when his horse suddenly recognised Whitey as its stablemate and whipped around to follow him. 'But I figured that I should try to find out what makes the woman I love tick, and why she's so hooked on it even though she claims it does nothing for her. I owe it to her. After all she joined a band for me.'

'True.' Dilly looked across to where Nell was jumping the practice fence with ease, oblivious of the rain. Lucky Nell, she found herself thinking. Always going after what she wants. Always getting it.

'I'm sorry about last night,' she muttered into the wind, staring guiltily at Whitey's rain-soaked grey mane. 'We should both have had more sleep before doing this.'

'I had a great sleep thanks to you.' Magnus cantered alongside. 'Who d'you suppose FGM is?'

Dilly looked across at him, the rain in her face. She had wanted it to be him more than anything. But she now knew that it wasn't. He loved Nell. He had just said it. She was the woman he loved, just as Dilly was the friend whom he loved. And it was his misfortune to be everything she loved, but he could never know that.

'Pixie, maybe?' she suggested, shouting through the rain. 'She was around when I was reading Mystic Meg, after all. Who else could it be?'

Magnus didn't have a chance to answer, his face turning several shades paler as a rumble of thunder sounded overhead and his horse suddenly put on an alarming burst of speed that propelled them both to the top end of the field in record speed.

'Don't wear him out before the chase!' Flipper, who had drawn alongside Dilly's other flank, called after Magnus. 'Christ, he's going to be a liability.'

'Give him a break,' Dilly snapped at him, tears welling stupidly in her eyes. Tears of pride and hurt and anger on Magnus's behalf.

'You know why I love you?' Flipper rode so close their thighs and boots bashed against one another.

'Do tell,' she hissed, almost too livid too speak around the boulder in her windpipe.

'Because I know you can love as much and as hard as me. And I can't wait until you admit it. Like me.'

The boulder in Dilly's throat exploded with a sob.

'You just wait until you're out there.' Flipper looked across to the course. 'It's better than hunting. The biggest rush. The truth drug of all rushes. You know who you are out there. You know who you love.'

Dilly nodded, trying to swallow the sharp shards of her sobs.

'This game isn't for wimps, Dilly,' he said, echoing his sister.

'Are we talking team chasing or love here?'

'The whole shooting match.'

With that, he peeled away and hurtled over the practice fence. The next moment, the team were called to the start.

Dilly's heart was thrumming so madly in her ears during the countdown that she missed 'Go'. The first she knew that they were off was Flipper blasting past her shouting 'Get a move on!'

And White Lies did. Boy, was he fast. Compared to Otto's bucking, squealing, fat procrastination, he was turbo-charged.

They raced through the first quarter of the course. Dilly had no real idea what was going on amongst her team mates behind – she was just enjoying her front seat view in a blind, excited flurry of mud, rain and blood-pumping adrenaline. It was amazing. All she had to do was point and shoot. Chased by the weather, she and Whitey flew. She thanked Rory for the chance to ride this fast, this freely and this ecstatically. It was a world apart from Otto.

They flew over hedges, rails, stone walls, brush and railway sleepers. Hardly checking, she whooped into the driving rain and felt a great wave of elated affection for poor Rory and the horse he had always adored more than any woman he had ever claimed to love, including herself. She was riding his dreams and, aware of that amazing responsibility, she rode like Rory.

Rory was a great rider, but he was also a spoiled, adrenaline-junky show-off.

Shouts came from behind and Dilly craned around as best she could, but the rain made it hard to see and the thrill of speed made it hard to think. It was a few seconds before she heard what the yells were about.

'Dressing fence!'

A vague trigger clicked in her brain as she glanced around

whilst hurtling towards a wide hedge and rails with a clutch of spectators and photographers close by.

It was compulsory to jump the dressing fence together as a foursome.

'Blimey!'

The rest of the bedraggled, muddy team was miles behind and desperately strung out.

Dilly sat back and took a cautious pull on Whitey's reins for the first time, only to find herself almost falling off as he braked immediately and looked for direction, so obediently trained that he would have made her a cup of tea had she asked.

Sitting herself safely back in the plate again, Dilly pulled up and patted the amenable Whitey, only to find herself on the end of a tongue-lashing from Flipper once the team caught up.

'For fuck's sake, lead the team – don't just blast off into the distance. We're carrying Mags here. Have a heart.'

Looking back, Dilly saw Magnus – white-faced and teeth gritted – desperately trying to control the careering ex-racer, who had his head in the air and the finish line in his sights, eyes rolling and mouth foaming. But he was hanging on in there, and even managed a big smile as he caught up. Beside him – not a hair out of place or a bead of sweat among the raindrops on her tanned face – Nell was in tears of laughter.

'You okay?' Dilly asked him.

He nodded, blue eyes smarting, smile as wide as the horizon, so much love radiating from both that it was as though the sun had suddenly come out.

They flew the dressing fence together, the twins so close on their heels that the photographers on the far side of the fence caught the shot of the day – two pairs of horses in flight, one seeming to be suspended above the other in mid air.

On they raced, desperate to make up time, Dilly leading them safely now, always keeping Magnus in her sights, knowing that Flipper had been right, that she would know once and for all how strongly she could love.

And they all flew. Alongside his stable-mate at last, Magnus's racehorse lost his single-minded fervour and started to enjoy the day out. Easy-going, louche Magnus rode more like a cowboy than a pro jockey, but his ease and kindness inspired trust and stability as the little hurdler tried his heart out for him and valiantly kept up with the heroic Whitey.

'I love you!' Dilly called across as they turned for home, knowing that the wind would whip the words from her mouth and far from Magnus's ears as the rain finally hit their faces full-on and they crested the hill and blinked down at the long line of hedges and ditches separating them from the finishing line and a celebratory drink.

It was a belly-lurching, steep drop. They could see the roofs of the horseboxes far below, the tiny, windswept spectators and steaming horses that had already braved the descent.

Dilly led the way carefully from hedge to hedge towards the final leap, checking her team mates all the way – especially Magnus.

'Faster!' Flipper drew alongside her.

Almost immediately she was flanked by Nell, too. 'Faster! We'll never win at this pace.'

Dilly dallied. Her fatal flaw. As the twins drew ahead, she stayed with Magnus, checking he was still in control. He looked across at her, face beaming.

He *was* in control. Total control. Not just of the horse, but of his life and his heart and his guts – those lion-brave guts – for the first time in years. And he looked ecstatic, blue eyes blazing through the rain like lanterns.

'I love you, too. I love you with all my heart!'

His words were snatched away by the wind.

As he said it, up ahead Popeye somersaulted.

Neither Dilly nor Magnus saw it happen. Afterwards, they were told that it was a freak accident – the horse pecked on landing and his hind end was travelling so fast that it simply overtook the crumpled front, the rider so securely tucked into her side-saddle that she had no escape hatch, simply disappearing beneath the great mass of body and hoof and mud as the horse rolled over his trapped passenger.

After that, Dilly could only think straight in dulled snatches as fast-framed slow motion set in.

Flipper was there first, Olive galloping away as he fell to his knees beside his sister and her equally lifeless horse, a desperate, hunched figure in the driving rain, seeking out vital signs in both.

Dilly and Magnus leaped the fence, landing together just yards away from the muddy tangle of fallen horse and rider, before turning suicidal, hillside circles trying to pull up their excited horses. When they did, they both leaped off and, knees buckling, stood hopelessly in the rain, asking Flipper how badly Nell was hurt, what they could do, how they could help.

'Just fucking well shut up!' he yelled. 'And catch my horse.'

Far below them, the ambulance tried and failed to scale the hill, sliding back every time.

After what seemed like an eternity, a Land Rover made it through the mud with an eager paramedic aboard, who attended to Nell and immediately called for the air ambulance.

While they waited for it to arrive, Pheely, Anke and Pixie panted and slithered up the hill to lend support and hysteria.

'Is it bad?'

'Is she breathing?'

'I've got some Bach Flowers Rescue Remedy if it helps. I always carry it.'

Flipper started to cry.

Magnus sank to his knees and told an unconscious Nell that he loved her.

Flipper elbowed him out of the way.

'Leave her alone, you bastard. She only rode for you.'

'For me?'

'Yes. She wanted you to stop her doing it, but you didn't.'

'I couldn't stop her!'

'Of course you fucking well could. This is your fault.'

They were almost exchanging blows by the time the paramedic booted them both into touch.

'Think of the patient, for God's sake!'

Dilly held horses and wept.

After a few minutes an air ambulance appeared noisily over the black, windswept woods to the east, descending through the rain clouds like a great black wasp landing on the sticky toffee pudding of muddy hill. Dilly led the horses away and let her tears rip, fear and agony shredding her lungs, certain that Nell had done it deliberately.

Titch's words kept ringing in her ears. 'Sloe gin and fast cross-country riding. Takes a brave girl to do it, but that's the Irish for you.'

Frozen, numbed and soaked through, she watched without seeing as Nell – a tiny, fragile figure in a muddy riding habit – was carefully transferred to a stretcher and lifted into the belly of the helicopter.

It was Anke who shook her from her hysteria.

'Nell's just come round, Dilly. She insists you travel with her.'

Teeth chattering, mind racing, Dilly shook her head in confusion.

'What about Flipper?'

'Has to stay here to deal with the horse. It's in a bad way.'

'Magnus?'

'She doesn't want him, Dilly. She wants you.' Sensible, practical Anke patted her firmly on her cold cheeks and stared into her eyes to get her attention. That blue gaze had the same open honesty as Magnus's, and Dilly suddenly came to life again, nodding furiously.

'Of course I'll go.'

'Make sure they know about her condition,' Anke said in sudden horror, thinking about her future grandchild. 'I'm not sure anyone's told them.'

Dilly handed over the reins and ran, ducking beneath the fierce, blinding blast of the chopper wings and clambered aboard, shouting 'She's pregnant!'

The journey to hospital was a stomach-lurching race.

Dilly hardly got to look at Nell as paramedics checked her constantly, fluorescent backs blocking her out.

Nell screamed. She screamed for Dilly and for Milo. She screamed apologies and Our Fathers. She screamed, most of all, in sheer pain.

'You do know she's pregnant,' Dilly explained again to one of the paramedics as he leaned back to fetch something from a box, but he wasn't listening.

'She's pregnant!' she yelled.

The paramedic glared at her furiously. 'Why didn't you say so earlier?'

25

An hour later, Dilly sat in a hospital corridor with Magnus, sipping vile vending machine coffee out of a plastic cup.

He was breathless and overwrought, still wearing his mud-splattered riding gear. Hearing that Nell wasn't in critical danger, he'd hugged Dilly so tightly that for a moment she was in danger of being admitted herself as her ribs creaked.

And his blue eyes had been tight with strain when he told her that Popeye was heading by horse ambulance to the equine clinic's operating table with only a twenty per cent chance of survival.

'Flipper says the vertebrae of his neck are all but wrecked.'

They both knew that Nell, also in theatre, had had a lucky escape, and still wasn't entirely out of the woods.

The impact of the fall – and of half a ton of horse on top of her – had caused a collapsed lung, broken ribs and internal bleeding, plus such severe concussion that she had only regained sporadic consciousness, triggering fear that she would suffer a swelling around the brain.

'Did she say anything that made sense?' Magnus asked.

'She just wanted to make sure the baby was okay – and called out for you,' Dilly lied, hating herself for the need to make him feel better.

Magnus went very quiet, just nodding and sipping coffee.

Dilly knew that he was thinking about the baby. He hadn't been able to bring himself to say the word yet, but his eyes gave him away totally, darting this way and that, narrowing and widening, fighting tears.

'I'm sure everything'll be okay,' she reassured him.

'I'm sure it will,' he agreed.

'Is Milo safe?'

'What?'

'She was asking after him,' she explained apologetically.

'He's fine. Titch is looking after him.'

They lapsed into silence.

Magnus picked holes in the rim of his coffee beaker. 'Why d'you say you love me?'

'What?'

'You said you loved me. When we were chasing.'

'I do love you – as a mate.' She stared at the plastic cup in her hands, drenched with shame. 'And I was *so* proud of you.'

'Because you love a man in breeches?'

Just for a moment she glanced involuntarily at his muddy breeches, and those mile-long thighs. She avoided his eyes.

'Of course.'

He nudged a shoulder against hers. 'I was proud of you, too.'

She relaxed enough to giggle for a moment. 'For galloping so far ahead that I almost forgot about you?'

'Exactly.'

'Meaning?'

'You had faith in me. You knew I'd be okay, which was more than the twins. They flanked me like a pair of outriders, issuing instructions all the way.'

'They did?'

'All I wanted was to catch you up and enjoy the ride.'

'Why didn't you?'

'I did. But then it all went wrong.'

Both were suddenly aware that they had been leaning against one another, faces close despite diverted eyes. They pulled politely apart and fixed their eyes on the health warning posters on the opposite side of the corridor.

Dilly read about the horrors of sexually transmitted diseases, while Magnus focused determinedly upon flu jabs for the elderly.

'She *will* be okay,' Dilly said eventually.

'I hope so,' he muttered.

'And the baby will be fine too. They're fighters, that family.'

'I couldn't agree more. We fight all the time. Or, rather she tries to make me fight.'

He sounded so utterly dejected that Dilly instinctively reached out and threaded her fingers through his.

'About what?'

'Everything.'

'Why?'

'Because that's what makes her tick. And I roll over and take it – just the same way you do. She has this incredible power over both of us. It's like we're under her spell.'

Dilly tried to deflect him. 'She's carrying your baby. Maybe it's just hormones.'

'Yes, the whore moans a lot,' he said without thinking.

Dilly quickly let go off his hand.

'Sorry! Sorry! That was unforgivable.' He rubbed his muddy face. 'I'm just in a bit of a state. I'm so angry with her, you know? For doing this to herself – to our baby, just because she's so stubborn and bloody minded. But I'm terrified for her at the same time. I don't know what's going on in my head any more. Most of all, I'm angry with myself. I should never have let her ride, but I did. I let her ride because she wanted to so much, because I didn't want another fight, because she called me gutless and I wanted to prove something, because I – because . . .'

'Because you love her.'

'She's my lover.'

'It was her choice to ride, Magnus – not yours.'

'And was getting pregnant her choice?'

Dilly didn't know how to answer.

'Where's that bloody Fairy God Mother when you need her?' he laughed bitterly. 'Call herself a mate . . .'

'Whoever it was couldn't have seen this coming.'

'Checkmate.' He stared ahead at the poster, muscles so tightly quilted in his cheek that Dilly could have played noughts and crosses on them.

'Soulmate,' she nodded, watching those two lovely, familiar little pale moles by his left ear blur as her eyes filled with tears.

His hand slid into hers again and they sat in silence, both staring at the posters.

'You'd have thought some of her family would have arrived by now . . .' Dilly said eventually.

'They're a pretty selfish lot,' Magnus pointed out. 'They were still planning to run the Gavels team when I left. That legendary Cottrell stiff upper lip means you'd have to have at least a double amputation to merit a bag of grapes.'

'Not too keen on the in-laws then?'

'I'm working on it.'

'How did they take the news of the pregnancy?'

'As far as I can tell, Flipper's the only one who knows.'

'Oh, God.'

'He's the culprit.'

'Flipper?' Dilly turned to him in shock, heart hammering.

'No – God,' he smiled despite himself. 'I'm a musician. You'd think I could master the rhythm method, but whoever thought it up had better self-control than I do. Bloody Catholicism.'

'You'd better get used to it.'

'I guess so.'

'I quite liked it at school.'

'Of course, you went to a convent,' he remembered. 'Tell me, why does a puritan old Anglican like Ely send his daughter to a Catholic school?'

'The fees were cheap,' she smiled.

'And that's where you met Nell?'

'Mmm,' she mumbled vaguely.

'But she was expelled?'

'Mmm.'

'Why?'

'Oh, just being Nell. You know.'

'I know,' he laughed, but his eyes were trained on her face. 'She had a huge impact on you then, didn't she?'

'Mmm.'

'Odd, given she's a few years older than you.'

'She was my dormitory monitor.'

'Tucked you up in bed?'

'Something like that.'

'Listened while you told her your secrets?'

'Mmm.'

'One secret in particular?'

She glanced across at him, 'Why are you so interested?'

He watched her face worriedly. 'I know something happened between you two at school. Don't pretend it didn't. And I know it's why you are the way you are with her.'

'What way's that?'

'Obsessive. Guilty. Hopelessly tender.'

'I think she's amazing. I always did. All the girls idolised her.'

'What happened, Dilly?'

'Nothing.'

'What happened?'

'I can't tell you.'

'You have to. We're soulmates.' Squeezing her hand tightly,

he dropped his face alongside hers, his other hand reaching up to her chin, blue eyes forcing her to look at him, breath soft on her cheek. 'You tell everything to your soulmates. That's why you told Nell about my real father. She's your soulmate, too – or she was then.'

She stifled a sob, trying and failing to look away. 'Sorry. I should never have told her, it's just . . .'

'You tell her everything?'

She nodded. 'Like I tell you.'

'So tell me this. You owe me this.'

He could always break her down faster than anyone – that soft, smoky voice, the intense gaze, the way he seemed to already know what she was going to tell him.

'If I tell you . . . you mustn't let Nell know I've betrayed her.'

'You're not betraying her. You're helping her. We both are.'

So Dilly told him what had happened all those years ago, when she had been too young to really understand what she'd done and how she had helped Nell almost kill herself.

'She'd been at the school about a year and was always getting in trouble. When she came back after Christmas, she was different – subdued, not as bright and bubbly. She was snappier, too – she used to make me cry a lot without meaning to and then got angry with me for it.'

'I know that feeling,' Magnus murmured.

'The dorm mons were allowed to accompany the younger girls into the village to buy tuck and have "healthy walks",' Dilly went on. 'One day, Nell took me to the village and we got into a cab and went to this housing estate on the outskirts of town. She told me that she'd get me into serious trouble if I told anyone. Then she called in at this house – I remember it had huge, painted butterflies above its door, and a little windmill thing in the front garden. She came back out with a package.'

'Drugs?'

'I suppose I must have thought that, but I was too young to really know. She had a real rock and roll reputation. She made me hide the package and promise not to look at it. The nuns were always searching through her stuff, but I was too young to be checked that often.'

'And you didn't look at it?'

She shook her head. 'I was too frightened. I just hid it in my trunk. The next day, she took some of whatever it was out and hid the package again. Then I heard that she was in the sick bay.'

'What was it?'

Dilly started to cry. 'She was really ill. She told them it was stomach cramps, but when I went to see her, she was grey, you know? She looked awful. She begged me to steal as many sanitary towels as I could.'

'Steal sanitary towels?'

'The nuns used to ration them – I have no idea why, but girls had to ask for their supply every month. I asked her why she couldn't just get them from the nuns, but she was hysterical. So I went around the dorms stealing every one I could find – I couldn't get at the cupboard they were kept in because it was kept locked. Those poor girls. There was such a fuss about it. The nuns went ape.'

'I can imagine.'

'When I took them to Nell, she looked worse than ever. I really thought she was dying, but she was still making out like it was just a stomach bug. She told me to get the rest of the package I'd hidden and bring that too. There were pills inside – two or three little boxes with foil strips inside. I didn't see what they were exactly, but she took the lot.

'She was in sick bay for almost a week, refusing to admit just how ill she was. Afterwards, she just said it had been a bad period.'

'But it wasn't?'

She shook her head. 'She'd been pregnant – almost four months. The drugs she'd bought were the Morning After Pill. It's only supposed to work for a few days, but the amount Nell took was plenty. And she took two whole months' worth of contraceptive pill as well. She took enough to abort a bloody elephant. It almost killed her.'

'And the baby?'

'There was no baby after that.'

'Oh God, Nell.' He sank his face in his hands.

'The school found out that I was the one who had stolen the sanitary towels, of course. I've always been a useless crook. I was too young to have periods, so the nuns were baffled. I couldn't tell them why. In the end, they brought in the priest who asked me all sorts of embarrassing questions, playing the child psychologist. I never told him why I'd done it, but I blamed myself.'

'How did you find out what Nell had done to herself? That she had been pregnant?' He looked at her curiously as it struck him.

'She told me. I suppose she had to – like a confession. It was eating her up. She was suicidal, I think. She sat on the end of my bed one night and told me that she had killed her baby.'

'And was it you who told the nuns?'

She shook her head violently. 'I've never told a soul what really went on until today.'

'If no one apart from you knew the awful truth, why did she get expelled?'

'We'd been seen in the taxi. She told the nuns that she'd taken me to an amusement arcade to cheer me up. I backed up the story, and she left a week later.'

'Christ.'

'Only Nell could stage an abortion in a nunnery.' Dilly shook her head in tearful wonder. 'She could have died. I think she almost did.'

'Do you know who the father was?'

She shook her head. 'She just told me that she would be damned more for having the baby than for getting rid of it. She said that she had told God what she was going to do and that he understood. She still really believed, you know? I suppose I did a bit then. I thought I would be damned for helping, even if she wasn't. I thought . . .'

'You were just a little, frightened child.' He reached across to hug her.

'So was Nell,' she breathed, closing her eyes tightly as his arms circled her shoulders.

Just for a moment she let him fold his warmth around her and buried herself in the safest place she knew on earth.

Then she ripped away and bolted to the loo to sob in a cubicle, guilt raging upon anger upon love upon hurt.

'You're more Catholic than she'll ever be,' he told her when she returned. He was staring fixedly at the poster once again.

'I'm an atheist.'

'Who lives with a rigid morality structure, self-reproach, utter faith in kindness and conviction in a greater – greatest – love that can never be matched by mortal life.'

'If you say so.'

'I do.' He buried a smile in anxious fingers that rubbed at his chin.

'I guess that means I'll burn in hell then.'

'For what?'

'Well, I'm sure God might have something to say about girl-on-girl action with a pregnant woman – not to mention the father of her child joining in, too.'

'In that case, I'll burn as well. We'll be lost soulmates.'

By trying to joke it off – awkwardly, almost politely – they lifted a great, guilty weight from both their shoulders. But then, without warning, the weight kept lifting, making then both light-headed and almost giddy. The tension and stress of the day had given them a strange flood of adrenaline that they couldn't shake off. The intimacy of the recent confession and the pure, simple pleasure of sitting together and talking again as friends after so much awkwardness had passed between them liberated them. And, even though neither of them was aware of it, their flirtatious hearts couldn't stop themselves.

'So you're secretly Catholic too?' she asked him.

'I'm me.' He turned to look at her at last. 'Just like you are you.'

The blue eyes were alive with meaning. Too much meaning. The light-headedness made Dilly almost faint with longing.

'Mates,' she spluttered.

'With souls that can never be saved.' He leaned forward to kiss her.

She felt his breath on her cheek, his lips touch hers, her heart and head pump and spin, her whole body floating and flying and soaring.

His tongue was inside her mouth, laced against hers, the sweetest of tastes and sensations that pulled a hot streak of lust up inside her like a broadsword being drawn from a scabbard.

There was a squeak of rubber sole against polished floor as a plump, button-nosed nurse approached them.

'Stabilised and out of danger,' she beamed as Dilly and Magnus looked up guiltily. 'Baby's heartbeat is as strong as an ox. I gather the father is trying to save the poor horse?'

Mortified, they split apart like a pair of clay shots fired from a field mortar.

'I'm Nell's boyfriend – the baby's father.' Magnus stood up.

The nurse looked from him to Dilly, her eyebrows shooting up archly, before leading Magnus away.

Dilly retreated to her loo cubicle to stifle her sobs in her arms.

In a room that beeped and blipped regularly, Magnus took Nell's soft, long-fingered hand and held it to his lips.

It smelled of leather and horse sweat.

He closed his eyes and breathed deeply. 'Forgive me.'

26

Otto and Bottom reappeared in their field that evening. The strange sports car was once again parked outside Giles's house but, undeterred, Dilly knocked on the door. Giles took a long time to answer, and was wearing a silk dressing-gown when he finally appeared, his cheeks very pink and champagne froth on his moustache.

'Ah, Dilly – I was, er, about to take a bath.'

'I see.' She nodded, glancing over her shoulder at the soft-top. 'New car?'

With perfect timing, the call came down the stairs. 'Who is it, darling?'

Giles had the decency to blush, moustache twitching guiltily.

'I'm sure she's "marvellous",' Dilly said carefully.

Blue eyes darting guiltily, Giles cleared his throat. 'I'd invite you in, only . . .'

'You're about to take a bath, I know.' She tucked her hood tighter around her head as the rain drummed down on it. 'I just wanted to know if you saw anyone bring Otto and Bottom back?'

'Back?' His tanned forehead creased. 'I wasn't aware that they'd gone anywhere.'

'Oh – right. Don't worry about it, then.' She turned to leave.

He hopped a few paces after her and stood barefoot on his front doorstep, holding the door half-closed, hissing. 'Did you give your mother that money?'

'In a manner of speaking.'

'What did she do with it?'

'Drowned her sorrows.'

Giles was so shocked he let go of the door which banged closed behind him, locking him out.

Listening as he called urgently through the letterbox to 'darling', Dilly headed back along the drive and kissed her horse and donkey goodnight, grateful to have them back.

'*How's Popeye?*' she texted Flipper once she got home, using her sim card in her mother's mobile handset.

'*Touch and go, but we think he'll pull through.*'

'*Well done you.*'

Dilly then slotted the ring-box sim card into the mobile and checked it, but FGM had left no texts and she felt no desire to make contact.

Instead, inspired by Giles, she took a long soak in the bath, trying to think about anything but Magnus.

It was no good. There he was in her head, talking to her, looking at her in that amazing, open way he had, laughing his whooping laugh, reassuring her with his kindness, his best-of-all hugs and – when she closed her eyes to try to blot it all out – he was kissing her and she was flying high, high up in the air.

A great tidal wave of water splashed out as she disappeared totally beneath the surface and let out a huge silent, bubbly, drowned scream.

Then, sopping wet and naked, she stomped out to her mother's charging mobile, slotted in the mystery card and texted FGM.

'*You are right. I love him, I love him, I love him. Now wave your magic wand.*'

She was drying her hair by the fire when she heard the door open behind her.

'Mum! There you are! I was worried about you. You left your phone behind.'

'No I didn't. It's right here.'

Her heart flipped and skipped as she buried her hot face in her towel for a moment of nerve-jangling gratitude.

It was Magnus.

'I tried calling you, but I kept getting voice mail.'

'Oh, my handset's broken. I just used Mum's to check the card.' She leaped up, hanging on tightly to the towel that was wrapped around her. 'Is it Nell? Is everything all right?'

'Fine – she's conscious now, still very groggy, but she managed to tell me I'm a rubbish rider, so she must be feeling okay. Then her family finally turned up and they all started barking and braying around her bed, so I thought I'd come back and change.'

Which was when Dilly realised that he was still dressed in his muddy riding gear. He was also soaking wet – his blond curls darkened by rain and shedding great drops every time he moved, his clothes absolutely wringing and his teeth chattering.

'So why didn't you change?'

'Fairy God Mother texted me.' He squelched a little closer to her, moving away from the wet puddle he had been creating on the kitchen floor to start a puddle behind the sofa.

On the other side of the wall of chintz upholstery that divided them, Dilly unwound the towel from her head and handed it to him.

Smiling gratefully, he took it and rubbed his hair.

With a sudden twinge of *déjà vu*, Dilly remembered Flipper drying his hair on the day of Basil's naming ceremony. The day she had suddenly started to fancy him like mad. The day Magnus had followed her into the old greenhouse and told her he wanted her to sing with him when they were both old. The day Flipper had looked at her instead of through her for the first time and she had felt both excited and very vulnerable. That day, he had seen what she hadn't yet been able to work out for herself – Flipper had seen just how much she loved Magnus, and he had recognised his own unacknowledged fire and passion in her.

A great stitch of emotion pinched at her windpipe.

'What did Fairy God Mother say?'

'To come here and see you.'

'But I'm fine.' She smiled artificially brightly.

'I can see that.' He looked up from under a furl of red towel, blue eyes unable to hide their admiration.

Lit by just the fire and the old table lamp beside the sofa, wrapped in only a blue towel, skin still hot and pink from her bath and hair falling around her face in damp tendrils, Dilly knew she should feel self-consciously vulnerable as well as excited. But she just felt excited. Crazily, explosively excited. Excited enough to want to cartwheel, to sing, to drop her towel and shimmy her booty in front of the dancing flames.

She didn't do any of these. She was too stunned by happiness to move. She just smiled, without a trace of artificiality. She smiled so widely – and excitedly – that her cheeks ached.

And Magnus smiled back, blue eyes darkening as his pupils slid wider, the lovely creases beside them reaching right across to the two little moles by his ear. Standing in a puddle, water still oozing out of his hems, droplets scattered across his shoulders and shirt plastered to his chest, he smiled a smile as wide as an ocean.

They both knew, as they smiled, that they had to break the moment. In their kindness and politeness, and their open-hearted way, they were duty-bound to pull the plug, break the electrical current running between them and pull the trip-switch for good measure.

'Good old FGM,' Dilly laughed.

'Don't you just love her?'

By mentioning her name, they had broken her spell.

They both knew that they had saved the moment. Catholic atheists that they were, they had shown great self-control and – in truth – chronic coyness.

Dilly sank down on the sofa and patted a spot beside her, which Hamlet lumbered into before Magnus could get there, giving him a resentful look as he squeezed damply into the far corner beside the big dog.

With another guilty pang of morality digging in, Dilly pulled out a few cushions to hug, covering the skin that the towel didn't reach.

'I'm just dying to know who FGM is.'

'Me too,' he agreed, pulling out a few cushions of his own.

'Is Nell really going to be okay?' She nervously butterflied from subject to subject.

He nodded. 'She's even saying she'll be pulling out all the stops for the hunt ball.'

Dilly registered a thudding ache of dread in her chest. 'Will she be well enough?'

'She insists she has to be there.' Magnus reached out a hand to stroke Hamlet, who groaned appreciatively. 'Seems to think it's going to be an extra special night.'

Remembering the proposal pact, a cold finger of jealousy prodded its path along Dilly's sternum. She extracted the largest cushion from beneath Hamlet and hugged it beneath her chin.

'That's great,' she managed to say flatly.

'Will you still be there?' he asked awkwardly, still giving Hamlet a thorough ear-rubbing.

She shrugged, sinking her teeth into the cushion.

'I need you there.' He glanced across at her.

'Why?' Heart skipping, she searched his eyes for clues.

He looked at Hamlet. 'The band is nothing without a female vocal – not to mention keyboards.'

Feeling deflated, Dilly shrugged again.

'You and Flipper not getting on?' he asked casually, nose to nose with Hamlet now and pulling silly faces to hide his curiosity.

'You could say that.'

'Things did seem a bit strained between you today.'

'Well, the fact someone deliberately hid my horses didn't help my mood. And Flipper's always been an arrogant sod.'

Looking up from Hamlet's nose kisses, he watched her closely. 'You'll have to patch things up if you're going to propose to him at the ball.'

'Propose?'

'Nell says that's what you're planning.' He stroked his hands along Hamlet's huge neck, troubled blue eyes catching hers again and again as her gaze flitted around the room, her heart in turmoil.

'That was just a stupid bet. There's no—'

'Don't do it, Dilly,' he interrupted urgently. 'Flipper's not right for you. He'd never make you—' He stopped himself with an apologetic grimace. 'Sorry. Sorry. Not my place to say. Forget it.'

Her restless gaze at last taking a break from its nervous patrol of the room, Dilly stared at him, realising to her astonishment that he had no idea their relationship was over. She opened her mouth to put him right, but he was already hurriedly asking whether she had heard how Popeye was doing, covering up for probing.

'Oh, fine apparently,' she said, flustered. 'He'll pull through. The thing is, about Flipper and me—'

'Thank God,' he interrupted again, still too jumpy to concentrate. 'Nell loves that horse more than life. More than me.'

Seeing his forlorn face, Dilly felt a desperate need to assure him. 'She loves you.'

He shook his head, smiling. 'She loves Milo, Popeye, Flipper, her family and you in that order. That doesn't leave a lot for me.'

'She doesn't love me,' she scoffed.

'Oh, she does.' His eyes blazed into hers now. 'She wants to be you.'

Dilly shook her head violently, all thoughts of turning the subject back to Flipper forgotten.

'She does. You're her little avenging angel. I never understood it fully until you told me about what had happened between you. Now I see.'

'See what?'

'You're the one thing that links her to the moment she lost her faith – not just in God, but in that bright bubble dream we all have of happy-ever-afters when we're kids. She did something that she will never forgive herself for. She can tell herself that God forgives her, but her own conscience won't let her go there. You never judged her. You were the only one in on the secret apart from God, and you never stopped loving her or being loyal to her. Imagine that? She loves you for that.'

'And hates me for it too, surely?'

He shook his head. 'She wants to punish you, maybe, but she will never hate you. You became a part of her that day.'

'The triplet,' Dilly echoed Nell's words hollowly.

Magnus said nothing, just reaching out again to stroke lucky Hamlet who up-ended his freckled belly and threw his long legs akimbo hoping for some action.

All Dilly's childish, horny hopes of action had long-since fizzled out as the great weight of her actions pressed down on her. She closed her eyes and curled tighter into the corner of the sofa.

'Poor Nell.'

'She was lucky to have you.'

'Lucky? By helping her I could have helped kill her.'

'But she *was* fine. That's the point. It was an awful, awful thing to put herself through, but she did it and even got away with it. She should never have got you involved.'

'I wanted to help her,' she muttered.

'You want to help everyone.'

'Yes, but I just fuck things up, don't I?'

There was a loud grumble and thump as Hamlet was forcibly ejected from the sofa and Magnus bridged the chintz divide to hug her.

It was a steamy hug for all the wrong reasons – he was still rain-soaked, but now fire-warmed too. It was like being hugged by a warm, wet, friendly bear in a sauna. Yet it was the best hug he had ever given, and the best taken. Dilly coiled into it, hugged back for all she was worth and stayed there for what felt like hours, breathing in safety, steam and comfort.

She could have stayed there for ever had Magnus's phone not rung, making them both leap from the embrace like salmon from a stream, yet again shot through with jumpy politeness.

It was a short call.

'Yup – yup – yup – of course.'

When he hung up, Magnus's blue eyes sought hers out with customary openness, if still indecently close to her face. She could feel his breath on her nose as he spoke.

'That was Finn Cottrell. Nell wants to see me.'

Dilly nodded, heart heavy with jealousy and guilt.

'Will you come with me?'

She realised that her fingers were still laced in his as they tightened their grip involuntarily.

'Of course. Whatever you want.'

*   *   *

'I took Otto first thing this morning,' he confessed as they drove to the hospital. 'I hid him.'

'Why?'

'To make sure you were safe. I had a dream – after we spoke on the phone – and you got hurt in it. I don't trust that horse.'

'Me neither,' she smiled across at him. 'But you could have told me.'

'You're stubborn. You'd have made a stand and fetched him back to prove a point.'

'You're probably right. Where did you hide him?'

'A little field behind Rectory Cottage. You can't see it from the road.'

He drove ludicrously fast, changing CDs without looking where he was going.

Yet, as always, Dilly felt completely safe with him.

'Did you really dream about me?'

'I dream about you a lot,' he said quite matter of factly.

'I dream about you too.'

'Friends do that.' He cleared his throat awkwardly.

'Yes, of course they do.' She cleared her throat too. 'And you really moved Otto and Bottom all the way across the village on your own?'

'Trudy Dew helped me – she was on one of her up-all-night song-writing blitzes when I texted her. It's her field. She put them back this afternoon.'

'I didn't know you were close.' She tried not to feel jealous.

'She's really behind what I do. She's a nice woman. We text quite a bit. I know she works strange hours, so I took a gamble and she was only too happy to help.'

'I'm sure.' Dilly couldn't help lacerating her heart with the image of blowsy, buxom Trudy Dew doing a bit of moonlit rustling with Magnus.

'You still had no right to do it.'

'I think I did. He might have killed you.'

'He's just a horse. *My* horse.'

'You attract the same qualities in men – meanness, unpredictability or just downright bloody-mindedness.'

'That's my right,' she muttered.

'I attract the same qualities in women.'

'Attraction is mutual.'

'Isn't it just?'

As she let this sink in, Dilly heard a Bach cello concerto ring out of the stereo, knowing that they were edging closer to the truth, one painful roundabout question or comment at a time. She knew it, but she didn't dare say it in her head or her heart just yet. It was too delicate and too easy to lose.

Instead she asked: 'Why does someone who writes such heartfelt modern ballads listen to classical music so much?'

'Why does someone who is heartbroken yet still believes in love fall into bed with a well-advertised heartbreaker?'

'Why do we breathe?'

'Eat?'

'Sleep?'

'Watch TV?'

'Talk nonsense?'

'Platitudes.'

'Small talk.'

'Skirting issues.'

'Avoiding truth.'

'Insinuating.'

'Hinting.'

'Lying.'

'I've never lied to you,' she lied.

'I've never lied to you either,' he lied back, both knowing they had spoken untruths out of love and kindness. It's what they did.

'Or with you. Never lied with you.'

'We've never lied verbally *or* biblically.'

There was an awkward moment of recognition.

'Actually we have lied down together,' she admitted, face burning. 'Twice. Three times if you count last night on the phone.'

'Of course.'

They laughed, and there was an almost audible crack as their broken hearts splintered in a furnace-hidden love, desperate to be molten and melded again.

They couldn't help themselves dancing around it, yet neither of them said it.

Nell did. Drugged up to the eyeballs and yet still in pain, she let rip.

'You arsehole! Talking to Dilly behind my back, texting, calling and whispering sweet nothings behind my back! And who the fuck is FGM?'

Coward that she was, Dilly deposited her garage flowers at the door and fled. She knew the way to the loos blindfold, let alone blinded by tears. Besieged in a cubicle by her own shame and fear, she twisted herself into a tiny jealous prawn, staring at her feet.

Magnus was no braver. He was inside the ladies' loos and hammering on Dilly's cubicle door within minutes.

'She wants to speak to you.'

'Tell her I'm busy.'

'Occupied?'

'Engaged.'

'You haven't proposed yet.'

'I'm still very much engaged in this loo right now.'

They couldn't stop themselves, even when they were both

hoarse with fear and guilt, a gland kept pumping out mutual support, affection and shared jokes that offered succour and hid the truth.

'I'll be out in five.' She sniffed, then blew her nose noisily on a hunk of toilet paper.

On the other side of the door, Magnus's great big feet moved around for a few moments before there was a clatter of heels and a furious female voice demanded that he get out before she reported him as a pervert.

Nell looked beautiful. There was no other word. Dilly stopped in the doorway for a moment, taking in her golden skin against the white sheets, her short black ink stain of hair, her long, angular lines – a perfect, quick sketch of a wild animal caught unawares.

Then the wild animal sprang to life, hackles raised.

Her first words were confusing.

'Have you spoken to Milo?'

'Milo?'

'Yes!'

'He's fine.'

'Well I'm glad. Bully for him. The shit.'

Dilly realised that the drugs she was on must be pretty high grade. Already on eggshells, she practically dropped to her knees in supplication.

'Would you like me to bring him here?'

'Yes! Yes, yes, yes!'

'I'll do it.'

'*Now.*'

Dilly hovered. 'It might take a bit longer than that. Sorry. I'll have to okay it with the hospital.'

'Okay what?'

'A dog coming in.'

Nell burst into tears.

Dilly raced to the bedside to comfort her

A long bony hand flapped about, longing to be caught.

It was caught and squeezed hard.

'Oh, Dilly – Dilly – Dilly. My better half. Forgive me.'

'For what?'

'Stealing your innocence. Again and again . . .'

'You're talking nonsense, Nell. It's the drugs.'

'I adore you.'

'I adore you, too.'

'You make me happy.'

'Likewise.'

'You're better than me.'

'Nobody is better than any other person. There is no better.'

'Saying that makes me know that you're better. That's why Flipper found it so easy to love you. You've broken his heart, you know?'

'I haven't?' Dilly was astonished.

'He probably deserved it.' The grey-green eyes looked up at her with a wicked sparkle. 'He has behaved very, very badly in the past. As have I . . . as you know . . .'

Dilly had to ask it. 'Today were you – did you – did you think that by riding so fast and hard you might . . .'

Nell squeezed her hand and shook her head. 'Never. I want this one. Back then, it was different, I could never have gone through with it.'

'Was that because of the father?' Dilly tried and failed to stop Godspell's words running around in her head, insinuating that Flipper and Nell had an unnatural coupling, that his great love was denied because it was morally heinous.

Nell looked up at her, drugs robbing her of her usual cool as tears eked from her eyes. 'Daddy would have killed him if he found out. And me. Or he'd have forced us to stay together until we were old enough to marry, and that would have been almost worse. I didn't even like him very much. I just wanted to know what sex was like. But he got really obsessive. He wrote to me endlessly. And I shouldn't have told him about the pregnancy, but I was so frightened. I thought he'd pay for an abortion. Instead, he flipped out completely, wanted to be a father, saw us marrying, pretty much stalked me. I was terrified by the end. I hated him, *really* hated him and his baby. That poor little thing . . .' She wept harder.

Dilly hugged her but, as always, Nell shrugged her off.

'I'm so sorry.' Dilly felt tears choke her own words.

'For what?'

'For not really understanding what you were going through. Such an awful thing.'

'Stupid, silly Dilly.' Nell grabbed her hand again. 'It's me who should be apologising. You saved my life at that place. You were the best thing that ever happened to me. A funny little kid I couldn't shake off.'

Then Dilly suddenly remembered Magnus telling her that Nell would never stop punishing her for helping her because her own pain and guilt were so great that everybody else associated with it got sucked in, too.

She wanted so much to make it better for Nell – and for herself, but the only thing that she could think of to say was, 'You'll be a wonderful mother to this baby. You really will. And Magnus will be a great father.' It sounded banal and weak, and she knew it.

They stared at each other for a long time, tears rolling. After a few moments, Nell seemed to crack and started to howl.

'Get Milo,' she sobbed through her tears. '*Please*. Now!'

Dilly headed for the door, but Nell called out to stop her.

'The namesake!'

'Sorry?'

'Not the Mexican dog. The man. The love of my life. The only man I have ever loved. Milo!' She closed her wet, turbulent grey-green eyes and conked out.

Hugging herself, Dilly wandered back into the corridor, her head exploding with everything she had just taken in.

Magnus was at her side in an instant.

'You okay?'

She nodded numbly, not thinking to question that they naturally threaded their arms together and leaned against one another as they walked towards the exit. She just breathed in his warmth and comfort as they walked.

As soon as she was outside, she started to roll a cigarette, but Magnus pulled the papers and tobacco from her grip and she laughed tearfully, leaning heavily against him as they headed for the car park.

'Can I use your phone?'

'Sure.'

She scrolled through Magnus's stored numbers until she found Flipper.

'What do you want Magnus?' he answered the call defensively.

'It's me.'

'That figures.'

'Can you text me Milo's number?'

'Nell's ex, Milo?'

'Yes.'

'That doesn't figure.'

'It will. Can you just do it?'

'Sure.'

'Thanks.'

'I miss you.'

'No you don't.'

'You're right.'

As she and Magnus clambered into Anke's car, Dilly called the number Flipper had sent through.

'Hi . . . Milo. My name's Dilly. I'm not sure quite how to put this, but if I said that Nell Cottrell was in hospital and—'

His answer was a most emphatic declaration of love and anger.

She pressed the phone to her cheek afterwards, uncertain what to say – if anything.

'So?' Magnus chose the shortest of words to cue the longest of pauses.

Still not knowing what to say, she looked across at that familiar profile and felt a great wave of affection, hope and love drench her.

'I'm not sure the baby's yours.'

She let out a little squeak after she had said this, appalled at herself. Oh God. She hadn't meant to put it like that. She hadn't meant to say it at all. She was just voicing wish fulfilment. But by doing so, she hurt the thing she loved most with a mortal blow to his pride.

He answered very carefully. 'What makes you say that?'

'She wants to see her ex – the one she was briefly back with again just after we formed the band.'

'And you think this "brief" back together may have led to her pregnancy?'

'I don't know,' she said in a small voice, realising that she was wrecking everything. 'I just think you should be prepared.'

'To find out I'm not going to be a father?'

Remembering Nell's parting words, Dilly went for broke, knowing that she would never again lie to him or with him after this.

'I think,' Dilly said eventually, 'that Milo was actually Nell's greatest high. She says he was the only man she's ever loved.'

He drove her home in silence, cranking up the volume on the CD stacker and the blast from the heater.

Déjà vu hit her along with the sound and the hot air.

It was like being in a car with Flipper. Or Nell.

'I'm sorry,' she muttered.

But her words were lost amid the beat and heat. Apologising wasn't enough. She had humiliated and hurt him without intending to. And he would, she was certain, never forgive her. He wanted to be a father. He wanted to be one with the woman he loved, bringing up the fused little being their blood, DNA and souls had created.

And his so-called friend had just blown his dreams. There was no apology known to man – even to Dilly, the mother and father of all apologists – that made up for her clumsy, blurted poison in his ear.

27

'So what *did* this Milo say that made you so convinced he loved Nell?' Ellen asked the following morning, when Dilly checked in for one of her increasingly rare but precious Goose Cottage invasions.

'He said "If she fucking dies, I'll kill her".'

'And that's *love*?' Ellen was confused.

'Undying.' Dilly settled the teapot on the coffee table, edging the usual mess out of the way.

'Sounds pretty mortal to me.'

'You had to hear his voice. There was so much choke in it.'

'Probably a smoker.'

Dilly shook her head. 'He loves her. Face it, everyone loves her. I do.'

'I don't. I mean, I like her, but . . . ah. Oops.'

Dilly was staring fixedly at a point just to the left of the teapot. A point occupied by a spread of promotional freebies sent to Spurs' company, Con. Not very well hidden beneath complimentary tickets to a film première were several jazzy phone sim cards in little plastic pouches that had gold lettering suggesting 'Call On Us'. They were unmistakeably the same as those Dilly and Magnus had received as gifts.

'How do you feel about motherhood, Ellen?' Dilly asked quietly.

'Terrified.'

'And Fairy God Motherhood?'

'It wasn't my idea. I was just the fairy . . .'

Dilly gritted her teeth. 'To my godless mother?'

'Well, Pixie thought it up first and Pheely did the product placement, but Anke is better at texting than any of us . . .'

Dilly stomped back home, but her mother and Basil were AWOL, although Pheely's phone was prominently plugged into its charger.

She pounded up the little rickety stairs to her room and gathered all her sketches together before carrying them downstairs to feed them into the stove.

Then she slotted the FGM card into her mother's phone and took it, and Hamlet, for a walk along the River Folly, noticing to her shame that the vile-coloured people carrier now had a Police Beware sticker on the windscreen and lots of stripy tape along the river bank behind it. Several villagers were standing around, including the ubiquitous Glad Tidings.

'Isn't that your mother's new car?' Gladys asked her.

'Left the handbrake off,' Dilly explained, dashing past.

'Poor girl.' Gladys watched her go. 'With a mother like that, it's no wonder she's a bit touched, too.'

Dilly texted Magnus on the FGM sim card number, but he didn't reply.

She sat on a stile in a cold blast of windy drizzle, looking down on a milk-misted Oddlode, waiting, but nothing came back and eventually she trailed home to find her mother in a vile temper having had the police on her doorstep asking about the waterlogged car.

'They seemed to think *I* caused the bloody thing to get in there. And give me my bloody phone back!'

'Here you go, Mother. Or should that be Fairy God Mother?'

Pheely feigned innocence.

'Thank you for fucking up my life.'

'Thank you for fucking up mine.'

'I didn't ask to be born.' Dilly found the classic teenage rebellion cliché a year too late.

'Oh, for God's sake. Your birthday was the best day of my life. My love is come to me.'

Dilly wavered, outgrown teenage anger and misunderstood spite dying on her tongue.

'I love you more than ever,' Pheely said simply.

'Why?'

'Because you are more than me.'

'Why more?'

'Stronger. Sweeter. Better.'

'I'm not. I wish people would stop telling me I'm better than them. If I was better I wouldn't have messed everything up like this.'

'You haven't messed anything up.'

'I have!' she howled. 'All I ever wanted was to find a soulmate, someone to love and to love me, but when I do the timing is all wrong and I'm too frightened to believe it's there and then he falls for someone else and I still just can't stop myself falling, you know? Falling so far.'

'You *have* found that love Dilly.'

'How d'you know?'

'Because it's been waiting for you all along. For God's sake, you and Magnus are so devoted to each other, everyone else can see it except you. You two only have eyes for one another, but you're still the only ones who can't see what's going on.'

'But Nell—'

'Nell saw it from the start and wanted a little bit of it. Who wouldn't? It's the most beautiful thing in the world. Unconditional love. I've never kept a hold of it with a man, but I do know what it feels like. It's how I love you. How I love Basil. It's a love you can't stop, whatever obstacles you come up against. It's forever love.'

'And you really think I have that?'

'In your grasp.'

Head spinning happily, Dilly pressed a hand to each of her mother's soft, pink cheeks and kissed them in turn.

'You are more than a Fairy God Mother. You are the best mother. Beyond fairy-tales and religion and maternal instincts. You are my life, too.'

Pheely's big green eyes filled with tears.

'So let go and love. You have me and Basil right behind you.'

'What do I do?' Dilly asked in a panic.

'I'd say that anything I didn't do would be a good start.'

'What did you do so wrong?'

'Nothing.'

Dilly laughed. 'There is a time and a place for your ego, Mum, but this isn't . . .'

'I did everything wrong by doing *nothing*,' Pheely extrapolated. 'That's what I've always done wrong. Doing nothing; waiting for something. *Do* something, Dilly.'

Dilly changed clothes hurriedly and dashed to River Cottage to tack up Otto.

He was in a curiously compliant mood, even tolerating the traffic on the Lower Oddlode road so that Dilly could hack – slowly – past Wyck Farm. Several times. No cars were parked outside. Magnus didn't rush out and whisk her off to the woods as she had daydreamed he would. She and Otto just got bored and damp trailing back and forth.

She was dilly-dallying. Just like her mother. Just as her mother had warned her not to do. Pheely – a classic passive self-dramatist – liked to drape herself seductively on every park bench in Oddlode in the hope that Giles would jog past and notice her, when the painful truth was that knocking on his door was far easier. Yet Dilly, for all her mother's wise advice, was just like her. She wanted life to happen to her and not vice versa.

And she was already almost an hour late for work.

Despite this, she rode Otto determinedly along the Wyck Farm drive.

The place was deserted; both house and annexe were locked. Had Dilly been brave enough to check earlier, she could have saved herself wearing Otto's shoes down on the tarmac and annoying the traffic.

'Oh God, how lovesick can you get?' she apologised, giving him a pat before trotting him back through Oddlode and turning him out for a roll. Having brayed himself hoarse with separation anxiety, little Bottom was beside himself with delight to have his field-mate back.

'Know how you feel, chum.' Dilly hugged him guiltily before heading to the market garden and apologising to Pixie for being late.

'How's life?' Pixie's sparkly grey eyes were more mischievous than ever. '*Truth*fully?'

Dilly gave her a curious look, but said nothing, leaving her to guard the till and read the recycled papers while she took on the mammoth task of forking piles of manure into the veg beds. She didn't feel like bonding with her Fairy God Mother right now any more than with her own mother. They both gave lousy advice and mucked up her life. Women of a certain age were, she decided, a liability. Although some had useful lifestyle accessories . . .

Half an hour later, dripping with sweat, she steamed back to Pixie.

'Can I have a couple of hours off and borrow your car?'

'I thought you'd never ask.' Pixie handed over the keys to her ancient Land Rover and reached for her phone to call the Fairy Godless Mothers with the good news.

With the Land Rover parked illegally in a doctor's bay, Dilly thundered to Nell's bedside.

A very dishy medic was leaning over her in a moment straight from *ER*.

'Sorry!' Dilly backed away.

'Stay, Dilly!' Nell ordered, then looked at the medic. 'You – go.'

Such was Nell's magnetism, Dilly stayed and the dishy doctor left, casting her a furious look as he passed.

'How do you make people do that?' Dilly asked Nell after he had gone. 'Anything you want?'

'I dunno. I just do.' She opened her arms. 'Come here.'

Dilly did as told.

It wasn't a Magnus hug, but it came close.

'I didn't think you *did* hugging.'

'I don't. And now I have broken ribs I know why. Ouch! You can get off now.' She sagged back against the pillow, her grey-green eyes twinkling mischievously from her tanned face. 'But you saved my life, so you get anything you want.'

Dilly laughed, cupping her cheeks.

'I love you.'

'I know. I wish I were a bloke. You and I could be something else.'

'How many drugs have they given you?'

'Hardly any.' Nell grinned, showing off a broken front tooth. 'In fact I can't wait to get back home for a top-up from my own supplies. I'm coming out tonight.'

'Really?'

'We Cottrells are tough.'

'Telling me.'

'Look at Flipper. He should be in this bed. Broken hearts take much longer to mend than collapsed lungs.'

Dilly hung her head. 'He didn't love me.'

'He did – he does. He loves the same people as me. It's always been agony for us.'

'So you love this woman that he can't get over?'

'Absolutely.'

'Who is she?'

'Well it sure as hell isn't me.' Nell pinched Dilly's nose playfully. 'You know that.'

Dilly watched her eyes closely, her own crucified with shame. 'Oh God. You know I thought that?'

'Stop apologising. Yes, I knew you thought it. You're not the first.'

'I can't bear the fact I almost believed—'

'Forget it. I lost my heart a long time ago. So did Flipper. We share that. It's *our* pact.'

Dilly nodded, not asking for more of an explanation because she knew for certain that she wouldn't get it. Instead, she stuck a small, guilty spear in her own side to remind her that the fantasies and daydreams, good and bad, were well and truly over.

'Magnus will be a good father. The best.'

'I agree.'

'He'll look after you.'

'Always.'

'He loves you.'

'Totally. I know.'

Dilly blinked away the tears and nodded in time with Nell.

'Like you love me.' Nell touched her nodding cheek.

Dilly kept on nodding, like a plastic dog on a car's parcel shelf.

'Because he loves the things you love.' Nell smiled tearfully.

Still Dilly nodded.

'He loves you so much – you love him so much – you can't differentiate between your desires. Like me and Flipper.'

Dilly nodded. Then stopped nodding.

'Are you saying . . .'

'You're twins. Soulmates. You and Mags. I can't tell the two of you apart – and I've slept with both of you,' she couldn't resist joking, although her sea-green eyes were turbulent.

'But I thought you said – you and Flipper—'

'I love Milo. He is my greatest – only – true love.'

'Your *dog*?'

'He is a bit of a dirty dog,' she grinned.

'Hardly a responsible father.'

'Flipper says that, too. That's what gets me. He just can't love Milo like I do.'

'Well, it's pretty unnatural.'

'That's what Flipper says. He thinks Magnus is a much better bet.'

'Good on Flipper.'

'Good on Flipper.'

There was a pause – confused on Dilly's part and drugged-out and exhausted on Nell's.

'I told Magnus about what happened,' Dilly blurted.

'About what?' Nell asked groggily.

'What happened at school before you were expelled. The house with the butterflies, and me taking the rag – the rap. Whatever you used to call it.'

Nell snorted, unable to resist laughter. 'Darling Dilly – always falling into *double entendres*. The rag! You took the rap with wings and lock-in core. Oh, Dilly, what did I do to you?' She started to cry again.

'I never minded.'

'That's why I love you.'

'And hate me?' Dilly echoed a previous conversation. 'I mean you want to punish me?'

'Maybe,' she admitted, blinking away her tears and reaching up to affectionately pull Dilly's hair from her forehead. 'It was my greatest low at that time.'

'Milo,' Dilly kept echoing.

'Milo,' Nell soothed, then looked up. 'Milo! Hi. You're back.'

Dilly looked across at the door where the dishy medic had reappeared.

'*You're* Milo?'

Tall, broad-shouldered, chisel-jawed and high-cheeked, he had the bluest eyes and the blackest mop of shiny, tousled hair.

He smiled and kissed her cheek, and Dilly's *déjà vu* went haywire. He looked like Flipper. He looked like Magnus. He looked right through her and right at Nell. It was the best sort of *déjà vu*.

It was starting to make sense.

Without thinking, Dilly held up her palm. Nell high-fived it.

The Land Rover had been clamped. Dilly had no mobile phone to call the release number, no change for a pay-phone and no time for practical sense.

She walked home. Twenty miles. It gave her lots of time to think.

'I love you,' she repeated through the rain. 'I love you.'

It kept her going. She just had to conjure up his smile and she walked another mile without noticing.

With burning feet, burning heart and sodden shoulders, she hammered on the annexe door. There was no answer. She reached up for the key.

'He's gone back to Essex,' announced a voice behind her.

'Essex?' Dilly turned to find Faith at her shoulder – all mad, frizzy hair and familiar blue eyes.

'County just to the east of Cambridgeshire.'

'I know where it is. Why?'

'Guess.'

'Looking up old friends?'

Faith's wide, sandy eyebrows shot up into ironic arcs. 'Looking for his heart. He lost it there first, after all.'

'Meaning?'

Faith, defensive and spiky as always, gave Dilly a shuttered look.

'You always return to your roots in times of crisis. He's looking up his exes.'

'Essexes.' Dilly backed away, feeling sick. 'Lovely Ess-exes.'

'You don't know him,' Faith said firmly.

Dilly closed her eyes for a moment, remembering the evening that Magnus had come to the Lodge cottage and told her, in his honest, straightforward way, that he wanted to get to know her. But, as well as knowing, they had inevitably started loving each other. Until loving eclipsed knowing each other. Loving had blinded them to the things they really knew in their hearts.

'I want to know him,' she told Faith now, desperate for an ally; certain she would understand. 'I really want to know him.'

Faith feigned indifference. 'Yes, but you don't really know my brother at all, do you?'

'I do!' she pleaded urgently. 'I *know* him like you *know* Rory. And I want to know him better, like you want to know Rory better.'

Faith hung on the door edge, sensitive and clever, getting the gist immediately. 'Does Rory *know* me?'

'He will.' Dilly nodded confidently. 'One day, he will know you better than he knows anyone.'

Faith's familiar blue eyes creased with familial wonder –

straightforward, honest and grateful. 'Magnus knows you better than anyone. That's why he's gone away.'

'I don't understand . . .'

'He's trying to be as brave as you. I think he's a bit hung up about how brave you are compared to him.'

Dilly baulked. 'Me? Brave.'

'You faced up to your father after all those years.' Faith pulled awkwardly at a strand of frizzy hair.

'He told you that?'

She nodded, blue eyes looking away, already damp. 'I have a bit of an issue with my father, you see. He thought it might help – knowing someone like you, someone so cool, had a similar . . . *thing* going on.'

Dilly nodded, seeing instantly around the scuffy-toed teenage language to the burning, misunderstood heart.

'He was right.' She reached out to stroke Faith's arm, absurdly flattered at the idea of being 'cool'.

And, at that moment, despite her own angst and panic and lovesick, lovelorn urgency, Dilly felt her heart go out to Faith, knowing exactly where she was coming from. 'You really want to get to know your father, don't you?' she asked.

Faith sniffed, shrugged, glared at her feet and stepped back before thrusting her chin up and staring fixedly at Dilly, blue eyes no longer friendly or familiar.

'You're going to marry Flipper Cottrell, aren't you?'

'Whoever said that?'

'Nell told Magnus. Ages ago. When they were first getting together.'

'Oh God.' Dilly closed her eyes. 'I'm so, *so* not.'

'Why does Magnus think that then?'

'I didn't tell him otherwise.' She pressed her palms over her clenched eyelids in horror as she felt her own shortcomings coming up to short circuit her mind. 'Just like I didn't really tell him I love him. Just shouted it to the wind.'

'Shame.' Faith had a good line in surly lack of reassurance. 'I think you lost him there.'

'You do?' Dilly bleated.

Faith curled her lip thoughtfully, shrugged again and then nodded. ''Fraid so. He just can't compete with Flipper. The guy is a god. Even I fancy him and I'm in love with—'

'Flipper is an arsehole!' Dilly wailed, fingers still laced across her eyes. 'A lovable, hateable arsehole! He's arrogant, unsympathetic, workaholic, anal, self-obsessed, not to mention madly in love with somebody else, who he'll never reveal – and he can't bloody *talk*.'

'Don't you love him then?' Faith asked simply.

'I hardly *know* him.'

She said it without the double-meaning, but Faith picked up on it anyway.

'You're someone worth knowing. He's not.'

'You are someone worth knowing, too.' Dilly fought more tears as she realised that Magnus might never forgive her now.

Letting her hands fall from her face at last, she looked into those blue eyes opposite her – so like Magnus's – and felt a great oil geyser of emotion erupt from her chest as she exploded forwards and embraced Faith in a tight hug.

At first it was like hugging a particularly stubborn ironing board that was half-open and clanking its metal limbs around awkwardly. Then, just as suddenly, it turned into a Magnus hug. Dilly and Faith hugged like the oldest and most loyal of compatriots.

Unfortunately, Faith's empathy wasn't quite on the same Magnus scale. 'I'm sorry you lucked out on my brother,' she muttered over Dilly's shoulder. 'You two would have been pretty cool together. But at least he's got Nell – and the baby. And you're pretty, so you can have anybody . . .'

Dilly held herself together surprisingly well given the numb shock of truth that was fast-tracking its way through her bloodstream. Magnus thought she loved Flipper and would marry him; Magnus was looking up exes in Essex; Magnus was going to be a father; Magnus had no idea how much she loved him; Magnus might – just might – love her as much in return. With amazing grace, she thanked Faith for her time and then ran all the way home, heart burning like a furnace as she sobbed inconsolably.

The cottage was in semi-darkness, lit just by the wood-burning stove.

Her mother was asleep in bed with Basil tucked beside her. Dilly checked, as she always did – and drew solace as ever.

She fed logs into the fuel burner and fed one sim card after another into her mother's phone.

'*Please play the hunt ball. I'll be there,*' she tapped with clumsy fingers, needing to go back and forth endlessly to correct mistakes.

No response.

'*I miss you.*'

No response.

'*You were right all along.*'

Nothing.

'*Are Essex exes distracting you?*'

There was no laughter in her jokey desperation. And no response.

Dilly went for broke: '*I love you, I love you, I love you.*'

It was three days before she got an answer. Three days of begging, borrowing and stealing her mother's phone to check her sim card almost hourly. Three days of twisting herself inside out, working every possible scenario in her head, convincing herself that he was everything from dead to shacked up with a footballer's wife, and feeling everything from hatred for her to complete lack of interest.

His text was by far the best thing that she had ever read in her life – and that included all the works of Jane Austen, the Brontës and Helen Fielding collectively.

'*In Sweden, not Essex. Figuring out fathers. Mobile only works up mountains here. Have climbed a mountain to tell you I love you too.*'

'*I love you to death, too!*'

'*I love you better alive.*'

'*I love you with all my heart.*'

'*I love you with all my body.*'

'*I love you with all my soul.*'

'*I love my soulmate.*'

'*I love mine too.*'

'*I want you with me right now.*'

'*Me too.*'

'*Want to get naked.*'

'*Me too.*'

'*I want you night and day, even in sub-zero temperatures.*'

'*Prove it,*' Dilly texted back.

He sent her a photograph of a lot of snow, a big smile and a deliciously pink rock face. '*Small mountain,*' he captioned modestly. It wasn't.

Dilly sent back something equally X-rated, captioned '*Steep, deep valley.*'

'What *is* this?' her mother asked in horror when she discovered the photograph on her phone whilst trying to change her ring-tone as she did on a daily basis.

'Oh, that's just a close-up of Otto that went wrong.' Dilly waved her arms around before racing along the lanes to apologise to Otto.

He flattened his ears and bared his teeth.

Dilly kissed him on the nose and danced along to Manor Farm.

Ely eyed her suspiciously down his long nose.

Dilly managed to resist hugging him although she took his hands in hers and squeezed them fiercely. 'Can I borrow a car?'

He withdrew his fingers from hers with clinical precision. 'Will you drive it into the river?'

'No.'

'Then you may.'

He handed over the keys to his precious Range Rover.

'I ripped up your cheque,' she told him as she took them.

'I know.'

'I just wanted a hug.'

'I gave you that.'

'You did. Thank you. And this is the last favour I will ever ask, I promise.'

He smiled – a rare and sacred Gates event. 'I hope not. I'm rather enjoying you coming of age at last.'

'You mean that?'

'Don't spoil the moment with frivolity.'

'Sorry. Can I have another hug?'

'No.'

'What then?'

'Respect. Every respect.'

Dilly beamed at him, shook the keys, promised to take care of his precious car and then drove it like a maniac all the way to Fox Oddfield.

Flipper let her into the attic flat, cool and defensive.

Dilly hugged him, throwing him off guard.

Nell was draped on the sofa in a white silk kimono, reading *The Da Vinci Code*, fragile and beautiful as ever, despite the paw-prints up one arm and the spliff dangling from her mouth.

'I want to talk about Magnus,' Dilly announced breathlessly.

'Milo's here,' she warned, nodding towards the kitchen, from which Milo was emerging with a brace of beer bottles, blue eyes narrowed. He handed one to Flipper as they exchanged matching suspicious expressions. Just for a moment, it was almost impossible to tell them apart.

At ankle level, dressed in a nurse's uniform, Milo the chihuahua gave Dilly a friendly yap, rubbing a small paw across his muzzle and then tilting his head up to her with a poppy-eyed expression that clearly said, 'For God's sake, sort this mess out.'

Dilly grinned, marching up to scoop Milo – both Milos – into a big hug.

'I want Entwined to rehearse a new song,' she told the twins and the Milos. 'I want us to perform it at the hunt ball.'

'Are you going to propose to Magnus?' Nell asked expectantly.

'No,' Dilly shook her head. '*You* are. Like we always planned . . .'

28

Eastlode Park looked spectacular, a shimmering jewelled box on the frosted cushion of its plump lawns, its tall windows beaming out golden warmth from the cool of silvery floodlit walls, carved out with intricate, luminescent relief work

By seven thirty, the small procession of cars and taxis that had been making their way along the carriage sweep towards the famous hotel had turned into a gridlocked jam.

At its rear, Dilly was crammed between Pixie and her mother in the Land Rover cab.

It wasn't quite Cinderella's coach, but it was good enough for Dilly.

'Magnus is definitely going to be back in time to perform?' Pixie checked for the fifth time.

'Anke is collecting him from the airport as we speak,' Pheely assured her.

'I wanted to collect him,' Dilly grumbled.

'You'd both never make it back here if you did,' her mother pointed out.

'I would. I have to play him a special song. We've been rehearsing it all week.'

'Which is why you and Magnus must be kept apart until you do.'

'I don't understand why,' complained Dilly, who had been exchanging such long, hot and steamy calls and texts with Magnus all week that she had broken her mother's mobile handset and was now texting furiously on Pixie's.

'You will,' Pixie smiled reassuringly, casting her precious little phone an anxious look. Dilly texted like a maddened virtuoso pianist taking it out on Rimsky-Korsakov's *Flight of the Bumble Bee*.

'This was supposed to be my idea!' Dilly fumed. 'I wanted to be there when he landed. I can't believe the bloody Swedish air traffic controllers have been striking all week. Oh!' Her face lit up along with the phone as it announced a message. 'He's on the ground.'

'I hope you land soon, too,' Pheely muttered, knowing that like anyone newly and obsessively in love, Dilly had spent the past four hours convincing herself that the plane would crash and that she would lose him for ever.

'Why can't I be there with him now?' she groaned, so desperate to be reunited that she resented any interference.

But the Fairy Godless Mothers had taken over the show, ably assisted by the Three Disgraces.

Deep within the Eastlode Park cellars, Sperry, Fe and Carry Sixsmith were in charge of setting up for the live bands and the DJ. Between them, they had overseen the transformation of the vaulted subterranean space from a whitewashed, brightly lit wine storage chamber to a magical grotto.

'Best thing I ever did, roping these girls in,' Ellen told Spurs when they headed downstairs to check on progress.

The space looked amazing, lit by countless long strings of fairy lights and votives with flickering candles. At one end, the cave-like cellars had been filled with squashy red velvet sofas and stools, along with low tables. A temporary bar was set up alongside, backing on to the old stone wine shelves. A long empty dance floor led to the 'stage' of raised rostra backing on to the long corridors of tall, modern wine shelves which provided plenty of privacy for the bands to prepare.

There would be two live sets – firstly Trackmarks, immediately after dinner had taken place upstairs in the ballroom, and then the DJ would fill the floor for an hour before Entwined took the stage.

Rumour was rampant that Trackmarks were only playing after a huge cash bung from Ely; gossip was also rife that Entwined were missing their lead guitarist, singer and lyricist; and the word on the street – or lane – was that the two bands enjoyed such a violent rivalry that a fight was inevitable.

Spurs, still on his best behaviour after deceiving Ellen about the team chase, went to check that the Three Disgraces were happy with progress.

'We're cool.' They looked at him in their blank, beautiful way. 'We'll just have to try to stop Trackmarks stage-diving and beating up Entwined.'

'God, I hope it's not going to get violent?'

'With Saul Wyck, you never know . . .' Ghosts of naughty smiles crossed three sets of lips. They were secretly rather hoping for a fight.

Spurs ran his finger around the tight collar of his dress shirt and blew out through his mouth worriedly. He had fought hard against his mother posting older chaperones in the cellars all night to ensure the younger generation were 'behaving decorously', but now he wasn't so sure it hadn't been a good idea.

He helped Ellen up the winding stairs. She was panting heavily by the time she reached the top.

Just days away from her due date, she was finding even quite short walks heavy going as Heshee weighed down between her legs and in the small of her back.

'I don't think I'll be tackling those stairs again until Entwined plays,' she laughed. 'But I have to be there for that.'

'What exactly *is* Dilly planning for tonight?'

Ellen raised her palms. 'I'm not sure. I just know that she's just a *little* bit out of control right now.'

'God help us.'

Standing at the top of the sweeping steps to the hall, alongside Lady Belling and two of the Vale of the Wolds MFHs, Ely Gates looked spectacular in black tie as he greeted arriving guests. He had just the right breadth of shoulders and narrowness of hips, the sharp contrast of black and white set off his silver mane, and his blue eyes positively glittered with self-satisfaction. Flanking him proudly, Hell's Bells, dressed in an ancient but serviceable Hardy Amies ball gown, had been shooting him furtive looks of approval from over her broad, taffeta-encrusted shoulders all night.

Ely was certainly at his most dashing and convivial. The night looked set to be a triumph. He was particularly pleased with the reaction to his much talked-about Look Before You Leap prize. It had been kept a complete secret, with just enough carefully-worded rumours allowed to get out in order to whip up speculation and interest.

Only Ely knew that the first couple to take advantage of the Leap Day tradition and become engaged that evening would win their wedding at Eastlode Park – an all-expenses-paid day to remember set in the hotel recently voted amongst the top ten wedding venues in the world by Condé Nast.

All the guests had been told was that any woman who proposed and was accepted that night was in for a big surprise.

Ely liked surprises, just so long as he was the one behind them.

And tonight, he was not at all surprised to find that his daughter was amongst the most beautiful women to arrive. He had provided a substantial share of her genetic make-up, after all.

Dilly looked exquisite. Poured into a borrowed turquoise silk dress that had once carried Jemima Cottrell around the ballroom of the Dorchester in the admiring arms of childhood sweetheart and husband, Piers, she radiated anticipation. Her blonde curls were drawn back at the nape of her neck with the simplest of jewelled clips; her huge green eyes, brought out by the colour of the dress, had just the lightest of kohl and mascara adorning them. Her cheeks glowed pink from excitement, not the war-paint so heavily applied by most of the other women.

To Ely, she was perfection and at last he could admit it – to himself, to her and to her mother.

'You look beautiful,' he told Dilly with a gallant kiss. 'I'm very proud of you. Good luck tonight.'

Standing behind her daughter, Pheely almost fell back down the steps.

'And you look – well, dear Ophelia,' he added to her courteously. 'Very well.'

Pheely, who had gone rather overboard with costume jewellery despite an already intricately beaded dress, actually looked like a large and colourful chandelier, but she suddenly felt like the most attractive woman in the valley. Ely's admiration had that effect on one. He always had.

Dilly reached up a hand to his neatly bearded face and, balancing on tip toes, planted a kiss on his cool cheek. 'I'm proud of you, too,' she told him happily.

'Oh, cut the sentimental crap – I need a drink,' hissed Pixie, who had just spotted estranged husband Sexton rolling up the steps with blowsy new girlfriend, Jacqui.

Resplendent in an electric-blue velvet body tube that matched her hair, Pixie dragged her companions at speed through the grand entrance to the foyer bar like a small, shiny blue balloon losing air fast and trailing its rounder, shiny chums behind her.

$\star$ $\quad$ $\star$ $\quad$ $\star$

The Cottrell twins arrived amid the usual family chaos, all squabbling and chatting and hailing hellos left, right and centre. The various Cottrells alone took up a table of twelve and, with a succession of friends, house guests and business associates in tow, the family party spilled on to two further tables.

Flipper and Nell were stuck on a table with Giles and his mother, Great-aunt Grania, along with impossibly boring banking friends of their brother-in-law and two of the Cottrell auctioneers whom they knew from experience had the loudest voices in the county and no table manners.

As such they had little or no intention of sitting down to eat, much to the horror of their hungry dates for the night.

Flipper had invited one of the prettier veterinary assistants from the practice; Nell's date – much to her father's fury – was Lloyd Fenniweather, the good-looking senior negotiator from rival estate agents, Seatons.

She and Dilly immediately hosted a much-needed briefing in the loos.

Dilly had been so busy keeping up her frenzied text life with Magnus all week that the two had hardly caught up between rushed band rehearsals.

Still battered and bruised from her team chase fall, Nell boasted a scarred cheek and a temporary ultra-white tooth in her smile, along with a bandaged chest and sling, but she still out-classed all the thick-set, healthy hunting women around them who were frantically hoiking up drooping cleavages and calming wind-chapped complexions in the plush Eastlode Park cloakrooms.

Still absurdly tanned, Nell was swathed in a tight, white velvet body-stocking of a dress with a high collar at one end and a fish tail at the other. It was pure vamp, softened by smudged kohl eyes, pink lips and tufted, urchin hair. She looked, to Dilly, unutterably beautiful.

'No Milo tonight?' she asked in surprise.

Nell pulled a face. 'I never said we were going to get back together.'

'But he's so obviously nuts about you.'

'As am I about him. I just don't think his wife would be so keen.'

Dilly's jaw dropped.

'She lives in Amsterdam – some sort of hot-shot promoter out there. They have a pretty good thing going on,' Nell said matter of factly, reapplying her mascara.

'So he's not – you're not . . .'

'We'll always be something to each other – friends, lovers, enemies—'

'Parents?'

Nell cast her a sideways look, those amazing verdigris eyes characteristically direct, despite a ghost of a wink. 'Magnus *is* the father.'

Dilly took a deep breath and turned to look at her own reflection, which had drained of colour.

She felt Nell's shoulder lean against hers. 'You still want me to propose to him tonight?'

'Are you still prepared to?'

'I'd do anything for you.'

'Likewise.' Dilly felt a great quiver of strength run across every muscle.

Their eyes met in the mirror and they smiled. Real smiles. Brave smiles. Radiant smiles.

'I adore you.'

'I adore you.'

Rory arrived late – as usual – with new girlfriend Justine Jones in tow. One of his favourite pupils at the riding school, she was a deliciously bright-eyed, buxom devotee swaddled in plunging black lace and satin, glossy brown bob swishing this way and that as she turned constantly to take in the amazing hotel.

Faith Brakespear, corseted in chest-flattening burgundy silk that had looked better in the Monsoon dressing-room, regarded her beloved's date with something close to hatred as she stalked them around the ballroom. Frizzy mane pinned into submission like a helmet, badly applied mascara already running, she skulked self-loathingly from corner to corner, observing her opposition at play.

Justine was a social climber extraordinaire, Faith noted bitterly. Within minutes she had air-kissed Rory's blowsy, raven-haired sister Diana and her sinister, glowering lover, Amos Gates.

Faith was briefly entertained by the distraction of watching Amos spot his ex-wife Jacqui in the arms of new squeeze Sexton, both shimmying ostentatiously across the room – her gold ball dress perfectly matching her dyed hair and his cummerbund. He looked furious.

Then she scowled at Justine Jones again as she split away from Rory and fell into the arms of Spurs and Ellen. How dare Justine know them, Faith thought furiously. She and Rory had barely been going out more than a week or two. Acting so familiar with his family was far too soon. Justine was beyond impertinent.

Too angry to watch, she glanced around the room at the white-clothed circular tables with their gold-sprayed, red-seated chairs, their loaded wine coolers, lavish place settings and flaming candles. It was just like every hunt ball she had ever imagined – only better. A far cry from the piss-ups in rugby clubs she remembered being hosted by their old Essex hunt. This was the posh Cotswolds, she reminded herself. It was grown-up stuff.

Had it not been for the alternative party taking place in the cellars – and the fact that she was so intrinsic to it – she might have gathered up her shapeless burgundy skirts and run home in fright.

Instead she glared at Justine again and noted with interest that her bra strap was showing and that it was a grubby grey one. It made Faith feel better, despite watching Justine flipping her glossy bob as she talked to Flipper Cottrell and a ravishing blonde.

You just wait, Faith thought murderously. You just wait until you realise just how cool I am.

At that moment, Rory looked across at her.

Faith froze, forgetting to smile.

But Rory had been brought up with rigid good manners and, despite the black look from his teenage *protégée*, he raised his glass and flashed his widest, sweetest smile.

Faith almost keeled over.

'Steady on!' brayed an eager young party-goer dressed in trad hunting pinks as she cannoned back against him. 'Dance later?'

Faith was so fuelled by unrequited love and lust that she dusted him down quite amiably and patted his arm.

'Believe me, you'll be dancing to my tune later, buster.'

Hamish – a young vet from the same clinic as Flipper – turned to chum Trist and muttered, 'Be a bloody corker in a couple of years that one – ugly as sin now, but I know the type. Mature well.'

'Want to stake an early claim?'

'God, no – like drinking wine before it's ready.'

'Your corker's best left uncorked?' Trist snorted.

'Just so. I say!' His eyes locked on target across the room. 'Rory's bagged a drinkable bubbly.'

'So has King Gorgeous,' Trist sighed as he spotted a slender blonde in light blue sequins. 'I asked Tots along weeks ago and she said she was busy. Bastard KG got in there first.'

'Unlikely. He was seeing Dilly Gently until a week ago, remember? Tots was very much second choice.'

'In that case, I am going to get very drunk.'

It was set to be a night of lusting and lushing. With their red cheeks matching their red coats, bloodshot eyes narrowed against their cigar smoke, Hamish and Trist reeled around the room like loose hounds at a meet.

The ball was on.

The formal dinner passed loudly, raucously and in classic hunt ball tradition – food flew between table settings, many a meet and chase were compared and contrasted, colour flooded cheeks and wine bottles were drained as quickly as they could be replenished by harassed staff. Everyone table-hopped, everyone exclaimed at the amazing venue, and everyone guzzled up the food with astonished relish. It was beyond edible. It was hot – a hunt ball rarity. It looked good – a hunt ball one-off. What's more, it was absolutely delicious.

Between courses, hunting horns sounded and the more raucous of the hunt members – including Hamish, Trist, most of the Cottrells and – surprisingly – Hell's Bells – charged around the ballroom in a strange congo line issuing view halloos and anti-ban chants.

Lounging back in his gold chair with a Rothmans between his lips, Sir St John Belling watched his wife galloping along the sides of the ballroom and, loins stirring, realised that he might be in for some action later. Hunt balls and taking up their debenture seats at the Wimbledon Men's Finals were the only rituals guaranteed to jump-start his wife's libido these days. As his gaze refocused across his family table to his sister-in-law Truffle feeding grapes to lover Ingmar Olensen, he was almost grateful for Isabel's sexual scarcity. Public shows of affection appalled Sir St John.

It was perhaps a good thing, then, that he wasn't watching Giles Hornton applying his wide, sensual, manicured fingers to the silken thighs of new MFH Christine Purnell – a thoroughly seductive blonde with a racy red sports car to match her satin dress, whose workaholic banker husband spent long months overseas.

Pheely Gently, whose coven of Godless Mothers was on a table just yards from Giles and his Cottrell clan, could see the thigh-fondling only too well.

'Pig!' she snarled.

'He's a cad,' Pixie muttered, still glaring at estranged husband Sexton and his ridiculous girlfriend three tables away.

'A very silly man,' Anke agreed, automatically dabbing her napkin into her water glass and sponging a gravy dribble from husband Graham's dress shirt.

Dilly – sitting opposite them and so hopelessly excited that she hadn't eaten a thing – suddenly registered something.

She looked up at the stucco ceiling, at the paintings of fat, earthy cherubs and fleshy women with coy wisps of gauze wafted across their pink bits, at the ornate cornicing and panelling, at the chandeliers and the formal waiting staff and the perfectly laid tables, flower-decked centre-pieces and candle arrangements. Most of all she looked at the raucous guests with their vivid expressions of laughter, gossip, happiness, shock and mirth.

'Magnus will love all this,' she sighed. 'It's the best sort of people watching. He'll love it.'

'Of course he will.' Pheely forgot all about Giles and minxy Catherine Purnell for a moment as she reached a hand across the table to clasp her daughter's. 'We're all loving this.'

'Liar,' Pixie hissed bitterly, and lit a blue cocktail cigarette that matched her hair and dress. Then she laughed. 'Bugger it, you are right. Even *I'm* enjoying this and my bloody husband is dressed like something from *Strictly Come Dancing* to match Jacqui's shock frock. I hope to God she knows he has two left feet.'

Long before petit fours and coffee cups were cleared, tables moved back and the dancing started, it had been universally agreed that this was the best hunt ball the Vale of the Wolds had ever staged.

The hunting horn conga lapped the ballroom several more times; Catherine Purnell's silk stockings descended a few more inches beneath Giles's expert fingers and Ingmar Olensen became so adept at being fed grapes by Truffle Dacre-Hopkinson that she was lobbing them into his mouth from several feet away.

When Foxy Lady struck up the first tune in the set – a jazzy cover of Van Morrison's *Moondance* – the ballroom dance floor filled with lumbering hunt followers, all so high from an excess of good food, wine and bonhomie that they danced like tomorrow might never dawn.

Sir St John clasped Hell's Bells in his arms and dashed her this way and that; she watched around his shoulder as Ely manoeuvred Felicity as expertly around the room as his Range Rover towing a small, overloaded trailer; Ely studied his daughter – birth daughter – over his wife's rigid hair, but Dilly dashed away to join the party downstairs.

In fact, anyone under thirty fled as Foxy Lady moved seamlessly from *Moondance* to Nina Simone's *My Baby Just Cares For Me*.

Singing along under her breath as she let husband Finn dutifully frog-march her up and down the room in a military fashion, Trudy Cottrell watched sadly as the youth disappeared, and she felt herself age as they did so. She was already cast with the octogenerians, her blonde hair feeling grey instead of ash, her vintage oyster-pink dress drab, her ankles fat and her make-up too heavy. She stared fixedly at Finn's shirt studs – monogrammed little silver beads that bullet-pointed his wide chest and flat belly. She reminded herself how grateful she should be. He was one of the best-looking men in the room by far, especially now that the young bloods had left.

Looking up to check that this was true, and catching Giles Hornton giving her a hot look nearby as he twirled a blonde in a red dress beneath his arm like a matador's cape, Trudy clutched her husband tighter.

Then a tall shadow fell across her as brother-in-law Flipper cut in.

'Sorry old chap,' he apologised to his brother. 'Got to take your wife for a spin for a last-minute briefing on stage technique before I head downstairs.'

Finn – gasping for another drink and cigarette – relinquished her rather too gratefully before lurching away.

Taking Flipper's warm left hand in hers and wrapping her right arm around his solid neck, Trudy felt herself spirited to a dark, quiet corner of the dance floor as the band's Nina Simone cover blended seamlessly into a soulful rendition of *You're Just Too Good To Be True*.

'You are just that.' Flipper kissed her cheek.

Trudy shied away politely, as she always did at hunt balls, wedding parties, Christmas celebrations and New Year festivities.

'You are the son I never had.' She squeezed his shoulder, repeating her standard line.

'You'd have been twelve when you gave birth to me,' he reminded her, as he always did.

Her flecked hazel eyes glittered up into his as she touched his cheek.

'Thank you for making me feel better. You're so sweet.'

Flipper tucked her head beneath his chin and felt their bodies move in easy unison, knowing full well that Trudy was the only person in the world who could get away with calling him sweet.

Boogying alongside with wife Jemima, his oldest brother Piers handed across a fat cigar, followed by a cutter and then a lighter.

Juggling all three, Flipper reluctantly let Trudy return to arm's length, the moment lost.

'Fantastic hunt bollock!' Piers boomed over the music as the Andy Williams track switched to Abba's *Dancing Queen*. 'You think you'll get a proposal tonight?'

'What?'

'Your bird going to propose?'

Just for a moment Flipper caught Trudy's wise, copper-flecked eyes before adopting his familiar louche, arrogant front.

'Brother, I expect more proposals than a student union debating chamber.'

'That's the spirit!' Piers slapped him on the back so hard that the cigar shot straight from Flipper's mouth into Trudy's cleavage.

Extracting it, she popped it in her own mouth, took a light from Flipper and walked away.

'Bloody nutter that woman,' Piers trotted out his usual line as he extracted another cigar from his dinner jacket and handed it to his brother. 'Drinks too much.'

Flipper chopped off the end of the new cigar and studied it. 'Don't we all?'

'Only at hunt bollocks.' Piers extracted a PLC hip-flask from his jacket and raised it in a toast. 'We all drink too much at hunt bollocks. Family tradition. And God, this one is good. Might even skinny dip in the Odd later. Foggy Farquar has a bet on –

last man breast-stroking gets a magnum of Krug. Hell's Bells is game apparently.'

'Oh God,' Flipper drew on his cigar and closed his eyes. 'I'm out of here.'

'Where are you going?' Piers asked indignantly.

'To join civilisation.' Flipper handed Jemima his cigar and headed for the cellars just as *Dancing Queen* gave way to *Fly Me To The Moon*.

Beneath many floorboards and layers of bricks, Trackmarks struck up their set just a few seconds later.

Godspell, resplendent in a widow's shroud of black lace and henna tattoos – part flamenco dancer, part dead bride – sang her lungs inside-out from the start. Hidden beneath a gauzy veil that shrouded the microphone from the audience, she screamed into the rounded foam head with erotic zeal, covering it with spit, tasting it with her lips, even biting little chunks from its side. She had never been so unleashed and so sensual.

Behind her, the band wove their magic – Saul, rebellious in a torn T-shirt and painted, ripped jeans, tearing chords and riffs from his guitar like echoes from heartstrings; Ket thudding a heartbeat of a bass: cousins Jobe and Moses echoing that lifeblood beat on drums and keyboards. And, a descant to them all, the true spell-binding ingredient to the supernatural fusion, was the figure on decks at the back, mixing the samples and complex layers that made the music an unholy religion.

The cellar was filled within minutes – old and young, twisting and grinding together to the sexiest music known to the valley. Word spread. Soon they were queuing up the stairs.

Rory ground his hips against Justine's as she flicked her glossy bob; Spurs and Ellen bobbed at the sidelines, both holding the Heshee bump; Flipper and veterinary nurse Tots bumped and grinded in the shadows; Nell and Lloyd

Fenniweather tottered drunkenly to the bar, hips swinging as they joined Hamish, Trist and the other young bloods who were playing drinking games and trying to score.

'This is seriously good ambiance.' Hamish swung his head around in what he hoped was a Glastonbury-hardened way, but came across as more Stevie Wonder meets weaving horse.

Nell hooked her arm through his and demanded a drink.

'You are a god, Hamish – and I have the perfect girl lined up for you.'

'Who?' he asked eagerly, ordering champagne. He hadn't got laid in seven months.

'Called Faith. Fantastic body. Shy, though – needs breaking in.'

'Lead me there,' he panted, handing her a frothy flute.

But when Nell scoured the room, she realised that her little frizzy-haired acolyte was nowhere to be seen.

Meanwhile, the Three Disgraces stood by proudly as Track-marks wowed their audience. Dressed in identical orange satin mini-dresses with long red boots and matching ribbon chokers, they were a three-way knock-out as ever – too terrifying for a single man to approach.

Rory knew no such fear, but with Justine and her flicking bob reapplying her make-up in the loos, he was hardly single these days.

'Just *who* is on their decks?' he asked Sperry Sixsmith as they regarded the character in the hoodie who was carrying the show. 'Magnus has always said they're absurdly talented.'

She smirked. 'Our little mole.'

'Meaning?'

'You should know her.' Sperry glanced at him coolly. 'You spend most days with her, mate.'

At which point Rory recognised the chin, the mouth and the nose poking from the hoodie. He knew the way that tongue was clenched between the very white and slightly crooked front teeth when she was concentrating – she did the same when she was riding her stallion, especially when he was teaching her and giving her a bad time. He knew the freckles on the end of her nose – one was almost a mole and shaped like a new moon; he had noticed it over coffee in the tack room once and found it strangely compelling. He knew the way her chin tucked neatly back into her neck when she was looking down as she was now – he bawled her out about it all the time when she rode, reminding her that she should look up at where she was going, not down at her horse's neck.

'That's Faith!' he gasped.

Sperry winked happily.

'The little cow!' Rory fumed, registering the disloyalty to Entwined – Faith's own brother's band, sworn enemies of Trackmarks.

Sperry shook her head. 'It's cool. She and Godspell are buddies.'

'And Magnus?'

'He's not here.' She shrugged. 'Besides, he doesn't know the history.'

'What history? Why do the bands hate each other so much?'

Sperry glanced across at him, wishing his almond-shaped eyes weren't quite so appealing, or that she wasn't quite such an unscrupulous gossip.

'Saul Wyck went out with Nell Cottrell once – as teenagers.'

'You're kidding?' he spluttered, looking across to where Nell was flirting happily with several men by the bar.

'Rumour has it he took her cherry.'

'When?' Rory demanded, having been under the illusion that he'd performed that task.

'I dunno – she was thirteen or fourteen I think.'

'Ah.' Rory conceded defeat, looking back from Nell to Sperry. 'And?'

'They say she got pregnant.'

'You *are* kidding now?'

'Nope. That's what they say. She got rid of it, of course – but Saul has never forgiven her.'

'Hang on – isn't *she* the Catholic?'

Sperry raised her Hooch bottle. 'Go figure.'

Rory watched Trackmarks again, taking in the anger in Godspell's voice and in Saul's playing. The song – lyrics lost in screams apart from the repeated phrase 'Killing my Future' – suddenly took on a new meaning, interlaced with samples from '*Crying Game*' coming from the decks.

'So why is Faith involved?' he asked Sperry.

'She needs a passion.'

'She has horses.'

'She needs to defend someone. She's a fighter.'

Rory found that hard to believe of the gawky, shy, diffident Faith he knew. She was surly and sulky at times, granted, but she was also very easily led.

'Did you set this up?' He looked at her askance.

Sperry cocked her head. 'I have Godspell's ear and Faith's trust.'

'Meaning?'

'Never under-estimate that girl. She has soul, mate.'

'Meaning?'

'Just you wait. I have Faith. You'll have Faith, too.'

He laughed disbelievingly, turning gratefully as Justine re-joined them, her bob flicking so much that she singed it on his cigarette and then almost blinded him.

Sperry looked away in despair and glanced at her watch worriedly. Magnus was cutting it fine. Rumours and jokes were already circulating that Entwined was under-rehearsed and lacking their star turn. At this rate, they would be a laughing stock. With half-price drinks already being offered at the bar – a hunt ball standard after ten o'clock – they were going to be crucified if he didn't turn up in time.

But she was distracted by Fe tapping her Hooch bottle against her corseted orange chest and announcing that she was going to propose to someone that night.

'Who?' Sperry asked, appalled.

'I dunno – just seems a shame to miss out. I'll be *twenty* next Leap Year. I have to be engaged at least once before then.'

'Who then?' sister Carry demanded.

Fe blew thoughtfully into her Hooch bottle, eyes scanning the room.

'Who?' her sisters demanded in unison.

Fe ran her eyes up and down every man in turn.

'So.' She shrugged. 'Twenty's a good age to get engaged. Nice round figure.'

Her sisters looped arms around her and hugged her tightly as they all dissolved into giggles.

Pheely was the first woman to take Leap Year advantage and propose.

Beads dangling and jangling, she cornered Giles by a large cheese plant and went for broke. She knew that Giles was currently after-darking with Christine Purnell – who was infinitely slimmer, classier, blonder, richer and probably more adventurous in bed than she was – but that didn't matter. She'd had more than a bottle of Sauvignon, two spliffs in the loo with Pixie, and the conviction of a new mother whose old affair had never really gone sour.

'I love you. Marry me.'

Giles pressed his moustache affectionately to her ear and declined.

'I'm just not the marrying sort.'

'You've been married four times.'

'There's proof.'

'Of what?'

'My utter inability to marry for life. Whereas you, Pheely Gently, will be someone I love for life, as will Basil.'

She pressed her nose to his moustache.

'Do you mean that?'

'I've had three glasses of champagne and the best part of a bottle of Shiraz. What do you think?'

'That I will never trust you.'

'Which is why we can never marry.'

Nose and moustache danced happily, although the few tears that crept from Pheely's painted eye into Giles's left sideburn went unnoticed.

Trackmarks were playing their last number. The hired DJ was lurking in the background, ready to start his set.

The atmosphere was electric, the audience astounded at such raw, sensual talent housed beneath the brick arches of a wine cellar, performing at a parochial hunt ball in a backwater.

Godspell's voice rang out, curiously softened by the looping, repeating beat of the sampled tracks spinning from the curious girl in the hoodie on the decks behind her.

And the sampled tracks were even more curious than the girl.

It was the crackling demo of Magnus's *Jealousy*, mixed in with Fauré's *Requiem*. Why it worked was anybody's guess, but it worked. And it rang and sang behind Godspell's carrion call. It was strangely beautiful. Those who danced made out. Those who didn't made eyes. The stairs filled as even the most hardened hunters sought out the sweetest and strangest of new calls.

And in its midst, Godspell proposed to Saul.

Very simply, very shyly, very truthfully.

She stopped the music around her, stepped closer up to the mike and, in her small, strange voice, told the assembled crowd that she wanted to spend the rest of her life with one man, and that man was standing behind her.

'I love you Saul,' her strange, creaky voice cried out finally. 'I love you, I love you, I love you. You are my future.'

Saul, battered-faced and broad-shouldered, moved up to her shoulder.

'I'll marry you,' he breathed, his undertone words only just audible through the amplifiers. 'I'll die if I don't.'

At the top of the cellar stairs, Ely Gates turned away in despair.

Behind the wine racks, smoking a spliff and chewing hard on a fingernail, Nell wished them luck, but felt her heart go out to odd, innocent Godspell. Saul Wyck was not a man she was going to forgive in a hurry. She hoped he'd changed in the past decade. She really hoped he'd changed.

29

Dilly waited, shivering, at the top of the Eastlode Hall steps. She had Rory's dinner jacket over her shoulders and was swathed in Pixie's electric-blue cashmere wrap. She was still so cold that her teeth chattered uncontrollably. He was late. Entwined were due on in three minutes. The big joke of the night was about to become the belly laugh.

Even outside, she could hear the booming beat thumping up from the cellars as the DJ finished his set, clashing with the jazzy tones of Foxy Lady playing Lionel Richie cover versions in the nearby ballroom.

Dilly hugged herself and twirled around on the spot. Through the tall windows to the left, she could see couples dancing in the ballroom, stumbling around together now as they suffered the consequences of half-price wine and *digest-ifs*, a hunt ball tradition to ensure as much debauchery as possible. Several couples were openly kissing, including Giles Hornton and the very married Christine Purnell. Dilly's heart went out to her mother, until she spotted Pheely lurching around with one of the local farriers, her tongue in his ear. Dilly looked hastily away, checking her watch again and cursing her borrowed mobile for running out of battery an hour earlier. Last time she had heard from him, Magnus and Anke were leaving the M40. They should be here by now.

Her heart lurched in panic as she envisaged an accident, the big car twisted and crumpled off the road, Magnus stolen from her before she could kiss him again, tell him that she loved him and shout it to the world.

Not that she would necessarily be able to do that if Nell proposed as intended.

Teeth chattering more than ever, Dilly wondered whether Nell would keep her promise. She had to. It was their pact. She felt sick with nerves, knowing that what she had asked was wrong. But she had to know for certain that she had his heart – and the only way to find that out was for him to make the ultimate brave gesture and turn down a proposal of marriage from the mother of his child. Nell was the one who had insisted that she must do it in public. All Dilly wanted was reassurance – childish, certainly, and very underhand, but Nell was a soulmate too and understood why she needed it to happen. She was willing to take the risk, and she insisted it had to be in front of a room full of witnesses. Dilly, who had been so battered and bruised by love in her short life that she no longer trusted its existence, needed proof. Nell would get that proof for her. That's what friends did, wasn't it?

But, downstairs, the witnesses were getting restless. The thumping had stopped in the cellars and Dilly could hear jeers and slow clapping. Entwined were due on stage. Where *was* he?

Then, a set of headlights racing towards her through the frosted mist set her heart beating faster.

Through the tinted glass, she could just make out the gleam of blond curls and the triangle of a white collar. He was doing up his bow-tie with fumbling hands, sun visor pulled down so that he could use the mirror. As he flipped it back up, he saw her at last, blue eyes widening in shock and delight – and Dilly's racing heart put on a sprint finish.

The way he threw himself from the car as it drew level with the steps made that heart skip too many beats to count. The way that he limped up the steps towards her two at a time and grabbed her in his arms made her heart seem to stop for countless seconds. The way he kissed her made her heart restart and beat like a furious drum-roll heralding a grand entrance. Everything added up when he kissed her like that. Lips searched lips as tongue caressed tongue and two bodies merged tightly together with great slamming hearts and thrumming shots of sexual adrenaline pumping through arteries and veins.

'We're on,' she told him, knowing the seconds were counting down, hearing the jeering and shouts far below, knowing that she was about to test him to the limit.

'I love you.' He couldn't stop kissing her.

'I love you, too,' she repeated, kissing him back for all she was worth.

And suddenly she didn't want him to have to go through Nell's proposal test. It wasn't fair. She trusted him with all her heart. He didn't need to prove anything to her any more.

He was dragging her along beneath his arm towards the cellars, stooping to kiss her again and again.

'Mags – wait – there's something I need to tell—'

But the shouts and jeers and clapping that greeted them from the crowded, steamy chamber drowned her words completely.

'King hell!' At the top of the steps, Magnus took in the packed room, its cool décor and louche basement club feel. Suddenly he was in performance mode. He was a singer-songwriter to be reckoned with and he was going to knock them dead, the impatient, braying heathens. Clutching Dilly even tighter to his side, burying his smiles and kisses in her hair, he steered her down through the throng and they joined the twins on the stage.

'About fucking time,' Flipper hissed, picking up his drumsticks. 'This lot were about to bloody eat us.'

Nell blew Magnus a kiss and shot Dilly a mischievous wink that made her feel sick, but there was no time to do anything but sing her heart out.

Without time to sound-check, Entwined launched into their first number.

Feedback shrieked through every mike. Flipper's amp died instantly. Nell had no sound whatsoever. It was just Dilly and Magnus – and they sounded awful. They were distracted, breathless from kissing and over-awed by excitement at seeing one another again. With lumps in their throats and chests full of emotion, their voices simply didn't carry in the strange, echoing space.

The jeering started almost immediately. The drunken hunt followers had no tolerance, especially after Trackmarks' brilliance – plus half an hour's diving and grinding to professional mixes. Their blood was up and they wanted to chase their quarry back to earth.

The next song was worse. Magnus's beautiful, heartfelt lyrics were overlooked completely, the crowd braying and cat-calling throughout. Someone started blowing a hunting horn. Shrieks of laughter and shouts of conversation drowned the music. By their third number, food was being thrown.

Dilly felt tears clutch at her throat, strangling her singing voice. It had all gone horribly wrong. Such an anti-climax. Such a bad omen.

Heart tearing apart with desperation and shame at greeting Magnus home with such a fiasco, she pulled her microphone from its stand and marched on to the dance floor, yelling for all she was worth.

'This next song means something. Please! Give us a chance! Listen!'

But the jeering and food throwing continued unabated. It was a hunt ball. It was close to midnight. For all their lyrical, clever, accessible sexiness, Entwined were just too personal to go public in this crowd.

In defeat, she turned away from the mocking laughter and saw Magnus looking back at her from the stage, his blue eyes so full of love that she knew it shouldn't really matter. He didn't care at all. Being with her at last was all he cared about. And she felt the same.

With that big security blanket of love and sexiness comforting her, she walked towards him, shrugging and laughing in despair. And then suddenly she paused, her eyes lighting up as an idea struck her. With a big smile and a wink, she blew him a kiss and leaped back on to the stage.

Standing behind her keyboard again, Dilly started to play the *Black Beauty* theme tune for all she was worth. Behind her, Magnus immediately cottoned on and joined in, hamming it up to Jimmy Hendrix proportions. Their old party piece.

Laughing as she recognised the tune, Nell danced, tambourine hitting her thigh with maddening speed.

When Flipper added an extraordinary, wild percussion to the familiar cheesy theme tune, cymbals ringing and snare thrumming, the room fell silent in awe and amused respect.

The crowd didn't know what to make of this at all, but they liked it. They liked it a lot – kitsch, nostalgic, rollicking and strangely sexy, it caught their imaginations and brought their drunken, cheerful mischief-making on side.

Then, as the tune finally came towards its end, Flipper rolled a drum faster and faster with hyperbolic frenzy before letting one stick crash down while holding up his free arm, stick twirling, demanding attention. The room quietened dramatically.

He looked across at Dilly, grey-green eyes cueing her in with a ghost of a wink.

Nodding, she glanced across at Magnus with a worried smile and hit the first chords of their newly rehearsed song.

The crowd listened, entranced, as a simple, sweet melody rang out.

She looked at Magnus again.

He raised his eyebrows, confused.

Flipper hit the skins at speed. Fighting painkillers and stiffness, Nell banged tambourine and Dilly started to sing, her sweet descant at last finding an audience attentive and hushed enough to appreciate its warmth and richness:

'*You ride the finest horse*
I've ever seen
Standing sixteen one or two . . .'

Magnus started to laugh, heart crushing with the force of his love.

It was *Ride On*. And the crowd loved it.

At last they had a captive audience. Milky-eyed and docile, they were putty in the band's hands.

When the song finished, the crowd was rapturous, calling for more, more, more.

Dilly and Magnus stared at one another, eyes blazing, smiling stupidly and unstoppably.

It was almost midnight.

Nell had stepped up to the mike.

'I'd like to make a proposal.' She set her jaw as a few cat calls came flying back at her.

Realising what was about to happen, Dilly turned hastily away from Magnus and closed her eyes, powerless to stop Nell.

'I'd like to make a proposal!' she shouted louder. 'Not for me. For soulmates everywhere!'

There was a brief lull.

'I want to propose to Magnus.'

There was a shocked silence, followed by a few wolf-whistles.

Eyes as wide as a hare caught in headlights, Magnus swallowed anxiously.

'I want to ask for his hand.' Nell smiled foxily.

As word flew around, the cellar stairs crowded with yet more interested onlookers desperate to catch the action.

Nell Cottrell was proposing. Nobody could quite believe it.

'Some men are just too polite to admit they are in love.' Nell's voice rang out through the speakers. 'They think it indecorous. A while ago, I issued a far from polite introduction over dinner,' she winked at Dilly, 'but he still didn't get the hint. I am very loyal to my family. My nearest and dearest. My blood relatives. I love my family with a fury. I love this man with the same fury. And I love his unborn child. And I love his future wife. And I'd like to introduce them formally this time. Magnus – meet Dilly. Dilly – meet Magnus. I'd like to propose that you marry. I love you both, because you love each other so much. If you don't marry, I'll personally kill all your pets. Happy Leap Year.'

Flipper let out a drum roll.

All eyes turned to Dilly and Magnus.

Under such intense public scrutiny, Dilly smiled anxiously from behind her keyboard, not daring to look at Magnus. That hadn't been what she was expecting at all. Darling Nell wasn't testing Magnus's bravery after all – she was testing the pair of them, the hopeless romantics that she had kept apart too long. Her heart was jumping from her chest to her ears to her belly and her trembling knees as she realised what was really going on.

His own heart performing identical tricks, Magnus hugged his guitar to his chest and stared at Dilly's quaking back, wishing he knew what to do.

Both knew what they believed in their racing, crazy-in-love hearts. Both knew that they were natural performers who hated to disappoint a crowd, whether it be an audience of two or a room of over a hundred. Both trusted the other. Neither believed in marriage – just soulmates. But did they trust the crowd to understand them?

It had started to chant.

'Kiss! Kiss! Kiss! Kiss!'

'Kiss! Kiss! Kiss!'

Hunting horns cried out. Whoops and catcalls cried loud. The chant rang on.

'Kiss! Kiss! Kiss! Marry! Marry!'

Dilly turned her back on them all and looked at Magnus.

He shook his head, slowly and deliberately, blue gaze resting so trustingly in hers that she knew she had been right all along.

Beaming back at him, she shook her head too.

'Soulmates,' he mouthed.

'Soulmates,' she nodded.

They smiled at each other until – unable to help themselves – they exploded into each other's arms, hands gripping tightly to the solid warmth of living, breathing love, lips colliding. The heat that emanated from the kiss that followed probably spoiled all the carefully laid vintage wines behind them for ever.

The crowd, taking it as an acceptance, roared delightedly.

At the top of the stairs, Ely Gates narrowed his eyes in approval, tightening his arm around Godspell's narrow shoulders.

'I think we have our Look Before You Leap prize winners.'

She reached up and pulled at his beard.

'Saul agreed to marry me half an hour ago, remember? I win.'

'I thought you wanted these two love-birds to be together?' he reminded her in return.

Godspell's black-rimmed eyes blinked thoughtfully as she watched Dilly and Magnus kissing and laughing their way from the back of the stage and disappearing behind the high wine shelves.

'I do. They are perfectly matched, as are Saul and me. But *I* want that wedding, Pa. And I want it here. You are giving me away, old man.'

Ely swallowed a large lump in his throat and, hoist by his own petard, managed a brave smile as he watched the Cottrell twins striking up a beat with drums and tambourine that matched the clapping, foot-stamping demands of the crowd for another song.

'Encore! Encore! Encore!'

Hidden from view, Dilly and Magnus tumbled, kissing and laughing, into one of the narrow corridors formed by the racks of wine. Slamming excitedly up against a curving brick wall, they touched and tasted as fast as they could.

Blood pumping so fast through their ears that they were deaf to the demands of the crowd just a few metres away, they were almost too hungry for one another to know where to start.

Dilly dropped to her knees to unzip his fly.

Shaking his head, he pulled her back upright by her chin and dropped to his haunches to lift up her skirts.

Shaking her head, she pulled him back up by his chin and looked in his eyes. Blue, honest, direct and so drenched with love they seemed to see right into her, they danced between hers questioningly.

'We have nothing to prove,' she whispered. 'We're just soulmating.'

He laughed and nodded. 'Soulmating.'

His fly and trousers dropped as quickly as he could engineer, the magnificent Swedish mountain joyfully released – all hers to scale.

Her skirts lifted as fast as she could gather them and her legs spread eagerly, the deep, pretty Cotswold valley all his to explore.

And they soulmated furiously. Simply. Hard, fast, deep and pure, they came in quick, effortless, feverish succession and, in sweaty and breathless sweet nothings afterwards, agreed that they were years away from marriage. They were far too deeply in love for that. Pressing hot foreheads together, they told each other that they loved more than they had ever loved. They had soulmated. It was enough.

'Flying.' Dilly pulled a brace of clarets from behind her and, laughing, crossed them above her head in a vintage red semaphore.

'Soaring,' Magnus agreed, extracting a matching pair of classic white burgundies from hip level and crossing them in front of his chest.

'I am never going to get drunk again – stoned again – even smoke again, while I feel this high,' she promised him.

'That means you'll get razzled the moment we argue.'

'Who says we'll argue?'

'I do.'

'I disagree.'

'Like hell.'

'I'm right.'

'No way.'

'Get lost

'Screw you.'

'I hate you.'

'You're dumped.'

Tears slid from Dilly's eyes – laughter and relief combined. 'I love you *so* much.'

He held his arms wider. 'I love you so, *so* much.'

They were kissing so greedily at first that they didn't hear the twins striking up another song on stage. The slow clapping and shouts of encore had at last faded away and in their place came a vaguely familiar melody.

Dilly and Magnus looked at one another curiously. A guitarist was picking out chords, and wasn't that a sample track jumping in and out of Flipper's drum beat? Someone was humming into a mike far more tunefully than Nell could. Who was playing alongside the twins?

It took a while to cotton on to the tune. When they did, they laughed, kissed and hurriedly pulled up trousers and smoothed down skirts to join in, bursting on to the stage to take their places beside Godspell, Saul Wyck and Faith who had joined them for one final showpiece song. And it was the old eighties favourite that Entwined loved to play for its bittersweet truth and fantastic chorus. It was the ultimate love song.

The hunting fraternity loved it too as they crowded in to dance and sing along. Upstairs in the ballroom, Foxy Lady – twanging out *Lady in Red* as a last waltz – had two drunken dancers and a waiter in attendance. The cellars were packed as two rival bands played together, burying their differences and lighting up a crowd.

'*I have a picture,*' Magnus sung in his beautiful, smoky voice, '*pinned to my wall.*

An image of you and of me and we're laughing and loving it all.

Look at our life now, tattered and torn.

We fuss and we fight and delight in the tears that we cry until dawn.'

As Dilly and Godspell joined in for the chorus, they all smiled at one another.

'*Hold me now, warm my heart*

Stay with me, let loving start

Let loving start.'

In the crowd, Rory Midwinter danced with Justine Jones, his chin resting on her shoulder as he watched Faith on stage, amazed that his shy, dowdy weekend girl could have such a secret talent.

Cheek pressed lovingly to Rory's arm and propping him up because he was even drunker than usual, Justine watched Lloyd Fenniweather dancing nearby with a pretty blonde veterinary nurse and decided he was by far the best looking man in the room. When he winked at her as they shuffled past with their partners, she blushed like a furnace.

'*You say I'm a dreamer, we're two of a kind*
Both of us searching for some perfect world we know we'll never find
So perhaps I should leave here, yeah yeah go far away
But you know that there's nowhere that I'd rather be than with you here today.'

At the top of the cellar steps, Ely Gates and Hell's Bells stood companionably side by side watching proceedings, feet unwittingly tapping along to the music. Hell's Bells even opened her mouth to point out that this youth band lot were really rather good but, realising that she hadn't a hope of being heard, she closed it again and settled for a mildly baffled expression of enjoyment.

'*Hold me now, warm my heart*
Stay with me, let loving start
Let loving start.'

Steering Ellen and her Heshee bump around the crowded dance floor, Spurs felt his first child kick him squarely in the stomach and grinned, turning to watch Magnus and Dilly on stage. Ellen had been right all along. They were magical together.

'*You ask if I love you, well what can I say?*
You know that I do and if this is just one of those games that we play
So I'll sing you a new song, please don't cry anymore
And then I'll ask your forgiveness, though I don't know just what I'm asking it for.'

Dancing with brother-in-law, Piers, her feet being trodden on regularly as a result, Trudy Dew watched Flipper drumming and felt a great swell of pride lift her on to her squashed toes. They were a seriously talented bunch, all of them, and they brought out the best in Flipper. He was showing signs of growing up at last.

'Hold me now, warm my heart
Stay with me, let loving start
Let loving start.'

Dilly and Magnus looked at one another for a long time after the cheers and laughter had died away, the cellar and its stairs had emptied, their vaulted cave had quietened.

'Let loving start.' He traced her lips with his fingers.

She nodded. 'Let loving start.'

And they held one another, intending never to let go.

High up on the Eastlode Hall roof, the Three Disgraces were staring up at the heavens, all their texts sent for the night.

'Orion!' Carry pointed out obviously.

'Cornucrespia!' Fe jabbed up a victorious finger towards the famous W.

'Cassiopeia,' Sperry corrected, her own eyes drifting right. 'Gemini can't be here already, can it?'

Her sisters followed her gaze.

'Isn't that the rugby club's floodlights?'

Sperry shook her head. 'Not at this time of night. It's Gemini. The Twins. It never normally appears over the horizon this early in the year.'

'So what's that?' Carry pointed to a little cluster of lights to one side.

'The sewage works.' Sperry clutched her shoulders comfortingly.

'I'm going to miss him,' her little sister sobbed briefly.

'He's happy.' Sperry squeezed her tightly to her side. 'We have other jobs to do.'

On her other side, Fe looked across at the Gemini stars on the horizon and flicked a finger against her nose. 'Who put you up to it? You never would say.'

'Godspell.'

'*Godspell* wanted Dilly and Magnus to get together?' Carry checked in disbelief.

Sperry nodded, smiling contentedly. 'She knew they'd work out – and take the heat off her and Saul. She saw the chemistry before any of us – or, indeed, either of them.'

'And our next target?' asked Fe, not wanting to dwell on the past any more than her sister did.

'Oh, please say Rory!' Carry pleaded.

Sperry shook her head.

'Flipper Cottrell.' She raised a challenging eyebrow.

Both her sisters gaped at her.

'Who could we find to love *him*?' Carry sneered. 'He's an arrogant—'

'*Loser*,' Fe finished for her, making a big L sign with finger and thumb.

'The woman he loves, of course.'

'And who is that?'

'That's the tricky bit.' Sperry rubbed her neck and shrugged, lifting her shoulders apologetically in time with her eyebrows.

Her sisters joined forces and linked arms in support as they embraced the new challenge.

'We'll find out. We can find out anything.'

'Of course we can.' Sperry hugged them both to her sides.

'Bound to be someone gorgeous.'

'One of us?'

They linked arms tighter and stared up at the sky in time to spot a shooting star dive from Orion to Cassiopeia.

'You won't fall in love with this one, will you?' Fe asked her big sister worriedly.

'And you didn't?'

'Well, Carry did.'

'Fe did more!' Carry sniped.

Sperry watched the last glow of the shooting star disappear

'One day . . .' She drew her sisters' heads into her chest and rested her chin on the point at which their shiny crowns met. 'Our turn will come. We might be Faith, Hope and Charity, but patience is our true virtue.'

On cue, three mobile phones rang out with text messages and the girls returned to what they knew best.

EPILOGUE

Unlike his father Spurs three decades earlier, Garfield Belling chose to emerge into the world two days before the start of Cheltenham Week.

'Sensible little chap,' Hell's Bells told Ely proudly when she marched around to Manor Farm to display a rather alarming digital photograph of something that looked like a pink, creased Shar Pei dog. 'Ugly as sin, but all Constantine men start out that way and end up as strapping chaps. Spurs looked just the same. Worse, possibly.'

While Felicity cooed over the picture, Lady Belling drew Ely to one side.

'Just want to let you know the hunt ball made an absolute mint, dear man. The VW coffers look healthier than they have in years. We have you to thank for that – plus Godspell, of course.'

Ely gritted his teeth as Hell's Bells' little silver bullet eyes bored merrily into his. 'I am *so* looking forward to another wedding at Eastlode. Spurs' and Ellen's was quite magical.'

'Indeed,' he muttered gruffly, snapping at Felicity to run along and make coffee.

'Of course, darling.' She blinked her nervous, pale eyes and handed the photograph back before waddling towards the kitchen.

'Oh, I can't stay.' Hell's Bells stopped her. 'I've got to go and check progress on the River Folly restoration. Should be finished by the end of the month – St John and I are planning to host a little celebration once it's complete. You must both come along.'

'We very much look forward to that.' Ely saw her to the door.

'Oh, I almost forgot.' She tapped her forehead absent mind-edly. 'Have you heard what Trudy Cottrell has done for that young Olensen boy? The musician?'

'Magnus?' He looked across at her sharply.

'Yes – handsome young chap. Going out with young Dilly, I gather.' She gave him a wise look.

'So it seems.'

'Well, he is certainly going to make her a very happy girl if they stay together. He's been signed by some sort of recording company – a label do they call it? "Snapped up", I think that's the way it was described. They are paying him *rather* a lot of money, too.'

'How very fortuitous.' He smiled uncertainly.

'Isn't it?' she beamed. 'Frightfully exciting thing to hap-pen to the village – our own home-grown pop star in the making.'

'I thought he hailed from Essex?'

'He is an Oddlode man now,' she insisted sternly. 'And it was an Oddlode connection that helped him. Trudy is such a charming woman – I always feel that we haven't really taken advantage of her talents as a village.'

Ely, who had long admired Trudy Dew and even allowed himself the odd daydream of taking advantage of her, tilted his head with interest. 'How do you mean?'

'One was thinking perhaps she could sing at the River Folly opening. Do you think she'd like that?'

'I don't think she performs publicly any more.'

'Pity. Never mind. I'll ask her to join the Help a Neighbour campaign instead. I'm sure she'd love getting involved in that. And maybe she'd like to help with church flowers? Must get her more involved. Lovely woman. Very bubbly. Reminds me of young Dilly somehow.'

'Indeed.' Ely watched her march out on to his front step and take her leave with a regal wave as she gathered her patiently waiting brace of black Labradors and strode off along his daffodil-lined drive.

Stalking the other way, kicking the odd daffodil head as she passed, came Godspell, swathed as always in several indistinguishable black layers.

Ely regarded his daughter thoughtfully as she scuttled up the steps and made to duck and dart past him without greeting.

He caught her arm before she could, levelling his gaze towards hers.

'Godspell, look at me.'

She did silently as she was told.

Behind them, in the shadows of the hallway, Felicity wrung her plump, red hands anxiously.

Father and daughter had not spoken since the hunt ball. He refused to acknowledge her engagement to Saul Wyck, although she now sported a rather alarming ring shaped like a serpent with a ruby for an eye. She lived in fear that her bugs would start meeting untimely deaths any day now.

'I have been thinking,' he said in surprisingly soft tones. 'And it occurred to me that a wedding in Eastlode Park would probably not really be your and – Saul's – first choice of venue, would it?' He managed to say his future son-in-law's name without snarling.

Godspell gaped at him in surprise, then gave a very small shake of her head.

'You – Gothic – people prefer rather more *dramatic* settings, don't you?' he said condescendingly, but still quite kindly, his blue eyes creasing in concentration.

This time Godspell gave a little nod.

'Crypts and graveyards and whatnot, am I right?'

Another nod.

In the hallway, Felicity had stopped wringing her hands and was pressing them excitedly to her mouth.

'How about a castle?' he suggested.

Godspell raised her eyebrows.

He smiled. 'I have a friend who owns a rather spectacular Gothic pile in Scotland – right on a cliff. They've used it to film several horror movies, I gather. It has its own private chapel. Very atmospheric.' Also damp and falling apart, he remembered, but that was an irrelevance. 'It has a licence to host wedding ceremonies.'

Godspell let out a cry of delight.

'Shall I have a word? See if he can let us have it?'

This time she nodded furiously and, raising up on tiptoes, she flapped a small, delicate hug around him, a little like a moth crashing into a light bulb, before dashing off to phone Saul.

As he watched her go, Ely found his wife panting eagerly to his side to squish her bulk affectionately against it. 'That was such a lovely thing to do, Ely. It means so much to her that you accept them.'

Ely patted the top of Felicity's head much as he did Mosely the dog and smiled to himself with satisfaction. Moving the wedding from Eastlode Park to the Highlands would not only save him several tens of thousands, it would also ensure that the event could be kept as small and private as possible. And, with any luck, he might even be able to push his unwanted future son-in-law off a cliff while they were there.

Putting an arm around his wife's shoulder, he stooped to pick up a daffodil head that had fallen from Godspell's shoe and, pressing it to his nose, steered Felicity back into the house.